PRAISE FOR KRISTINE KATHI
DIVING UNIVERS

"The Diving Universe, conceived by Hugo-Award winning author Kristine [Kathryn] Rusch is a refreshingly new and fleshed out realm of sci-fi action and adventure."

ASTROGUYZ

"Kristine Kathryn Rusch is best known for her Retrieval Artist series, so maybe you've missed her Diving Universe series. If so, it's high time to remedy that oversight."

ANALOG

"This is classic sci-fi, a well-told tale of dangerous exploration. The firstperson narration makes the reader an eye witness to the vast, silent realms of deep space, where even the smallest error will bring disaster. Compellingly human and technically absorbing, the suspense builds to fevered intensity, culminating in an explosive yet plausible conclusion."

RT BOOK REVIEWS (TOP PICK) ON DIVING INTO THE WRECK

"Rusch delivers a page-turning space adventure while contemplating the ethics of scientists and governments working together on future tech."

PUBLISHERS WEEKLY ON DIVING INTO THE WRECK

"Rusch's handling of the mystery and adventure is stellar, and the whole tale proves quite entertaining."

BOOKLIST ONLINE ON DIVING INTO THE WRECK

"The technicalities in Boss' story are beautifully played.... She's real, flawed, and interesting.... Read the book. It is very good."

"Kristine Kathryn Rusch's Diving into the Wreck is exactly what the sf genre needs to get more readers...and to keep the readers the genre already has."

"Rusch keeps the science accessible, the cultures intriguing, and the characters engaging. For anyone needing to add to their science fiction library, keep an eye out for this."

"Rusch's latest addition to her Diving series features a strong, capable female heroine and a vividly imagined far-future universe. Blending fast-paced action with an exploration of the nature of friendship and the ethics of scientific discoveries, this tale should appeal to Rusch's readers and fans of space opera."

"Rusch follows Diving into the Wreck and City of Ruins with another fast-paced novel of the far future... [Rusch's] sensibilities will endear this book to readers looking for a light, quick space adventure with strong female protagonists."

"Filled with well-defined characters who confront a variety of ethical and moral dilemmas, Rusch's third Diving novel is classic space opera, with richly detailed worldbuilding and lots of drama."

RT BOOK REVIEWS ON BONEYARDS

"...a fabulous outer space thriller that rotates perspective between the divers, the Alliance and to a lesser degree the Empire. Action-packed and filled with twists yet allowing the reader to understand the motives of the key players, Skirmishes is another intelligent exciting voyage into the Rusch Diving universe."

THE MIDWEST BOOK REVIEW ON SKIRMISHES

"A combination of first-person and third-person narrative and flashback segments makes this a complex and compelling story. It's like having three tales in one, with an added peek into the bad guys' activities, all of them intriguing, classic science fiction. It leaves the reader eager to explore this universe again and see what will happen next with these characters."

RT BOOK REVIEWS ON SKIRMISHES

"A skillful blend of science fiction and murder mystery which keeps ratcheting up the stakes."

WORLDS WITHOUT END ON THE FALLS

"[The Runabout] is so good, it will make you want to read the other stories."

SFREVU ON THE RUNABOUT

"Amazing character construction, building a plot that riveted me almost from the moment it began. I will now absolutely have to read the preceding titles and I cannot wait to see what will come as a result of *The Runabout*."

"By mixing cerebral and investigative elements, emotional character segments, and the adrenaline of action, Rusch tells a complete yet varied tale that will please science fiction readers looking for something different from the usual fare."

"One of the most amazing science fiction series in recent years now has an exciting new installment."

"...a story of exploration of an artifact on an alien world, a bit reminiscent of the sort of story that Jack McDevitt writes."

"*Escaping Amnthra* is a full-fledged action adventure filled with high stakes and near-death experiences."

"...as suspenseful and mysterious as any of the tales that came before."

IVORY TREES

A DIVING UNIVERSE NOVEL

KRISTINE KATHRYN RUSCH

Ivory Trees
Copyright © 2023 by Kristine Kathryn Rusch
All rights reserved
Published 2023 by WMG Publishing
Cover and layout copyright © 2023 by WMG Publishing
Cover design by Allyson Longueira/WMG Publishing
Cover art copyright © Philcold
Parts of this novel have appeared in *Asimov's* in slightly different form
in the novellas "The Death Hole Bunker," July/August 2023 and "The Break-in,"
September/October 2023

ISBN-13 (trade paperback): 978-1-56146-887-4
ISBN-13 (hardcover): 978-1-56146-888-1

THE DIVING SERIES (READING ORDER)

ALSO BY KRISTINE KATHRYN RUSCH

THE RETRIEVAL ARTIST SERIES

The Disappeared

Extremes

Consequences

Buried Deep

Paloma

Recovery Man

The Recovery Man's Bargain

Duplicate Effort

The Possession of Paavo Deshin

Anniversary Day

Blowback

A Murder of Clones

Search & Recovery

The Peyti Crisis

Vigilantes

Starbase Human

Masterminds

The Impossibles

The Retrieval Artist

The Fey Series

THE ORIGINAL BOOKS OF THE FEY

The Sacrifice: Book One of the Fey

The Changeling: Book Two of the Fey

The Rival: Book Three of the Fey

The Resistance: Book Four of the Fey

Victory: Book Five of the Fey

THE BLACK THRONE

The Black Queen: Book One of the Black Throne

The Black King: Book Two of the Black Throne

THE QAVNERIAN PROTECTORATE

The Reflection on Mount Vitaki: Prequel to the Qavnerian Protectorate

The Kirilli Matter: The First Book of the Qavnerian Protectorate

Barkson's Journey: The Second Book of the Qavnerian Protectorate

(coming 2024)

WRITING AS KRIS NELSCOTT

THE SMOKEY DALTON SERIES

A Dangerous Road

Smoke-Filled Rooms

Thin Walls

Stone Cribs

War at Home

Days of Rage

Street Justice

AND

Protectors

IVORY TREES

THE DISCOVERY

TWO YEARS AGO

ONE

Six mummies on the stairs leading into the bunker. And it was an actual bunker too, not some cave that had much-too-smooth walls. Hogarth adjusted the pack he'd slung over his shoulder. He was wearing an environmental suit, and he had climbing gear, not that he needed it so far.

He was a bit surprised about that. He was surprised about all of it.

The mummies were sprawled on the stairs as if they had all fallen while running. They were dressed in tattered clothing that looked deeply unfamiliar. The mummies he'd found in the past were wearing clothing that usually followed some kind of style from the Enterran Empire's history, something he could recognize.

But these were different in ways he couldn't quite process yet.

He didn't try to process the mummies at all. He had learned long ago not to look at them too closely—their wizened faces, their crabbed hands. Years ago, one of his early team members had quit after encountering a mummy, saying the sunken eyes and the mouth, curved into a circle, looked like the person had been screaming when they died.

Hogarth couldn't get that idea out of his own head, so ever since, he'd tried not to look at the faces. They all ended up like that, the lips sunken inward so that only the teeth remained, the eyes sunken as well—sometimes with eyeballs and sometimes not. He tried not to think about expressions or how, exactly, these people died, and he always, always failed.

These days, though, he prepared his team for a gruesome discovery. No one had been truly surprised in years, not this team, anyway.

The team was one level up. They moved a lot slower than he did. He was team leader, not because he owned the company (which he did) but because he was willing to risk death every time they explored one of these caves.

Or what he had thought was going to be a cave. The fact that this was a bunker did surprise him. Stairs, actual walls designed by a human being, all of them leading somewhere. He'd never really encountered that before, not when he was exploring death holes.

Death holes had appeared all over Wyr for decades, maybe centuries. Some kind of energy blew through the surface, creating the death holes, which often destroyed homes or entire blocks, sometimes entire sections of a city.

The city of Vaycehn had relocated twice that he knew of because of the death holes.

Within the last year, though, there had been no new death holes. No repeated problems with existing death holes. Nothing.

Some thought it was just a lull, but Hogarth believed something was different.

He had made his living exploring the caves found underneath a lot of the death holes, unable to go too deep into some of them because there was a feeling that he would get. He'd told some of his team members about the feeling, but no one else. Refusing to explore based on a feeling sounded strange to him, but he had relied on that gut instinct from the start.

The feeling was powerful. His skin would crawl or the hair on the back of his neck would literally rise, even though he had seen nothing to cause the sensation.

Every now and then, he had a guess. Some of the caves had once been inhabited. Someone had shored up the walls or built ceilings—which the death holes had blown through. The remaining ceilings would sometimes have lights that would flare on, always startling him.

A member of an earlier team had once asked him if the lights had caused his feelings, and Hogarth had thought about that for a while. Then he remembered that he'd had feelings in dark caves that had clearly been tunneled by the power of a death hole. So the lights, the former habitation, none of that had caused whatever it was that he felt.

And he was always the only one who felt it. It didn't matter who else was on his team—none of them could feel the skin tingle. None of them ever had their hair rise up.

He'd even lost a few team members back at the beginning, when they wouldn't listen to him about the change in the air. They would put on helmets and say that their environmental suits would protect them.

Then they would march inside an area that something in his inner being shouted was a death trap.

Two of them never came out. One had stumbled and fallen near the part of the cave he'd entered, close enough that Hogarth could grab his feet and pull him out.

But the man was already dead. Maybe a minute inside that strange area, and the man had died, his oxygen gone, his body dehydrated so badly that the coroner had thought Hogarth was lying about how long the man had been in that cave corridor.

That incident still gave Hogarth the shudders, but it hadn't stopped him from exploring the tunnels blown by the death holes. Sometimes the tunnels revealed nothing, and sometimes they contained little treasures—a dropped piece of jewelry or mysterious bits of technology that no one seemed to understand.

Hogarth believed that people had lived in some of the tunnels centuries ago, maybe because the surface of Wyr was uninhabitable and an entire civilization repurposed the caves. There was nothing in the history of Wyr that confirmed any of his theories, from the surface being uninhabitable to some strange civilization lost to memory. As far as recorded history knew, people had lived on the surface. But he had found throughout his career, though, that there was a lot that recorded history didn't know.

There was a myopia in anything the Enterran Empire did that he found annoying, a requirement, really, to ignore what had come before the Empire. So whoever had established Vaycehn had been lost to time.

Hogarth did know that Vaycehn came first, because its citizens often left the beleaguered city and founded other towns, other cities, other villages. That history was clear and linear.

But the history of Vaycehn was not.

Just like the history of the death holes.

People said the death holes had always been a part of Wyr, and maybe that was true. But there were communities all over the planet that had not had a single death hole explosion ever in their recorded history.

The communities around Vaycehn did, and of course, Vaycehn itself had always had death holes.

Some believed that was because Vaycehn was in the SeBaze Mountain Range. Death holes often appeared in the range, even in the uninhabited areas.

Hogarth believed that the death holes did emanate from something underneath the range, but what, he wasn't certain. Still, others believed that the death holes were simply a feature of Wyr, even though they didn't appear in other parts of the planet.

Many people did listen to Hogarth, though. He was considered an expert on the caves.

That was because he mapped them. After nearly a decade of work, he'd gotten the city fathers in Vaycehn to pay for his explorations. Having the cave system mapped meant that parts of Vaycehn wouldn't succumb to a death hole.

Hogarth believed—and so far, nothing had proven him wrong— that the death holes came from inside the caves rather than creating the caves, as some scientists thought. He also believed—even though he couldn't figure out how to do the research to back his ideas up— that the feelings he got, those back-of-the-neck creepy-crawlies, were caused by the same thing that caused the death holes.

But no one wanted to do the research based on his hunch. He wasn't going to do the research either. He was an explorer, a sometimes treasure hunter, and an adrenaline junkie. There was no way he was going to sit in a room and run all kinds of diagnostics or whatever it was scientists did just to explore a hunch.

When he explored a hunch, he literally explored. That was how he started mapping death holes in the first place. He had a hunch they led somewhere, and he had been right. They did.

They always did.

Since none had appeared in the past year—the longest stretch without even a small death hole—he had started exploring death holes far from Vaycehn.

Death holes had a look, even if they occurred in an unpopulated area. Vaycehn was surrounded by mountains that left the city in a bowl. There were other, smaller valleys that were also bowls, a few where Vaycehn had originated.

But some had been unoccupied forever, at least according to existing records. He'd explored two unoccupied valleys and hadn't seen any obvious death holes.

Then he moved farther away from the city and its previous sites and he found a hidden box valley that showed evidence of massive death hole activity.

Death holes always left a mark on the land. The hole wasn't really a sinkhole, even though that was often the cumulative effect. Death holes blew the ground outward and upward, as if someone had fired a weapon underground, a weapon with enough power to cut through layers of rock and dirt. The rock and dirt flew into the air and sprayed across the surface—or what was left of the surface after the death hole had blown through it.

Sometimes the holes collapsed in on themselves, filling the tunnel, always leaving a dip on the land. The dip was a sign of a death hole, just like the mounds of dirt around it.

Ancient death holes had the dip, but it wasn't always visible. What was visible were the mounds. They fell only on one side of the dip, so the pattern always looked like a hole and then a series of mounds.

That was how he had found this particular death hole. The dip was more of a divot now because so much time had passed. The mounds were tiny inclines, but the pattern was familiar. He'd gone over it several times, looking at it from all angles, even measuring it from above.

After many years of doing this work, he had equipment to dig out the tunnel without ruining its edges.

He had done that here, then encased the edges so that the hole wouldn't collapse in on his team. He had gone in first, rappelling downward until he found what he believed to be the cave. It had looked like any other cave that had sparked death holes, and it hadn't caused any uncomfortable feelings for him.

He'd brought the team down, and they were going to explore.

Which was when Raemi found the stairs. Raemi was his second; she had been with him almost from the beginning.

Sometimes he thought she looked like a mummy herself. Over the years, her skin had grown darker, wrinkled, and tighter against her skull. She spent too much time in the sun along the SeBaze Mountain Range, and as long as he'd known her, she hadn't eaten enough.

She had beckoned him over, and he had gone, and they both stared down into the extreme darkness that the stairs disappeared into.

When they had stood at the top, discussing their next move, Hogarth hadn't even seen the mummies.

Neither had anyone else. All eleven of the other team members had looked and none of them had seen anything. So, Hogarth put Raemi on notice: she was to follow him if he gave the signal. Then he put Mehmet, his third, in charge of the team on the surface.

Then Hogarth had pulled on his helmet and turned on the oxygen as a precaution. He was going deep into another hole, and the surface had been covered for a long time.

For all he knew, the oxygen was limited down there to whatever had accumulated after they had dug out the cave.

The farther down he went, the fresher the air got, though, at least according to his suit. The suit also told him that the temperature was comfortable, not the chill he usually found when he went deep underground.

Those two facts made him uneasy. He'd encountered this kind of strangeness one or two times before, registered it, and then had to flee the cave because he got that creepy-crawly feeling.

There was no such feeling here. Nothing except human-made walls, perfectly cut stairs, and a darkness that the lights on his palms couldn't really penetrate. He was loath to turn on his headlamp only because it distorted things.

And then he found the mummies. Six of them, sprawled. Six of them, all of whom seemed to die at the same time—but he wasn't sure of that. They had tumbled face first, though, which led him to believe that they had fallen going *up* the stairs, not down.

He couldn't know that either.

So he contacted Raemi through the comms in his helmet.

"Mummies," he said.

"Plural?" she asked.

"Six of them. I want to travel deeper, but I also need someone to record all of this. A second witness at least."

He needed one more witness because the Mummies of Wyr were considered valuable. The City Museum of Vaycehn preferred to acquire the mummies—usually as a donation, claiming that since the mummies had once been people, they needed to be treated with respect.

Others, though, were willing to pay exorbitant prices for any Wyr mummy. Hogarth could take advantage of that if he wanted to. Because this part of Wyr was uninhabited and unclaimed by Vaycehn, which was the only place that mummies had been found (so far).

He could claim ownership of them, and sell them with impunity.

He didn't want to do that though, because he partly agreed with the museum. The mummies had to be treated like the people they had been. Except the museum sometimes failed at that. The museum was often as guilty of exploiting the mummies as the antiquities dealers were.

He was going to need scientists and forensic specialists and others who could identify these mummies, in case they had still-living families. He also had to protect the mummies.

In the past, former members of his team had talked about mummy discoveries, and a couple of former members had actually stolen the mummies from him and sold them.

Of course, the thieves had never worked for him again, but that didn't really matter. The damage had been done—to him, to his sense of trust, and to his reputation.

Raemi understood. Now they had one person on their team who was in charge of contacting the experts, even before the rest of the team learned about what was going on.

Raemi would initiate the procedures, and then she would join Hogarth. That way, if one of the current team members got it in their head to steal a mummy, Hogarth and Raemi would be in the clear. They would have tried to do the right thing.

Hogarth paused on this part of the stairs, crouching to look at the mummies. That was when he noted the strange clothing, even stranger because it had started to decay—and the decay was recent. In the past, when he discovered mummies, the clothing was often intact, sometimes looking as fresh as it had when the mummy had put it on the day of their death.

Here, though, as Hogarth looked, he realized that not only was the clothing starting to decay, but the mummies didn't look quite as fresh as the ones he had found in the past. It actually looked like something had nibbled on the skin of the closest mummy before giving up.

He shuddered a little and peered into the darkness. The stairs continued as far as he could see, even when he turned his palm lights down there. He finally relented and turned on his headlamp—broad beam, so that he could see as much as possible.

He still couldn't see the bottom, although he did see a landing, and the beginnings of another flight of stairs. His heart was pounding harder than it had on a job in a long time.

He wanted to continue down the stairs alone, but he needed to wait for Raemi. The procedure they were using wasn't official—no authority recognized it—but it had worked in previous cases where someone had tried to steal from one of the sites that Hogarth had discovered.

Authorities might not recognize his procedures, but they certainly relied on them when they needed evidence.

It took nearly ten minutes before Raemi picked her way down the stairs. She hated stairs, particularly those without handholds of some kind. She saw them as a dangerous enemy, preferring a steep incline in a death hole tunnel to something carved out of stone, like these were.

She stopped one step above him, two steps above the closest mummy. She turned on her palm lights as Hogarth turned off his headlamp, so that he wouldn't blind her.

She looked at the nearest mummy, then went down a few steps to the next, and the next and the next, until she had seen all six. Then she climbed back up to Hogarth, and made a point of gesturing at the comms.

He had thought they were on a private channel, but clearly, she wanted him to check.

"You know these are worth a fortune, right?" she asked.

He nodded.

"We can't let the others down here," she said. "I had Mehmet contact our experts, but I had him climb out of the tunnel to do so."

"These look different," Hogarth said. "Clothing, decay, positioning."

"We've never found so many at once," she said.

She was right; they'd found more mummies in a different cave near the edge of Vaycehn, but not gathered in one place.

Then she tilted her head toward him, her eyes looking big inside her helmet. "You usually feel that tingly thing whenever we find mummies."

"I know," he said. "I'm not feeling a thing."

"Maybe it's the helmet...?" she asked, her voice trailing off.

He shook his head. "It's never been a problem in the past."

But that didn't mean it wasn't a problem now.

"My readings say that the air here is fresh and normal." Raemi sounded just as surprised as Hogarth felt. He had never encountered air this fresh in one of the caves. "You think there's another exit somewhere?"

"Maybe," he said, "but you usually don't encounter that when you go down."

He resisted the urge to call up the map of the area on the visor of his helmet. He knew where they were. The tunnel went underneath the hidden box valley. From mapping others had done nearby, and the things he had seen, there were no other points where a person could enter this area from below.

Air like this—fresh air like this—usually came from a nearby entrance. He supposed he could have missed it, but he didn't think he had. He had mapped this part of the valley floor himself, augmenting the flyover he had done of the entire valley. He had seen no obvious death holes, no obvious entrances, and certainly nothing lower than he was right now.

And there was one other thing.

"Air wouldn't regulate the temperature," he said. "Not like this."

Every other cavern he'd been in had been cold this far down. Fresh air coming in might have been warmer, but it wouldn't have warmed this area and made it comfortable. His suit told him that the air was thirty-two degrees—what his father used to call "sleeveless weather." Certainly not cold, and definitely not that underground chill Hogarth had braced for.

Raemi nodded. Then she took off her helmet. Her black hair was tousled, her cheeks a bit flushed. She took a deep, ostentatious breath.

"This air is fresh," she said. "There's nothing tainting it that I can sense."

She waited, as if she expected Hogarth to remove his helmet as well.

He looked down at the mummies. She was right; he had never found mummies in such an accessible place, where he could touch them and extract them. He'd never found mummies without feeling at least a little bit of a tingle, one that bothered him so much that he wouldn't retrieve the mummies.

He wouldn't allow his team to do so either. He always let the so-called experts do it, and often, he would leave before the mummies were extracted. He didn't even want to know if any of the experts were injured or died. He knew it had happened, but he tried to ignore it.

He never considered mummy retrieval part of his business.

He let out a nervous breath. Sometimes, when he found a mummy, the tingly feeling was faint, almost nonexistent. Maybe Raemi had a point; maybe Hogarth couldn't feel a truly faint tingle because of the environmental suit.

He brought up his hands and slowly disconnected the helmet. He took a step down, past the first two mummies. Then he took another, and another, until he was at Raemi's side.

No tingle. Not even one he could conjure with his imagination. He felt fine, maybe better than fine, because now he was breathing fresh air instead of oxygen from his environmental suit.

The very idea of that made him shaky. Not the kind of shaky that went with the creepy-crawly feeling. The kind of shaky that he felt whenever he encountered a situation he didn't entirely understand.

He peered up the stairs. He couldn't see the cave level. He had gone down too far. And if he continued down, he—and possibly Raemi—would not be able to run out of here quickly.

In the past—the long ago past, when he was first exploring caves —a moment like this wouldn't have stopped him. He had thought that he was fearless, and maybe he would have been if the stairs had been empty.

But the mummies were a warning sign of something.

He glanced at Raemi. She shrugged, as if saying, *This is your decision.*

If he left, he would never come back. He knew that. The mummies would upset him even more in hindsight. Besides, there would be experts here, trying to figure out what the mummies were.

And mummies sometimes led to other things. Little bits of treasure that he could use to continue his work, to augment the money he earned from the City of Vaycehn to map the caves.

He would always wonder what was down there. If his experience in other caves was any measure, he wouldn't find anything at all. Or he would find a blockage, beyond which there was something that made him deeply uncomfortable.

Maybe the tingle-causing energy was farther down now. Maybe it had receded. Maybe he wouldn't be able to go down all of those stairs.

He didn't know at the moment, and he needed to know.

"All right," he said. "I'm going to see what's down there. You want to come?"

"Yep," Raemi said. "That's why I'm here."

He put his helmet back on. He didn't trust that fresh air. After a moment, Raemi put her helmet on too.

Then they followed the usual procedure. He went first, and she followed a few meters behind.

There were a surprising number of stairs. He should have started counting them from the moment he encountered them, but he did not. He started at the first landing.

The stairs were steeper than he was used to, and there were a dozen of them that went down to the next landing. The landings were wide and square, turning the stairs in a zigzag pattern.

According to his suit, the air did not get colder nor did the freshness fade. The suit wasn't recording a breeze, either. There were no lights, other than his helmet light and the lights on his palms. Raemi had turned on her headlamp as well, and the light bobbed as she made her way down the stairs.

Finally, Hogarth reached the bottom of the stairs. They ended in another square landing-like platform, but he suspected this was the actual floor. At the opposite end of the square, a door loomed. It was partially open, which bothered him more than it would have if it had been closed and locked.

He hesitated before stepping on the floor. It looked uneven. Then he realized that he was seeing particles. They had gathered like dirt around the open door, and they also covered the floor itself.

He waited until Raemi joined him, then dipped a foot onto the floor. The particles stirred, looking like black snow in the light of the headlamps.

He recognized the particles. He had seen them in death hole caves, usually in the ones where he found mummies—or saw mummies in the distance, just before fleeing because of the creepy-crawly feeling.

"You're still not feeling anything?" Raemi asked.

Apparently she had had the same thought.

"No." He checked and double-checked, then felt a thread of worry: Had he lost the ability to have that feeling? Did that feeling really matter or had he always been reacting to the strangeness of the circumstance?

He shook off that last thought. The feeling had been caused by something external, and it was always visceral.

"I've never seen the particles settle like this," he said. "There are usually some that float."

So that was a difference too, something that he had seen but not entirely understood until this moment.

He took a deep breath of the air in his environmental suit. It tasted metallic, and he found that incredibly reassuring.

"You stay here," he said to Raemi, without turning around to look at her. If he did, he might see concern on her face, and he didn't need that at the moment.

He stepped onto the floor. Particles rose around him, circling as if they were attracted to his suit. As he walked, they continued to float. They rarely went higher than his head.

The particle pile was deep, though. He shuffled as he walked, stirring up the pile all the way to the door.

Some of the particles were stuck underneath the bottom of the door, and looked almost like some kind of dried sludge. He wasn't sure if those were different or not.

What was different—what just registered—was that everything in this space, from the stairs to the landings to the walls to the ceilings and floors, were at straight angles. Like buildings in Vaycehn. Like land-based design throughout the Empire.

The death hole caves were usually arched, without angles or corners, except in a few odd places. The death hole caves reminded him of the military space ships he had served on. Most had rounded designs in their corridors and public spaces because, he was told, it was a better use of the space.

He reached the door, and examined it for a moment. He didn't want it to cut his suit or to transfer something unidentified onto him. He saw nothing dangerous, though. No sharp edges, nothing obvious that might hurt him.

He threaded his fingers together, and pushed his gloves into his skin, making sure they were tight. Then he grabbed the edge of the door, and tried to move it outward, ever so slowly.

For a moment, it wouldn't budge. He wondered if that was because of the material underneath or because it had been in the same position for a long, long time.

Then it moved with a loud squeak and groan. Particles floated everywhere, brushing against his visor, but not sticking to it.

He peered inside the door, seeing blackness for just a moment, before realizing that it was simply particles floating in front of him.

He pushed the door a little farther, so that he could fit inside the opening, then waited for the particles to settle.

It took longer than he expected.

As the particles settled, he couldn't see the outlines of a room like he expected. He saw edges of things and because he had no context, he couldn't tell exactly what he was seeing.

He slowly shoved an arm inside the room, not wanting to disturb any more particles.

When his elbow breached the space, something hummed, like some kind of circuit. He nearly jumped backwards. He had experienced that humming sound before and it usually presaged the start of the creepy-crawling feeling.

He waited. No feeling. But the light inside the room was changing. Far from him, he saw a faint light—pale grayish white and horribly thin. As he watched, the light moved toward him along the ceiling.

Something he had done had activated motion sensors, maybe, or maybe opening the door to this width had done the same thing.

Whatever it was, it was clear that these lights hadn't been used in a long time. Some of the lights were yellow, others had a layer of particles along the bottom—although he couldn't tell if that layer was inside the light fixture or attached to it, like the sludge beneath the door.

Some of the light was coming out of the sides of the fixtures, which was why the light seemed so thin. Other light seemed to almost rain down on him, as if there were holes in part of the fixtures.

"What do you see?" Raemi asked. She sounded impatient.

"Lights came on," he said, and slipped inside the room.

It wasn't as big as he had expected, given the lights. The room was long and narrow, with walls that looked like some kind of brushed metal. The metal surprised him. Metal hadn't been used for buildings or for ships for centuries.

The metal wasn't rusted, which he found somewhat amazing too, considering most places he went underground were dank and cold.

The room itself was filled with tables and shelves. From what he could tell, they were also metal. But he only saw parts of them, since they were all covered with various items.

Close to the door, he couldn't see what the items were, because they were covered in particles. Farther back, there seemed to be fewer particles, but that might also be his perspective.

"I think it's safe to come in here," he said, and walked in just a bit further, stirring up more particles.

He stopped at the nearest table. The table itself came up to hip height, but with the items on top, reached his ribcage. He gingerly ran his gloved hands over the items, trying to dislodge the particles without making too much of a mess.

They rose up and floated. Beneath them were what appeared to be blankets and bags. They were remarkably intact for being in a room like this.

He stepped past them to the next table.

The items on it didn't form neat piles. They were scattered, of varying heights and shapes. Some of them seemed to have toppled on the far side of the table.

He peered at that first, and then gasped.

He recognized the shapes. They looked like twigs entwining off a branch. No one stored twigs and branches in a room like this.

His heart started to pound. He tried not to make an assumption, but as usual, his mind was leaping ahead of him.

He brushed the twig nearest him, touching it very carefully, because if it was what he thought it was, it would be very fragile.

The particles floated and circled, but they wanted to return to the surface of the twig. Still, he got close enough to see the color—a whitish ivory—and some writing engraved on the surface.

Familiar writing.

His breath quickened.

"Raemi, I need you," he said.

"Almost there," she said.

He didn't want to move quickly. He didn't want to damage anything.

"Behind you," Raemi said.

"Look here," he said, "and tell me what you see."

He stepped slightly to one side and pointed.

She bent at the waist, and carefully brushed the twigs. Then she stood up quickly, losing her balance ever so slightly.

He caught her so that she didn't try to stop herself from falling by grabbing a table or one of the branches. She pivoted slightly and gripped his arms.

"These are Ivory Trees!" she said, breathlessly. "And there are a lot of them."

His mouth went dry. That was what he had thought as well, but he had been afraid to admit it to himself.

Ivory Trees were not real trees, nor were they made of ivory. In fact, ivory would have cheapened them, since ivory was a substance that could be made in any lab.

Ivory Trees were made of a material that no one seemed able to replicate. Even trying to extract part of an Ivory Tree didn't really work. Bits of them didn't seem to have DNA, which meant that they were not organic, and the parts that were removed by someone didn't respond well to most tests, dissolving or disappearing as someone experimented on it.

Occasionally, some scientist would do something that would cause a bit of an Ivory Tree to explode, but no one knew what that something was, since the scientist who triggered an Ivory Tree explosion never survived.

Ivory Trees were valuable, though, because they were beautiful and rare. They always came in branches and twigs, suggesting that there might actually be an Ivory Tree somewhere.

Where, no one knew. The bits of Ivory Tree that had floated around the Enterran Empire had come from different sources. Hogarth knew of only three sources—a derelict ship found far from here more than a hundred years ago; an escape pod filled with Ivory Tree bits found close to the shared space with the Nine Planets; and one small Ivory Tree that appeared to be intact. The intact tree was in the Enterran Empire Museum on Ukhanda.

That small tree had been captured in a space battle centuries ago. Its beauty had inspired countless people to search for more Ivory Trees, but with little luck.

Some claimed they had found bits of an Ivory Tree only to lose those bits or claim (when someone tried to take one) that the bits had been stolen. He believed the theft claims, even though the Enterran Empire and most of its art and antiquities dealers did not. They didn't seem to account for the fact that there had been at least three attempts to steal the Ivory Tree in the Enterran Empire Museum over several decades.

"If this is really an Ivory Tree," Raemi said, "we are rich beyond our wildest dreams."

Hogarth didn't say anything. She had leapt from the discovery to selling the bits of Ivory Tree. He hadn't had that thought at all. He had been dealing with the practicalities. How did he get the bits out of this room without his team knowing? Or did he want them to know?

He trusted his team, but he wasn't sure how much.

He pressed his hands together and looked around the room. Every surface was covered in particles. Every surface had a different shape, which meant there were other items here.

And in the back was another door.

He and Raemi had found some kind of treasure trove, and it was one he couldn't just walk away from. He would have to report those mummies because part of his team knew about them, and if someone from City Museum of Vaycehn or the Empire's Antiquities Division showed up, then they would explore this area just like he had.

He wasn't even sure how to lay a claim to all of this. Had he been in space, he could have registered a shipwreck with the Empire. The first person to find the wreck and claim it would be the person who could profit the most from any treasure inside.

But on land? It varied from community to community. The problem was worse here in Wyr, because there was no planetwide government. Some areas were unaffiliated and this was one of them.

He wasn't sure, though, if that made them subject to Empire salvage laws or subject to something else, some kind of regional division or something.

And of course, he hadn't asked about that before he arrived here. He had never discovered a trove this big.

He had figured if he found a few items, he would pocket them. If he found a dozen or more, his team would pocket them as well.

That was what he had done in the past in any unaffiliated area. He'd fought to keep some of his salvage in the cities and villages around Wyr, and he'd tangled with the Vaycehn government more than once.

But something this large? If everything on these tables was valuable, then it would take him a year or more to properly catalog it all.

He didn't have that kind of time—not and keep this space secret.

Raemi was looking at him, not at the pieces of the Ivory Tree.

"We're not going to keep this, are we?" she asked.

"Some of it, maybe," he said. If they found small Ivory Tree pieces, the kind that they could pocket.

Then he realized that if any of them sold Ivory Tree bits, even to private collectors, the authorities would know where the bits came from.

He sighed. "This is too big for us, Raemi."

She glanced at the bits, then frowned at him. "We can do it," she said.

"Not with the mummies," he said, and hoped she would understand.

She brushed the particles off some items on another table. Nothing from an Ivory Tree, but some black pottery with a white design along the curved sides.

Raemi picked up a vase. "That's a drawing of an Ivory Tree."

He peered at it. She was right: the branches of an Ivory Tree were unmistakable.

He walked carefully toward the first table, with the blankets and bags. Many were plain, but one of the blankets was made of fabric that had a repeating design—and that design appeared to be an Ivory Tree.

What had he stumbled into? Now he wanted to climb the stairs and look closer at the clothing on the mummies. Did the clothing have an Ivory Tree design as well?

Raemi set the vase down. She inclined her head toward the back of the room.

"What do you think is through that door?" she asked.

More rooms. More items. More mummies? He had no idea and for the first time in his life, he wasn't sure he wanted to know.

He took a deep breath, forcing himself to think. What he needed was time, time to sort this out, time to figure out who was entitled to the salvage, and time to hire someone to help him, someone who was not Raemi.

She saw only the money, and while he valued that, it wasn't everything. She would probably laugh if she knew he was thinking that. But there was more here, a history that had clearly been lost, and something else, something mysterious.

He wasn't sure he dared keep it to himself.

"Are we going to explore?" Raemi asked.

Hogarth was shaking his head before he even realized he was doing so.

"Not yet," he said.

"So we'll figure out what's here?" she asked. "Catalog it?"

"Record it," he said. "We have to make a visual record."

That was simple enough. But the rest of it? He had no idea.

"Are you going to talk to me or not?" Raemi asked.

Particles had adhered to her environmental suit, making her look like she was part of the room, something covered and abandoned, maybe for centuries.

He had to get ahold of himself. He needed to move forward, needed to make some choices.

But he couldn't make any choices until he knew what they had found. And he wouldn't know that until he figured out how big this place actually was.

That settled it: he was going to have to trust the team, with some information, anyway. Not all of it.

Certainly not about the Ivory Trees.

"We're going back up," he said.

"We can't just leave this here," Raemi said. "We've opened it up. Others will find it. We'll lose—"

He held up a hand, stopping her.

"We're going back up." He spoke slower, as if she couldn't understand him otherwise. "And we're going to tell the team that we found an underground bunker. We're going to see where the rooms lead, which might take the rest of the day. They're to wait on the surface. If they don't hear from us by morning, they can come searching."

She suddenly looked alarmed. "You think we can get trapped down here?"

"You think we can't?" he asked.

Her mouth opened slightly. Apparently, the thought of riches had chased anything sensible out of her head.

He didn't need someone beside him who wasn't thinking clearly.

"Look," he said, "you go up, and tell them that I'm going to explore. Don't take them to this room, but maybe catalog what you can from the mummies. Come get me if I don't come back by morning."

She shook herself, as if she realized she had just been demoted from his main assistant.

"No," she said. "You need me."

No, he wanted to say, *you just want to see what other treasures are here.*

But then, didn't he as well? Wasn't he thinking about what kind of treasures he might find in this very strange place?

"Then shape up," he said as harshly as he could. "You're going to need to be thinking clearly about *exploring*, not about getting rich."

She snapped her head back as if he had hit her. Then she nodded, just once.

22

"Fair enough," she said. "Let's go tell them what we're going to do."

"Not all of it," he cautioned.

"Not all of it," she repeated. "But we will impress upon them the fact that we might die, and that's why they're not coming."

He sighed silently and struggled not to shake his head. That was not why she wanted to do this with him. No matter what she said, she wanted to see what other treasures this bunker held.

She wanted to treasure hunt, in a way that the two of them never had—which was why he had never seen this side of her before.

It worried him.

He hoped he could control her, if he needed to.

And of course, he hoped he wouldn't need to.

TWO

The team was not happy about being left behind, especially when Hogarth asked them to catalog the mummies. Cataloging was meticulous work, but it had to be done if something was going to be sold.

Hogarth wouldn't sell the mummies. If he sold anything, it would be something a mummy was wearing, something it held, something that was currently hidden beneath the body. He'd sold a lot of rings and other jewelry that way. He'd sold some mysterious tech that he hadn't understood, primarily because the mummy it had come off of had been catalogued, and that intrigued the buyer.

So he wanted the mummies catalogued, and he made sure the team knew they would share in any profits...if they did the cataloguing right.

That mollified them, but not as much as telling them how dangerous this excursion would be. He stressed the risks, not just for them, but so that Raemi could hear it as well. He talked about dying because of one unforeseen mistake, part of his life that he had accepted. More than accepted, really. It was a part that made him feel alive.

He didn't confess that. Instead he made himself sound like a bit of a martyr: *I do this so you don't have to, so that we can all do this job well.*

They seemed to buy it. The discontent eased and they were willing to do the work while he explored.

He couldn't dissuade Raemi, though. She wanted to know what was down there, and that meant she was going to take risks she hadn't taken in years.

He would have to keep an eye on her, which annoyed him.

Before going back into the cave, he had taken a pack from one of the team members, and asked others to hand him things the pack was missing. Door wedges, blocks that would make sure that nothing closed on him, extra oxygen, a knife, and one laser pistol. He attached three huge oblong water bottles the size of his forearm to his utility belt, but didn't attach them to the system inside his environmental suit.

The water bottles were only for emergencies.

He made Raemi do the same, and for once, she didn't complain about the fact that water bottles added a lot of extra weight.

He was as prepared as he knew how to be. He wanted to survive if the ceiling fell in on him, blocking his way back, or if one of those doors closed and locked him in.

He believed his team would be able to get him out. He had to believe that or he wouldn't be able to explore anything.

He and Raemi walked down the stairs again. He reached the mummies, with the team behind him, and stopped to remind them that at this stage, they couldn't touch the mummies, not until the experts showed up.

"Under no circumstances," he said before leaving the team, "are you to tell *anyone* about the bunker we found. Just tell them we are going deeper in the cave network and we're not sure what we're going to find."

The team remained silent. No one nodded, no one acknowledged him.

Mehmet stood toward the back.

He looked weak, at least by Wyr standards, but he had been raised in space on a trading ship he couldn't wait to leave behind. That skinniness hid a wiry strength that Hogarth had relied on more than once.

Mehmet looked doubtful, as if he didn't believe anything that Hogarth said. If Hogarth had to guess, he would have thought that the mummies made Mehmet nervous.

"Both of those things you're going to tell others are true," Hogarth said, mostly to Mehmet. "We *are* exploring deeper in this cave network and we are not sure what we're going to find."

Mehmet nodded, and that made Hogarth feel better.

He had to trust his team, and ever since Raemi's response, Hogarth did not. He felt very alone here.

Maybe the mummies bothered him as well.

He pivoted, and headed down the stairs again, putting his helmet on as he went. He was going to wear a full environmental suit the entire way. He had already told Raemi that she would have to as well. At any point, they could get trapped, or that strange fresh air could stop. He wanted them protected, not gasping for breath or inhaling something they shouldn't while they tried to assemble their suits.

She said she understood in a voice that led him to believe she wasn't paying attention. So he added one more caution:

"I have no idea what those particles will do to our bodies," he said. "I don't know what they are, and you don't either. In all of my years exploring like this, I have not ever inhaled a lot of particles. I plan to keep it that way."

That little speech got her to check the connections for her helmet. He had finally gotten through.

He walked down the stairs, making sure he catalogued the route, recording everything from his helmet. He had it set to take in the entire space—from the front and back and sides to whatever was above him and the stairs below. He would review it all later to see what he missed.

He usually missed quite a bit when he was as focused as he was now.

He hadn't told Raemi to do the same thing, like he normally would have. He hadn't told her for two reasons: first, if she failed to do so, he wanted to use that as an example of the fact that she wasn't thinking clearly; and second, he didn't want her to have as much access to information as he did.

If she thought of it all on her own, well, then everything was well and good. But if she didn't, then he had reasons to bar her from further exploration.

He didn't wait for her to keep up with him as he descended. If he had been on his own—or if Raemi had been acting like herself—he would have slowed down, maybe even figure out when or how these walls and stairs had been built.

But he didn't. He had given himself a deadline with the team and that deadline might not have been sufficient.

When he reached the landing at the bottom of the stairs, he pushed the door all the way back. He used a wedge to hold the door open, and then he placed a block on the wall near the doorjamb, something that would (in theory) keep the door from closing all the way.

The door was heavier than expected. Metal doors often were. He found them more dangerous than regular doors, because metal doors sometimes succumbed to their weight; they often closed on their own.

He looked over his shoulder at Raemi. She watched him do the work and didn't help, just like he had instructed her. He did hope that she would speak up if she thought he needed to do more.

After all, her life would be at risk too if he did anything wrong.

"We're not going to see what's on those tables or even beside them," he said for maybe the dozenth time. He was so worried that she was going to be distracted. He couldn't tolerate that. "We're going to map out this entire place first. Then we figure out what we've found."

"I got that," she said with more irritation than he wanted to hear. He wanted her to be the old Raemi, the one who was as cautious as he was, the one who usually instructed the team to slow down and think before doing anything unusual.

"All right," he said, "You're going to follow me. Do exactly what I do."

Usually he added, *Unless it proves too dangerous to do so*, but he didn't want to give her any excuses at all.

He stepped into the room and paused. The lights had remained on, which bothered him on some level. Were they set to shut off long after they were activated? Or had they been activated by something else?

He deliberately had not moved near the door until he was ready to enter, so the lights couldn't have been reacting to him—could they? They hadn't activated when he had been at the bottom of the steps earlier.

Nothing else pointed to some other kind of movement activation. The particles had settled from his first visit here, and his arrival in the room hadn't caused any of them to rise—or at least to rise very high. Some were floating around his feet now, but he supposed he had to expect that.

The settled particles made everything in the room look like it was coated in black and gray gunk. He couldn't even see the Ivory Trees any longer, but he recognized the shape of them on that second table.

He counted ten tables—five on each side of the room. The tables were wide and all seemed to have something on their surface. Some also had items underneath, and to the side. The walls deeper in seemed to be shelves, but he wasn't certain. They might have been something odd, like the trees, something he didn't recognize.

No matter. If he had to label this room, he'd call it the storage room. Or the front room. Right now, it was all he had.

There was an aisle in the center and that was where he walked, going as slowly as he could so that he would disturb the fewest number of particles.

He realized, halfway through, that he was breathing shallowly, a side effect of moving slowly and of thinking about the particles. He made himself stop and take regular breaths. Then he pressed on, without looking back to see how Raemi was doing and without asking for her input.

The door on the far side of the room was the same size as the door in which they had entered. This new door was metal as well, and judging by the actual hinges on the side, it opened inward.

He wasn't sure he would be able to open it at all. He expected it to be locked. Then he would have to cut through it, which made him uneasy. Maybe he could simply remove those old-fashioned hinges.

With that thought, he looked over at the hinges. They did seem removable, which was good. He had no idea what awaited him in the next room, and using some kind of heat or a laser or something else to open that door might activate—what? More particles? Something that might explode? Bad air?

He wasn't sure, and he really didn't want to find out accidentally.

Raemi was being unusually quiet. He turned, half expecting her to be inspecting something on one of the tables. But she had followed instructions. She was walking slightly behind him.

She had paused because he had paused. Particles swirled around her, but not around him. It was as if his passage through the room had blown all of the particles backwards.

He didn't say anything. He wasn't sure what there was to say. So he turned back to that door.

This was where he made the decision. They could just as easily go back, deal with the mummies and all of the treasures in this room, and not know what was farther ahead. What was ahead might complicate things.

But it would be better to know, especially if one of the experts got it in their head to go down the remaining stairs. Usually the experts that Hogarth had brought in did exactly as he told them, particularly when they were in a dangerous area, like one of the death hole caves.

But this area looked a lot less dangerous to the untrained eye because of the stairs and the finished walls and the familiar furniture, like tables.

He thought this area much more dangerous because of it.

"Are we still getting fresh air?" he asked Raemi. He needed her to do something; monitoring the environmental system might be more than enough.

"Yes," she said. "But there's no breeze, not in here."

Or the particles would be constantly disturbed.

"Thanks," he said. "Keep monitoring that, would you?"

"Oh, trust me, I am," she said. "I'm concerned about the entire environmental system."

Good. Let her worry about that. He would worry about the door, and the room beyond.

He took a deep, steadying breath, and reached for the door handle.

It was a lever that should either go up or down, depending. He tried down first, and heard something click.

So he pushed slightly on the door.

It gave.

He pushed harder, and it moved. Then it got stuck, as if it were blocked by something. He cursed ever so slightly.

"Can we get in?" Raemi asked.

"Don't know yet," Hogarth said. He put more effort into his push without leaning his body weight on the door. The last thing he wanted to do was tumble into the room and activate something that shouldn't have been activated.

The door slid even more, its old-fashioned hinges creaking.

He let out a breath he hadn't even realized he'd been holding.

The door was open wide enough that he could peer inside.

He leaned in just a little and saw only floating particles in darkness. He turned on his helmet light, which made the particles look like snow on a particularly dark winter night.

He blinked, trying not to let the odd reflection off of them interfere with his ability to see.

His eyes couldn't adjust though, which told him that the darkness was profound.

He pushed the door just a bit more, and it stalled yet again. Only this time, the opening was wide enough for him to step through.

Rather than do so, he illuminated one of his palm lights and turned his hand toward the interior of the room.

Ghostly shapes appeared in the thin light. Chairs. Another table. Some kind of equipment on a counter. Dishes that actually looked like they'd been used.

The particles continued to swirl, but less furiously now. Their presence told him something else: there was no one else in this area.

He put a block on the doorjamb to make sure the door wouldn't close on its own. With the hinges on the outside of this room, going in was even more dangerous than the other room.

That thought caught him.

"Don't follow me yet," he said to Raemi. He'd never experienced a setup like this, and he really did not want to get trapped.

"Okay," she said, and she didn't even sound reluctant. He was a bit surprised. He would have thought that she wanted to go with him.

Unless she wanted to stay so she could look at the items in the other room.

He made himself take a deep breath again. He had never experienced distrust like this with Raemi before. With other team members —the ones who had betrayed him, yes, but not Raemi.

Perhaps he was feeling this way because she was acting like they had, and it was having an impact on him.

He had to shake them from his head. Raemi had been trustworthy for years. He had to give her the benefit of that doubt.

He slipped inside, and a light came on. The light first appeared above him and then it ran forward from his position, heading all the way to the back of the room.

The light was thin and brownish. He looked up. Particles had adhered to the long fixture, but he couldn't tell if the particles were inside or outside of it.

The light made the entire room look like it was tinged in sepia, even though the floors, the furniture and the walls were coated in particles. They looked brown here, instead of black, and he wasn't sure if that was the light or if it was the particles themselves.

There didn't seem to be as many particles either. They had swirled slightly when he stepped into the room, but they had settled down quickly.

He surveyed the area before him. It couldn't be any more different than the room before it. This one was set up for living. There were chairs in a small grouping near the door, with some kind of smaller table in front of them. There was a longer piece of furniture, which he would have called a couch, but he couldn't be sure, on the far wall. To his right was a counter that appeared to have equipment on it, but not equipment for work. Judging by the dishes beside it, that counter was used for meal preparation.

There were open shelves behind it with more dishes and what appeared to be a sink of some sort.

And then there were doors on either side of the counter, leading who knew where.

His heart started pounding. He didn't want to go through more doors without Raemi behind him.

He also didn't think he had enough items to brace all of the doors.

He turned around, and let out a small breath. Raemi was standing behind him, waiting patiently. She didn't move guiltily like people had in the past when they were concentrating on the treasure instead of the job at hand.

She was completely focused, just like she was supposed to be.

"We need to double-brace this door," he said to her, "and you need to come in here."

She pulled out one of her door wedges, and handed it to him. He pushed the door as far as it would go, and stuck the wedge underneath it.

He hadn't located whatever caused the door to stick initially. He hoped it was nothing more than the door itself, not having been used in years (decades? Longer than that?). Then he went deeper inside, and grabbed the nearest chair.

Particles rose off the surface, but didn't go very high. They seemed heavier here, and he wasn't sure exactly why. A mystery for later, then.

He scooched the chair toward the door. When he reached it, he shoved the chair in front of it.

Raemi raised her head, her eyes wide with surprise. "You're worried about this."

"I don't want to be trapped here," he said. He had never encountered rooms before, and he was discovering that he feared them a lot more than a basic cave—even one that had suffered cave-ins in the past.

She nodded ever so slightly, as if she didn't want to think about it. Then she peered at the room.

"Someone lived down here," she said.

"Yeah," he said. "And I want to see what's behind the doors by the counter."

"I'll wait here. I'm going to record all of this before we change it too much." Raemi was back to being herself, and Hogarth was profoundly grateful. The mistrust, piled on top of the strangeness of this place, had him more on edge than he had been in years.

"Thanks," he said as he walked to the nearest door.

The particles swirled again, but didn't rise past his thighs. He was right: they were heavier in here, and a different color. The brown that overlaid everything in this room was coming from the particles themselves.

"Still monitoring the environment?" he asked, because he was suddenly nervous about it.

"Only that breeze is missing," Raemi said. "The air is weirdly fresh and the temperature hasn't changed."

It should have. The air should have been stuffy and unused in here, and the temperature should have been different, especially behind that metal door.

A shiver ran down Hogarth's spine. He waited a moment, to see if the shiver was caused by the creepy-crawly feeling that came with whatever trouble he'd encountered before, but the hair didn't rise on the back of his neck nor did his skin crawl, not exactly.

The shiver had come from the strange situation—or so he hoped. Since he had never encountered metal doors and rooms before, he had no idea if they muted the energy that caused the tingly feeling.

With that thought, he moved more slowly toward the door. Part of him stood aside in his own mind, astonished that he was acting so cautiously. He used to love exploring, but this—this just felt odd and dangerous.

And, he reminded himself, it was completely in his control. He could abort.

He swallowed hard, then went forward. He hadn't gotten this far in his life by being a coward or by overthinking. He was doing both at the moment.

So he reached the door, examined it, and saw that it too opened inward. He grabbed the lever and pushed it down. Something clicked, and this time, the door started to move on its own.

He had to let go of the lever because he was, essentially, holding the door closed.

The door swung easily and slowly inside the room. He wondered if all of the doors had been designed like that—to move with such ease into another space.

Another question he couldn't answer immediately.

He peered in, illuminating the room with his headlamp. The beam found a bed, another chair and table, and clothes sprawled along the surfaces, as if someone had left them there planning to use them.

There was an open closet on the wall to his right, and a partially open door on his left. If he turned his head just right, he caught a hint of what was behind that door.

It looked like a bathroom.

But he wasn't going to check on any of it—at least not right now.

He pulled the door closed and walked behind the counter to the other door. It opened just like the first, swinging inward, revealing another bedroom that couldn't have been more different. The mattress was barely above the floor, and the room was incredibly neat. No clothing anywhere except in the open closet, which was on the opposite wall from the one in the first bedroom.

There was another door on the wall to his right this time. Clearly the bedrooms shared a bathroom, and it was behind the area designated as a kitchen.

This underground windowless space, hidden from above, was clearly set up for at least two people to live in, and maybe more with the other door in the main room, waiting for him to explore.

He pulled the door closed, feeling truly uneasy. Something bad had happened down here.

Were the mummies that he found the people who had lived here? Had something happened to cause them to flee and collapse on those stairs? A loss of this near-perfect environment, perhaps? Or something else? Something that usually caused the creepy-crawly feeling for him?

"What is it?" Raemi asked. She sounded almost scared.

Or maybe she did sound scared. Because Hogarth was beginning to realize that he was.

"Bedrooms," he said. "Two so far."

Raemi visibly shuddered. "I'd hate to live down here. There's no windows. No real light."

"And so far," he said, "only one way out."

She clasped her hands together tightly, then looked around. "What is this place?"

He shook his head. "I'd be suggesting that we leave, but it's pretty clear that no one has been here for a long time."

No one alive, anyway.

"Maybe we don't go farther...?" Raemi said.

Another decision point. He took a deep breath, thinking about it. He doubted he'd be back down here—at least this far in. He was tempted to leave it all for the experts, and never see this place again.

But he had promised himself early in this career not to let fear of the unknown stop him, and yet he had allowed himself to become comfortable. Too comfortable. Even though he was exploring death holes all over Wyr.

Here, he was encountering a fear of the unknown like he hadn't felt since he was starting out.

"We're not going to deeply explore," he said, "but I'd like a map of this place, even if it's just in my head. If you don't want to go deep inside, then you can monitor the doors for me."

"You're uneasy too," she said.

"Yeah." He didn't like the fact that his mood was so obvious. "But right now, I'm not going to let it stop me."

She tilted her head a little, making the light reflect off her visor. He couldn't see her expression, but he didn't have to. That movement meant that she didn't agree with his plan, but she wasn't going to argue with him.

Hogarth walked around the counter and went to the third door. It also had a lever handle, but it opened outward, into this room. The third door was also wider than any of the other doors, and it looked a lot more rusted.

He frowned at it, then grabbed the handle before he had the chance to change his mind. He pulled down and the door shook, as if he had put force on it.

He didn't like that, but he didn't like much about this suite of rooms. He hadn't heard a click, but that didn't mean anything. Maybe there was no latch here.

He pulled the lever toward himself, and the door swung open easily. Raemi came to his side, and handed him a block for the door-jamb. Then she helped him prop the door open.

More particles swirled out. They were dark, but he couldn't determine the actual color in this brownish light. He turned his palm lights at the open door, and let out an involuntary sound of surprise.

The room appeared to be bigger—a lot bigger—than these others. He couldn't see the ceiling and he couldn't see the other side of the room. Something large and ungainly blocked his view.

Raemi peered over his shoulder, added her helmet light to his. All of the lights—from the palm lights to the headlamps—did little to dispel the gloom.

"What the hell is this place?" she asked.

He shook his head, and stepped inside, because if he didn't, he never would.

His suit told him that the air was cooler in here, but just as fresh as it had always been. And, his suit told him, there was a breeze.

As he moved, the particles swirled just a little, then settled. There didn't appear to be as many of them here as there had been in the other rooms.

His heart was pounding. His palms might actually have been sweating. No lights went on as he stepped in, so he couldn't see what was in shadow, but whatever it was, it was large.

He looked up. He couldn't see a ceiling, even though that didn't mean there wasn't one.

The walls were curved upwards, as if the room was more of a dome than an actual square room with a ceiling.

Then lights went on all around him, bright and vibrant. He blinked, the lights hurting his eyes.

"There," Raemi said.

Hogarth turned just a little. Raemi had pressed a gloved hand against the wall. Apparently something beside the door activated the lights.

"Thanks," he said, and whirled around again.

The large thing—the unbelievably large thing—was also an impossibly large thing. It was a spacecraft. Not a huge one, not like the ones the Empire usually flew for its military exercises, but a medium-sized one, more like a pleasure craft or something that someone would use for their own personal travels.

Only, he'd never seen this design before. It was as boxy as the rooms he had just left, square and ungainly, with something that looked like skis underneath. The ski-like things were turned upward on each end, pointing to the ship itself.

He had never seen a ship design with an obvious up and down. Nor had he seen one with a series of what looked like windows around one end. There was a ladder that had been deployed on the side of the ship that he stood on, and that ladder led to a closed door.

Hogarth wasn't about to try that door. He wasn't going to get into a strange ship at all.

He walked deeper in the room, and realized that it was much bigger than he had initially thought. Ten or more ships like that might have fit in here. On the wall directly in front of him, there appeared to be display screens and other equipment, as if someone would stand there and work some kind of controls.

He looked behind himself, but didn't see anything similar on the far wall. Instead, he saw containers lined up against the wall. Dozens of them. They looked vaguely rusty, which meant they were made of metal. Or maybe something had dripped on them from above.

"Where are we exactly?" he asked Raemi.

She had known him long enough to answer, "What do you mean?" instead of explaining that they were in some kind of underground bunker.

"What's above us?" he asked.

He rarely looked up that information with his own equipment. When he was underground, he focused on exploring. He would figure out where the death hole had carved its path of destruction when he returned to the surface.

This time, though, he needed to know. Raemi usually tracked such things.

"We've left the valley," she said. "If my coordinates are right, then we're under one of the mountain peaks."

Coordinates on their equipment weren't always right. Being underground sometimes confused the system.

He let out a breath.

There was no way to get a ship in here—at least from this direction. He had no idea what existed on the far side of this room, but he would doubt that any of the doors were large enough to bring a ship like this inside, let alone a lot of small ships.

This room could accommodate more than the small ships, though. It could accommodate larger ships. Or one very large ship.

He walked a little deeper inside and looked up. The light from his helmet couldn't penetrate the darkness, and there were no lights coming from above. All of the interior lights that Raemi had activated ringed around the entire large room, revealing its emptiness and its preparedness for more ships.

But Hogarth knew he was deep underground. There were only two ways the ship got in here—either it had been assembled here or it had come from somewhere else, maybe above.

"Are you getting recordings of this?" he asked Raemi.

She nodded.

"Let's walk around the space, see if we see anything else that we can...I don't know...try to figure out." Hogarth wasn't sure what he was looking for. Maybe a platform on the floor that rose up to the ceiling—wherever that might be—or maybe an indication that this ship had been assembled here.

He started to walk around, when Raemi grabbed his arm.

"I've had enough," she said. "I think this is beyond us."

He peered at the ring, the empty space, the possibility of more doors. He and Raemi had gone a long distance underground, if her positioning was correct. And, if she was correct, there was an entire mountain on top of them.

It *was* beyond them. Mummies, artifacts, abandoned living quarters, and now this ship with all of these containers nearby. This had been something a long time ago, but what kind of something, he did not know.

He wondered if he should even tell the experts about it when they arrived or maybe just leave it at the mummies. He didn't make that suggestion to Raemi, though. He would consider it as they made their way out of here.

"You're right," he said. "Let's go."

They turned around, and Raemi went through the door first. Hogarth groped for the lights as he left, somehow pressing them off. He felt the weight of the darkness behind him.

He took the wedges and blocks off the door.

Then he stepped into the creepy living quarters. The lights were still on here, but he couldn't control them. Raemi almost ran forward. She was more unnerved by this place than he was.

But when she reached the room filled with artifacts, she stopped, and he braced himself for whatever she was going to say. He wasn't sure he was going to like it.

"Let's at least take one piece of an Ivory Tree," she said. "We might be misidentifying it. And knowing what we've found might make a difference."

One piece of an Ivory Tree might fund their work for years. Or make them both well off.

"No," he said. "Either we leave everything or we work on figuring out how to excavate this thing."

He stalked past her and reached the main door, leading to the staircase. She had better follow, or he'd remove the Ivory Tree from her grasp and put the damn thing back.

For the first time in his career, he had found something that was better excavated by people with real experience, people like some archeologists from a university or experts connected to the City Museum of Vaycehn, or maybe even the Death Hole Council, even though he personally thought they were useless. Still, letting them deal with all of this would get him off the hook.

Off the hook for what, he wasn't certain. But this was bigger than him, bigger than his ego, bigger than a simple exploration and a minor theft.

Raemi still hadn't joined him.

He leaned toward the door. The lights were still on, and sure enough, she was standing near the Ivory Trees.

"Raemi," he said. "We're not bringing those."

She held up a piece no larger than her fist. It had broken edges on each side, so it clearly had come off of something else.

"This will be enough to let us know what we found," she said.

"We don't need to know," he said.

"*I* need to know," she said. She tucked it under one arm and picked her way out of the first room.

She had dislodged a lot of particles. It looked like she was in a storm of black snow. As she picked her way out, the particles continued to swirl and rise, almost like they were attacking her.

His stomach flopped. He had no idea what those were or what their purpose was. It wasn't until this moment that he actually thought of them as some kind of defensive weapon, designed to keep people from doing exactly what Raemi was doing.

He wanted to caution her, but he already had, several times.

All he knew was that this action on her part was going to end their working relationship, and maybe their personal one as well.

He moved into the stairwell. She could take the pieces off the door. He wasn't going to go up those stairs side by side with her, just in case the experts had arrived. He didn't want them to think he was complicit in what they might call a theft.

Still, he couldn't stop himself. He paused on the first step, and looked, watching her step out of the door. She stopped long enough to grab the door block and yank it.

Then the door swung closed as if it was being pushed from the inside. It hit her on the arm holding the Ivory Tree.

A loud bang echoed in the small space, and a light flared so bright that it hurt.

Something shoved Hogarth to the stairs. He stumbled, fell, caught himself, even though his ears were ringing and he couldn't see anything except a fritzing black-and-green light in front of his eyes.

His breath caught. His suit wasn't saying anything about being compromised, which was good, since his hands and knees were bruised. He didn't remember falling, but he clearly had fallen.

He scrambled upward, feeling his way as he went. He couldn't hear. He couldn't see. At least the air in his suit was fresh.

He climbed on his hands and knees until he reached the next landing, getting away from whatever had happened. His brain was foggy, his balance compromised. He couldn't stand up, no matter how much he wanted to. He only knew he was on the landing because he couldn't feel another step.

He sat there for a moment, blinking, wishing he could see. His head ached and his ears were ringing. He had no way of gaining information from his suit or in any other way, not until his sight and hearing returned. Right now, he had no idea if the air in the bunker was compromised, if there was smoke or even flame, because he couldn't feel anything through his suit.

He had never thought of environmental suits as dangerous before. He didn't know if his was saving his life or forcing him to make terrible decisions. He had no idea what was going on, not exactly.

And Raemi. He had no idea if she had followed him. If she was all right. If something had happened to her down there.

He leaned forward, conscious of the fact that very little in his body was working at the moment except his sense of touch. He felt the exterior of his suit with his gloves on, feeling for rips and tears or sore spots on his skin.

Up from his ankles, his calves, his thighs, his hips. Nothing really —or rather, nothing unexpected, considering he had fallen against stairs. Nothing he could feel through two layers of thick protective material either. No rips that he could find.

He would have no idea if the suit was compromised, no idea if it was blaring a warning, or trying to flash a bright light at him.

He didn't even try to talk to Raemi because he knew he wouldn't be able to hear her response.

He kept blinking, waiting. He had to breathe slowly, calm himself. He hoped all he had was flash blindness, not something more permanent. He didn't want to think about something more permanent.

But his hearing—after a sound that loud, he might not get that back for a half hour, an hour, maybe more.

He wasn't sure if he should pull off a glove maybe, try to see if the air was hot or if some debris was falling. He might actually be in danger by being on the landing. Maybe he had to go higher.

Maybe he had to go for Raemi.

He kept blinking and he thought something was emerging. It looked like fuzz and then he realized that he could see, but what he was seeing were those damn gray particles.

As if he was in a blizzard, as if the snow visibility was maybe a meter, maybe less.

But he breathed out a sigh of relief. He could see and his suit wasn't telling him that it was compromised.

"Change to text only," he said aloud. At least, he hoped it was aloud. He could feel the words emerge from his throat, but that amplified quality that every human took for granted when they spoke was gone. He wasn't even sure the words had come out as words until he realized that a red cursor blinked in front of him, just like it was supposed to do.

"Is there smoke?" he asked. "Fire? What's the air quality? The ambient temperature?"

Probably too many questions for the suit to deal with in this mode, but it had to. He needed answers. He needed to go get Raemi, if she hadn't already passed him.

The suit told him with numbers that took a moment for him to comprehend that the air was unbreathable due to the amount of debris and dust that surrounded him, but the suit detected no smoke, no fire that it could register.

There had been an explosion and the suit hypothesized, in its mathematically precise way, that this part of this bunker might be compromised.

Recommend extraction, the suit said.

Extraction. As if someone could come and help him.

Maybe someone could, but who would help Raemi? If she was still behind him, anyway. He had been blown forward. Maybe she had too.

Part of his foggy brain wondered what they had touched. What had they altered? What had they triggered?

Not that knowing right now would make any difference. His ears still rang and it felt like his entire head had swollen to five times its normal size. He still wasn't sure he could stand up.

"Can you locate Raemi?" he asked the suit. "Can you contact her? If so, answer me in text. I can't hear."

The cursor blinked. Whoever had designed that as a prompt should have been crushed the moment they suggested the idea. He had never seen such an annoying blinking light in his life.

Finally, the cursor stopped blinking, replaced with *Raemi is offline.*

"What does that mean?" Hogarth asked. "Does that mean you can't contact her or does it mean that she's not in her suit?"

Communications appear to be down. Raemi does not show up on any normal proximity measure.

Or at least one that the suit could reach.

His heart rate increased. Offline. Raemi was offline. And she shouldn't have been. She was suited up just like he had been, so her suit should have talked to his. But maybe it took the force of that explosion differently.

If she had passed him, then she would have been accessible, right? Or maybe the entire communications system was down.

"Contact the others," he said. "Let them know we're in distress."

Emergency beacon was activated the moment that the explosion hit, the suit said. *Help should arrive soon.*

He knew better than to ask if the suit had some kind of knowledge about help arriving. It had already told him that communications were down. That "help should arrive soon" crap was probably something the manufacturers installed to make people feel better.

Even though he wasn't sure if he could stand, he had to go back down and find Raemi. If she had gotten past him, maybe the others would find her, but he had a feeling—a horrible, sick feeling—that she was still down there, in the dust and debris.

He tried to stand, swayed, and nearly fell forward. So he sat back down, and scooted toward the stairs. He climbed down them like a toddler just learning how to negotiate stairs, feet, then butt, then hands. His hands found ragged bits of something hard—rock? Metal? He didn't know. His feet pushed against even more hard things.

That horrible sick feeling was growing worse. He made it down to

43

where he thought he had been standing when he was catapulted forward, and there, the particles no longer looked like snow.

They looked like the aftermath of a snowstorm—rock formations, small hilly inclines, trees—all covered in centimeters of snow. Too much snow.

Sensors show no path forward.

The suit sent him that in bright red flashing letters.

"I just came from here," he said.

You left before the explosion. Now, there is no path forward.

He'd never had an environmental suit argue with him before.

"There has to be," he said.

The cursor blinked. Apparently the suit had no response to that.

He stood on the lowest step and used his hands to push at the snow-, well, particle- covered items. They didn't budge.

He yelled Raemi's name, even though he suspected it would do no good, through his helmet, through the debris before him, without comms.

Even if she could hear.

Her hearing was probably as damaged as his. Maybe more, if she was near that stuff.

He hoped whatever had fallen had come from the ceiling, not from somewhere else.

Then he looked up, and realized that his helmet light was still on. That was why the particles had initially looked like snow. Because they had been visible in the light.

But the ceiling in this stairwell looked like it was intact. So were the walls.

His heart sank, and his breath hitched. He made himself breathe again, stunned that the air was fresh in his suit when everything around him was covered in dust and dirt and particles.

Everything.

All that material—it had to have come from the door. It obviously hadn't come from above.

Obviously.

He was shaking. He felt it.

If he pushed against the rock, he might push it onto Raemi. He couldn't do this without equipment, equipment that he had on the surface. Equipment he had used a hundred times when he explored death holes.

But not like this. Never like this.

He turned around and climbed up the stairs on his hands and knees, going faster than he thought possible. He was still grabbing rocks and debris and bits of items he couldn't quite identify. He had to reach the nearest level. Or the surface.

He needed to get to the surface, and to help.

He needed his team.

He needed someone to help him.

And save Raemi.

THREE

Hogarth had no idea how long he climbed. The climb up seemed to take forever. The climb down hadn't taken that long. And with his brain fog, he couldn't remember how many landings this staircase had, how far up he had to go.

When he reached the next landing, the air cleared a bit. The particles were scattered on the stairs like dirt after a dust storm.

Then, suddenly, hands grabbed him and pulled him up. Helmeted faces peered at him, and people were waving their arms.

It took him a moment to realize that they were talking to him. He shook his head, and pointed to his ears.

The movement made him so dizzy that he nearly fell over, but the hands holding him held tighter.

He pointed behind him, gestured, didn't know how to tell them without comms, without any way to send information, that Raemi was down there.

Finally he tried to take off his helmet, but the hands kept him from doing so.

He waved his hands even more.

"Raemi," he shouted. "You have to get Raemi."

A few people nodded, then started down, but he grabbed at them.

They stopped, confused, and he gestured with both hands, going down and then up, miming digging with a shovel.

They didn't seem to understand. How could they?

He tried to take off the helmet again, and the hands held him firmly. He shook them off, staggered, nearly fell down the stairs, but someone else caught him.

Dammit, they had to understand. They had to listen.

He grabbed his helmet before they could stop him, shut off its connection to the suit and pulled up the visor.

The air tasted of chalk and dirt. He coughed, then said, as loudly as he could, "You'll need equipment to get Raemi. The passageway came down on us. She doesn't have comms. Neither do I."

Someone gave him a thumbs up, then the nearest person grabbed his helmet and pushed the visor down, activating the seal from the exterior, like people could do in an emergency. He protested, then realized, yes, indeed, this was an emergency.

Two team members ran up the stairs, while others ran down. Some stayed with him.

He was swaying and coughing, and those damn dots were in front of his eyes again. There hadn't been another flare, but his eyes weren't acting right, and he was dizzy, and his stomach had grown queasy.

He grabbed the nearest arm to brace himself. He would climb the rest of the way up, get out of this hellhole, explain what kind of equipment they needed.

He started up, swayed again, and started to fall backwards. Someone caught him, then turned out all the lights. His head lolled, and he thought: *I need to keep moving.*

But he couldn't.

He couldn't.

So he stopped.

FOUR

Hogarth was surprised to wake up in a bed, under cool crisp sheets. The room was dim and had a trail of pale lights that ran around the edges of walls, floor, ceiling, and door, as if marking all of them. An open door, with a pale light illuminating a bit of the interior, revealed a bathroom.

There were handles on the side of the bed, but they were in a lowered position, so no one thought he needed to grab something when he got up.

They would have been wrong. His head ached so badly that turning it slightly made him nauseous. His ears still rang, and his eyes burned as if the room was filled with smoke.

He raised his hands gingerly. He watched them come up, but looking at them move made him dizzy. He closed his aching eyes, and reached for his ears.

They were bandaged.

He felt the rest of his face, found no more bandages but as he worked, he realized his throat ached, and his entire torso was sore.

"You have a concussion," a woman said. Her voice sounded loud and underwater at the same time. "But we had to keep you unconscious, despite the risk, because we are doing a lot of repair on your lungs. In those few minutes that you had your helmet off, you inhaled something that pretty much destroyed them."

"What?" he asked. At least he could hear himself now. His voice sounded raspy beneath the constant ringing in his ears, but he had a voice and something that passed for hearing.

He was surprised at how much that relieved him.

"And it didn't do your throat any good. Fortunately, you had breathed through your mouth only, not your nose, or you'd be sore there too. We were able to repair most of it in the first try, but we're tweaking it all now. You were very badly hurt."

He blinked his eyes open. The woman, a shadow in the dim light, was standing near the main door.

"What happened to Raemi?" he asked.

The woman let out a small sigh. "Raemi was so close to the blast that she died instantly. You do not want me to tell you anything else."

But he did. He needed to know all of it. He had never made a mistake this big in his work. People had died, but not because of him. Not because he wanted to explore something. Not because he hadn't foreseen any of it.

Raemi. Raemi was dead.

He couldn't quite wrap his brain around it. He had never lost someone this close before, someone he actually cared about.

"What happened to us?" he asked.

The woman shook her head. "I'm your doctor. Let me get someone who actually knows."

And then she walked out of the room.

Hogarth closed his eyes, his heart pounding. He was upset, but unsurprised. Somehow he had known that Raemi might not make it. Maybe he had known that she was already dead.

If only he could have blamed it on her greed, but he couldn't. After that conversation in the first room, she had calmed down. She had helped with the exploration. She had acted like herself...

Hadn't she?

Something tinged the front of his aching brain. She had, but then

49

she had taken part of an Ivory Tree. A small part. And she had a reason for it, although he couldn't remember the details.

That couldn't be it, though, since no one else had ever had an issue with an Ivory Tree. They were pretty and valuable, but useless, as far as he knew.

The more likely scenario was that the bunker itself attacked the moment she tried to carry something out of it. That had probably been some kind of failsafe, something that protected whatever was inside that space.

Or maybe it had nothing to do with the items in the bunker, and everything to do with the bunker itself. Maybe no one was allowed to leave without some kind of code. Maybe it had a wide variety of ways to attack whoever had breached its systems.

The door to his room opened again, and this time Mehmet entered. Hogarth recognized him just from his body shape and his stance. Mehmet always leaned a bit to the right. His skinny shoulders were never properly aligned with the rest of him.

"They finally woke you," Mehmet said.

Hogarth could barely hear him. Unlike the doctor, Mehmet wasn't speaking loudly. Instead, it sounded like Mehmet was speaking through a bad comm system, one that didn't work well at all.

"I woke up on my own," Hogarth said.

"Yeah, because they let you," Mehmet said. "I wanted them to keep you awake the whole time, but I had no say."

Why would Mehmet want him awake? Something was going on. Hogarth had no idea how long he had been unconscious, how long Mehmet had been waiting.

How long Raemi had been dead.

"They told me they needed me unconscious to repair damage," Hogarth said.

"That's what they say," Mehmet said. "I guess they did a lot of risky things to save your life."

"What happened?" Hogarth whispered. He wasn't talking about the blast as much as he was talking about himself. He had no idea what happened or how it happened or how he ended up here.

Mehmet knew him well enough to answer the question that Hogarth wanted to ask, not the one he did ask.

"You inhaled those strange particles. They coated your lungs. Tried to seal them. You barely survived," Mehmet sounded matter of fact, even though his voice was shaking.

Seal his lungs? Hogarth tried to understand what Mehmet meant. The particles—they formed something that closed up his lungs?

How had people lived with those particles then? Was that how they had become mummies?

Mehmet was shaking his head. "You shouldn't have taken off your helmet."

The words stabbed at Hogarth, making him feel as if his injury— as if Raemi's death—was his fault. Maybe it was.

They didn't have to go in that room.

"I thought Raemi was alive." Hogarth's voice broke. Maybe she had been. Maybe if he had gotten to her quicker...

"No one could have survived that blast," Mehmet said. "It blew out the door, collapsed a wall, and caused a crater that went even deeper underground."

Hogarth blinked. He didn't understand. That wasn't what he saw at all.

"But the debris," he said. "It was piled high, not like something that went underground."

"Yeah, it was piled," Mehmet said. "You only saw the top of it."

The top of it. Hogarth had seen so much, and it had been just a bit.

"And Raemi was under it?" he asked.

"No. She got blown sideways." Mehmet shook his head. "I'm not telling you anything else, because I don't want to think about it."

"Mehmet," Hogarth said. "I was with her. She couldn't have died in that blast. She is probably still there, trapped somewhere. She—"

"We found parts," Mehmet said. "Okay? We found pieces of Raemi, just like we found pieces of the door and the floor and the wall. We found *pieces*. I'm not saying anything else about that. Not another word."

Pieces. Parts. And Mehmet, cutting off discussion because he was so traumatized.

That wasn't Mehmet at all. He had always been sensible. The man that Hogarth could go to if Raemi wasn't around.

Now Raemi wasn't around.

And Mehmet—he wasn't sensible. He wasn't calm. He snapped at Hogarth, and Hogarth was the one who had been injured.

Who had nearly died.

"Do they know what caused the explosion?" Hogarth asked. He had to bite back the rest of the question. He'd almost added *besides the exploration.*

Because he knew—they probably knew—that nothing would have exploded if he hadn't gone down those stairs. If he had waited with his team by the mummies.

If they had figured out what those mummies were, exactly.

Like he had assigned them. The team had probably recorded everything, done everything they could for the experts.

"Who are *they?*" Mehmet spat out the words, and Hogarth finally understood what was going on.

Mehmet was furious. At Hogarth. Probably rightfully so.

Mehmet had been the one to deal with the aftermath. Mehmet had been the one who found Raemi, and Mehmet had been arguing that they wake up Hogarth sooner.

To accuse him? Or to talk to him?

"Anyone," Hogarth said. "Does anyone know?"

"I thought maybe you did," Mehmet said.

Hogarth frowned, remembering. Trying to put everything together.

He had gotten out of the door but he had been empty-handed. Raemi hadn't been.

He shook his head, and stopped almost immediately. The movement made him both dizzy and nauseous.

"We were leaving," he said. "I was just a bit ahead of her. She seemed fine. Everything seemed fine. And then..."

The flash. Something forcing him forward. The stairs, colliding with him or him colliding with the stairs.

He had clearly been blown free.

And Raemi hadn't.

Mehmet waved a hand, as if he didn't want to hear.

"I stayed until they finally woke you because there are some things you need to know. I figured you'd have questions. After that, I'm gone."

"Gone?" Hogarth asked. What did that mean?

"The team disbanded," Mehmet said. "They want nothing to do with any of this. Ever. Neither do I."

"This?" Hogarth asked. Everything was moving so fast that it made his head spin worse than it already was. Was he having trouble understanding because he just woke up or was it because of his injuries?

"The bunker, the mummies." Mehmet waved a hand. "I'm done. You know, I should have known. We've been exploring *death holes*, for godsake. *Death* holes. At some point it would catch up to us, I suppose. We were stalking death. Of course it would catch us."

And finally everything crystalized.

Death holes blew outward from underground. Death holes usually blew upwards with such power that it ripped through layers of dirt and stone and rock, sometimes tearing buildings apart, destroying entire blocks.

Sometimes the sides of mountains blew off. And people died.

There hadn't been a new death hole in more than a year, but that didn't mean they had stopped.

This one had blown sideways, not upward.

"You think this was a death hole?" Hogarth asked.

Mehmet tilted his head, just like he always did when a new idea hit him.

"I didn't say that." He spoke slowly. "Do you?"

"The mummies," Hogarth said. "They usually show up near death holes."

Inside the area where the death hole had originated, in fact.

He had to squint to maintain his concentration. He was exhausted. Just this much conversation was hurting him.

"It would have been a small one," Mehmet said. "The stairway is still intact."

"You said the explosion went down, not up." Hogarth brought his hand to his face, one of his nervous gestures. He usually ran the hand along his skin, but he had to stop.

His hand was trembling too much to even touch his skin.

"If death holes go down too, then everything on Wyr is unstable," Mehmet said.

"Everything on Wyr *is* unstable," Hogarth said. "We just lie to ourselves about it all the time."

He thought Mehmet knew that, thought the team understood it. Maybe Hogarth hadn't understood it fully either, though. He had been taking items from the death hole passages, not doing some kind of scientific exploration.

No one was doing scientific exploration, and everyone was happy that the death holes had stopped, at least for a while. But if they went deeper underground, then at some point, the surface would just cave in, not blow out.

"Well, it doesn't matter," Mehmet said. "I'm not doing this anymore. That's part of what I need to tell you."

Part. Hogarth frowned, then stopped himself. Even that movement of his forehead hurt. He had to think hard to smooth it out.

"The team needs you, Mehmet," Hogarth said. "*I* need you. With Raemi gone—"

"There is no team," Mehmet said. "They left. All of them. This was the end of it, for everyone. They're gone. That's the other thing I needed to tell you."

Hogarth wanted to shake his head. He had to grip the sheets hard. "It doesn't matter," he said. "We can hire new people. I've done that half a dozen times. That's how I found you."

But not Raemi. She'd been in the first group, all the way back.

His heart twisted. He regretted this entire trip, everything. He had treated her so unfairly, thinking of her as greedy, when she'd been at his side forever.

Why did the last trip have to be so negative? Why, if someone had to die, couldn't it have been at the end of some victory, something—

"No," Mehmet said, bursting into Hogarth's thoughts. They had gone along a strange side trip, which, again, was how he knew he wasn't well.

"No?" Hogarth asked, wondering if he'd missed more.

"No, there will be no new team, at least not with me." Mehmet took one step closer to the bed. Hogarth still couldn't see his face clearly. "And not with anyone else you've hired. No one is going into those death holes again."

Hogarth had been through this before. When he'd lost the two greedy bastards, years ago, his entire team left, blaming him. He could get through this again.

Once he healed. Once he figured out what was going on.

"Can we talk when I'm better?" Hogarth asked. He was getting woozy from exhaustion.

"No," Mehmet said, "because I am leaving Wyr. I have no idea where the others have gone, either, but I stayed, to tell you about Raemi and the team, but mostly to let you know that this—everything —it's your problem."

Hogarth frowned, and this time, despite the pain, he couldn't quite relax his face. He was concentrating hard, and trying to figure out what was happening in this conversation, and he was feeling light-headed. He needed to track it.

"Everything?" he repeated.

He usually wasn't slow on the uptake, but he was on this day.

"I didn't know this but maybe you did and didn't tell us." Mehmet's voice dripped contempt. "This part of Wyr, there's no real government here."

Hogarth knew that. He had told the team that, so how could Mehmet say he didn't know it?

"Which means that the entire area is a kind of finders-keepers place," Mehmet said. "You find something valuable, you own it. It's yours if you want it."

Had Raemi known that? Was that why she was so focused on the Ivory Trees?

A shudder ran through Hogarth.

"The mummies, whatever is behind that door, it belongs to you now, Hogarth," Mehmet said. "The damage, that's on you too. And if someone wants to go after you for Raemi's death, then that's on you as well."

That would have been on Hogarth no matter what. That was the way that the team worked. But he didn't say that, since there was no need.

The team had been Raemi's family. She had no one else.

Hogarth took a deep breath. He had to say this clearly.

"If that's true," he said, "whatever we found, it belongs to the team, not to me."

"We don't want it. The others have already left, didn't you hear me?"

"I heard," Hogarth said. "But..."

He almost mentioned the wealth inside that room, the Ivory Trees, the entire bunker. But he had no idea if the death hole, or whatever it was, had blown backwards as well, destroying what was inside.

"The mummies," he finished. "They're worth something."

"You said you would never sell human beings," Mehmet said, viciously.

"They're not human," Hogarth said. "They're the remains of human beings."

"Fine distinction to make now," Mehmet said. "You going to sell the pieces of Raemi too?"

The words hung between them.

Hogarth supposed he deserved that.

"No," he said. "That's not what I meant. I'm not being as clear as I want, Mehmet."

"Then be clear." The words were whip sharp, as if Mehmet didn't want to hear any more. But he didn't move, so there was that, at least.

"The mummies were dressed. They had to have had items on their bodies that had value. You catalogued them, Mehmet, or you were supposed to. There was value, right? A lot of value."

"We had never seen anything like what they were carrying before," Mehmet said. "I was going to tell you that when you came up, but you were in such a hurry. You and Raemi wanted to get back to that room. You wanted something from down there or to explore. You were so sure that there was more to it—"

"There was," Hogarth said. "We found other rooms."

But he wasn't going to mention the spaceship. That just stressed credulity, particularly when he had a head injury.

He wasn't going to mention the Ivory Trees either. He didn't want Mehmet to react like Raemi had.

"I'm just saying," Hogarth said, as carefully as he could, "there's money. We would be able to handle whatever came our way."

"I'm not going down there again," Mehmet said. "I'm not going in any caves again, and neither is anyone else. We don't want any money. We just want to get away from here. It's all yours, Hogarth. That's what I'm here to tell you. It's all yours."

The bunker, the death hole, the pieces of Raemi.

Hogarth closed his eyes. He didn't really want any of it either, and yet, there was a mystery here. Something that still intrigued him.

He opened his eyes, afraid he had fallen asleep, afraid Mehmet was gone.

But Mehmet remained.

"The experts," Hogarth said. "Did they ever arrive?"

"No," Mehmet said. "We were left to try to rescue you all ourselves."

Hogarth tried to imagine it—the team hearing (feeling?) the explosion, and reacting. He didn't even know if they had been on the surface or beside the mummies.

The team had come—he remembered them coming, as a unit, and he had pulled off his helmet to talk to them. He had no idea who ran into the dirt and debris. Nor did he know who had gone up to the surface for more help.

Did the team try to get to Raemi and fail? Did they try to dig her out? Did they wait for some authorities?

He wanted to know all of it, and he didn't want to know any of it. He was getting so tired. He needed rest, and he had a feeling that he might never really rest again, not deeply. Not securely.

He would think about Raemi, about bringing her in deeper into that bunker, about the Ivory Trees and the disaster.

"But," Mehmet was saying, "I did take the mummies to the experts you had hired for the last job. They'd seemed honest enough. They're using the recordings that we made and the location, and the information about the bunker, to figure out what we—what you —have."

That was a commitment then. Because the experts cost money. It was probably too late to stop them. They would have already racked up a lot of charges.

"Thank you," Hogarth said. He wasn't sure he meant it.

Mehmet nodded, then took another step forward. His face was no longer in shadow. He looked older. Lines had formed along his mouth and nose, and his eyes were sunken.

This disaster had taken a severe toll on him.

He surveyed all the medical equipment, then looked Hogarth directly in the eye.

"I hope you recover quickly," Mehmet said. Then he flailed with both arms, as if he wasn't sure what to say next. He was clearly too angry to be as kind as he usually would have been.

"Thank you," Hogarth said.

"I've left detailed notes in the team systems. You'll be able to find everything. We recorded a lot too, so you'll have that." Mehmet's tone was flat, as if he didn't want to say much more.

"May I contact you when I start into all the materials?" Hogarth asked.

"No," Mehmet said curtly. Then his expression softened. "I mean...I'm only available for the next week or so. Then I'm going home."

Home? Mehmet didn't have a home.

It took a moment for it all to register.

"The freighter?" Hogarth asked. "You're going back to space?"

Mehmet hated space. He hated the way he had grown up. He hated traveling everywhere and never stopping anywhere.

"Yeah," Mehmet said. "It's safer than living planetside. I'm done exploring. And if you were smart, you'd be done too."

He pivoted and stalked out of the room before Hogarth could even think of stopping him. As the thought flitted across Hogarth's sore brain, he considered yelling after Mehmet.

But he didn't. Mehmet had the right to make his own choices, and he had done so while Hogarth was still unconscious. Judging by the way Mehmet looked, there would be no argument that would convince him to stay.

Everything was on Hogarth now.

Although he could probably walk away from it too. He had a variety of excuses. He'd lost his team. He might have lost his health. He certainly lost mobility, at least for the foreseeable future.

But he wasn't ready to give up yet.

He wasn't a sentimental man, so he couldn't convince himself to stay and work for Raemi's sake. Raemi was gone and that hurt his heart, but her death had no impact on his choices.

He wanted answers. He *needed* answers. And he wouldn't even be able to get them until he had healed.

He wasn't even sure how he would get them. A team like the one that had just left him wasn't the answer. If he wanted to know what happened in that death hole, then he would need real experts, not just some random hired folk, but the people who studied it all for a living.

Maybe he and Raemi had activated whatever it was that caused death holes. Or maybe their presence—and the explosion—beefed up the automated security down below.

Or maybe there was another entrance. There had to be. Not one created by a death hole, but somewhere else.

His heart rate increased and he felt more awake than he had moments ago. He was interested again.

This was just a setback—a particularly nasty one, true—but a setback nonetheless.

He would need to raise funds (maybe sell the mummies?) and he would need a new team, a lot of planning, and a real goal.

Maybe he could even get one of the universities to participate, with a promise of the proceeds.

He smiled for the first time since he woke up.

He could lie to himself and say that this was what Raemi would have wanted, but it wasn't. Raemi would have stopped at that first room. She would have looted it for the Ivory Trees and everything else that was down there.

And maybe he would do that too. But he had to assume that all of that got destroyed in the explosion. Or maybe that it was all blocked off.

He wouldn't be able to do any of the planning from here. He needed to recover. He needed to take the time to become whole.

And he would do all that, as soon as he woke up from this next, most necessary, nap.

THE AUCTION

NOW

FIVE

Khelan Māhoe sat alone in an automated aircart built to transport at least ten people, and regretted his choices. He should have landed his skip illegally on an empty patch of land near the warehouse area. But he had chosen to be cooperative, which was clearly a mistake.

Instead of ending up a few city blocks from his skip, he was kilometers away, and getting farther with each passing second. He had landed at Vaycehn's space port, on the opposite side of the city, and he had subjected himself to Corporate Treasures' whims right from the start.

Would a man of means do that? Usually, Khelan was sure-footed when he used his wealthiest Empire identity, but he usually used it in space, instead of planetside. The very idea of attending an auction on Wyr made him uncomfortable, and of course, that had had an impact on his decision-making.

His assistant, Idil Palakiko, was too new to understand the differences between planetside work and space work. He had brought her from Amnthra for all of her expertise—especially her piloting skills—but she had only been here a year. He hoped that she would take his place one day, but he had hoped that of every assistant from the beginning of his work in the Empire.

Those hopes had been dashed for more than twenty years.

Still, he couldn't remember ever allowing himself to be this vulnerable. The aircart was built for ten or more, with seats toward the back that could be folded to make room for cargo. The cart was too big, especially considering that he was by himself.

He had expected to join others on the trip to the warehouse, and listen to gossip along the way. He had not expected to be completely alone.

That made him nervous as did the design of the aircart. It was open to the elements, even though it had a rigid structure that suggested it had side and top panels that could be activated when needed.

Of course, he didn't know how to activate anything here. He'd ridden on aircarts before, but they usually had an obvious control panel or an actual operator (read tour guide) who could handle the cart in an emergency.

He didn't need a tour guide. In fact, he had turned one down. Early in his years in the Empire, he had lived in Vaycehn, until he realized how dangerous the city was. He hadn't known about the death holes when he moved here, and the moment he found out about them, he fled.

Still, he found the SeBaze Mountains, which rimmed the city, to be the most beautiful in the Empire. They reminded him of the Naramzin Range back home on Amnthra, which shouldn't have been a surprise. The Fleet had probably had the same thought many millennia ago, when they chose those two sites for sector bases.

At least, Khelan was assuming that there had been a sector base in these mountains. All the signs pointed to it.

He tried to concentrate on the mountains as the cart veered around building after building. Even after all these centuries, the mountains were jagged. Time had not smoothed their edges. They were tall, imposing, and at the highest elevations, snow-covered. In this early morning light, they looked vaguely purple, except where Wyr's sun illuminated their tannish-brown sides.

He had to look away from the snow, though, because it made him focus on the wind blowing in through the open sides of the cart. The cool air of a Vaycehn morning felt actively cold at this speed. He wished he'd worn an actual coat, not that it would have helped. The black tunic and matching pants should have been enough, but they weren't. He resisted the urge to put his hands in his armpits because he had no idea if he was being observed, and the movement was slightly rude by Vaycehn standards.

It felt like he was completely alone. He didn't even see people moving about the city, no matter how many neighborhoods he passed. It wasn't that early, but then, Vaycehn wasn't a walking city. People liked their own transports, probably because danger lurked around every corner (and underground).

When he had lived here, he had been startled at how accepting the city was of its strangeness and its difficulties. It wasn't like people from Vaycehn had no choice but to live here. They could live anywhere within the Empire (or outside of it, if they were smart). But they chose here. Most of them had been here for generations, something he truly did not understand.

He gripped the edges of his seat. The cart had restraining belts, which he used although they made him uncomfortable. He had debated it, though, because if something happened to the cart, he couldn't escape quickly.

He finally decided that, since he wasn't even certain how to find the control panel, he might as well acquiesce to remaining in one place. Besides, if he was honest, he wouldn't know what to do with the control panel if he found it. The Empire's technology was centuries behind Amnthran tech, and even though he'd lived in the Empire for decades, he had never mastered the intricacies of their technology.

He hadn't wanted to, and he really didn't now.

He usually tried not to put himself in situations like this, but he hadn't been thinking. He had been scurrying to get to the auction, and to put all of the correct funds in the correct accounts. That was harder than it sounded, given that the notification of the auction had come at the last minute to his Khelan Madani identity. Madani was a collector who had made his interest in rare items known throughout the Empire.

Madani also owned a space yacht filled with rare collectibles. It was that yacht, with Idil at the helm, that was in orbit around Wyr right now.

Khelan was not going to contact her, except in the case of an extreme emergency. He hadn't expected any, but then, he hadn't expected this damn cart either.

Finally, the warehouse district appeared ahead. The district used to be on the very edge of the city, but time and the need to move after a death hole had brought the city to the district. Now he could see homes and businesses dotting the mountainside on the other side of the warehouses.

Apartment complexes rose around the district, which had surprised him when he had looked on a holographic map before coming here. He had wanted to know exactly where this auction was being held.

He had been to hundreds of art, antiquities, and collectible auctions in the Empire since coming here, but he had never been to one in a warehouse before.

The contact had claimed that more than a thousand items had been discovered along with six mummies. It was the mummies that had caught his attention. Sadly—and creepily—the mummies were collectible. They even had a name, "The Mummies of Wyr."

The mummies were created inside a malfunctioning *anacapa* field. There were a few such fields in the Empire, which was one reason that Khelan knew the Fleet had come through here. One of those fields, at the Room of Lost Souls, might have been shut down a few years ago.

He didn't know that for certain, and on most levels, he didn't care. It wasn't his remit to study the Fleet or its sector and star bases. He certainly wasn't going to tell anyone in the Empire about the malfunctioning *anacapa* drives. No one would believe him, or if they did, they would see him as someone other than a person raised in the Empire.

The malfunctioning drives did bother him, though. Clearly, when the Fleet left the sector containing the Empire thousands of years ago, something had gone wrong. Either the *anacapas* were left behind or they had needed to remain active to deal with some threat.

There were two reasons he was convinced the sector base had been on Wyr—the SeBaze Mountain Range and the mummies that were being discovered here.

Anyone caught inside a malfunctioning *anacapa* field experienced time differently than someone outside the field. From the perspective of someone outside the field, the person inside could die within hours. A handful got pulled out of the field, usually by using some kind of automated tool that could fetch them without sending another person into the field.

But others who got trapped inside a field couldn't be recovered until the field retreated. Those mummies were forgotten explorers, unknown to anyone from Vaycehn. And they had become artifacts, because they were usually discovered with art or antiquities that the people of the Empire considered valuable.

Many of those artifacts were from other places. He had discovered nearly a hundred Amnthran weapons at auctions like this over the years. The Empire did not understand Amnthran weapons—didn't even see them as weapons—so they were usually included as artworks or historical artifacts.

That was why Khelan had the Mandani identity. He posed as an exceedingly rich man who collected rare items. So far, he had managed to purchase every Amnthran weapon he had found, and he had sent them back to Amnthra, sometimes with an assistant who wasn't working out.

This auction had six mummies—more than had ever been auctioned at one time before. He wasn't going after the mummies. He hoped he wouldn't have to go near them.

He wanted to see what they had been found with. Corporate Treasures, the group in charge of the auction, had promised beautiful surprises.

Beautiful surprises were often code words for Amnthran items. Amnthra, unlike the Empire, believed that everything, no matter what its function, should also be a work of art. Just because something was useful didn't mean it had to be ugly.

That philosophy worked well in Amnthran culture, but here, in the Empire, where everything was ugly, and art was something to be displayed, beauty signified "useless." Most inside the Empire dismissed beautiful items as something that belonged to the idle rich.

So far, no one here had discovered how to use Amnthran weapons, and Khelan was here to keep it that way.

There were maybe a hundred people like him in various sectors, tasked with recovering Amnthran weapons, usually stolen so that they could be reversed engineered. Amnthra did its best to keep its culture and its cultural knowledge closely held. Their fierceness in guarding their secrets, and their willingness to build on the technology and science left behind by the Fleet thousands of years before made Amnthra the most feared culture in their sector—and maybe beyond.

The Empire was so locked in its own belief that it, and its culture, were the greatest in the universe that they hadn't looked beyond their own borders for more information. Usually, Khelan played on that ignorance.

Right now, it was making him nervous.

The cart slowed as it reached the warehouse district. He let out a small breath, then glanced at the mountains again.

The warehouse district was built on a flat area near the foothills. He had forgotten that.

He wondered where Corporate Treasures had found the mummies. He hoped it wasn't close to here.

The cart reached the center of the district, and then lowered rapidly. It went almost straight down onto a gravel-strewn area outside what appeared to be the largest warehouse.

There were no skips here, no other carts, and no people outside.

His heart started beating hard. He hadn't expected a crowd, but he had expected a greeting committee of some kind.

The cart landed and a mechanized voice said, "You have reached your destination. Please disembark."

It wobbled a little, as if it was going to disgorge him itself. So he undid the restraint and climbed out.

The cart immediately rose and left him, unprotected and alone.

At least he had his laser pistol, even if it was of Empire make. It was good enough.

He hadn't expected to be stranded.

He suddenly wondered if the invitation and the mummies were a ruse to get him here. Or rather, Madani. Kidnapping wasn't something that occurred in the Empire much—the military tended to overreact and kidnappers (successful or not) usually died—but that might not stop someone from taking one of the richest men in the Empire.

He let out a breath of annoyance at himself. He had done a proper background check on Corporate Treasures. They had a sterling reputation. The invite had been real. But that didn't stop him from feeling uneasy.

He would give them five minutes before he walked away from the warehouse and contacted Idil.

Five minutes, and not a second more.

SIX

Khelan stood alone and tried not to fidget. He did not look at the time, although he could feel it ticking down.

The neighborhood was old, for this part of Vaycehn anyway, with lots of flat white rectangular buildings. The buildings were built into a large depression which, if Khelan were a betting man, he would wager was probably part of an ancient caved-in death hole.

The warehouse at the end of the gravel area before him looked abandoned.

He had been stupid not to bring his own security, but then, as Madani, he had never traveled with security. He had maintained the image of a hugely private rich man.

The lack of security (here in the Empire anyway) was seen as a sign of trust. It also prevented any information about the items for sale being leaked outside of the world of collectors.

He had been through this rigmarole before, and knew that the locals would expect the same behavior from him. That was one of the few downsides of a well-established identity. He had to behave the way he had behaved in the past. He never kept notes about what he did, and the longer he was here in the Empire, the harder it was to remember what action had been performed by which identity.

A slight breeze toyed with his black hair, making the tips fall into his eyes. He pushed the hair away, deliberately revealing the tattoos that ran along the left side of his face.

They were the only thing he had refused to change when he came to the Empire. People here didn't tattoo their bodies much at all, so his face tattoos were not only unusual, but highly noticeable. People commented on them.

He kept them for the Madani identity, but not for any other identity. In his early days here, he hadn't wanted to hide the tattoos at all. Now, he covered them as often as he needed to, particularly when he didn't want to be identified.

Here, though, in front of this warehouse, he wanted the people inside to know who he was.

The breeze was stubbornly determined to move his hair around his face. He decided to stop fussing with the hair, although he couldn't stop adjusting his clothing. He had already shut off some of his trackable tech. Now, he activated a chip in his wrist so that Idil could track him from orbit.

They didn't have a team to back them up at the moment, so he wasn't sure what she could do if someone did try to take him.

That would be Idil's problem.

He had enough problems of his own.

The warehouse he had been invited to looked no different on the exterior than the ones around it, except that it was shiny white. The gray skies made the other warehouses look a bit tattered and faded, but not this one.

There were roads leading to all of the warehouses, roads that did not run in a straight line. He had no idea if that was deliberate or if that meant they had once been built around other buildings or problems on the ground.

This warehouse had no windows and no obvious doors. The place was designed to hide whatever was inside, unlike some of the more dilapidated warehouses nearby.

He also did not recognize the material that the warehouse was made out of. It did not attract dirt, which led him to believe either the Empire's military had built this place to store weapons, or Corporate

Treasures' parent organization—whatever it was—had done so for the very purpose of storing valuables here…and making it impossible for anyone to steal them.

After three long fidgety minutes, perfectly aligned cracks appeared in the wall he was facing. The cracks revealed the shape of a door, which opened outward. A man stepped out, followed by a woman and another person whose face was obscured by some kind of helmet. All three people were wearing matching green uniforms with gold piping, and a logo across the back.

Clearly not military uniforms.

The woman stopped in front of him, and her greenish-gray eyes examined him as if she had never seen anything like him before. She probably hadn't. Her gaze rested on the intricate pattern of his tattoo. It went straight down the side of his face, all angles and sharp edges, except for the oval around his left eye, which she now looked at directly.

"I had heard about your strange habits," she said as if there was something wrong with him. "You must be Khelan Madani."

"I am," he said, clicking his heels together and bowing his head ever so slightly in the usual greeting among members of the Empire. Normally, he would have added some kind of honorific or claimed he was happy to make her acquaintance, or say that he was happy to be here, but judging from the uniforms and the other two people, she was just security.

Although she was a bit rude for security.

"I'm told you carry a laser pistol when you're alone," she said. "Give it to me."

"Once you tell me where we're going," Khelan said. He made sure he sounded bored with a touch of irritation.

"Inside, obviously," she said.

He stared at her and did not remove the pistol. "I'm not fond of your tone," he said. "I need to know who you are before I turn over anything."

She sighed, and looked over her shoulder at the helmeted person. "My name is not important," she said. "I'm in charge of keeping all of you safe."

"I only count one of me," he said.

"There are two dozen invitees, all of whom seem to think that buying corpses is a good idea." Her mouth turned upwards ever so slightly in what might have been a smile. "And before you ask for more information, I'm hired security. The firm I work for is the best in the Empire, partly because we don't play games or pretend that you're better than we are because you have enough money to waste on things that shouldn't be purchased in the first place."

He did his best to keep his expression neutral, but he was surprised. He had never met someone who worked security quite like her before.

"Now," she said, extending her right hand, palm up, "give me the pistol. You'll get it back when you leave."

He raised his chin ever so slightly so that he could give her a look he had worked on specifically for this identity. It was an *I can destroy you in ways you can't imagine* look, one that wasn't based on physical power, but on class differences.

Her gaze did not waver. Nor did she close her hand and retract it.

He maintained his gaze on hers, his expression deliberately darkening as he removed the laser pistol from the holster he had inside his tunic. He put the pistol on her palm, knowing if he said anything else about it, he would look weak rather than strong.

She handed the pistol as if it were nothing over to the man beside her. He put it in a belt around his waist that Khelan hadn't noticed until now.

Then both the woman and the helmeted person nudged Khelan forward, walking beside him as they headed into the warehouse. He felt like a prisoner, someone who could be grabbed and shoved into a cell, which he suspected, was exactly how the woman wanted him to feel.

They reached the door. There seemed to be darkness beyond. With her right hand, the woman indicated that he needed to go first. He gave her a condescending smile.

"I never am the first one to walk into a building," he said, finally using the full contempt that he allowed himself as Madani.

He deliberately leaned back, just a little, so that his body language made it clear that he wouldn't move until the woman did.

She shot him a look of fury, then swept that hand forward again, this time with her gaze on the man to Khelan's left. The man shrugged and stepped inside, disappearing into the darkness.

Khelan waited a beat. He knew that the woman wouldn't precede him, and he wasn't going to push her to do so. He'd pushed hard enough to make his point; that was all he needed to do.

He walked through the door. The room was lighter than he expected. What his brain had registered as darkness was actually gray room dividers that walled off the entry from the rest of the warehouse, maybe so that no one could easily record what was going on inside.

He threaded his way around the dividers. There was no sign of the man who had preceded him and he couldn't hear the woman or the helmeted person behind him.

The entire setup was designed to make Khelan nervous, but he'd been through such things a dozen or more times before. For some reason, the Empire believed that more barriers—inexplicable barriers —were some kind of security rather than an actual annoyance.

He finally stepped out of the dividers into the warehouse proper. The main room had not been divided up. It was large and ran the entire width of the building. In the far back, half a block away, he saw a few doors and an unprotected entrance to what might have been a hallway.

The lights on the ceiling made everything washed out and pale, including the solid gray floor. In the center, though, was a stack of boxes as tall as Khelan was. Gold light spilled from that area, and he heard echoey conversation.

That, then, was where the mummies were.

He walked toward the boxes, half expecting that irritating female security guard to try to stop him. She didn't. Now that he was inside, no one seemed to care about what he was doing.

As Khelan got closer to the boxes, he realized that the area he had thought of as small was maybe the size of the living room of a rather large house. What he had considered to be boxes were actually crates made of wood, which the Amnthran part of him flagged as wasteful.

He hoped that momentary surprise and judgment did not show on his face. If it did, he would have to explain it from Madani's perspective, as a native of the Empire, not as Khelan experienced it.

The crates were actually taller than he was by a meter or more. They had been set up as another one of those silly barriers, creating a slight maze.

He was half-tempted to shove his way forward, to prove to the folks inside that the barriers were useless.

But he had to cooperate, because he might want to bid on what he saw inside. Collectors didn't always take the most money for an item. Sometimes they took the most money from the people they liked and respected, making sure that the assholes never got anything at all, no matter how much they were willing to pay.

Khelan pasted an insincere smile on his face—which was easier to do than usual—and stepped around the last few crates.

The interior here was what he had expected. Mummies, separated by several meters from each other. Each mummy was upright, being held in place by some kind of stand that gingerly clamped around the neck. At least the poor creatures hadn't been posed any more than that.

He wasn't alone here. The heads of at least ten museums were pacing around the mummies, and a few exceptionally wealthy collectors were using a sanctioned handheld to examine the mummies more closely, pretending at authenticity.

He had one of those sanctioned handhelds as well, stashed in a pocket of his tunic. He had forgotten he carried it, but he might have to pull it out, just to fit into the group.

Two official-looking women, with hair pulled away from their very serious faces, watched the entire group move. Neither of the women appeared to be the owners of the material.

Khelan looked for other items beyond the mummies, but saw nothing. The mummies were clearly the main attraction. The other items had to be hidden in another location, probably a more controllable one.

Unlike most occasions when he was supposed to see and bid on mummies (something he abhorred), this time, he was truly interested.

He wanted to know how old they were, and, if he could figure it out, where they had come from.

The stands holding the mummies in place accented their wizened faces. The one that faced Khelan as he entered had a narrow jaw, an open mouth stuck in an oval, and eyes that had sunken deeply into their sockets. A wisp of hair fell behind one ear. The shrunken skin looked like dirt had accumulated in the wrinkles.

It took Khelan a moment to realize he was looking at tattoos, maybe like the ones on his face. The mummy's tattoos were faded and misshapen because the skin was so badly desiccated.

He might not even have recognized what he was seeing if he hadn't had much experience with tattoos. He'd seen a lot of older tattoos, fading and altered by time. He'd also seen tattoos on the skin of the newly dead, although never anyone mummified before.

He resisted the urge to touch his own skin, which would call attention to his tattoos. He doubted anyone had figured out what those markings, those "dirt" lines, were on the mummy's face, and he needed to keep it that way.

The invitation had mentioned uniforms of unknown origin. The mummy before Khelan wore one of those, a rather dull olive green, ripped and tattered, unlike clothing on previous mummies he'd seen. The mummy wore heavy black boots. Several rings were embedded into the skin of its crabbed right hand. The left wasn't quite in Khelan's range of vision, but he suspected that hand was covered in rings too.

He probably could guess what the rings looked like as well.

Because the origin of the uniform wasn't unknown to him. These uniforms were from Amnthra—centuries ago. They belonged to a military unit that used to work around Denon, where the Spires had originated.

He let out a breath, hoping that his discomfort wasn't showing on his face. He had expected to be upset by the mummies—that always happened to him—but not because they had clearly been Amnthran.

The fact that they were Denonites surprised him even more.

Denon had been built over some of the ruins of a Fleet Sector base. That base had been properly shut down, and wasn't subject to death holes, unlike Wyr. Denon itself had been settled by a Fleet group that had decided they wanted to remain on Amnthra.

After several centuries, Denon was abandoned, for reasons no one would communicate, but eventually, Amnthrans resettled the area, after a number of architectural digs run by off-worlders brought attention to the beauty and wealth of the area.

The new Denonites were well-known for their military prowess. They resurrected the Spires, which had been dormant, and sold much of that technology to other cultures all over the planet. It had been the Denonites who had determined that the Spires, modified and improved, could protect the entire planet, not just one small section of it.

Gradually, the attention turned from warring between local cultures to becoming a unified military presence throughout the sector. Mostly acting on defense, with some dramatic history and even more dramatic results.

This uniform came from the early period, when Denon was reestablishing itself as a major power. Khelan had seen a number of the uniforms, but they were holographic representations. The ones that were stored in museums around Denon and on Amnthra were preserved, yes, but had that fragile look that ancient textiles often got.

This uniform looked decayed. Something had nibbled on one of the sleeves, disturbing the four ribbons of embroidery that encircled the edge. Those ribbons went from yellow to blue to red to white, in the colors of the old Denon military. A flag covered the left breast, made of those colors in that order as well, but it looked well chewed.

There should have been more along the lower edge of the waistcoat, but either the mummy had tucked the edge into his pants before he died (at least, Khelan thought he was looking at a male) or whoever had dressed (fixed?) the mummy's uniform had done so.

Khelan peered even closer at the waist. There should have been some kind of utility belt, with weapons, attached to the pants, but he saw none. Nor did he see evidence that it had been recently cut away.

Instead, he saw more wear, the kind that appeared in an already damaged area.

He wasn't sure if he could even ask about a belt, because that might imply too much knowledge.

He didn't pull out his Empire handheld, even though it made him look like he wasn't as interested as his compatriots were. He hated those handhelds. They weren't supposed to damage anything, but the light used, the way it was designed, often did, especially over time.

He had become enough of a collector by posing as one that he didn't want to damage anything.

He saw the items that mummies wore as historical pieces, something to be preserved and to be examined as part of the past. The fact that none of the collectibles were *ever* considered as a part of the past, as something that belonged to everyone, not just some lone collector, usually irritated him.

Right now, though, he was glad that very few people in the Empire cared about the past. Because they should have been a lot more concerned about the unknown uniforms. The others probably assumed that the uniforms belonged to someone in the Empire, some group, some locale that they weren't familiar with.

They would have staff or some expert try to locate the uniforms, not to see how they fit into history, but to see how much they were worth.

It might take months, maybe years, for anyone to figure out that these uniforms were completely unknown in the Empire. These Empire collectors and museum directors might *never* figure that out.

Khelan, however, was shaken by this. Ancient Denonites here, ending up dead in some former sector base. He wasn't sure what would have brought them here or what might have killed them.

They would have recognized a malfunctioning *anacapa* drive, and they would have protected themselves against it. Either they didn't have the chance, or something else killed them.

He was shaking as he looked at the one in front of him, trying to keep his expression as neutral as possible. There was a low murmur of conversation around him as the other people talked about what they were seeing.

He made himself slowly walk around all of the mummies, as if he was interested in buying them. They had been different heights, although most had shrunken. A few had wisps of black hair still attached to the skull. Some were in worse shape than the others, as if something really had tried to nibble on them.

The one near the entry—the one he had studied first—was in the best shape of all of them, which made sense: it was the one everyone first saw. It was the one designed to whet everyone's interest, to get them to buy.

Several of the others had gathered near the mummy farthest from the entrance. That mummy also appeared to be mostly intact. It was smaller than the first one, thinner—which was probably what the person had been like. It also had a full head of hair, and a less repulsive face. The desiccation process had been kinder to this one—the eyes had shrunken less and the mouth wasn't in that screaming death oval.

It also didn't appear to have any visible tattoos, which he found curious. The others did, which had led him to believe that they might have been part of a culture that insisted on tattooing everyone.

This mummy, though, was disproving that assumption.

He didn't want to stop and examine this one. Nor did he want to eavesdrop on the conversations too much, because the ignorance behind it all would just irritate him.

So he made his way through the group, nodded at his acquaintances and smiling at the others, almost as if he were reassuring them.

Then he went to one of the women who was clearly in charge.

She gave him a fake salesperson's smile, one that didn't reach her dark eyes. If he hadn't been looking for the insincerity, he wouldn't have seen it, though, because she was very practiced at what she did.

Her black hair was cut in a wedge, and her slacks and long sweater were a matching muted gray. Underneath, she wore a faint lavender blouse that added radiance to her skin.

"Khelan Madani," she said, placing a hand on her shoulder in greeting. "It is a pleasure to finally make your acquaintance. I'm Serena Walters. I helped organize this gathering."

Her words were chosen with care. She wasn't in charge of the gathering. She was an organizer.

She probably expected him to ask who owned everything and what they wanted.

"We will be having a presentation soon," she said in that practiced tone. "I'm sure it will answer many of your questions."

"I look forward to it," he said, as if her brush-off was working. "But..."

He paused, mostly for effect. She braced herself ever so slightly, standing up straighter. The look in her eyes sharpened, as if she was seeing him as more than a customer now, as someone she needed to pay attention to.

"...I am interested in more than the mummies. I heard tell of other items found with them, including some Ivory Trees. I collect them, you know."

"I had heard," she said. "We have a secondary part of this exhibit. Unfortunately, we need to charge everyone just for the pleasure of viewing it."

His heart rate increased. He had only been to two other viewings that charged for the "pleasure" of viewing other items for sale. Those viewings had not included Ivory Trees, but they had included items so rare that essentially the collectors invited into the private screening had to prove they had sufficient wealth to bid, if the time came.

It would make sense that they would charge extra to see something like an Ivory Tree.

"If there are Ivory Trees," he said, "I'll gladly pay your price."

He had learned long ago that people with a ridiculous amount of money never asked how much something cost. They always assumed they could afford it.

Her eyes brightened ever so slightly. She had hoped to hook him; instead, he had hooked her.

"We will be showing those who want to join us the other items in about thirty minutes," she said. "After the presentation."

"I'd like to see it now," he said, his tone hardening just a little. As himself—not as Madani—he would have added a softener, an "if I may" or an "if you don't mind." But Madani was not that man. He demanded, and he usually got what he wanted.

"We weren't planning on private showings," she said with just an edge of firmness. He could almost hear the argument now, the argu- ment adults gave misbehaving children: *If we do that for you, we have to do it for everyone.*

"I don't really care what you planned." He let his expression slip even more into a slight haughtiness he was beginning to feel. "I need to know if this visit was worth my time."

Her eyebrows went up. That was clearly an unplanned reaction, because she struggled to regain control of her face.

"You aren't interested in the mummies?" she asked.

He waved a hand dismissively. "They're damaged," he said.

Again with the eyebrows. He was surprising her in ways she clearly hadn't experienced in some time.

"You didn't mention the damage in your contact," he said, pushing the point harder. "If you had, I wouldn't have come."

A glimmer of panic showed in her eyes. She wasn't the person in charge of the event; she managed it. Which meant if she lost him as a contact, then she might lose her job as well.

She glanced over his shoulder, clearly looking to see who else might have heard this conversation. He waited, keeping his expres- sion steely. He could almost read her thoughts: she wasn't sure she had the authority to give him a private showing.

But she also didn't want anyone to know that she was about to lose him. When her gaze met his again, she had lost the edge. Her expression hadn't changed, but her eyes had. She was almost pleading.

"If I show you the other items," she said, her voice low, "we have to do so now, and quickly. You can't spend a lot of time there. We both have to be back for that overall meeting. You can examine things more closely afterwards."

He didn't like that, but it was as good as he was going to get.

"Fair enough," he said, nodding ever so slightly. "Let's go."

SEVEN

Khelan saw Walters take a deep breath, as if she was steadying herself to break the rules. Her gaze went over Khelan's shoulder one last time. Then she beckoned him, and walked outside of the wall of crates and toward one of the doors that suddenly seemed impossibly far away. It seemed that walking there and back would take the entire half hour.

But they reached the door in just a few minutes. Something in the design of this building tricked the eye. He made a mental note of that, so that he could figure out what it meant later, if need be.

Walters pressed a spot on the wall that Khelan hadn't seen before and a keypad came up. He wasn't sure if her touch activated the keypad or if the activation was tied to her DNA.

If it was, then he had a problem. Those kinds of locks weren't easy to overcome. They would take a lot of finesse, if he needed to do that. He hoped he wouldn't need it. If he did need to open the doors himself, that meant he had to have a team, and the last thing he wanted to do was bring in a team.

The room Walters led him into wasn't really a room. It was an antechamber for staircases and for elevators. There were two separate staircases, to the right and left of the door. Directly in front of him were elevators. They were labeled with different numbers—18, 32, 6, and 221—which made no sense to him.

The woman took him to the elevator marked 18. Again, she had to use her palm on the very large button that accessed the elevator. The hair on the back of his head rose.

This was or had once been a military facility. This level of security in a warehouse was not something that most warehouses inside or outside of the Empire actually used.

The elevator door opened. The interior was large. She hurried inside, and held the door for him. He slipped in beside her. She was acting like they were doing something wrong—and maybe she was. He was just getting what his very rich persona had asked for.

The doors closed, and the elevator jolted. It was long and wide, clearly made for hauling large items, like the crates. There was another door on the opposite side, so the elevator opened differently on different levels.

It went down quickly, but there were no obvious numbers, so he couldn't see how deep they had gone down. His stomach twisted. He didn't want to be in a cavern beneath Vaycehn.

He couldn't back out now. He would raise suspicions if he did.

He was suddenly relieved that he wouldn't be down here longer than thirty minutes. The chances of a death hole blowing during his limited time below the surface were slim.

He hoped.

The elevator stopped with another jolt, and the doors opposite him opened. He couldn't tell if something the woman had touched indicated that those doors should open instead of the one through which they had entered, or if the doors only opened in this direction on this particular floor/landing, whatever they were on.

The area ahead of him was dark, so he waited for Walters to go first. Khelan's heart was pounding too hard as he suddenly realized how vulnerable he was. He had left his weapon with those guards and no one knew he was down here, not even Idil.

She could probably track him, but he wasn't sure the tracking would make sense to her, especially if he was deep underground beneath the warehouse.

Walters walked to the opposite door and stepped through it, giving Khelan a slight measure of relief. Her demeanor hadn't changed. She still felt a bit off, a bit worried, a bit tense.

She triggered lights as she walked into a very large room. He paused, taking a breath to calm himself.

She had promised only a few minutes down here. He would keep her to that.

Then he followed her into the room.

Items were scattered all over, but the pattern was organized. Some were on tables, while others were on display on the floor.

Directly in front of him was what everyone in the Empire called an Ivory Tree. It looked like a birch tree, with branches reaching toward a ceiling that he couldn't quite see from his vantage point. He could see other "branches" and "twigs" scattered throughout the room, placed strategically, to show them off as the centerpiece of this part of this exhibit.

Khelan tried not to panic. All of these trees were part of the Spires. From this vantage, he couldn't tell how old the parts were, nor could he tell if they were offensive pieces, defensive pieces or both combined.

Not that it mattered. If they were mishandled, any one of them could explode. If the "intact" tree before him was mishandled, then the explosion could bring the entire center of the warehouse down on top of him.

He almost asked *May I look more closely?* but caught himself before he did so. Instead, he walked up to the large Ivory Tree, making sure he was thinking in Empire terminology, not Amnthran.

He didn't touch it. Instead, he read the Amnthran words scrawled on the side. The words were in an older form of writing, one designed to look like square block letters, which in theory made each word easy to read from a distance.

The words were labels and part numbers. The part numbers seemed low to him, and the labels were unfamiliar. They didn't use the modern system. However, they were in Amnthran, and they did make sense for the piece they were placed on.

Fake Ivory Trees often had Amnthran words, but they didn't make any sense for where they were placed. Sometimes they didn't make sense at all. Sometimes they were merely names, or random words like "number."

These, though, made sense. But their labeling, their numbering system, and the slightly yellow color to the manufactured materials told him that this tree was very old. It probably dated from the same period as the uniforms he saw on the ground level.

There was not enough information, either here or near those mummies, to tell him if this particular tree was dangerous.

All he did know was that this tree, and the pieces farther back, had been brought to this site, assembled, and placed in position without an incident. The lack of an incident argued that these were not easily triggered, and were probably intact.

"What are you asking for all of them?" he asked Walters.

Her eyebrows went up, and her lips tried to turn upward into a smile, but she stopped herself just before it happened.

"I've been instructed not to sell them as a group. The owner would like the pieces to go to different institutions as well as to collectors. The owner does not want them hidden entirely from the public."

Khelan felt a surge of impatience. "Who is this 'owner'?"

"The person who discovered the pieces," she said. "He believes there's an Imperial interest in studying the history around these pieces and the mummies, since they're unfamiliar. You'll understand when you hear the presentation."

"I'm not interested in a presentation," Khelan said. "I collect Ivory Trees. I would like these. I would like to buy them as a unit."

"I'm sorry," she said. "You'll have to bid like everyone else. I am not authorized to make this kind of deal."

"Get authorized," he said. "I'm sure I will meet your owner's price."

"But not his conditions," she said. "He had initially planned to donate all of the pieces to the various museums and universities in the Empire. You're here only because he needed to recoup the cost of recovering the pieces."

Khelan let out a small laugh. "One mummy alone would cover the cost of any recovery expense."

"You'll understand when we have the meeting," she said. She threaded her hands together. He was making her nervous.

He let out an exasperated sigh. "I'm willing, just with the trees alone, to make your owner wealthy beyond his wildest imaginings."

"I'm sure he understands that," she said in a tone that said *Of course he does*. "He is not interested in money."

"No one is uninterested in money," Khelan said. "Everyone has a price."

Her expression flattened. He had clearly gone too far. He felt a surge of irritation at himself. He knew better than to seem too eager in a negotiation. He had lost a lot of the leverage he had had when he entered this very dangerous room.

"Let's go back to the rest," she said, and pushed the door open. She swept her hand toward it, ordering him to go to the elevator.

Since he could probably be trapped down here with the weapons that she didn't even know she had, he had no choice but to comply.

He stepped into the elevator, shaking his head as he did so.

They didn't speak as they rode to the top, and he had the uncomfortable sense that he had ruined any chance he had of purchasing the trees outright.

86

EIGHT

The meeting was held in a small auditorium that Khelan suspected was right above the room with the Ivory Trees. He stood near the back, as close to the doors as he could get. Maybe, if something happened—and if he was lucky—he could sprint through the doors and get outside of the warehouse before everything toppled downward.

Or maybe he was just deluding himself.

No matter what, he felt safer in the back.

The small auditorium had eighty seats and a small stage. He had no idea what kind of warehouse this had been, what kind of business it had housed, that it needed something this old-fashioned. Most businesses didn't use stages or in-person meetings—not even in the Empire.

This auditorium was only half full. Everyone had crowded into the front, except one of the other collectors, a heavyset man who had come to almost every event that Khelan had also attended over the years.

The heavyset man always insisted on wearing threadbare shirts that were at least one size too small, often revealing his rounded belly.

Right now, he had his arms crossed over that belly, as if he was feeling as uncomfortable about this entire meeting as Khelan was.

Khelan saw only three other major collectors here. Everyone else seemed to be associated with a museum or with one of the universities. The administrators were seated away from each other, as if sitting too close compromised not only them, but their institutions.

He looked for someone who might be the owner of all of this material, but didn't see anyone who might possibly be that person. They could have been watching a livestream of the event somewhere else, either on Wyr or in orbit.

Then a woman stepped onto the stage. She was tiny, with black hair cut into sharp spikes. Her face was narrow, her chin almost pointed, and her green eyes were alive with intelligence. She had a *don't mess with me* air.

She wore a tailored white tunic over matching white pants. Pink, purple, blue, and green embroidery in a small geometric shapes ran down the sleeves and around the wrists. Matching embroidery also decorated the right leg of the pants.

Her shoes also matched the embroidery and seemed to be made of cloth, with some kind of rope sole. They were the most impractical part of an impractical outfit, clearly designed to impress the people in the audience, rather than deal with collectibles, antiquities, and a half-full warehouse.

She introduced herself as Ethel Hazleberg, with Corporate Treasures. She ran through the usual platitudes, thanking everyone for accepting the invitations, and saying there were surprises ahead.

Then she waved a hand at the back of the stage. Some images appeared, but they were out of focus, most likely deliberately.

"Before we get any farther," she said, "let me explain where these items were found."

Khelan's entire body stiffened ever so slightly. He hadn't expected to hear anything about the history of the items, except vaguely.

"The owner of these items found them in an uninhabited box valley in the SeBaze Mountain Range," she said.

Much of the SeBaze Mountain Range was in an unincorporated part of Wyr. Most of the mountain range was too steep and too harsh for day-to-day life. If the discovery had been close to Vaycehn, she would have said so, because Vaycehn's laws would have applied. If the box valley was truly outside of the city, then Empire salvage laws applied.

"The owner recognized the signs of an ancient death hole," she was saying, "and decided to dig it out. The owner has found many items that we've represented in the past by this habit of exploring death holes."

"Don't be cagey about this owner," said the heavyset man, his tone filled with contempt. "Just tell us who he is."

"I can't tell you anything about the owner," Hazleberg said. "We're under strict instructions to keep the owner's name quiet."

"Why?" the heavyset man asked. "Because we might want to deal with him directly?"

"I have not given you any identifiers," Hazleberg said. "I'm sorry. It's a condition of the sale."

"You already gave us identifiers," the heavyset man said, his tone growing harsher. "This owner has a company that explores death holes."

"I did not say that," Hazleberg said.

"Enough." The word came out of Khelan's mouth before he could stop it. "Let's hear the provenance."

Then added silently, *And get the hell out of this place.*

Hazleberg smiled and inclined her head toward him, as if thanking him. He did not acknowledge the gesture.

She turned again, waved a hand at the back wall, and the unfocused image crystalized into a square stairwell, with well-worn steps.

"The owner was surprised to find a developed area beneath the surface. Usually, death holes carve caves and tunnels, but they're not square, nor do they have stairs leading down."

The heavyset man shook his head, as if he couldn't believe what he was hearing.

"The mummies were found on these stairs, quite some distance down from the surface." Hazleberg moved to the next image.

The six mummies were sprawled on the stairs as if each mummy had tripped running up. Hazleberg showed several different images of the mummies.

"I have several holographic representations of this moment as well," she said, "and will show them to interested parties."

Khelan's mind flagged the word "representation." That meant the holograms were based on static images from several sources, and the information missing from those sources—maybe some stairs heading down or a bit of wall—would have been added by the computers as an approximation.

Using representations was not normal, particularly when a reputable company was establishing provenance.

Usually, when mummies were found, they were captured entirely *in situ* and then holograms were made, before anything happened to the mummies. But no one had done that here, and Khelan would wager that Hazleberg wasn't going to explain why.

"The mummies were intriguing," Hazleberg continued, her tone level, "but the stairs were even more intriguing."

She changed the image behind her to show a small antechamber.

"At the bottom of the stairs, a bunker was found," she said, "and inside of it, over a thousand artifacts, many of which you will find in the second part of our presentation."

Khelan had not seen enough to know if all of those thousand items had been Ivory Tree parts, but they might have been. And that made standing above that basement room even more dangerous.

Anything could set them off.

"It took nearly two years and a tremendous amount of expense to excavate the artifacts," Hazleberg was saying, "which is ultimately why we will be selling some of the mummies."

"Not all?" the heavyset man asked, sounding even more disgusted.

"No, not all," Hazleberg said. "This bunker was quite a discovery. It hints at the history of the Empire in general and of Wyr in specific. The bunker needs a great deal of study, which will probably take decades."

Khelan's heart sank. He had used the wrong identity. He had needed to come here, not as a collector, but as some kind of administrator—someone who was heading a program of archeology or geology or history or maybe even art history—something that would have given him an excuse to help with the excavation.

He silently cursed himself. It was too late to make the change, and there was only him and Idil. He didn't have the resources to shove someone else into the mix or to come up with some kind of expert company that would investigate this bunker.

"In fact," Hazleberg said, "we have to follow the wishes of the owner of these items. Not everything will be sold. Many pieces will be donated to smaller universities and museums, none of whom are here today."

"So," a woman sitting in the front said, quite loudly, "whatever is left over from today's auction goes to them."

"Not quite," Hazleberg said. "Some items have already been set aside so that each organization with get something of great value."

Khelan felt his heart sink. Everything he had seen, then, was not everything they had.

"Including Ivory Trees?" he asked, since her staff already knew he wanted all of them.

"Including Ivory Trees," she said. "We have quite a few available for auction, however, and that should be enough to satisfy most collectors."

The heavyset man put an arm over the back of one of the chairs, and then looked back at Khelan.

"It's almost like she's never met real collectors," the heavyset man said loudly.

Khelan gave him a thin smile. Khelan knew he was being lumped into the same category as the heavyset man, but something about that man put Khelan's teeth on edge.

The heavyset man noted Khelan's thin smile and turned back, saying as he did so, "Collectors like to buy as much as we can, especially when price is no object."

Khelan wasn't sure if that comment was for everyone else or for Hazleberg alone.

It didn't matter how the heavyset man intended the comment. Hazleberg heard it, glanced at Khelan whose actions had said the same thing, and said, "As an organization, we would love to conduct a full auction."

Khelan's heart rose. So, perhaps there was a chance to bid against the heavyset man and others for the full one thousand or so items.

"But," she said, causing the hope that Khelan had momentarily felt to fade, "we are bound by contract to follow the directive of the owner. His wish is simple: he wants to make sure that enough of these pieces are available all over the Empire so that students and scholars can study the materials found in the bunker and perhaps learn something about the history of the Empire."

"Ivory Trees are just decorative," Khelan lied, hoping that he sounded convincing. "I don't understand why the decorative pieces are lumped into the category of historical."

"Then, sir, you don't understand scholarship." A woman from the front had turned. She had a narrow face and brown hair that was pulled back from her face into a small bun. "Everything that represents a culture helps us understand the culture."

"I understand scholarship," Khelan said, his voice chilly. Then he looked directly at Hazleberg. "Perhaps you should consult with the owner and find a middle ground. I'm sure that collectors would be willing to sign a contract that would allow their pieces to be studied."

The heavyset man slouched in his chair as if he had no stake in this whatsoever, but he was clearly listening. Khelan didn't remember the man collecting Ivory Trees, but Khelan was also uncertain if the man had been anywhere near an Ivory Tree auction. There had been so few of them throughout the Empire.

"We suggested that to the owner," Hazleberg said. "Unfortunately, he said he had no idea how those contracts could be enforced. He was concerned that they would not be honored."

Then she gave the entire group a small smile.

"Those of you who are here would never do that, of course. You would honor your contracts. But you can't guarantee that your heirs would or that their children or their grandchildren would."

Her voice had lost some of its confidence as she spoke, and it was clear—at least to Khelan—that she had been quoting this mysterious owner.

"And that," she said without a lot of conviction, "is how opportunities for complete understanding get lost."

She looked at Khelan and the heavyset man as if they were the only collectors in the room, even though they weren't. Khelan narrowed his eyes, letting his annoyance show.

"Universities, museums, public-facing entities," she said, "they all have an obligation to make their collections available to everyone who needs to see it."

Unless the university closed or the museums went out of business or the "public-facing entity," whatever that meant, decided to sell some pieces to, say, a collector.

But Khelan wasn't going to say anything like that, and neither, apparently, was the heavyset man. He was shaking his head, as if he couldn't believe what he was hearing.

Khelan now realized he had lost the argument before he even knew these pieces existed. So he was going to have to take matters into his own hands.

He already started making a list in his head. He would need a team, and quickly. He would need to contact Idil and make sure they had some kind of plan.

But in order to get the plan, he needed a lot more information. He wasn't sure he could get it all right now. But he was going to try.

"All right," he said, as if he was conceding, "how will this auction work? Will we be able to remove our items today?"

"You have not worked with our company before, have you, Mr. Madani?" Hazleberg's voice was just a bit too condescending.

"She makes you pay and then they deliver," the heavyset man said.

"Oh," Khelan said. "Had I known that, I wouldn't even have come here. There's no guarantee that I would get my items after the sale. I don't do business with companies like this."

Another lie. He did business with whomever he could to recover items stolen from Amnthra.

Hazleberg straightened, her lips thinning in disapproval. "Our reputation is unassailable, Mr. Madani. We pride ourselves on—"

"I don't care what you pride yourselves on," Khelan said. "The fact is that you, or if you were to lose your job tomorrow, whoever replaces you could take my money and refuse to give the items to me."

"This is ridiculous," the narrow-faced woman said. "If you don't want to participate, then don't. But the rest of us do."

"It's simple, Mr. Madani," Hazleberg said as if the narrow-faced woman hadn't spoken at all. "Our items, our terms."

A bubble of anger rose and Khelan actually had to clamp it down. He wished he could tell them all they were sitting on top of a cache of weapons so big that they'd make death hole explosions look small. He wished he could tell these people how ignorant they all were, and how they never ever seemed to understand what Ivory Trees and half the other items they had in their universities and museums were. He wished he could tell them that what they called stealth tech was really a drive that allowed rapid travel through sectors.

In short, he wished he could tell them just how damned stupid they all were.

Instead, he nodded once, and let himself lean against the wall as if he had been defeated. He probably should have made the argument about payment and deliveries later, because he really did need to see the inventory.

"How many items are we allowed to purchase?" he asked, his voice dripping with contempt.

Hazleberg smiled. She clearly believed she had won—and in this small skirmish, she had.

"It depends on the item," she said. "For example, with the mummies, only four are for sale, and each successful bidder may only have one. We have more leeway with the Ivory Trees, but each successful bidder may only have one large Ivory Tree. The number of smaller tree bits—which our owner is calling 'twigs'—"

Of course he is, Khelan thought, allowing that sentiment to cross his face.

"—will vary as to size and amount. Same with the other items."

"Is this random or do you have an inventory list?" Fortunately, the heavyset man asked that question. His voice trembled as if he could barely contain some rage as well.

"We have an inventory list," Hazleberg said. "It's available to any serious bidder."

The heavyset man leaned forward. "I thought our presence here in this *place* proves our seriousness."

The way he emphasized *place* made it clear that he thought this was all beneath him.

"It does allow you to bid on some items," Hazleberg said.

The heavyset man's face flushed. "Some? We all had to put down a hefty deposit just to be here."

"Yes," Hazleberg said, "and that's customary."

Which it was. It proved that each collector had the financial wherewithal to make good on their bids.

"For collectors," the heavyset man said. "But what about them?"

He waved his hands at the front seats.

"Each institution provided us with a guarantee," Hazleberg said. "Their representatives have a budget that they can access."

"A budget," the heavyset man said. "And then you'll give them a donation anyway."

"You misunderstand, Mr. Zimmer," Hazleberg said.

Khelan let out a small sound of surprise. Zimmer. They had met at several auctions in the distant past, but Khelan had never put the name with the face. Zimmer had outbid him many times on items that were unusual or considered extremely rare.

"I misunderstand, do I?" the heavyset man—Zimmer—said, no longer hiding his anger. "I don't think I do."

"The donations will go to small institutions that simply do not have the budgets to participate in something like this. The owner wants these items to be accessed all over the Empire," Hazleberg said.

"And yet," Zimmer said, "if the owner was so set on preserving the history, he should just make the bunker itself into a damn museum and have done with it."

"He considered that," Hazleberg said. "But the...the distance people would have to travel, and the...the proximity to death holes makes it too...too dangerous to use as any kind of public facility."

She had not been this visibly uncomfortable before. Something had happened at that bunker that she was not telling everyone.

"Then he should just donate the damn contents to one institution so they can replicate it all," Zimmer said. "Because these games are ridiculous."

"I agree," the narrow-faced woman said. "We would be happy to recreate the bunker, based on any holos you have. We would take as many of the materials as we can and make it into a display. And as you know, we are centrally located within the Empire. People would not have to travel far, and price is no—"

"Thank you," Hazleberg said, clearly recovering from whatever had made her nervous a moment ago. She smiled, but the smile did not reach her eyes. "I can reassure all of you that we discussed *all* of these options with the owner. He is adamant. He wants many items donated. He wants much of this inventory scattered throughout the Empire. He is completely unwilling to make any of these modifications that you are suggesting. So, we are wasting time—"

"You said there's an inventory," Zimmer said. "I want to see it."

"You will all have a chance to glance at the list," Hazleberg said. Her eyes seemed a little brighter than they had a moment ago, and her cheeks appeared darker than they had a moment before. "If you would like to keep a copy of the list, you will have to—as I said—put down an additional deposit."

"You did not say," Zimmer said. "You implied."

"Well, then, let me be clear. There is an additional deposit for a full copy of the inventory list, complete with holographic images." She didn't even try to smile at him this time.

"You could have given that to us before," Zimmer said.

"The list you will receive will be personalized for you, with identification marking it as yours. That way—"

"If we try to sell it or give it away, you'll be able to track it," Zimmer said. "Believe it or not, I've done this before. I'm beginning to wonder if you have, though."

That kind of tracking usually had more features than the ones that Hazleberg mentioned. Khelan felt even more irritation. He wanted a list so that he could use it for planning, but he wasn't going to be able to do that.

Many lists that were "personalized" often had trackers built in so if copies were made, a notification was sent to the list builder. Sometimes any attempt to make extra copies would make the list completely vanish.

"There's no need to be insulting, Mr. Zimmer," Hazleberg said. She had clearly had enough of him.

"Me? Insulting? Lady, you have no idea." Zimmer stood. "You brought us here under false pretenses, tell us to leave our usual protections behind, and make us put down a deposit. Now you're telling us to put down *another* deposit? This feels like a scam to me."

"I assure you, Mr. Zimmer, our items are legitimate," Hazleberg said.

"You tell me there are a thousand items," Zimmer said. "I've seen six. And to see more, I need to trust you."

Khelan almost spoke up, almost said there were more, but he didn't. This was unusual, but most auctions had their quirks. He wasn't disturbed by the things that disturbed Zimmer, although Zimmer's complaints were making some of the other collectors squirm.

"Mr. Zimmer—is it?" The narrow-faced woman stood as well, and faced him. "I understand that you're unhappy with the way this is being run. Frankly, I think we're all uncomfortable here. But some of us are on a limited time schedule, and I'd rather spend my time examining and bidding on artifacts than I would listening to you voice your complaints. Perhaps there's someone he can talk with who will ease his mind…?"

That last, she directed at Hazleberg.

"Yes," Hazleberg said. "One of my assistants—"

"Yeah, take the guy who has legitimate complaints and move him aside." Zimmer waved a hand dismissively. "I'm not interested in your damn mummies. I'm here because in your invitation, you hinted at Ivory Trees. You say there are Ivory Trees here, but I don't see them. If there are, bring them out and let us inspect them."

"As you know, Mr. Zimmer," Hazleberg said, "Ivory Trees are fragile. We will bring you to them, rather than bring them to you. If you want to stay, that is."

Zimmer's face had grown so red that it seemed like he was on the verge of a medical incident. Khelan had never seen anything like it. Zimmer was angrier than he should have been.

Or maybe Khelan was not quite collector enough to understand Zimmer's rage.

"It was my understanding that the auction would be held today," Khelan said. "But with a thousand items, that seems unlikely."

Hazleberg shot him a look that was meant for him alone, a look that said, *You understand what's happening here, so stop getting in the way.*

"We have everything separated into lots," Hazleberg said. "Once we begin the auction, it won't take long to go through the items."

"Because most of the thousand aren't for sale, isn't that right?" Zimmer said.

"I promise you, Mr. Zimmer," Hazleberg said, finally allowing the contempt into her voice, "this entire journey *will* be worth your time."

"It damn well better be," he said, and sank back into his seat.

Khelan let out a small sigh of relief. He wanted to go back to the history that Hazleberg had started with, but didn't want to force this conversation to go on any longer.

He had a few things besides the inventory to investigate, though. The location of the bunker was a top priority. Hazleberg thought she was being coy, but she wasn't. A box valley in an unincorporated part of Wyr, in the SeBaze Mountain Range was easy to search for. And someone who investigated death holes or explored them or bought entire collections...all of that would have created some kind of record.

Khelan would need that later. He needed to find out if everything Hazleberg said was correct: If the bunker was emptied out, or if it still contained things that no one in the Empire understood.

He also wanted to investigate the hesitation that Hazleberg showed. Something had happened at the bunker, something that made the usual procedures for this kind of event impossible to conduct. Had the bunker been destroyed? Looted?

He didn't know, but he suspected as much, considering the lack of visual record. That "holographic representation" was something lawyers came up with, to protect companies like Corporate Treasures from misrepresenting something their clients had given them.

There was no complete visual record, which meant that some of these items couldn't be easily verified—for Empire collectors, anyway. But Khelan would be able to figure out whether all of the pieces of the Spire were real or not, if the Ivory Trees were manufactured somewhere other than Amnthra.

"The other items are stored on the lower level," Hazleberg said, turning so that she didn't have to face Zimmer at all. "We will go below, and you'll have time to inspect the items—without touching them—"

"It's hard to validate an Ivory Tree without touching it," one of the academics said, sending a shudder through Khelan.

"Ivory Trees are fragile, and should not be touched at all," Khelan said, before he could stop himself.

"Mr. Madani is correct," Hazleberg said. "You may not touch the Ivory Trees. Some of the other items may be picked up and examined, with the help of our staff, but the Ivory Trees are off-limits."

"I don't like this," Zimmer muttered loudly.

"That's clear," the narrow-faced woman said. She had clearly made it her mission to argue with him.

"Their items, their rules," someone else said, and a handful of people laughed bitterly.

"After you've inspected the items," Hazleberg said, "we will hold the auction. We should finish by late evening."

"And the promised meals?" another academic asked.

"Will be provided," Hazleberg said. "The auction will occur over dinner. Lunch will be on your own time. We will have food available, so that when you're done examining the items—or, if you so choose, when you're on a break—you'll be able to get something to eat."

A low murmur arose among the group. The very mention of food made Khelan's stomach growl. He had forgotten about eating until just now.

He debated getting food the moment it was offered, then changed his mind. He needed to see the items other than the Ivory Trees. Considering the uniforms on the mummies, there was an extremely good chance that the other items found in that bunker were also weapons or weapons-related material from Amnthra.

He felt nervous for the first time in years. He was also torn. He wanted to get out of here more than he wanted to stay, but he had to see the extent of the haul that had been hidden away for so long.

He also needed to talk to Hazleberg directly about transporting items, which meant he had to buy something today. If Khelan was lucky, all of the material would be transported to all of the buyers at the same time.

He waited until the other collectors, including Zimmer, finished with Hazleberg and headed down the elevator for their viewings. The administrators had already gone down, apparently not as interested in the inventory list.

Or, perhaps, they got one as a courtesy.

As an educated man, he appreciated the deference being shown to the academic and scholarly institutions. He rarely saw that in the Empire.

As a man with a mission, one who would prefer to gather the Amnthran materials himself, he did not like the deference at all.

It made his job that much harder.

He walked over to Hazleberg who had been tapping the top of a handheld tablet. He wanted to snatch the tablet from her, knowing that both he and Idil could easily crack its encryption, just like they had done with everything here in the Empire.

Instead, he folded his hands behind his back.

"I am going to give you the extra funds as a deposit," he said. "Reluctantly. I'm sure you know—and I suspect the owner knows—that collectors can't really operate without an inventory of their own, so this feels coercive."

Hazleberg looked up at him. "Yes, my company is aware of the way that collectors behave. As I told you repeatedly—"

"Our artifacts, our rules," he said, not remembering the exact quote.

"Well, that," she said, "and we did inform the owner of all of these things. He will not change his mind."

She seemed a little less hard-edged than she had on that stage. Now, she just seemed tired, as if she wanted this entire day to end.

Khelan recalibrated his level of snobbish aggression, toning down his attitude as Madani. But he didn't make it go away entirely.

"I would like to meet this owner," Khelan said. "I have questions, especially about the discovery of the artifacts."

The smile that Hazleberg gave him was thin. "I'm sure you do. We all do, honestly. I haven't seen that place either, nor do I know its location. No one here does. He is keeping that information from all of us."

"Well, perhaps if I could talk with him—"

"That's a hard and fast no," Hazleberg said. "The scholars and academics have already asked. I asked as well. We wanted him here to describe what he found. Provenance, as you well know, helps, and the history of the artifacts helps even more. He refused to participate in any of it."

Khelan frowned. None of this made sense to him.

"Why is he even putting these items up for sale? Why not just donate the site and all its contents to his favorite university and be done with it?"

Hazleberg shut off the tablet and lowered it to her side. She studied Khelan as if she could see through him, as if she was trying to understand him.

Then she let out a small sigh.

"My understanding is this," she said. "The site is compromised. That's why we don't have full holograms of the mummies. The owner was smart enough to have his team take images of the mummies when they were found. We also have images of the recovery, but something happened between discovery and recovery."

The hair rose on the back of Khelan's neck. "What kind of something?"

"I don't know exactly." She lowered her voice. "I do know this, though. The entrance to the site collapsed and killed one member of the owner's team. Because he had already put the recovery of the mummies into motion, though, he wasn't able to just abandon the site. I'm not sure he wanted to."

The entrance collapsed. Explosion? Some kind of accident that destroyed unstable walls? A small burst from a nearby malfunctioning *anacapa* drive? Or was the collapse caused by someone activating part of an Ivory Tree?

"After this incident, though, he removed everything?" Khelan asked.

"He supervised it. He's selling the mummies and some of the other items to pay for their recovery. I guess it was hugely expensive."

Given the number of items that Khelan saw, he could believe it. Plus, this owner would have needed to hire a trustworthy firm, so no fly-by-night operation that would do things on the cheap.

"He could have just left it all," Khelan said.

"I think he considered it." Hazleberg shrugged. "He ruled it out, although I'm not entirely sure why. Maybe because a lot of people knew about the mummies."

"I hadn't heard anything and I keep my ear to the ground," Khelan said.

"Well, no one knew in collector circles. But the incident—whatever it was—there were people who helped recover the body of his teammate, and the experts that the owner had initially called in, and then there was the rest of his team. So this was a secret that couldn't be kept."

She glanced over her shoulder at the open door leading down to the rest of the artifacts. Khelan resisted the urge to shift from one foot to another. He was feeling restless, and more than a little uncomfortable with all of those people examining weapons that they thought were collectibles.

At least they were collectors and scholars. They weren't the kind of people who would randomly grab something and wave it about.

Then she turned her attention back to Khelan, and lowered her voice.

"I think he was worried that others would die exploring this place. The secret, and the idea of hidden wealth, would draw treasure seekers, and there was no guarantee they would survive the exploration."

Khelan tilted his head just a little. "You make him sound like some kind of altruist."

He let the skepticism color his words. Altruists didn't sell human bodies for any reason.

"I don't think he is," Hazleberg said. "I think that first death weighs on him, and he's trying to prevent more. But that's all a guess, since I haven't met him either. I just know the rules he imposed on us, and a bit about the circumstances of this entire collection."

Khelan deliberately softened his position. She had been honest with him. He needed to be kinder to her.

"Thank you for telling me that," he said. "I should join the others and see what else is there besides the Ivory Trees."

"You'll get your personal inventory list as you walk into the room," she said. "You'll be able to access it from the moment you step off the elevator."

He nodded, then started to walk away, but stopped as he remembered that last question he had to ask.

"I asked earlier about delivery," he said, "but the answer you gave me wasn't clear. I take it you'll be removing the items from this warehouse when the auction is over...?"

She stiffened, as if his question bothered her. He probably seemed too eager. He had to be careful not to completely burn this identity, so he needed to modify his ask.

"Or," he said, before she got a chance to answer, "can we take the portable items from here after our payments go through?"

That second part of the question made her relax. The movements were subtle. If he hadn't been watching for them, he wouldn't have seen them at all.

"No, you may not take anything from this site. Moving the artifacts is delicate work, as you know, and we can't—"

"I have good assistants and the proper equipment," he lied. He had the proper equipment, but right now, he had no assistants besides Idil.

"Yes, I'm sure you do," Hazleberg said. "But that doesn't mean everyone does. I'm particularly worried about the academics, who try to do these things on a ridiculous budget, and often employ their students."

He hadn't thought of that. Since this mysterious owner wanted to make sure everyone had access to the various artifacts, then the artifacts had to remain in good condition.

"We have to treat everyone the same," she said.

He had no idea why that particular rule existed. But he held his tongue, at least for the moment.

"So," she said, "we will bring the items you purchase to you, as we discussed."

"I'd prefer to take them myself," he said. "I'll sign off on anything you want, guaranteeing condition or making sure—"

"Again," she said, and her tone was irritatingly didactic. "We must treat the purchasers the same. We will deliver the artifacts—"

"I don't like it." He decided to go full Madani, now. "I could spend millions and then I'd have to trust you to deliver them on your schedule? That could take weeks or even years. And I have no guarantee that whatever I buy would be in good condition."

"First," she said, "if something arrives damaged, we will refund your money—"

"And have a destroyed artifact," he said. "Not a good solution, at all."

"Second," she said as if he hadn't spoken, "we will begin the deliveries three weeks after this event closes. That gives us time to plan a route—"

"So, you won't deliver everything at once?" he asked.

"To you, we will," she said, slowly as if he were a child. "We will contact you with the delivery date, and we will make sure that your items go wherever you need them to go."

He didn't like this at all. That meant that different artifacts would be on different ships. He wanted one ship with everything on board. That was what he had planned for in his contingency plan, and that would reflect the size of the team he would request from Amnthra.

"In other words, you'll send a bunch of ships across the Empire with valuable cargo, and no guarantee that the cargo will be well tended."

She sighed. "Mr. Madani, those are *our* ships, *our* people, and *our* systems. We've had no complaints in the past. Feel free to check on that."

"I will," he said.

She nodded, acknowledging his curt little sentence, before continuing. "You will have a guarantee," she said. "It's *our* guarantee; You will get your items in perfect condition or you will receive a full refund."

He shook his head. "How many deliveries would I have to arrange? I travel a lot, and I don't like being tied to someone else's schedule."

"Just one delivery," she said, "depending, of course, on how much you buy."

"I wanted to buy all of the Ivory Trees, but your people won't let me," he said.

"That's right," she said. "Again, through the owner, we are making sure that items get scattered throughout the Empire."

Khelan emitted a theatrical sigh. Then, without saying anything else, he pivoted and headed toward that door.

Halfway there, he stopped as if he had gotten a new idea. He hadn't; he just didn't want to make this question obvious.

"Where will all of these items be stored while you make your deliveries?" he asked.

"Forgive me, Mr. Madani, but that's not your concern," she said.

"Begging *your* pardon," he said with a bit of sarcasm. "Of course it is. If the artifacts aren't protected properly, they could be damaged or stolen or switched out with some other item."

That flush returned to her cheeks. Her eyes sparkled. He had made her angry now.

"None of that will happen," she said.

"Because your company is so reputable?" he asked snidely.

"Because the items will remain here until they get packed for delivery, and this is a secure military facility." Then she gasped after the words came out of her mouth. Apparently, she was not supposed to say that this was an *active* military facility.

"I see no evidence of that," he said curtly, even though he knew better. Some of these facilities were guarded, not by people or overt means, but by covert means at the top of the Empire's technological abilities.

Those abilities were clunky and out of date from an Amnthran point of view. But it was easier to capture items off a ship than it was to dig them out of a well-protected warehouse.

He tried not to let the disappointment show on his face.

"And for that reason," she said, "you're not supposed to see evidence."

"So it's another *I need to trust you* situation," he snapped. "Amazing how many of those there are in this little transaction."

Then he pivoted again and stalked to the elevators. Part of him didn't want to go down them at all. He didn't like how dangerous this place was, and he liked it even less now that he knew it was an active military facility.

For all he knew, some of the Empire's tech could interact with the ancient Amnthran tech, causing problems.

But he didn't dare focus on that right now. He needed to make some bids on various items so that he didn't look suspicious, items he would want if his people couldn't recover them any other way.

He needed as many Ivory Trees as he could get, and he needed other weapons—if there were any below. He would have to see, no matter how uncomfortable it made him.

He reached the strangely marked elevators and showed his identification. The elevator to his right opened.

He hesitated for a half second before stepping inside.

The ruse had to continue. He needed to know what else was down there—no matter how uncomfortable it made him.

THE BREAK-IN

TEN DAYS LATER

THE BREAK-IN

TEN DAYS LATER

NINE

Khelan stood on the command deck of the cloaked ship, hands clasped behind his back. It had been a long time since he'd been on an Amnthran ship of any real size, which was one of many reasons why he wasn't in command of this vessel.

He had forgotten how beautiful Amnthran ships were. To honor its name, this one, the *anuenue,* had rainbows of mist that appeared in the corridors, and then disappeared just as quickly. The air in the entire ship was much more humid than he was used to, and the temperature warmer, just like most of the populated parts of Amnthra itself.

The command center here was smaller than the average command center for a larger ship. Those command centers were usually in the middle of a flight deck, but the *anuenue* did not have a flight deck. It was a medium-sized vessel with defensive and weapons capabilities. Its primary use was for stealth missions, like this one.

Despite its smaller size, he was comfortable here. The air had a slight hint of ocean breezes and the lights were set at an hour past dawn, so that the fake sun wouldn't seem too hot.

There weren't as many plants in this command center as on most Amnthran ships, but that was because this ship wasn't really run by any particular crew. The plants here were standard with a banyan trunk for the commander's pedestal, and some monkey tree trunks with branching sections for the navigator, weapons' specialist and one other person.

The pedestals toward the back were made of loulu and felt a bit wobbly for a palm tree trunk of that size. So he didn't sit. If the truth be told, he was too nervous to sit.

A lot could go wrong on this mission. They were putting it together very fast. He didn't like that. Nor did he like being in an unfamiliar ship, no matter how comfortable it was.

The *anuenue* had been closer to the Empire than any other ship. It had picked up a variety of team members, none of whom had worked together before, but all of whom had the benefit of being several sectors closer to the Empire than the teams that Khelan preferred.

He wasn't even sure this could accurately be called a team. But the members were the only people available, especially as Corporate Treasures seemed to be working faster than he expected.

There were only a few people in the command center.

The *anuenue* had two assigned pilots, but half of the team of twenty had enough training to get this ship into foldspace without being detected by the Empire's military. Heck, Khelan had enough training to do that too, although figuring out the controls in this beast would have taken some time.

There were no control panels, nothing to touch to activate the holographic panels. The two pilots had command buttons, assigned to them when they came on the ship. Everyone else knew some code that would enable them to create and activate their own buttons.

He had requested one as well, but Elikapeka, the main pilot in charge of the ship, turned him down.

We have enough backup here, she had said. *If something goes wrong, we can still escape orbit and get away undetected.*

Somehow, he had expressed his doubts without insulting Elikapeka. It was clear she had never operated in the Empire before, so she had no idea that even though the Empire's tech was clunky and inadequate, it shouldn't be underestimated.

He had tried to impress that on the team when they arrived, but they were more interested in the warehouse.

By then, he had already made the decision to leave Idil on the Amnthran vessel he had used for more than twenty years now. He usually lived on that when he was between jobs, keeping it cloaked as well.

He had thought he needed her there to monitor communications with Amnthra and to send any messages from his yacht, should Corporate Treasures try to contact him.

So far, Corporate Treasures had simply sent a date for the arrival of his purchases. He had given them an address at the auction, so they were using that, not that it mattered.

He had learned, when he monitored Corporate Treasures' chatter, that they planned to deliver the artifacts to each buyer and institution on the very same day, exactly three weeks from the auction.

Which meant that the warehouse would have to be emptied and the cargo ships loaded days before that. It would take a massive effort to move all of those items, making sure they went to the right places.

If they didn't blow up.

He tried not to think about any of that. He couldn't. Because he would end up doing something similar here. The reason that the Amnthran government had provided him with the *anuenue* was because this ship model came with a large armory, which was, at the moment, empty.

The armory was heavily reinforced. Something could explode inside the armory and it would contain the explosion—at least until the ship could jettison the armory and protect the crew.

Once the items were loaded onto the *anuenue,* which would be a task in and of itself, the *anuenue* would leave Wyr's orbit as quickly as possible. Should something go seriously wrong, he didn't want any other ship to see or run into that armory.

He also had requested two fighters, thinking they would probably be enough to handle any ships in Wyr's orbit who got too suspicious of the cargo vessels loading the artifacts into the ship.

He hoped he wouldn't need any of that. He had initially thought that Wyr was one of the least militarized places in the Empire. But the fact that the warehouse was an active military facility bothered him. His assumptions might have been very wrong.

What he did know was this: it was just dumb luck that none of the Spire bits had exploded or that the other, older weapons hadn't gone off. Corporate Treasures was treating the artifacts gingerly, given their age and rarity, but they weren't following Amnthran procedures for active weapons—not that anyone at Corporate Treasures could.

He had had a lot of difficulty explaining the Empire's ignorance of Amnthra to these team members. Most had never worked in the Empire before. He had been trying to keep a balance between giving them information they needed for this particular job, and making sure they understood that underestimating the Empire was a bad idea.

He wasn't sure he had succeeded.

The pilot, Elikapeka, had given him his own little command center around his uncomfortable pedestal. The little command center consisted of three holographic screens, one which monitored the rein-forced skip that brought most of the team to the surface as well as an Amnthran military vessel he did not approve of.

He didn't want any Amnthran ships on Enterran soil, but Olina, who was running the ground operation, wouldn't listen to his protests. She wanted to make sure her team had as much protection as possible.

She also promised him that the ship, called the *manu,* would remain cloaked, which he doubted. If the cloak worked like most Amnthran cloaks, then no personnel could leave the ship with the cloak engaged.

He had gotten the sense that she didn't believe a cloak on the ground was necessary. He challenged her, but she had just smiled at him. She was in charge of the ground mission, not him, because all of these ships belonged to the Amnthran Territorial Guard.

Most of the team were no longer guard members, but they acted in the Guard's stead. Team members, like Olina, answered to the Guard so long as she was using their equipment.

They—all of them, from Khelan to Olina to the pilots—were a recovery group, not a regular part of the Territorial Guard. The Amnthran Territorial Guard tried not to operate in other sectors, unless called to do so for some emergency.

That left workers like him without the benefits of rank, at least when he believed he needed them.

Olina had set up her own rank among the team. And, he knew, she had already scouted out the area. She believed she had a landing spot close to the warehouse. The team would still have to walk, but they were out of the range of the Enterran military's surveillance, or so it seemed.

At least they would start the op at twilight. Most Empire surveillance systems didn't work well in that crossover time between light and dark. If the team could get into the warehouse, then they would be fine.

He wished this particular surveillance visit was unnecessary. He and Idil hadn't been able to figure out if the items were moved out of that protected room in the basement after the auction.

Corporate Treasures planned to group the artifacts for each delivery and bind them together in some way (which gave him the shivers). But he had no idea if that had been done yet.

He suspected the delivery information was not in their usual system. He and Idil had been unable to find another system, which, if he had actually been a collector, would have made him feel better. Corporate Treasures had been very careful to have its inventory list in a different system and marked so that he couldn't transfer it to his team.

He had been unable to get rid of that tracking, so he hadn't done so. His own list went to them after he had shut off the Enterran-made safeguards. The provenance footage went to them as well as the still images that someone had used to compile that footage.

But it wasn't a complete list.

So the team was going to go in, figure out where the items were, and how to get them out.

If all worked according to plan, they would have that information within the hour. Once that happened, they would use reinforced skips to remove the items over several trips and bring them to the reinforced armory on this ship.

Then the third person in this command center would use her

specialty to deactivate those weapons. She thought she could do it without even going into the command center.

Khelan wasn't going to count on that. He wasn't going to count on anything.

In fact, he was going to take his skip and get out of the *anuenue* after everything was on board—maybe as it was being loaded. He trusted these people only so far. But he had seen the bits of the Spires and the old weapons, and he knew what they were facing.

He didn't want to trust his life to someone's overconfidence.

He let out a breath. No one was really paying attention to him up here. He was using his second screen to monitor the ships on their way into Wyr. They had to ask permission to enter the atmosphere but that was automatic.

Or rather, the skip did. The *manu's* cloak was holding up.

No one on Wyr really cared about skips or even about where they landed. The planet was in the very center of the Empire, and the over-confident military believed that anything away from their borders was safe from foreign incursion.

That was what happened when a culture had no idea what kind of technological prowess their neighbors and enemies had. But the Empire might have been getting a clue after a very strange battle took place at the Room of Lost Souls.

"They've landed," Elikapeka said.

Khelan blinked. He hadn't been watching as closely as he thought he was. Both the skip and the *manu* showed up on his middle screen, but he knew the second ship was invisible to the Empire at the moment.

Now, everything rested on the team below.

If they did it right and everything went the way he hoped, then the artifacts would be loaded onto this ship before the night was out.

He activated his third screen, which showed the warehouse area, and settled in to wait.

TEN

Olani preached respect. Respect for the culture, respect for the people, respect for the problems that might lie ahead. She had headed dozens of recovery teams, successful and unsuccessful. The successful ones succeeded because they practiced respect.

She stood in the near darkness at the end of a street filled with warehouses. What lights there were seemed to have a faint blue edge, which she had not expected. She had thought the lighting in this part of Vaycehn would be yellowish gold, like the lighting she had seen in the center of town.

That was the problem with a job like this. Planned in a hurry to be executed in a hurry. Those jobs always brought their own trouble.

She liked to say she hated them, but a challenge was a challenge was a challenge, although this job was more challenging than most.

Starting with the team. They surrounded her, except for the three she had already sent to the target warehouse. A dozen people, all in environmental suits at her insistence.

They had argued with her from the start because they didn't know her. She didn't know them either. They were all names and résumés, unproven, at least to her. A couple of them had Guard experience, but most of them did not. They were, like her, experts in raiding buildings and ships in a variety of cultures. Only some members of the team had very little expertise, which worried her.

They were the only people available when Khelan Māhoe contacted the Amnthran authorities. He'd discovered a cache of weapons so large that it scared him, and he needed people to recover them immediately. Normally, he discovered weaponry or stolen items, and he would purchase them. He had been unable to do so here.

Olina had no idea how much her team knew. She had briefed them and Māhoe had briefed them, but none of them had ever worked together before. It even showed in how they stood.

They weren't clustered in small groups, the way that a long-time team would have been. They stood apart from each other, backs to each other as they surveyed the area.

She had taken a few steps away from them, so she was as guilty as they were. She didn't have time to unify this team. She had only a few hours to get this job done.

Right now, they were doing reconnaissance. By the end of the evening, she should know how much work it would be to remove the weaponry.

Māhoe thought they'd be able to do it in hours, but the way he described it, she thought it would take days.

They didn't have days.

And, she thought, they didn't have the right equipment. He had gotten them Empire-made skips that were reinforced enough (he said) to handle the weaponry. She didn't believe it.

But the one thing she knew about this recovery team was that everyone had had experience with ancient Amnthran weapons and with recovering bits of the Spires. The team knew how to keep something unstable from blowing up—if it was possible.

She wasn't entirely sure it would be possible here.

She had tried to argue that with Māhoe. She thought that the best plan might be to somehow get the government to evacuate the area, and then blow the warehouse up.

He did not agree. He wasn't sure what lurked beneath the ground on Wyr, and he was worried that a huge explosion like this one would make matters worse—or maybe destroy the entire city of Vaycehn.

She thought he was being too cautious.

He thought she wasn't being cautious enough.

So they were conducting this mission in a half-assed manner, something that satisfied neither of them, even though he seemed weirdly optimistic about the chances for success.

She tried to chalk all of that up to his experiences with previous recovery teams. She had known some of them. They had been lucky in their work, returning to Amnthra with the bits of the Spires that he had found.

Or maybe they hadn't been lucky at all. There was an argument to be made that what she considered luck on the recovery teams' part was simply experience on Māhoe's.

Olani needed to respect him too. He had found this amazing cache of weapons all on his own, and had tried to purchase them all. Corporate Treasures had thwarted him. Nothing Māhoe had tried had changed their course. He'd also done his best, in the ten days since he discovered the cache, to track down the owner of it all.

He had been unsuccessful. Or at least, unsuccessful from Olani's point of view. Māhoe had information, but it was old, and it wasn't possible to track down the owner in the time frame that the team had.

That time frame was causing all kinds of problems. Even though Māhoe and his partner had been doing their best to study Corporate Treasures and figure out that warehouse, they were two people who didn't usually run these kinds of missions.

Which meant that Olina and her team only had seven days to plan what usually took months.

The most worrisome problem, though, was the technological one. The Enterran Empire was centuries behind Amnthra in its tech. She knew that, but she didn't know what that meant. She had no real idea how to breach some of that tech.

Māhoe had told her that this warehouse had active military tech, but she had no idea what that meant. He had also told her that the warehouse had been empty except for the artifacts, and from what he could tell, the military rented out the site rather than continuing to use it.

She hoped his research was correct.

No one on this cobbled-together team had any kind of expertise in the Enterran Empire. Half of them had never worked in the Empire before, and those that had had nothing but contempt for this backwards militaristic culture that believed itself to be the strongest and most advanced power in the sector.

Not that the Empire had traveled far inside its own sector. It didn't have the benefit of using a proper *anacapa* drive. So they couldn't travel through foldspace. While the Empire's drives were quick enough, they couldn't handle the vast distances that the Fleet, the Armada, and the Amnthrans traveled often within days.

And that was pretty much what Olani knew about the Enterrans as well. She was as ignorant as her team, although she had spent the short trip here studying what she could. She had worked in the Empire before, but she had been a green recruit, following orders and avoiding the locals.

Theory suggested that Amnthran tech would easily conquer Enterran tech. The team should be able to open any door, shut off any technology, and convince anything around them that nothing had happened during the theft itself.

But theory didn't always work well in practice. And Olani had learned that just because other tech was outmoded or less advanced, that didn't mean it was less effective.

Sometimes in fact, it was harder to understand, which made it harder to overcome.

She had sent three of her tech experts (and boy, did she hope they were truly *experts*) to examine the exterior of that warehouse. They had already scanned it from the *anuenue*, and Māhoe had readings from the space yacht he had used when he posed as a collector to examine and authenticate the collection.

Olani had also taken scans as she brought the skips to the surface. Māhoe had bought the best skips available. They traveled from the cargo bay of the *anuenue* and were able to land anywhere on the surface. The skips were Enterran tech as well, but quite intuitive.

Olani had used the skip sensors to examine the warehouse tech as well, knowing full well that the skip sensors might trigger the tech. She hadn't told Māhoe she was going to do that.

He didn't need to know.

Most people didn't understand her methodology. She *wanted* to trigger early rather than later. If something set off the tech, then she wanted it to happen before her people were anywhere near the target.

The skip had landed on an empty field just outside the warehouse district. The other skips still on the *anuenue* would come down if she needed them. They had floating carts that could travel the short distance, with some cargo. There was no way she could park the skips near the warehouse (nor would she, even if she had the ability).

Over Māhoe's protests, she had also brought one of her own orbit-to-land vehicles, the *manu*. She needed Amnthran tech. She needed a ship with an *anacapa* drive, in case she and the team needed to make a quick getaway.

The *manu* was faster than anything built by the Empire. The ship could also open a foldspace window inside the planet's atmosphere. The timing would be difficult, but Olani had done it all before.

She wasn't going to lose a team member to the Empire, unless she had *planned* to lose a team member.

She had scanned the warehouse with the *manu's* sensors as well, and found a few...well, what she could only call holes. She didn't know if that meant there were gaps in the security system—gaps that she and the team could use to their advantage—or if those gaps were some kind of tech she didn't understand.

All of the scans done by all of the ships showed that the warehouse had extreme security, just like Māhoe had assumed. The Empire was run by the military, and the military got the best tech.

It also had a lot of secret tech, the kind that wasn't easy to research, the kind that every military in every sector guarded as jealously as it guarded its territory.

The theory (there was that word again) was that *all* Empire tech wasn't advanced as Amnthran tech, but since some of the Empire's tech was secret, there was no way to verify this theory.

That was why Olani had sent three team members to scout. They each had different skills and were looking for different things.

What she didn't tell the three team members was this: she was using them as bait. If there was external tech that she hadn't found, that Māhoe's examination hadn't found either, then these three might activate it.

The one thing she really feared, though, was that there would be eyes on the exterior. Older cultures often used people to back up the tech.

She had found, in her decades of doing this work, that people—some people, anyway; *competent* people—didn't let a shadow on the tech go by without an investigation.

And then there was one other factor that she had seen over and over again: military cultures were paranoid cultures. They had a history of assuming the worst and punishing the offenders. Some people liked finding an anomaly. If that anomaly was a person, then the anomaly would be investigated and punished, no matter what the crime or even if there was a crime.

So, this moment, while her people literally walked around the building, doing what they could to find tech that hadn't shown up in the scans from orbit, she was probably the most nervous she ever got in a job.

She could lose three members of her small team right here, and then she would have to recalibrate everything she had planned.

She had already designed the recalibration, even though she hadn't told Māhoe about it.

She hadn't told the team about it either.

If they had been her usual team, they would have already known. A handful of them would have volunteered, thinking themselves invincible. Sometimes she had believed that they were.

That had bitten some of her teams, more than once.

She hoped this method wouldn't bite her again.

ELEVEN

Delores Lebede sat in her tiny tower on top of the apartment complex just outside the warehouse district. She called the little guardroom a tiny tower because it popped up on the roof, surrounded by the doors to the stairwell and another door to what the apartment manager ostentatiously called the "physical plant."

All that area did was house the controls for heating and cooling units, as well as for the water that flowed through the building. The entire system was nearly one hundred years old, and Lebede worried that it would fall apart while she was here.

It creaked that much.

She had received this assignment three months before, when some gigantic shipment entered the warehouse in the very center of the warehouse district. She had been told that the center warehouse was to be the main focus of her entire attention.

So far, there hadn't been a lot of activity. Sure, there had been some when the shipments were delivered. She'd actually had some representative from an auction house named (so pretentiously) Corporate Treasures, which was selling most of the items stored in the warehouse, join her for a short time.

That had been annoying.

The representative, a man in an inappropriately expensive suit that he had described as his "dressed down" look, had examined the interior of the tower with its four chairs, its open-door bathroom, and its one-table kitchen and had given Lebede a look of absolute horror.

He had worn more appropriate pants and a button-down shirt the following two nights, but even those looked like they would cost Lebede's entire salary. He had barely spoken to her either, just monitored the deliveries on a handheld that he had brought.

She had had to keep her own screens shaded and not use the holographic imagery at all because of his presence. He didn't have clearance to see all of the tech in the room, a fact she had argued when her boss, Oliver Fernsby, wanted representatives from the high-end auction house inside the tower.

She had lost that fight, as had her daytime counterpart. She and her counterpart had actually had a discussion about it at shift change —outside of the building, where they couldn't be recorded.

Because the presence of the representatives, with their tiny and inadequate (but expensive!) handhelds, actually made the tower less effective rather than more so.

Lebede hadn't been able to see half of what was going on while the visitor was in her tower, which, after the second night, she suspected was the entire point. She (and her daytime counterpart) weren't supposed to see what was being loaded into the warehouse.

Lebede didn't really give a crap about items that rich people wanted to buy. She assumed it was either old military technology or some discontinued (but secret) environmental suits or something. Or maybe it was *new* technology, and they were sharing it with some private brokers.

She didn't know, and she didn't care. She just cared about doing her job and doing it well. No one had broken into the warehouses on her shift. No one had lurked around them. No one had even pretended to visit them, or she would have shut them all down.

Not that she'd had much of a chance to do so. She'd moved from an outpost closer to the primary armory near Vaycehn to this dumb little tower. It had been, ostensibly, a promotion.

She was getting paid more, and she had been bumped up ever so slightly in rank. She had been told that six months guarding this sleepy little district would move her even higher on the food chain, maybe take her out of this kind of security altogether.

She couldn't wait. Most people loved postings where they had almost nothing to do, but she hated it. Lebede loved being in the middle of the action.

She had thwarted several theft attempts at the armory. The last one had been particularly notable because she had—singlehandedly, mind you—brought down an entire theft ring, which operated from inside the armory. They'd thought they were so clever, reworking the security tech and altering the delivery schedules.

They'd also changed some of the inventory and made it seem as if nothing was missing at all.

All of her predecessors in the previous four years hadn't noticed that particular ring but she had wondered why there had been so much activity at night. The activity had been small—the same people going in and out of the building—but that had been the problem: there had been no reason to go in and out of the building. Once someone had shown up for work, they had no reason to leave until the shift was over.

Of course, she had verified all parts of that assumption before deeming the activity as suspicious. And even then, she hadn't told anyone, because to speak might have been to alert someone. So she hadn't done that.

Her investigation had been slow and methodical and had resulted in a lot of arrests and recovery of stolen weaponry. Her reward had been this tower.

That wasn't an entirely fair assessment, of course. Her reward had been this tower, the promotion, and a chance to pick whatever job she wanted in the future. Or at least, that was what Fernsby was telling her right now. How it would actually end up, she didn't know.

This shift had started out like any other. She had made herself some of the best coffee in the city, ate a quiet dinner, and reveled in her alone time. Those few days with the representative from the auction house had been a nightmare, not just because of his attitude, but because of that open-door bathroom. They'd had to negotiate their bathroom usage, which also took eyes off the security equipment.

This shift, though, had felt strange from the beginning. She had a sense that something was off from the moment she arrived at work. Usually the neighborhoods around the warehouse district were empty. She might pass a pedestrian or an aircar, but rarely did she see other vehicles or even lights on in nearby buildings.

The apartment complex was full of young professionals and families who weren't certain which part of Vaycehn their employment would take them to. Lebede didn't interact with them much because the tower had its own elevator. When that wasn't working, though, she could take the main elevator, which she did once a week anyway. She wanted the residents to think she was a resident too, in case something odd was going on in the neighborhood. She hoped she would learn something from gossip before whatever that something was became a problem.

She had come to recognize the locals' vehicles and the rhythm of the public transport, which would drop off children from their various schools and adults who chose not to own a vehicle at all.

On this shift, though, she saw some things that really bothered her. At least a dozen people on foot heading into the warehouse district.

She couldn't remember when she had ever seen a dozen people walking in this neighborhood, let alone doing so together.

But there had been a lot of strange activity around that warehouse ever since the auction house had loaded in its goods. So she monitored, and made note, but didn't mark any of it as suspicious.

Finally, as she poured another cup of her very good coffee and settled in her work chair, the holographic map of the area flagged a major change. She had zoomed in and was startled to note that the old landing strip built for apartment complexes that had been destroyed by a death hole years back was in use.

Three brand-new skips had arrived at twilight. And near them was a ship of a make that Lebede didn't recognize. She hadn't seen it arrive, which she thought was odd. It had just appeared in her system.

Maybe the skips' arrival had masked it. She didn't have the most sophisticated equipment, even though she had asked for it.

Before searching for the make of the ship, she examined the skips. They belonged to some corporation she had never heard of, and it would take more digging than she had time for to find out who owned that corporation.

She did a quick scan, though, to see if the corporation had holdings in the warehouse district, and quickly discovered that it did not. She looked for holdings in the area, and found none.

She told herself that it didn't mean anything, that corporations could be layered—one owning another, which then owned another. But she had seen corporate skips in the area only twice before.

The first time had been when the big and important shipment arrived.

The second time had been when there had been some kind of viewing of that shipment. She had received a list of cleared vehicles, which was shorter than she had expected. Corporate Treasures preferred to have the participants arrive at Vaycehn's port, leave their skips there, and then be driven to the warehouse by aircart.

So the new skips and the strange ship bothered Lebede. Not to mention the fact that no one local would have put heavy equipment on that old landing strip. Locals didn't tempt fate.

A death hole had destroyed some buildings nearby years ago. There were systems for handling death hole repairs, and the city had done all of that. The engineers had come in to make sure all of the buildings (and roads) in the area were properly shored up, but locals had learned, maybe at birth, that doing anything near an old death hole could be a death sentence in and of itself.

Maybe there were locals dumb enough to ignore previous death hole destruction. After all, this apartment complex was perilously close to the hole. But the complex had been built before the hole blew, and had suffered no destruction at all.

So maybe whoever owned the skips (and that strange ship) had done the same kind of math that she had. Maybe they had figured that the chances of another death hole blowing near here were smaller than in other parts of the city, because death holes usually didn't strike the same neighborhood in the same decade.

That felt like a lie, but the math bore it out. And she liked to think she trusted math. Maybe the owners of the skips did as well.

Although there was something odd about those skips. Not to mention the ship her system couldn't identify.

She reversed the various recordings, searching for more information. She went all the way back to the moment the skips had arrived. They landed, one after another, as the sky grayed. Clouds had been moving in, making twilight even grimmer than usual.

At that point on the recording, she couldn't see the other ship. It must not have arrived yet.

Her mouth had grown dry.

Unless someone had been monitoring the area, no one would have noticed the skips' arrival. She had only seen them because she had set up the system to flag anything that occurred within thirty miles of the district, a system she was certain Fernsby would tell her was unnecessary.

It didn't feel unnecessary at the moment, particularly when the recorded imagery showed more than a dozen people descending from the skips.

The number of people was suspicious, considering the group that was currently walking around the neighborhood. These people emerging from the skips were all dressed in black, and they had hoods covering their heads.

Lebede couldn't tell if those hoods were part of an environmental suit or not. But the more she looked through all of this, the more uncomfortable she got.

Lebede couldn't tell from this distance, though, and she didn't scroll in. She was watching behavior first. She'd get the details of what had happened later.

Then she saw the unidentifiable ship. It was mostly hidden in the growing twilight. She frowned at it, reversed the imagery again, and the ship vanished.

It slowly appeared over the course of several minutes. She let out a breath. She had to be seeing some kind of cloak, of a type she was unfamiliar with.

Slowly, the people had gathered in front of the unidentifiable ship.

A woman, who walked with military precision, had emerged from the unidentifiable ship's far side. She had stepped into the group of people, and gestured.

The people were mostly figures, grayed and diffuse because of the darkness and the misty rain that had started about thirty minutes after the skips arrived.

The people put packs over their shoulders. A few had long thin items under their arms—some kind of weapon, perhaps? Or something else? And some people walked slowly, heads down, as if they were monitoring the area around them.

She watched two holoscreens—the old one, of the events that happened not long ago, and the current one. The current one was even harder to see.

Darkness had fallen, and there wasn't a lot of good light in the warehouse district. As far as she could tell, those dozen-plus people (and it irritated her that she couldn't get a good count) had become about ten, all of them still diffuse due to the mist and the bad lighting.

She was going by shape now, not by any real readings. The group stayed outside of the monitoring area, away from all of the tracking equipment, as if someone knew where the holes in the tech were.

Surely, Fernsby would tell her that she was being overly sensitive. People stood in strange places all the time, and it wasn't because they were trying to do something nefarious. It was because they were doing whatever it was they usually did.

But these folks seemed to be waiting and monitoring, not actually doing something innocuous.

The other holoscreen wasn't moving quickly enough for her. She could fast forward through the imagery but she didn't want to. She wanted to see if she could figure out what this group had been doing.

She didn't adjust what she was watching to make the group clearer. Not yet anyway. So, as they had walked as a group toward the warehouse district, the people in the center clumped together into a gigantic blob. They didn't quite walk in lockstep, but they didn't separate themselves out much either.

They passed two different warehouses, the two closest to that old landing strip. The group didn't seem to be in any kind of hurry. Nor did they look around much either, which caught her attention.

People in an unfamiliar place often swiveled their heads, trying to see what they could.

That argued for the hoods being part of environmental suits, which would give the wearer a 360-degree view, should they want it. But these things seemed to have hoods, if anything. They didn't stick out like common bubble helmets.

Which again, made her a lot more suspicious than she had been earlier.

The group reached the edge of the access road that separated the central warehouse from the warehouses that the group had passed earlier. The group stopped, seemingly without consultation (unless it was through environmental suits).

Then three members of the group peeled off, running in three different directions toward the central warehouse. One ran to the right, the other to the left, and, at least according to the imagery Lebede was getting, the third one went around to the far side.

So far, they hadn't tripped any alarms. They seemed to know where the blind spots were, the spots she had complained about from the moment she started here.

Then very little happened. The remaining members of the group stayed stationary. She checked the time stamp and realized she was now watching the same imagery she had seen in real time.

So she shrank the hologram of the past to the size of her fist. She couldn't see any of it, but she had it there, just to remind her that something odd was going on, and she was keeping track of it.

Then she looked at the main group.

She focused on the remaining image, clearing it up, getting rid of the fuzziness caused by what had become real rain. The exterior lights all had rings around them, caused by the moisture. She cleared up those rings first, as a way of making sure that her work was correct.

Then she went to the group. They still seemed diffuse. She could no longer blame that strange imagery on the rain or the twilight or the lack of excellent lighting in the warehouse area.

They had to be causing it somehow.

Her heart started pounding. This was definitely out of the ordinary. She weighed the options of what it could be. It could be a test, either by Fernsby or by Corporate Treasures themselves, just to see how good the security was.

But she didn't think that was the case. Corporate Treasures knew as much about the security as it could thanks to the monitors. And Fernsby usually did that kind of test early in someone's tenure at a new office rather than later.

Plus, tests were not usually this people-heavy. People cost money, and there were too many here for some kind of random test.

She had to try to count them. She adjusted the settings on her imagery as best she could, screening out the blurred edges, more or less, trying to separate each individual. She thought she managed. The group in the center still seemed like a blob, but she had the system track each individual by movement.

It took a few minutes, but she ended up with what she hoped was an accurate count.

Fifteen.

She hadn't expected that many at all. She had undercounted significantly. Counting the three that had peeled off, she had missed a full third of the group.

She was feeling deeply uncomfortable about this. She now faced something new for this job. She was going to have to decide whether or not to flag the suspicious activity.

And she was going to have to figure out how to flag it. As an emergency? Something she could handle? Something she needed assistance on?

She had a two-pronged risk. The first was that she didn't respond quickly or strongly enough, and this turned out to be something serious.

The second was that she responded with too high a call—an emergency when this wasn't serious at all—and got a reputation as an overreactor.

But she had just gotten a promotion. She had a reputation already for being someone who found thieves.

And what was she protecting here? A job that marked time in the tiny tower, watching empty warehouses with the occasional jerk at her side?

She scanned the third file, compared it to the events that occurred at the same time the night before. The file showed nothing different yet, but she had a feeling she would see something soon.

Lebede took a deep breath and let it out slowly, making herself think. They could demote her for doing too much or doing too little.

She would rather be demoted for doing too much.

She rubbed her hands together nervously. Her palms were sweating, so she dried them off on the front of her uniform.

Then she launched into the emergency system.

Immediately, it gave her a choice—a silent alarm and increased monitoring while she waited for backup, or an audible designed to scare off intruders.

She doubted the audible would scare off this group. It might embolden them.

She was going with the silent alarm. She made her choice, and watched as another screen lit up.

More choices. More to do.

She wiped her sweaty palms on her uniform again, and settled in for a long, and possibly consequential, night.

TWELVE

The door was old-fashioned, with an actual lock and a pull handle. There was an automated lock as well, and some kind of code panel on the right. The light above the door shed pale white light on the rust-colored metal surface.

This was the warehouse's only visible door. The doors that his other two team members had been sent to were deliberately hidden. Apparently, the man who had put this entire thing together, Khelan Māhoe, had seen at least one of them open, and had found a schematic for the other.

It had taken Iokua a while to get to this door, since it was on the far side of the warehouse from the team's landing area. The warehouse was bigger than it looked on the holographic maps. It also was a strange whitish-gray color that faded in the twilight.

The neighborhood was empty, but Iokua felt like there were eyes on him from all sides.

He had no idea why he felt that way, but he had learned to trust the hunches.

Iokua slid his laser rifle over his shoulder, hoping the damn thing would stay on his back. He hadn't wanted to carry a weapon, particularly since Māhoe had said there were probably bits of a Spire inside this warehouse, but Olina had insisted—and right now, she was the head of this mission.

Iokua had run dozens of missions in the past two years, and was as qualified as she was, if not more qualified, since he knew most of this team and she didn't.

But she had been on a mission or two in the Enterran Empire years ago, and he hadn't. For that reason, she got to lead this team.

Iokua wouldn't have had the team in full environmental suits with the individual shields on. He would have thought that such clothing would have seemed suspicious to anyone in the nearby community.

Not, he had to admit, that they had seen anyone in the community since they had arrived.

He would have also done more to hide the skips, and he certainly wouldn't have brought an Amnthran ship with its advanced tech— even though Olina had explained her reasoning. She had thought they would need a quick getaway vehicle.

He had figured the skips were enough, but she hadn't listened.

So he had (angrily, he had to admit) decided to volunteer to be on the first team. That way, he could see what was inside, and he could decide if they needed more time.

Olina had decided to hang back. Olina was waiting, something that he believed team leaders should never do.

And now, the door. He hadn't realized there would be an actual physical handle and a physical lock. Māhoe had said nothing about that, and neither had the schematics.

Physical locks would slow the team down. They didn't carry the equipment to pick one of those locks, which meant either using the rifle (not a choice, in his opinion) or somehow figuring out how to jiggle the damn thing open.

He didn't use the comms to contact Olina. He wouldn't do that until he had a chance to try the lock.

He was going to ignore the physical part first. That keypad was probably the security part of the entrance. Even if he managed to make the physical lock work, he'd have to contend with the keypad at one point or another. Or, if he failed to deal with the keypad, he would probably end up setting off some kind of alarm.

The environmental suit aided him in all that he needed to do, much as he didn't like wearing one on a job like this. He didn't like wearing the suit because it was skin-tight and made him feel like he was being compressed all over, a sensation he never had when he wore the suit in zero gravity.

But the suit had a lot of built-in tools, including the comm units that the team used on this mission. He did appreciate not having to carry scanners or any kind of pad, as well as lights and stun weaponry, which were built into various parts of the suit. He was carrying enough in his belt. He was one of the few who chose not to use a backpack.

He had a few doorjambs, and a knife, and a handful of other practical items, should something physically go wrong, but little else.

The suit's weapons, lights, and scanners were activated with either a look or a code word or a quick touch. He preferred the code word, so his suit was set up that way. Which meant he had to keep his comms toggled off much of the time, otherwise the team (and anyone else monitoring) would hear him mumble a bunch of nonsense phrases.

He mumbled one now, as he held his gloved hand over the keypad. The phrase activated the scanner built into the fingertips and palm of the glove. The slight blue light it sent to the keypad was undetectable on systems built by the Armada or with any kind of security on Amnthra. But he had no idea how this would register here in the Empire—or if the light would register at all.

The mechanisms behind the keypad were simple. They showed up on one side of his visor, as a schematic with recommendations about what to do next. He had no idea what the recommendations were based on, only that they existed and that they had rarely failed him in the past.

One thing that did catch his eye, though, were the wires that extended along the back of the keypad and down the side of the door frame.

Could he be that lucky? Could the door open when the keypad was disengaged?

He didn't ask for more clarification from the computer system built into his suit. If he had been working with a large crew and a team that remained on board a ship, he would send the schematic to them for a second opinion.

But the bulk of the team here was on the ground, waiting to find out what he and the other two team members discovered.

He inhaled slowly. The reason he and the other two were sent out was to scout, yes, but also to trigger the security systems around this warehouse. If the systems could be easily triggered, then the mission would either be called off—or it would become bloody.

The direction this would go wasn't his call. He just had to make the best decision he could, using his own judgment.

He moved his hand away from the keypad, keeping the scanner on, and let it penetrate the door frame.

He had been right: the wire went all the way to the back of the lock, which was on the wall-side of the door frame.

So the physical lock had two mechanisms, one in the door and one in the frame. And unlike some physical locks he had encountered, this one's locking mechanism was in the frame.

Or so it seemed.

Only one way to find out.

He shut off the scanner in his gloves but left the recommendation and its instructions on his visor. If the recommendation was correct, he wouldn't have to do a lot. He would simply have to push a few buttons on the keypad and step back.

He let out a slow exhale, then followed the instructions before him. He pressed six keys in the order that the scan recommended, biting his lower lip as he did so.

The keypad gave him no hints as to whether what he was doing was correct. The keys didn't seem more or less sticky as he worked them. They felt like normal keys.

He pressed the larger key at the bottom, which he assumed was some kind of final key—an enter key or an "ok" key or something—and pulled his hand back.

Nothing happened. The light above him did not change color. Nothing indicated that anything had changed at all.

He was about to turn his scanner back on when he decided to try the door handle.

He grabbed it with his left hand and tugged down.

And the door popped open.

He leaned his head back slightly, second-guessing himself. Should he have tried the door first? Or did the keypad give him permission to try the door without activating anything?

He had no idea, and he wasn't about to do another scan to find out. Instead, he pulled the door toward him.

A light went on inside, but it wasn't much of a light. More of a companion to the thready white light that was currently illuminating the exterior.

If anything, the interior light masked what was beyond it, which, at the moment looked like a lot of inky darkness.

This was the moment he could make a decision that might impact the team. He could call for more team members to come here, or he could step inside and explore a little, just to see what they were facing.

That wasn't much of a decision. He wasn't a call-for-backup kinda guy.

He pulled the door open as wide as it went, and, not willing to use one of his jambs, braced the door with a small rock that seemed to be set near it for just that purpose.

Then he stepped inside.

THIRTEEN

The main entry on the far side of the warehouse had been breached. Lebede felt vindicated and panicked at the same time. When she had caught the thieves at her previous site, she had done so from a distance, with evidence and a presentation to her bosses.

Not as some kind of crime actually started.

The emergency procedures at this site were not automated. She actually had to reach someone, which was a whole different level of communication. First, she checked to see where the security team that should have responded to the silent alarm was.

They hadn't left the other side of the city. She wasn't even sure they had been notified yet.

Then another notification flared on the hologram of the warehouse. A blinking light appeared on the left side of the building, then another on the right.

Two more doors had been breached.

Those three people she had seen peel off were now inside the warehouse.

She had no idea if they were going in to do damage or if they were going in because they wanted to commit some kind of destruction.

She fumbled with the controls, the ones she usually handled so well, searching for the correct dashboard on the correct machine.

Her heart rate had gone way up. As she sorted through her unusually messy desktop, she nearly knocked over the half-full cup of coffee—which had once promised a great night of quiet instead of this strangeness she was dealing with.

She finally found the correct handheld and hit the button that put her in immediate contact with the head of security, a man she didn't know.

His face appeared, florid and too wide, which she placed on top of the hologram of the warehouse and the area around it. Through his reddish-white skin, she could see the grayness of the night, the lamps around the warehouses and those flaring lights, as well as the blurry figures of the people still standing several meters away from that central warehouse.

"Yes?" he said into her silence.

"We have a breach," she said, naming the central warehouse by using its numerical designation. That at least had been easy to find. "I activated an alarm ten minutes ago, but the security team hasn't left yet. We need someone there now. There are three people inside the warehouse, with at least a dozen more outside."

She said at least a dozen because she didn't want to have a potential overcount on her record.

"Take your team in there," he said. "Do what you can until backup arrives."

"I do not have a team, sir," she said, pleased that she could sound so calm when his stupid statement caused a flare of anger. "I'm several buildings away in a security silo, monitoring the building."

"Well, then switch to the inside monitors and start blaring alarms," he said. "That'll slow these people down."

"I don't have clearance for that," she said. She did for all the other buildings, but not for this one. Because of whatever was being stored in there.

He cursed, then said, "Let me see what I can do."

An entire screen flared up beside him on the hologram, making everything muddy. She had to find what device he was sending it through, which made her scramble, even as she was trying to read it all.

She found the device, another handheld—hadn't anyone told them their emergency system sucked?—and slid the screen he had sent off to her left, so it no longer covered his face.

"Thank you, sir," she said. "I'll do as you suggest, but we need someone here now. I don't know what these people are going to do, but—".

"You let me worry about that," he said. "Activate the alarms."

And then he vanished.

She swallowed, hard. Before she used the screen he sent, she tried one thing on her own devices.

She checked to see if that supervisor she had reached had given her access on this machine. He should have, but she didn't know him and therefore didn't trust that he would do the right thing.

She saw a flaring light on her control panel that she hadn't seen before. She touched it, and sure enough, it showed the breached areas. She could pick and choose which ones she wanted to see.

She wanted to see them all, so she set them up as holograms and scattered them around her.

What bothered her the most was that each door was propped open. She could see white light from the exterior on all three of them, and then a matching white light inside.

But no people.

They had already moved deep inside the building in the short time she had been fighting a system made for monitoring, not for responding.

If she got through this and still had a job when it was over, she was going to volunteer to overhaul the entire system. Because this was stupid, and she was suffering for it.

She found the alarms control and set off the interior alarms. For good measure, she set off all of them, not just the ones near the door.

Surely, there had to be more she could do from here.

She just had to figure out what it all was.

FOURTEEN

A siren suddenly went off, blaring and echoing inside the warehouse, followed by maybe a dozen other sirens. The sound was piercing and so loud that it actually hurt Iokua's ears, before he did the very thing he didn't want to do, and shut off all exterior sound coming into his environmental suit.

He had only gone several meters inside the warehouse, surprised that the place looked empty, at least over here. There was no dust, though, and no indication that it had been abandoned. Maybe this part just hadn't been in use.

Then thirty seconds after the sirens started, bright white and silver lights flashed. They had the benefit of clarifying the length of the room—which was longer and wider than he expected—but they would effectively blind him if he wasn't careful.

He had to change the settings on his suit to filter out the rotating bright lights. He did so, cursing silently because that meant Olina had been right to have him wear the suit. He hadn't been able to imagine why it would be necessary.

He knew the alarms were meant to get him out of the building, but he didn't know what would follow them, if anything. The sirens and the lights didn't tell him that.

139

Most storage places did not have anything like foam or gas that would take intruders down, because that might damage what was stored here. For that, he was grateful, considering the weapons poorly stored on the premises.

But some places, particularly militaristic ones, followed with actual people—some kind of security detail or something—and he had no warning on that either.

So he also set his suit to monitor for other humans on the premises.

Immediately, he discovered that his two teammates had gotten into the warehouse as well. He didn't want to contact them yet to find out how they were doing. He figured they would let him know if they were in trouble.

He made himself focus despite the lights and the sound. Switching to a setting that filtered out the bright lights had taken a moment to adjust to. Everything was slightly darker. He used a feature of the suit to create a small two-dimensional image of the room he was in, and he placed it on the lower right side of his visor.

That way, he could double check what he thought he was seeing.

What he thought he was seeing was a large empty space, with no sign anything had ever been in it. That was not what Māhoe had described.

Māhoe had seen staged artifacts, like mummified bodies which, strangely, the people of the Empire sold. He had also seen several other items on this floor, items he didn't exactly specify because he hadn't been that interested in them.

There had been an auditorium filled with chairs in front of a stage, where someone had actually put on a presentation.

Iokua saw none of that, but perhaps it was not on this side of the warehouse. He remained stationary as he tried to parse the information that was coming at him, but he thought he saw very little.

The image that the suit created of the room (filtering out that bright light) was the same. This was a large empty space that looked like it hadn't been used in a long time.

Māhoe had drawn a map, though, of the layout as he had experienced it, and that more or less corresponded to what Iokua was seeing. There was a long wall to his left.

He decided to head that way, because the wall had to contain the doors that Māhoe had mentioned.

Doors, and behind them, stairs and elevators, which would take people to the lower floors.

He headed toward that wall, walking at a good clip. So far, no one other than his teammates had entered the warehouse, at least that his suit could monitor.

His teammates remained closer to their doors, maybe figuring out how to deal with the alarms there, or maybe just investigating something nearby.

He wasn't going to investigate much. Those alarms said that the system or someone or something had figured out that the warehouse had been breached, so the team only had a short time to figure out exactly where the weapons were and how to remove them from the building.

The wall was farther away than he expected. According to the information scrolling along the bottom of his visor, at least two of the sound alarms were blaring from that area. The decibel level was extremely high, probably ear-shattering if he hadn't been wearing the hood with the sound off.

Even if he hadn't known where the materials had been stored, he would have guessed that they were somewhere behind that wall, simple because of the protection and the noise.

He scanned, using both the small image and the visor's information, and saw a single door not too far from him.

He hurried toward it. It had a downward handle, and did not appear to be locked.

But before he grabbed the handle, he examined it, trying to see if there was another alarm attached. He used every scan in his suit to examine the area, and saw nothing—which, he knew, meant nothing as well.

Still, he grabbed the handle and pulled it down, expecting the suit to tell him that he had initiated another alarm.

But the suit remained silent. As far as he could tell, nothing else happened.

He couldn't see any way to prop the door open, so he had to use one of the jambs he had brought. He opened the door wide enough to slide through, clutching the jamb in one hand. With the other, he scanned, trying to see if there were any traps beyond.

The suit found none, which didn't mean that the traps weren't there. It just meant that the traps weren't visible to his tech.

He slipped through the door, then placed the jamb as tight as he could underneath it. Then he stepped aside, and used the palm lights on his suit to inspect the room.

Oddly, according to the scans, there were no bright lights or blaring sirens in here. There was residual noise from the sirens in the main area, but nothing new. Which meant exactly nothing.

Those warnings were for someone who had entered the warehouse, not for someone determined to breach it further.

He made sure his suit's seals were tight. He hadn't paid a lot of attention earlier, because he had thought wearing the suit was a joke.

He didn't think so now.

Then he looked around, saw the antechamber room that Māhoe had described, and saw several elevators. But Māhoe had mentioned stairs as well, and Iokua couldn't see them.

The scanner on his suit could penetrate some walls, so he tried here.

These walls were reinforced with some kind of material that his suit couldn't identify.

That meant nothing, of course. The suit was designed for Amnthrans, using Amnthran tech, built to find Amnthran materials. Every culture had different ways of building things.

He had seen that in the past, and had found that his scanners weren't always able to penetrate new material, even if it was thin.

Still, it disturbed him here, on some deep level.

That meant that this part of the warehouse was designed to store items that needed added protection of some type.

For a moment, he wondered if he should go down alone, if he

shouldn't contact the others who had arrived with him to see if they wanted to accompany him to the lower level.

But the three of them had all agreed on this initial visit that they would explore as much as they could on their own. That would bring the team more information.

It would also help them figure out where the alarms were.

He moved closer to the blank wall before him, and tapped it, hoping to see if whatever was behind it was hollow. He had his sound settings on his suit set up to recognize differences.

And the suit found one almost directly in front of him. But there was no door around that area, not even a carefully camouflaged door.

He was about to give up when he had an inspiration.

He felt along the wall to the right of the hollow area, looking for a hidden keypad.

His fingertips found one. It was recessed ever so slightly. There were no obvious keys or anything that really told him it was a keypad, but it was the same size and shape as the one outside the building.

He had the suit superimpose the image of the outside keypad on this one, and he used the same code that he had discovered for the outside door.

The wall opened inward. The opening was as wide as two doors, and reached almost to the ceiling.

There was no way to prop this thing open, so he either had to notify his colleagues that he was going in, or risk getting trapped in a place that no one knew existed.

He opted for a compromise: he sent both of his colleagues a map of the area, with the door open and the keypad visible, the code high-lighted.

Then he took a deep breath, and entered, hoping he would find the stairs.

FIFTEEN

"Well," Elikapeka said disgustedly. "They set off alarms."

She bent her foot and drove her heel into a spot on what looked like the root of the banyan tree that provided the pedestal. Dozens of plants receded into the floor, making the command center wider and clearer.

Khelan could now see all of his colleagues clearly, instead of through the leaves of various plants. The lovely scent of the ocean had faded as well, along with the breeze that carried it.

For a moment, the center felt even more humid than it had and then dry air filled the center, warm and a bit overwhelming.

Apparently, Elikapeka was prepping for some kind of battle.

Khelan didn't think they were anywhere near a fight. He had seen the alarm notifications too, and those had annoyed him, but he didn't believe that would cause the *anuenue* to take action.

He didn't like that Elikapeka's first response was to set the command center for battle. Nor was he happy with Olina on the ground.

He had wanted to know what the alarm capabilities were, but he hadn't wanted the team to trigger them.

Maybe he hadn't gotten through to Olina.

"Are you getting any readings from the interior of the warehouse?" he asked, keeping his tone neutral. No sense getting angry now. Now they had to see what kind of response the alarms would bring.

"No," the second pilot, Nani, said.

She was standing slightly away from the perch she should have had on the thick branch that extended from the monkey tree trunk. Her hands were moving quickly over a hologram that looked to Khelan like a silverish blur of light. This ship was filled with precautions he wasn't sure he liked.

Nani hadn't looked at him once since he had boarded the command deck. She kept her head bowed, which might have meant nothing or it might have been the placement of the holoscreen she was using.

All he could see of her were the semi-circular gold tattoos on the back of her neck. She kept her hair shaved back there so that the tattoos were visible, except where they disappeared into her shirt.

The tattoos were the same color as her hair. He had spent a good few minutes when he first arrived trying to figure out if he'd been seeing tattoos or hair styled strangely.

When he finally figured out what he was seeing, he had grown calmer. He didn't like it when his perceptions were off. Some of that might have been the discomfort he felt on this command deck.

"I'm not getting any readings from the interior either," he said, which wasn't as strange as he made it sound since he was piggybacking on the same system they were using. "I thought I was earlier."

"Me too," Nani said. "The alarms slammed something in place. All the readings I got from the interior are gone now."

"And we've got three people inside," Elikapeka said.

"They breached too early," Khelan said. "I told them—"

"Being judgmental will not help," Elikapeka said. Her hands were moving up and down slowly, and it took him a moment to realize that she was moving her own holoscreens downward, without giving any voice commands.

"I'm not being judgmental," Khelan said. "I'm just—"

"It doesn't matter whether they did what you wanted," Elikapeka said. "What matters now is what kind of response we see from Enterran authorities. An alarm should trigger something."

He did not like being cut off like that. So he spoke slowly, deliberately.

"What I'm trying to say is that our entire plan might not be feasible any longer. If there's some kind of military response, then we're not going to be able to liberate the items from the warehouse."

Nani stiffened, then turned slightly. Her face was narrow. The gold tattoos rose off her neck and decorated her chin, but didn't go past her cheekbones. He had not seen anything like that.

The structure of the tattoos accented her brown eyes, which looked annoyed.

"We couldn't have done that tonight anyway," she said.

He raised his eyebrows. "That was the plan."

"That was *your* plan," she said. "It was unrealistic in the extreme. There are too many items to take in one visit."

He straightened. "If you believe that, then you should have said something as we planned."

"We had no opportunity to say anything. You declared yourself in charge and told us what we would do. You seemed to think that we could handle offloading a thousand sensitive items from a military facility without being caught."

His breath caught. He almost said that his usual team could have done it, and they could have. They knew all the Enterran systems. They knew the alarms and the military capabilities. They would have known how to breach a building like this without triggering anything.

But what good would the comparisons have done? This team was not his. They hadn't even coalesced as a team.

Still, this Nani, this woman he had never met before, she didn't have any reason to lash out at him. He couldn't remain completely silent.

"I based this plan on my previous experiences recovering items in the Empire." His tone was frostier than he had planned. Clearly he was angrier than he wanted to be.

146

"Enough." Elikapeka raised an arm and waved it, without looking at them. "Fight about whose fault this is later. Maybe nothing will happen."

"The Enterrans are a rules-based military culture," Khelan said. "*Something* is going to happen."

"Maybe something has. Maybe the group is trapped inside," Nani said.

"Well," Elikapeka said, "they didn't use some kind of chemical agent or weaponry, because nothing has exploded."

"Or," Khelan snapped, "nothing of ours has exploded. Yet."

He was shaking now, a lot angrier than he expected to be. He had known this would be a hard recovery, but he had thought it not just possible, but probable.

These people weren't used to the Enterrans. Even if it took the authorities a lot of time to respond, they would acknowledge the breach and harden the site.

Activating the alarms had been a huge mistake.

"We need to call the team back," he said.

"It's too late for that," Elikapeka said. "They'll finish the mission."

"There's no mission to finish," he said. "Nani is right: we're not getting anything out of the warehouse tonight. And we have people on the ground who are going to draw attention to themselves."

"We'll see," Elikapeka said.

"No." He took a step toward her, angry that she was sitting and sounded so calm, so disgusted. "We won't see. *I* know these people. *I* know what they're capable of. They'll send a response team. That team will see the *manu* and they will do what they can to isolate it."

"They can't take the *manu*," Elikapeka said with that same disgust.

Khelan was shaking. He didn't like having to explain how the Enterrans thought, but that was what he needed to do.

"There's nothing else in that warehouse, so they're going to know that we're after the artifacts. Let's hope nothing explodes, so they continue to think it's all art and antiquities, because if they get a hint

147

that their so-called Ivory Trees are weapons, we have another problem."

"Wow," Nani said, "are you always this pessimistic?"

"No," Khelan said. "I'm not. And I'm not being pessimistic now. I *know* this culture and we just messed with them in the worst way. We're going to recall the team and then we're going to leave and figure out another way to get these artifacts."

"It's not your call," Elikapeka said.

Her flat tone infuriated him further.

"What?"

"Olina handles the team on the ground," Elikapeka said.

He hated this, but he knew better than to argue.

"Then get her for me. I'll handle her."

"We're not contacting anyone in the middle of a mission," Elikapeka said.

"We better contact her," Khelan said. "Because this mission is about to go seriously sideways."

"We'll be fine," Elikapeka said.

"No," he said. "We won't. If we're lucky, we'll only lose the team and a ship. If there's weapons fire around those artifacts—"

"He's right," Nani said, surprising him. He hadn't expected her to back him up. "That many weapons would crater the entire area."

Not counting what might happen with the death holes. If there were Fleet tunnels underneath the area, the entire city could implode.

That was why he had fought against destroying the warehouse in the first place.

"We have to call them back," he said, just a bit calmer this time.

Elikapeka leaned her head back, her eyes closed, as if the two of them were getting on her last nerve.

"We can't," she said. "Communications blackout. I can't reach Olani if I want to. She has to reach me."

"Are you serious?" he asked. "I hadn't heard that part of the plan."

"It's her way," Elikapeka said. "I can maybe get a message to Halia, the pilot of the *manu*, and hope she can reach Olani. But that kind of communication might trigger your military friends."

His military friends. As if he was responsible for the Empire.
"Do what you can," he said. He was defeated and he knew it.

He was just going to have to watch this play out—and then he was
going to have to live with the consequences, whatever they might be.

SIXTEEN

Lieutenant-Coronet Felicity Dunstan piloted the flightwing herself. The twelve members of her tiny unit sat in the back. Tegan Thatcher, the usual pilot, sat with them, peering around the edge of Dunstan's seat trying to see what Dunstan was doing.

The flightwing was a small craft, shaped like a tube with wings. The back end opened so that anyone inside could leave while the flightwing was in the air. There were side doors as well, and a nearly useless screen that could separate the cockpit from the area in back.

Dunstan kept that screen open, so that her unit could see what was happening. The cockpit had the only windows in the craft. The windows, which were on all three sides and above as well, were reinforced, but there was no way to barricade them, making the pilot vulnerable should someone try to shoot one.

That had never happened to Dunstan, but she was always keenly aware of it.

Before she had been promoted, Dunstan had been a pilot, and she didn't believe that anyone else was as good as she was at finding their way around Wyr. She knew the mountains (and had had no incidents flying through them, even with larger craft), and she knew Vaycehn extremely well—from its air currents to the vagaries of the ground.

The ground had a lot of vagaries. Some parts of its crust were thin, covered over by dirt and debris after an ancient death hole. Other parts were so thick that she had no qualms setting a very heavy machine on top of them.

She had a map in her head of all the good landing spots around the city, and by good, she meant safe as well as hidden.

She had worked this warehouse area before, primarily when it had been a central storage facility for the military. Now, though, some commander, with a much much much higher rank than she, had determined that storage facilities within the city limits should not hold anything dangerous like weaponry or explosives.

Dunstan had been part of a much larger corps that had moved all of the equipment and a full armory to a supposedly more secure facility in the foothills of the mountains outside of Vaycehn.

These city warehouses were porous, which, she understood, was a problem when they stored valuables, but they were also easy to access in an emergency—the kind of emergency that the armories around Vaycehn had been designed for.

If Vaycehn were under attack by an enemy unknown, then the military could easily access a wide variety of equipment, weaponry, and explosives. Or could have done so, in the past.

Now, it wasn't so easy.

Something she thought ironic, considering there had been an eyes-only report of a strange attack on the city, about three years ago.

Now this.

She didn't know what *this* was, but she did know that it was unusual. Skips, along with a ship of unknown origin, on an unused landing pad (with a surface too thin to carry a lot of weight) near the remaining apartment complexes not far from the warehouse district.

Eighteen people also of unknown origin, impossible to scan properly, apparently waiting outside of the central warehouse, the one built to store the most dangerous weapons of the Empire.

And three of those people peeling off to breach the facility, in a fascinating maneuver, designed to draw someone like her out.

For what reason, she did not know. Testing the system? Trying to figure out where the weaknesses were?

Three people couldn't remove all the artifacts in the warehouse. She had been given a list of them when she received the assignment. The list had more than a thousand items, separated by worth.

Which did her exactly no good, because she needed to know how big the items were and how easy they were to carry. If this was a theft, then three people wouldn't complete it unless it was targeted.

Unless they wanted only a few items.

That left a bunch of other options.

Maybe this group wanted to seize the warehouse itself, for what purpose she had no idea.

Or maybe they wanted to draw out the authorities, whether that be building security or law enforcement or the military.

Although she had no idea how anyone who wasn't affiliated with these warehouses, either now or in the past, would know that the response team to a breach in this building would be military.

She had been surprised when her unit was called up. The warehouses were no longer being run by the military. Civilians handled all of the rentals and security now, even though the building was still listed as active military. That listing was to make sure no one messed with it.

Or perhaps her assumption was wrong. Because any kind of emergency response had remained with the Vaycehn branch of the Imperial Combat Corps. She wasn't sure why and her commander told her not to question the assignment.

He said it didn't matter.

She had a hunch it did.

But hunches weren't going to get the job done, and that was what she was here for—getting the job done.

And the job, right now, as she had been told, was to get these interlopers out of the warehouse before they did any damage.

She would do that, and she might do a few other things as well.

She might figure out what that strange ship was, what its defenses were, and whether or not she could capture it.

SEVENTEEN

Olina shifted impatiently. Twilight was gone and night had officially fallen. The lights in this warehouse district were a harsh white, which cast strange shadows along the road and the hardened ground. Rain was falling intermittently, sometimes making the area even dimmer.

Her team waited for her next order. They stood in a square, facing outward.

Normally, she would have stood in the center of that square, but a few minutes ago, she had walked closer to the target warehouse.

She could hear sirens whooping in the distance, and on the side farthest from here, red, blue, and yellow lights flashed and flared.

They were far enough away from her that they looked like a light show, designed for entertainment. She doubted there was anyone in this neighborhood who could see them, except maybe a handful of people who lived in the upper floors of the remaining apartment buildings.

So far, there was no other response to the breach, which bothered her. She had expected something—maybe even a *help* notification from one of her people inside.

They weren't incapacitated. She was monitoring their vitals as they went through the building. She didn't have accurate schematics of the place, but she was able to have her suit's scanners create a makeshift floorplan of the ground level, based on the building's size, exterior configuration and the information Māhoe had given her.

What she worried about—what she had mentioned to her team before sending them in—was that when they went to the lower level, they might lose contact.

She had told them she would give them two hours before she sent a rescue squad inside.

If she sent a rescue squad inside. She might send a demolition team.

She had not told this to Māhoe, who was set on recovering the bits of the Spires and sending them home.

She might actually destroy them.

Her comm chirruped to life, which made her heart rate increase, even though she didn't want it to. She was a bit more tense about the team than she had thought she was.

"Hey, Olina."

The voice did not belong to any of the three team members who had breached the warehouse. It belonged to Halia, the pilot she had left behind on the *manu*.

"Yeah," Olina said tersely. Halia was sometimes prone to impatience, asking for a timetable when there was none or wondering what was going on with the rest of the team.

To prevent that, Olina had asked her to monitor the operation from the ship.

Apparently that hadn't worked.

"We have a low-flying air vehicle of some kind, heading toward us. It's maybe forty kilometers out, but it's closing the distance rapidly."

"You think it's heading here?" Olina asked.

She was surprised. She figured if there was any human response to the breach, it would be a ground response.

"It seems to be," Halia said. "There's no communication from the craft, and it has rudimentary stealth technology."

"Based on an *anacapa?*" Olina asked, since most of the Empire's stealth technology was a misuse of the *anacapa* drive.

"Clunkier than that. Something that might have predated it maybe." Helia sounded distracted. "Or maybe their *anacapa*-based stealth tech doesn't work in atmosphere."

That was possible. The *anacapa* drives could be used in atmosphere, but they worked best in space itself. Olina had only used a ship-based *anacapa* drive inside a planet's atmosphere a few times, although she had used a ground-based drive often throughout her career.

"They coming to us or you?" Olina asked.

"That I'm not sure of," Halia said. "I'm not even sure they'll arrive here or if they'll register our presence. But I know you like to be prepared, and we did just set off some alarms, so the timing is suspicious."

The timing was very suspicious. Halia had been right to contact her.

"Put your shields up if you haven't already," Olina said. The shield would protect the ship as well as cloak it.

"What about the skips?" Halia asked. She wouldn't be able to shield them remotely, unless she put the *manu*'s shield over them.

If the incoming craft was monitoring the *manu* and the skips, it would find the disappearance of all of them suspicious.

"No, leave them be," Olina said. "I'm less worried about them than I am about the *manu*. I don't want it—and its technology—to fall into Enterran hands."

"It won't." Halia was clearly bristling at the idea that she would let someone capture one of their ships.

"See that it doesn't," Olina said, and signed off.

Then she opened the comm link to the team around her. She purposely didn't include the three in the warehouse. They had enough to deal with.

"Some kind of craft is flying in," Olina said. "I'm guessing that we're going to have a human response to the breaches at the warehouse. Brace yourselves."

She got nods from the team. No need to continue chatter. They were in a defensive position already. They knew what to do.

The people in the corners would switch to heat vision, so they could see anyone approaching. It could be distracting, because random bypassers would show up, but that didn't matter now.

The entire team slid their weapons into position.

Olina scanned the area while her team prepared. They were in the open, and vulnerable to any attack from above. They were already using the shields built into their environmental suits, but on the lowest setting, mostly so that they wouldn't easily be picked up by any surrounding security tech.

"Olina." Halia again, sounding breathless. "That craft coming in? It's got Imperial military insignia."

Olina felt a thread of irritation. She had expected local authorities first. That was the way that most cultures responded. But the warehouse was an active military facility, so it made sense that there'd be a military response.

In her canvassing of the area earlier, though, she hadn't noticed any nearby military bases. Perhaps that was why the response was air-based, not ground-based.

The fact that the initial response was military was a problem. Olina could handle local authorities. They usually didn't know what they were doing. But a military response in a military culture? She and her team were not large enough to handle a proper military response.

"You shielded?" she asked.

"Yes," Halia said.

Olina's heart rate had slowed. She felt an odd little quiver of joy, and hoped it didn't turn up on any of her bio readings. She loved being in the middle of the action. It was one of her favorite things, and one of her biggest secrets.

As a trainee, she had been kicked out of the Amnthran military because she admitted to loving the fight. They believed that someone like her would be too reckless, initiating fights rather than following orders.

She had been that woman once, but she wasn't now. She had

learned how to tamp the emotions down, except for that whisper of joy.

"Personal shields on maximum," she said to her team as she adjusted hers.

Then she braced herself for whatever was coming next.

EIGHTEEN

They disappeared. Fifteen people vanished off her monitoring equipment. There was a visible hole in the main hologram that Lebede had been monitoring.

She pushed her chair back and rubbed her chin, breathing shallowly through her mouth. The small tower room felt too warm, almost sticky, but she suspected it was as comfortable as usual.

She had changed. Her nerves were getting to her.

That hole in the hologram was weird and floaty. She had been looking at the entire district on that hologram, all of the warehouses and the roads leading into it, with a focus on the fifteen (or so) people outside.

They had been standing in a box-like square, with one of their people roaming around it, when suddenly, they just winked out.

But they left a perceptual hole. The air where they had been didn't look black, it didn't look like a night sky with light filtering through it — both of which she would have expected.

No, instead, it looked like there was a flaw in the data. She could see her own wall through that little carved-out section.

She opened a second, smaller hologram and changed the settings on that, not wanting to do it with the one she was monitoring, in case she screwed things up.

The changed settings did not zero in on that group, as she had thought might happen. Instead, the hologram slowly filled in the gap with what had been there before, thinking it had a flaw in its own program.

She deleted that hologram, then swiveled her chair slightly and looked at the landing area near the apartment complex.

The strange ship was gone. The skips remained, but the larger ship seemed to have completely vanished.

She opened another hologram of that area, and this time, she changed the settings to reflect the one that was showing emptiness.

Sure enough, she saw the same kind of gap in the imagery that she got.

These people—whoever they were—were using some kind of weird stealth technology. Something her systems couldn't translate.

She had to let Fernsby know. She wasn't sure how to explain this without sounding crazy. No one had that kind of personal stealth technology, at least that she knew about.

But maybe, just maybe, her clearance wasn't high enough. Maybe this was kind of common tech for the Combat Corps.

Still, she had a duty to warn.

A bead of sweat ran down her back. She rubbed her palms on her pants. She hadn't been this nervous in a long time.

Usually she could make informed guesses as to what was going on, but right now, she had none.

Except that this might be bigger than some kind of simple breach. That tech suggested that these weren't common thieves.

Did they think the warehouse was still owned by the military? Were they trying some kind of raid of military equipment?

Or was something else happening here? Was there something in that building that warranted a major military intervention?

She didn't know.

But she did know that something could go very, very wrong.

NINETEEN

Iokua's environmental suit told him that the area behind the hidden door was six degrees cooler than the rest of the warehouse. He wasn't sure what to do with that information except note it. He had no idea if that was because the door wasn't opened much or because something below needed to be stored in cooler temperatures or if there even was something below.

The area back here was inky black. No lights came on as he entered, unlike the other parts of the warehouse.

He had the feeling that the people in charge of this place did not want any visitors at all.

He turned on some of his exterior suit lights—the ones on his palms and the one that he rarely used on the top of his hood. That light fell around him diffusely, making him feel like some kind of standing lamp. He'd seen it with his compatriots in the past, and always thought it strange.

But it was the best way to light up this place.

Not that the place was much. It was like the room he had just left, only without the elevators. It was a place that was a stopping point on the way to another place.

And just ahead of him was a flight of stairs, heading down.

Māhoe had described stairs and elevators in one place. Either Iokua had gone through a different entrance or the doors he just walked through had been wide open when Māhoe had come through here.

The stairs were wider than Iokua expected, making him wonder what their initial purpose had been. They looked utilitarian, without much decoration at all.

The sirens and lights from the alarms weren't back here either, and didn't appear to have been activated on the lower level of the staircase. More confirmation that those alarms were designed to scare someone away from this place, not to warn a person inside the building that something was wrong.

Iokua approached the stairs. They had handrails on one side only. The other side was open, maybe so that items too big for the elevators could be carried to the lower level.

He was making assumptions, something he tried not to do on jobs like this.

He trained his palm lights below, trying to see what was down there. Māhoe had gone down an elevator on his visits below, so he had no real sense of how deep underground this warehouse went.

Iokua almost sent another image of the floorplan to his colleagues inside the building, and then stopped himself. Time to contact them directly, since the building's security already knew they were here.

He sent a map of his trail from the door to here, and then said, out loud through the comm system, "I'm going to head down a flight of stairs. I'm hoping it'll take me to the items."

He waited almost a minute, peering down the stairs like a kid forbidden to go below. Just when he was about to give up on hearing from his colleagues, Leimomi answered. Her voice sounded faint, and he had to concentrate to hear her.

"I found stairs too," she said, then sent coordinates. "I'm also heading down."

There was no response from Akamu. Iokua hoped that meant he was out of range, rather than unable to respond.

They probably should have done some kind of check, back when they had entered. But no one had suggested it, and no one had been in charge.

Besides, for some reason, Iokua had thought this would be easy, even though they were supposed to trigger the security systems.

Maybe Olina had a point. Maybe he hadn't respected the Enterrans enough.

Then he grinned at himself. Lights and sirens? Those were silly ways to scare off serious intruders.

"I'm heading down too," he said. He wasn't going to wait any longer, and letting Leimomi know that he had gone down was enough.

Maybe Akamu just hadn't answered. Maybe he saw no reason.

Iokua moved to the farthest side of the stairwell so that he could grab the handrail if necessary. He didn't hold it, though, because he wanted to keep his palm lights ahead of him.

The stairs were long and flat, not at the height he had been trained to anticipate on Amnthra. These were shallow, only about ten centimeters. He could easily trip if he wasn't careful.

He didn't count the stairs, though. They seemed to go on forever, heading forward. He had no idea how deep he had gone before there was a wide landing, with a high ceiling.

He had the sense—again—that this was all built for transporting large materials. He admonished himself for the assumption, though, knowing it might have come from his paltry knowledge of this place.

Māhoe had told him about the materials on the lower level, many of them large—especially the parts of the Spires. Iokua hadn't gone into the elevators, but few would be wide enough or tall enough to handle large tree-sized Spire parts.

He followed the landing around, and then headed down the next section of stairway, which went beneath the section he had just climbed down. So the stairwell was built into one large space, that headed down a lot farther than he expected.

His suit told him that the temperature had dipped again. He wasn't sure what to make of that knowledge, although it did reassure him just a bit.

It meant that the Spires wouldn't activate themselves accidentally. They weren't as easily triggered in cooler temperatures.

There was no way that the Enterrans could know that, right? He would make a point of letting Olina or Māhoe know when this job was over, though. It suggested there could be some kind of knowledge about the items.

Iokua finally reached the lowest level. The inky blackness seemed even thicker here. The area where he landed was wider than it had been above.

He didn't see any elevator entrances, though. Just the opening to a wide corridor with a very high ceiling.

He used his suit to orient himself, because he felt turned around. He didn't know what direction he faced.

The suit told him that the building entrance he had used was behind him. He would have guessed it was to his side.

Enough caution now. They had to get through this quicker than he was going, anyway.

So he pinged Leimomi, and asked, "You hit the lower level yet?"

The ping seemed to echo. He got no response, and he wasn't going to wait for one.

He hoped that she heard him, but she might not have.

He set up the scanners in his suit so that they could monitor the materials in the walls around him. He had to assume now that the walls were made of something that was blocking his comms.

He also needed to know this to see if there was any way to get the rest of the team down here quicker.

He stepped into that corridor and walked quickly forward, feeling like he was on some kind of track, that he had no choice in the direction he was taking.

What he did know was this: there would be no easy way to get the materials out of this lower level. The team would have to cart them out up the stairs, which was possible, since they had brought air carts. But someone would have to drive the cart, and someone else would have to monitor it.

And if there were a thousand items like Māhoe had claimed, then it would take more than hours to liberate anything from this place.

It would take days.

Iokua wasn't sure anyone was prepared for that.

He sighed and continued forward, picking up his pace. He felt very alone down here, and he didn't like the feeling.

He didn't like it at all.

TWENTY

Ethel Hazleberg had found a bar in this corner of Vaycehn that suited her. It was smallish, with one main area, and a few private rooms off to the side. The bar was quiet, but not too quiet. It was usually full, except in the afternoon, but she wasn't an afternoon drinker. She had too much to do. Her work at Corporate Treasures kept her busier than she liked, particularly at this stage of a job.

The auction was over, the money was made and/or promised, and the delivery companies were hired. She had to supervise them and plan a route to deliver all of the artifacts, which usually wasn't as big a job as it had been on this one.

Thousands of items, all of them going to different parts of the Empire, most of them donated, a thousand of them paid for. Her head spun just thinking about it all.

She sat at the bar, not because she wanted to meet anyone, but because she didn't. The bar was made of some kind of honey-colored local wood, polished to a glossy sheen that didn't completely cover the grooves and the edges that proved this wood had once been some kind of tree.

As a woman who specialized in knowing what each piece she had ever sold was made of and where that material had come from, even down to the date it was harvested, she found it almost decadent not to know the provenance of something she touched.

Her long fingers were wrapped around a glass filled with three different kinds of local liquors, all made from the same berry at different stages of its existence. The bar sold each liquor individually, and she'd tried all of them, finding the young version too sour, the middle one too bland, and the aged version too sweet.

Combined, they were tart and rich and almost chewy, something she could linger over and relax before heading to the corporate apartment only two blocks away. There she would find some meal waiting for her, made for her and the other members of the auction team. The other members usually gathered in the community area to eat theirs, but she had asked that hers be delivered in a manner that allowed her to reheat it (if necessary) because she needed to decompress, and talking to her colleagues never allowed her to relax.

They didn't know about this bar, and she was going to keep it that way.

She sipped the drink, and watched the other patrons in the large mirror behind the bar. A handful of women, most of them in skirts and some kind of military tunic, all of them sitting at tables. A slightly larger handful of men, some of whom circled the bar, drinks in hand, as if looking for a table.

It was a nice gambit, but a silly one, because several tables were open. Ethel had placed her bag, filled with the traveling tablet and a scarf and the remains of her lunch, on the chair to her right. There was no chair to her left, so no one would even think of sitting near her.

She felt, and not for the first time, relief that this place did not have a regular bartender. No one to inquire about her day. No one to remember her drink. No one to smile knowingly at her when they thought they understood what she was thinking.

The bar had a rotating group of employees who apparently worked at other bars in the chain. The owners seemed to believe that relationships with the customers led to a little bit of price shaving and too many free drinks.

Ethel was glad that her employer did not try to shave fractions off each interaction, and that Corporate Treasures liked to pamper its employees. She was in such high demand as a managing auctioneer that she could work for dozens of rival companies or have a position at the universities that needed someone to head their museum and acquisitions departments.

Corporate Treasures knew that, and did everything to hang onto her and her people.

As if registering that thought, the tiny band on her wrist vibrated. She looked down and—surprisingly—saw a code red.

Emergency contact. She needed to get somewhere private immediately so that she could find out what was going on.

She bit back some irritation—she had wanted to nurse this drink for another thirty minutes at least. Instead, she downed half of it in two large gulps—suspecting she would need the fortification—and then grabbed her bag, and hurried out the door.

The night was darker than any she'd seen since she'd been working this job. The air was damp with an annoying mist, the kind that seeped into clothing and hair as if she was standing in some kind of high-end steam bath—without the heat, that is. Because this air was cold.

More people than she expected walked the street, most of them going home. Their heads were bent down, as if the rain was defeating them. There had to be at least twenty people nearby, and that wasn't counting any vehicles passing.

Everyone was strangely quiet, though, or maybe the mist was muting the noise.

She didn't have the secure tablet, just the one the team used to plan routes and handle the non-proprietary parts of the work. Still, an emergency contact was an emergency contact, and if she lost even five minutes to a quick walk home, she might screw something up.

She pulled the tablet out of the bag, and punched the emergency light, hitting the secure channel setting as she did so. The channel wasn't really secure, and out here anyone could listen in, but that was the best she could do.

Then she started to walk as the system hooked her up to whoever thought interrupting her evening was a good idea.

Her boss's face filled the screen. Bertram Blasingale had a round face that was smooshed flat in two dimensions, and made his eyes seem a little too small. Somehow, though, the look made him seem even snobbier than he was. She felt a smidge of amusement, and tamped it down. This was some kind of emergency, and with him in two dimensions, no one else would be able see him unless they looked over her shoulder.

"Ethel." His voice sounded watery and she hoped to hell that he wouldn't notice that she wasn't using the links that would enable them to converse privately.

Then his eyes sharpened, and he seemed to look right at her.

"Where are you?" he asked.

Damn. He had noticed. She made herself smile, and wondered if it worked. It felt more like a grimace.

"I'm about a block from home," she said, exaggerating by a half a block. "Figured this couldn't wait, whatever it was."

"Yeah," he said. "You figured right. We've had a break-in at the central warehouse."

She almost stopped walking. She was shocked. They had chosen that warehouse to store the exceptionally valuable art and artifacts because the warehouse had been built for the Imperial military.

There were top secret security features in that warehouse that even she didn't understand.

She had no idea how someone had broken into the place. She'd been assured that no one could.

Three people walked past her, and she realized that she had stopped moving forward, which was the opposite of what she needed to do. She needed to hurry. She needed to figure out what was going on and what needed to be done.

She forced herself to walk, holding the tablet slightly to one side so that she could see past it. The last thing she needed to do was trip.

"When was the break-in?" she asked.

"It's ongoing," he said, and she stopped again. Apparently her involuntary reaction to surprise was to stop moving.

She forced herself forward.

"Now?" she asked. "We were guaranteed rapid response from the warehouse's security team. Is that happening?"

"I don't know," Blasingale said. "I only just got the notification. You're the one with quick access. You need to activate our security."

He was right; she did need to activate that. But they had paid a fortune for the venue and that had included military-level security.

"We were promised a quick response," she repeated. "We need to know if it's happening. I'll activate our security, but you need to get the warehouse's security people on board right now."

She didn't care that he was her boss. The fact that he contacted her without checking the status of the project led her to believe he had no idea how much money was at stake.

Those artifacts were worth more than three times the corporation's annual budget. This auction had been the largest the company had ever held.

He had trusted her to handle it, but he should have known how much liability they had. If they lost the artifacts...

She didn't want to think about that.

"Security should act automatically," he said, and she felt a surge of fury.

She knew he was used to delegating, but this time, he needed to get his hands dirty.

"They should, but that doesn't mean they are." She reached the street in front of her corporate apartment building. It was square, with long balconies jutting off each side. It seemed like an oversized cube with too many fiddly design elements on the side.

She didn't quite hate the place, but it certainly wasn't somewhere should have chosen to spend three months of her life.

"Good point," he said. "I'll check."

And because he seemed so laconic about his role, she couldn't help herself. She said, "If we don't solve this, we could lose millions and be sued for even more. They'd have a case, too, because we guaranteed the items' safety."

She looked down at his flat face as she said that, and it seemed to change from a slightly mottled ivory to reddish gray. If that wasn't some trick of the golden light spilling from the corporate apartment building, then she truly had gotten through to him.

"Quickly," she pushed, then severed the connection. She dumped the tablet back in her bag and hurried to the front of the building.

This building had automated security augmented by two people who greeted the tenants. Apparently, someone (or several someones) in the past had managed to take the infinitesimally small identification chip, embedded in each person when they arrived, and had given it to someone else.

She had no idea how anyone accomplished that, and she suspected it had been part of an earlier and less effective security system, but she found that she didn't mind the added human touch to the security.

One of the two people was stationed outside. Today it was a young man who wore his long hair in a single braid that he kept tucked into his blue uniform shirt. His eyes twinkled when he saw her, and he greeted her warmly while tagging her with his handheld.

When she first moved in, she had bristled at the constant checking. Now, she anticipated it. She hadn't changed her opinion about it as much as she had gotten used to it.

She greeted him with a nod and hurried through the automated doors.

The lobby was filled with the building's trademark golden light. Supposedly, the light was supposed to lift someone's mood when they arrived home.

The light wasn't lifting her mood now. She wasn't sure what could. On the surface, she was quite calm, but she could feel a bubble of panic underneath.

If this went wrong...

She made herself breathe as she nodded at the second security greeter, without really seeing who it was. Then she wove her way through the thick chairs, all chosen for comfort, as if residents would rather spend their time in the lobby than in their apartment, and headed to the private elevator that took her to the top floor.

Once inside the elevator, which could uncomfortably hold maybe three people, she leaned against the golden wall, and closed her eyes for just a moment.

She couldn't quite get the idea that this was all a big disaster out of her mind. But she had to. She had to focus.

The elevator doors opened before she could get ahold of herself, but she did a reasonable facsimile thereof. She needed to take care of this problem and then she could deal with the fallout, if there was any.

Not that anyone was going to see her. This elevator opened directly into the apartment.

The corporation actually owned this apartment. They had bought it specifically for this job, with the idea that they would use that warehouse on several future auctions.

The apartment took up a full quarter of the floor, and had windows on three sides. It was colder than she liked, and had brown monotone furniture that looked drab on the tan tile floor. There was a second floor, which she could take the elevator to, but that was the "private" floor, with the bedrooms (five) and the bathrooms. There was one bathroom on this level, a catering kitchen, and a kitchen for the non-cook.

She kept that kitchen stocked, but she didn't go there now. Instead, she went to the main sitting area. She usually worked there, because she wouldn't arrive home until darkness fell. If she sat on the long loveseat, she could watch the city, which she found as beautiful as an ancient painting.

She had left her most important equipment on a gigantic ottoman in the center, the protected tablets and the business handhelds, the ones that connected her directly to the various auctions she was overseeing.

She set her bag beside the loveseat, grabbed the handheld for the central warehouse and flopped onto the loveseat, kicking off her shoes. In a flurry of commands, she turned up the heat, shut down the lights, and set the security system in the apartment at its highest level.

Then she had the catering kitchen serve her some hot tea and buttered scones. She wasn't sure she would have time for actual dinner, but she could munch while she worked.

She opened the tablet that led her directly into the security for the warehouse. She had minimal access to the actual warehouse security, the one that had notified her boss, but she didn't have access to the security controls in this.

Still, what she saw made her heart race. Three breaches on the exterior doors, which she had been assured had unbreakable security. She could see that part of the warehouse, so she knew that lights and sirens had been activated, which should have driven away any casual thief.

She'd been in this business long enough to know that any thief who could get into this warehouse—who even knew what it stored—was not casual.

She grabbed a handheld and tapped it, opening the list she had made of potential buyers who seemed a little off to her. She didn't really look at the list—not yet—but she wanted it open so that she could reference quickly.

Then she grabbed another tablet, the one that held the security *she* had installed in the warehouse. She had told the operators of that warehouse that she would not store items worth multimillions without having her own security around them.

Those items filled the lower level. She had been told that the security had to be approved through the warehouse security, and the low-level security had been approved. But she had also added security around each grouping of artifacts, security that didn't touch anything owned by the warehouse except the air around the items.

That level of security had been a failsafe on nearly a dozen jobs. There were thieves that worked high-end auctions, and she had always thwarted them.

She would thwart these as well—she hoped. Her damn boss had brought this to her much too late.

Because she couldn't open the warehouse security on the lower level, she was more or less flying blind when it came to lower level access. Three stairways that regular people used, and several elevators, none of which she could access.

She really hated the fact that she couldn't access the service elevators or the maintenance stairways. She'd only seen those things once, and, at the time, she had only seen them from the doors leading into those areas.

She had complained to Blasingale, but he was new to this kind of auction. He had no real idea how dangerous storing millions in artifacts could be.

When this was over, if she managed to save the artifacts, it would be time to talk to the head of the company. She didn't need a boss. Bosses had always been her problem.

She needed free reign to handle whatever auctions she got assigned.

Something bumped her left arm, and she looked over. A serving tray backed away slightly. It held her scones (four of them, because she hadn't specified), some jellies and jams and honey, and a teapot with two mugs on the side. She knew without checking that the pot was brewing her favorite tea, which actually came from a small bitter plant in the mountains nearby.

She commanded the tray to remain stationary so she didn't have to move anything. It immediately moved slightly forward and to the side, so that she wouldn't bump it.

She moved the security tablet closer to her and shielded it from prying eyes, in case someone had altered the programming in the simple items around the apartment, like the serving tray. Then she quickly put in half a dozen commands, making yet another mental note that while the commands were lovely and protective, they were also time-consuming.

Finally, she activated the hidden cameras around the artifacts.

So far, it looked like no one had entered the exceptionally large room with all of the valuables. That would give her time.

She worked backwards from the most expensive items to the cheapest. Normally, she would have worked from those closest to the door, to the ones in the center, but the thieves were already in the building.

She needed to protect the investment first.

TWENTY-ONE

The strange ship vanished from Dunstan's control panel. One moment it was there, and the next gone.

Some kind of shield?

Even though her flightwing was closing in on the site rapidly, she was still too far away to eyeball the landing area. Right now, the sky was dusty gray with unhelpful rain making everything look fuzzy through the windshields.

"I need someone next to me," she said.

Teagan Thatcher, the flightwing's regular pilot, moved from the seat behind Dunstan to the copilot seat beside her. Thatcher was slight and wizened. In her off time, she climbed mountains using little more than ropes, so her skin had the look of old worn-out shoes.

Only her eyes were alive, with both intelligence and attitude. Dunstan loved the intelligence and hated the attitude.

"The strange ship just vanished," Dunstan said, "and that group of people seems to have disappeared as well."

"Personal shields?" Thatcher asked. "Do we have that technology?"

"We don't," Dunstan said. "Whether the Empire does or someone in the private sector is anyone's guess."

And Dunstan didn't have time for guessing. She didn't even want to think about that. Her mission was to focus on the breach at the warehouse, and she would do that.

"I need you to do three things," she said to Thatcher. "I need you to find that group of people and see if the strange ship is still there or if it has taken off with its little shield on. I also need you to contact headquarters and tell them we need one more unit. Because we really should be going after those ships on the ground as well as guarding that warehouse."

Thatcher's lips thinned, as if she was clamping them together. She got that expression when she disagreed with orders.

Dunstan didn't care. She rarely consulted with her people. They were her unit, and when they had their own command (however small, like hers) they could do what they thought important.

Right now, she knew where her priorities were.

"Gear up, people," she said to the remaining eleven. "I'm going to bring us down just outside that warehouse, and we're going to go in, one-two-three formation."

If she had more time to do this right, she would have dropped one-third of her group on one side, another third on the other, and the remaining third on yet another, before bringing the flightwing down all the way.

But she didn't have that kind of time.

"What kind of backup do we need?" Thatcher asked, her voice a little harsh, as if the words were coming reluctantly.

"Two more flightwings where those skips are. One of the flightwings needs to have tracking capability in case that ship..." Dunstan paused.

She wasn't sure what the right word was, so she didn't say exactly what she was thinking. She didn't want to put ideas in anyone's heads. She had been serving as part of Combat Corps on *Daystar* which had responded with its squadron to the disaster at the Room of Lost Souls.

The squadron had arrived prepared for battle, but there had been none. Just the remains of Imperial vessels. The attacking ship had vanished, according to one of the survivors. Others thought he was exaggerating, but she never did. He claimed that the strange ship that had caused all the problems had opened a little door in space, and seemed to go through it. Then it hadn't been visible any more.

More than that—it hadn't been *there* anymore.

The higher-ups dismissed his report, and then buried it, but she had heard it firsthand. And it had stuck with her. There had been strangers at the Room of Lost Souls, and they had done something, and killed six hundred people.

Now there were strangers here, on Vaycehn, with ships she didn't recognize.

"...left," she finished. "In case that ship left and we had somehow missed it."

Thatcher gave her a sideways look, as if she didn't know what Dunstan meant or why Dunstan was being so coy.

"Now, Thatcher," Dunstan said. She had more than enough to concentrate on without dealing with Thatcher's moods.

Dunstan had to make a quick decision on where she would land the flightwing. And she finally decided, with a half second of consideration, that she would land it where that group of people had been.

She smiled.

If they were still there—if they did have personal shields—well then, this would test them. And scatter them.

And give her a hell of an advantage.

TWENTY-TWO

"They've brought a flightwing," Khelan said tightly. His mouth was dry, but his palms were sweating. He was staring at the holos before him, watching the disaster unfold.

He wanted to pace, but he was afraid to. It had been years since he'd been in this kind of command center, and he was afraid he'd trip on the tree roots around the pedestals.

Elikapeka was still sitting a few meters from him, but at least she had leaned toward her holoscreens. She looked engaged again.

Nani was doing something on hers, but he couldn't see what it was.

All he knew was that the *manu* had cloaked and the team on the ground had activated their maximum shields, which meant that to most Empire tech, they were invisible.

That was small comfort. The Enterrans were savvy warriors, and he didn't underestimate them, even if most everyone else here did.

"You say that like it's significant," Elikapeka said in that flat tone of hers. He couldn't tell if the tone conveyed disinterest or contempt, but it didn't matter. Neither were appropriate here.

"It is," he said. "A flightwing can hold up to twenty soldiers, who are all highly trained. The flightwing itself has weapons capability that will operate on the ground here."

"We can't handle that," Nani said, sounding panicked.

"Yeah," Khelan said. "Our people need to leave, now."

"They're cloaked," Elikapeka said. "They'll be fine."

Khelan opened his control panel, looking for a way to communicate with the team. He found the comms system, but he couldn't activate it.

"I need to talk to Olina," he said.

"No," Elikapeka said. "She said no comms."

"She's not up for this," Khelan said. "No one on the ground is."

"You underestimate our capabilities," Elikapeka said.

"You underestimate the Empire," he snapped. "Turn on my comms."

"No," she said again.

He left his screens and almost ran to Nani's work area, weaving in and out of the empty pedestals. He nearly banged into one of the extended branches of the large monkey tree pedestal.

He couldn't see Nani's screens. He knew that Elikapeka wouldn't let him use hers.

He had no idea how to activate another panel, not in the time he needed.

"They know a ship is coming," Elikapeka said, as she watched him. "They'll be fine."

"No," he said. "They won't."

If he wanted to talk to them, he would have to go to his quarters and get one of his Empire tablets. He could contact a skip with that, but no one was on the skips.

He had been shut out of the comms.

"You're going to get them killed," he said, almost yelling.

"No, I'm not," Elikapeka said. "They're cloaked. These Empire people can't see them, can't target them, can't find them. They'll be fine."

"Even the people in the warehouse?" he asked. "If someone starts shooting in there—"

"Then the artifacts will be destroyed," Elikapeka said. "And our job will be done."

She sounded so calm. A chill ran down his back. "Hundreds of people could die." He had told the group that before they went. "The entire neighborhood could disappear."

She shrugged. "My understanding is that they have learned to live with disaster on this planet."

For a moment, he couldn't breathe. She was talking about the death of human beings—entire families, innocent people, people who had no reason to die.

"You have to get me into the system," he said to Nani, "or innocent deaths will be on your shoulders."

She looked up at him, then glanced at Elikapeka.

"He's overreacting," Elikapeka said.

"And if he's not?" Nani asked.

Elikapeka shrugged again.

Nani toggled something on one of her screens, and the comm system came up.

"I can't reach Olani," she said, "but you can talk to Halia on the *manu*."

"Thank you," he said. He leaned forward, watching the hail and seeing the *manu*'s silent acknowledgement.

"Halia," he said, "this is Khelan. That flightwing is dangerous. You have to let the team know. They have to leave *now*."

"I told them something was coming," she said, her voice sounding far away and filtered. "They'll be fine."

"Tell them this is a real threat," he said.

"If I contact them now, it might give away their location," she said.

"If you don't, they might die," he said. Or others might die. He didn't add that.

"Okay, okay," she said. "I can't guarantee I'll get through. Olina hates to be contacted—"

"I don't care," he said. "Do it. Do it now."

Halia didn't respond. The light had gone off near the communications bar. She had severed the conversation.

He hoped to hell that she had heard that final command.

"How do I reach Olina?" he asked Nani.

"Let Halia do it," Nani said and opaqued her screen.

She turned her back on him and returned to whatever she had been doing.

He stared at her for a moment, but it was clear that she wouldn't change her mind. He had done what he could and it wasn't nearly enough.

He went back to his little cave of screens, and wondered if there was a way he could override Elikapeka's commands.

He would have to look, even though he doubted he could figure it all out.

TWENTY-THREE

Halia pinged her, but Olina silenced the ping. Everything felt off. She needed to warn her team. They were still standing in a stupid square facing outward, even though they had activated their shields.

She had heard nothing from the three inside the warehouse. This entire op was going slower than she wanted it to.

Then something screeched above her. A series of warnings activated inside her environmental suit at the exact same time, warning her of danger from the skies.

She looked up, saw that craft that Halia had told her about, and saw that it was coming in fast. That had to be what Halia had wanted with that ping, to let her know this craft was coming toward her.

It just wasn't coming in. It was plummeting downward in a controlled descent.

"Move! Move! Move!" she said to her team. Two looked up. The rest ran across the flat area around the warehouse, scattering in several different directions.

She body-slammed the two who looked up, pushing them out of the way.

Her suit warned her that she was too close to that craft, so she veered to the right, away from the two who were too stupid to follow instructions.

She had learned long ago that she had to save herself first.

The craft's engine sent out some kind of backdraft that made the air look hot and wavy. She couldn't feel it, but the suit warned her that the temperature around her had risen to dangerous levels.

"Get to the warehouse," she shouted at her team through the comms. "Find a door."

Screw doing this the proper way. She was going to do it her way.

Her heart rate had not increased. She felt ridiculously calm. Her brain was moving quickly though.

The craft—a military craft from the Enterran Empire—shouldn't have broken through their shields. There should have been no way that the craft should have seen them.

The problem was on her. She should have moved her team.

The craft must have seen some kind of hole in their security. And they had headed for the hole.

Which meant the craft had been flying blind.

She moved closer to the warehouse. Screw hiding the orbiting *anuenue* from the Enterrans. Olina didn't have time to think of niceties.

She contacted Elikapeka.

"I hope you see this mess," Olina said. "I need you to take out the craft."

"I don't have any way to finesse this," Elikapeka said. "Your people have to get as close to the warehouse as possible."

"Done," Olina said, and ended the contact. Elikapeka had better act quickly because they didn't have a lot of time.

Olina opened the comms to the rest of her team.

"We're shooting from orbit," she said. "That incoming craft will explode. You need to run as far from that craft as you can. Head to the far side of the warehouse."

And then she peeled out, running at top speed toward the warehouse.

Behind her, she heard actual gunfire, the kind that came with projectile weapons.

The environmental suits did not have much protection against projectiles shot with extreme force. And it was too late to tell the team to augment their shields to explosion levels, so that shrapnel wouldn't penetrate.

She hoped the team was smart enough to consider that, given what they were facing.

She doubted the two that she already saved were that smart, but what did she know? She hadn't worked with most of this team before.

She headed to the far corner of the gigantic warehouse and hoped she would make it before the explosion added its strength to the projectile weapons.

Shots pinged around her. She could see puffs of dirt rising, but she knew the shots were landing too far away.

Were they coming from the craft? Because so far, no one had exited.

She didn't turn to look. She needed to get as far as she could from that descending craft.

She didn't look back at it. She didn't want to slow down.

And then she heard it—a warning sound, like a hum. She didn't stop until she reached the far side of the warehouse, where three of her team were already huddling, weapons out.

She turned now, and saw the craft illuminated in red, one of the doors open, and a woman in uniform leaning out of it, a rifle of some kind on her shoulder.

They seemed to freeze, the woman's concentration etched on her face. Olina had a half second to wonder why such an Imperial military vessel that could hold a full team was responding to a security call and then the entire craft seemed to expand.

The woman turned, clearly shouting, and tumbled or was pulled inside of the craft, which suddenly reversed direction. It was trying to get away.

But its shield wasn't good enough to fight Amnthran weapons—if the craft even had its shield activated with someone leaning out a door. If the craft even had a shield.

The craft moved slightly up and forward, but it was expanding. It had to be unbearably hot inside. Everyone was roasting to death, and they probably didn't know it. They had probably passed out already.

Then the craft came apart, first in large segments, and then the large segments became smaller segments. The segmentation continued with each succeeding piece, a visible disassembly.

"We have to move farther away," Olina said. Because once this explosion ceased to be contained by whatever field kept it in place—a field created by the weapon from the *anuenue* or a field created by the craft itself—once that field disappeared, the tiny bits would go hurtling with great force in all directions.

Olina ran along the side of the warehouse. She didn't look to see if the others were following her or not. She didn't care.

She hadn't expected this level of response.

That meant the team was on an even tighter timeline or they would have to abandon this mission.

She had three people inside.

She didn't want to abandon them.

But she had no idea how they would accomplish the job now.

Shrapnel started pelting the warehouse, sounding like hard rain. She thought maybe she heard a grunt through the comms, but she wasn't sure.

She kept running until she had the warehouse between her and the explosion.

Then she stopped, grabbed her knees, and gasped for air. She hadn't run like that in years.

She hadn't expected to do it here.

TWENTY-FOUR

Khelan launched himself at Elikapeka, but she raised one of the floor plants, tripping him. He clutched at the plant. It was rubbery and smooth, so it bent. He nearly fell, but managed to keep his balance somehow. He used the movement of the plant to throw himself around it.

He slid on the floor, nearly hitting the roots of the banyan pedestal, and finally caught his balance.

Then he turned around, dizzy but not disoriented, so furious that he could hardly speak.

Elikapeka smiled at him. It wasn't a pleasant smile.

"That pesky little Empire vehicle is no more," she said. "The team can finish now."

"Are you kidding me?" He swayed a little, catching his balance. He couldn't remember the code he needed to use to get his screens up. He might have gone back to his station, but Elikapeka might raise more of the plants. He had no idea where they were supposed to be located.

Still, he needed to get back to his pedestal, needed to see. As he had that thought, a hologram appeared in front of him, flat and filled with information. Flaming parts of what he assumed was the ship was scattered all along one side of that warehouse.

He could see some of their people, huddled against the warehouse, but he did not count them. The air was filled with smoke.

He glanced at Nani. She inclined her head toward him, in acknowledgement. She had opened a communal screen.

Her expression was serious, and if he knew her better, he would have thought she was as furious as he was.

Elikapeka ignored the ship. "No, I'm not kidding you," she said, answering his rhetorical question. "As you can see, that little ship is now gone."

"Along with all of the lives inside," he said.

She shrugged. "Military culture," she said. "They had to plan for the inevitable deaths of soldiers."

A gasp came from behind him. Nani. Elikapeka's coldness was something he had never experienced before, and apparently, neither had Nani.

"They were attacking our people," Elikapeka continued. "We need to finish this mission. Now we can."

Khelan clenched his fists and took one step toward her. He had never wanted to hit anyone before in his life, but he wanted to hit her or kick her or push her off that pedestal. But if it was like the others he had known, it would balance her.

He didn't want that.

He wanted to do something physical, like slam his fist on a console or punch a wall—things he hadn't done since he was a child and taught to outgrow violent showings of anger.

He wasn't sure he had ever been this furious as an adult.

"First—I don't even know where to start." His voice was shaking. It sounded strangled. "First, you should have told me if we were going to fire on them."

"Olina is in charge on the ground," Elikapeka said.

"And I run this mission. I'm the one who brought you all here!" He was shouting. People didn't listen when someone shouted, but he wasn't sure how to stop.

He took a deep breath.

"You should have confirmed with me," he said.

"You would have said no, and Olina needed our backup."

"Damn right I would have said no," he said. "If you had missed—"

"I don't miss," she said.

"If. You. Had. Missed," he said deliberately, loudly, as he stalked toward her. "You would have hit the warehouse and activated the weapons inside. The explosion would have destroyed the neighborhood."

Maybe even the city.

"You don't know that," Elikapeka said.

"I do know that," he said. "You do too. You know what's in there."

"And you told me—hell, our readings tell us—that this is a military facility with all kinds of protections. There's no way of knowing if the shot would have penetrated."

He stared at her for a moment. Behind him, Nani murmured, "Oh, for…"

Then he said, "You also had no way of knowing if you were going to activate some kind of weapon built into that warehouse."

"We scanned it," Elikapeka said. "They don't have that kind of weaponry."

"You don't know that! I don't know that! No one knows that!" He stopped. He had to get control of himself.

Elikapeka seemed to hear him have that thought. "Get ahold of yourself. You're overreacting."

"You've just needlessly killed people—"

"Soldiers," she said, "who were trying to kill our people."

"—and you tell me I'm overreacting?" He took another step toward her. If only this ship was his. He could toss her out of her pedestal, take over the controls and deal with everything himself.

But even as he had that thought he now understood the ship's design. No one could take over the ship without somehow compromising the captain. Brilliant until it wasn't.

Like right now.

"It's done," Elikapeka said. "We need to finish this now."

"There is no finishing it, don't you understand? You just ruined our entire mission."

Her lips quirked, and she shook her head. "I saved it. Or rather Olina did. It's what she wanted."

"And neither of you understand this culture. It's pure military. If there's an incident, they respond. If there's aggression, they'll respond in kind. Or worse." He let out a breath. This entire mission was over now. He would never get the artifacts out of the warehouse. He would need a new plan—and he didn't have time to come up with one. Not right now.

"I'm not seeing any response," Elikapeka said.

"There's activity at the base where the Empire craft originated," Nani said. "I'm sure there's going to be a response."

"Of course, there's going to be a response," Khelan said. "And they're going to come in, searching for everyone. It's exactly what we didn't want. They're coming in, and they will find our ships, if we don't get everyone out of there now."

Then he put a hand to his forehead and cursed.

"First, move this ship to a different orbit," he said.

"They don't have the capability of finding us, based on that shot," she said.

"Every spacefaring culture we've ever encountered has the capability of finding a ship in orbit after something like that." He turned toward Nani. "Is there any way to get the control of this vessel away from this crazy woman?"

"Yeah," Nani said. She raised a hand rather flamboyantly, like someone putting the final touch on something important. "I just did."

"*What?*" Elikapeka stood all the way up, hands on her hips. "You can't."

"I did," Nani said. "I'm the second, not *your* second. And now you're out of this."

Too late, Khelan almost said, but he didn't.

"Let me know what you think we should do," Nani said to him.

He took a shuddery breath. He had to set the anger aside.

"She doesn't know what she's doing," Elikapeka said. "She has no idea—"

"Shut up," he said. "Go sit in the back or go get yourself something to eat. You're done here."

"I can get in just like she did," Elikapeka said.

"No, you can't," Nani said. She was looking at Khelan, not Elikapeka. To him, Nani added, "Can you pilot ships?"

"Yeah," he said. He didn't know the theory of this one, but he probably knew enough.

"Good, because if anything happens to me, you'll have to," Nani said. That time she looked at Elikapeka. "At least until the rest of the team gets back here."

"They need to move quickly," he said. "The military response will be swift."

Nani nodded. "I'm also moving this ship to a different orbit."

"Good."

"There's no way these people can threaten us," Elikapeka said. "They're backwards. They're—"

"Those weapons they were using?" Nani snapped. "Our environmental suits aren't designed to withstand a repeated barrage from projectiles. So, Khelan's right, Elikapeka. You need to shut up and get out of our way."

"That means I was right," she said. "That means—"

"Get out," Khelan said, approaching her. He would bodily toss her from this command center if he had to. Even though she was wiry and younger and could probably take him. He was angry enough to do anything.

Something in his eyes must have convinced her. She wiped her hands on the sides of her pants, then pinched her fingers together, clearly closing screens.

"All right," she said. "I'm leaving you two to handle this mess, but I'm going to report it."

Khelan didn't care. Even if the Amnthran government decided she was right, it would be too late, and it wouldn't really affect his job in any way.

Although he could make life unpleasant for her.

But that was in the future.

Right now, he had not just a sideways mission to recover from, he had a blown mission. The Enterrans knew that someone was after the items in the warehouse, and now the military had lost several personnel.

They were going to swoop in and kill everyone on the ground. After interrogating one or two of them.

And the Enterrans were vicious in their interrogations. Khelan doubted anyone could hold up.

"The goal now," he said, "is to get our people out of there and make sure we leave no tech behind."

Nani let out an audible breath. Not quite a sigh, more a sound of disgust.

"That might be a tall order," she said.

"I know," he said.

TWENTY-FIVE

After going through the endless corridor, Iokua finally found a door. He pulled it open easily, which stunned him.

What stunned him even more was a room—if he wanted to call it that—filled to the brim with Amnthran artifacts. Pieces of the Spires stood everywhere, set up to look like branches or, in some cases, actual trees. The writing on the sides was displayed.

Scattered around them were smaller weapons, little bombs designed to look like rocks and even smaller pieces of actual ammunition. Then there were the handheld lasers, designed just like the Spires, with the white exterior and instructional writing on the side.

This place looked like an armory stocked with ancient weapons to him, but he could understand why the Enterrans believed these were some kind of art.

Displayed this way, the pieces did look lovely.

What the Enterrans didn't seem to understand—and why would they?—was that the Amnthrans designed everything with an eye to beauty.

The breadth of this room, the number of items, the display, so confident in the artistry, took Iokua's breath away.

He actually couldn't see the end of it all. He saw the walls to his right and left—and there were more items attached, from daggers (how did anyone even hang those? The sides of the blade were so sharp they would slice skin at a single touch) to actual clubs with flat ends. The Amnthrans no longer used the clubs, but they were potent weapons, something that a person could put some real power behind.

Unless he missed his guess, there were enough pieces of Spire here to build a working Spire, one that could defend a section of this planet from whatever came at it, in orbit or on the ground.

The thought chilled him.

He took a step deeper inside, and as he did, a wave hit him, pushing him forward. His suit notified him that some kind of force field went up around the door.

Apparently, he had been noticed. He didn't try to flee, not immediately. Instead he let his suit probe the field.

It was rudimentary and badly designed, filled with flaws. He would have no trouble going through it when the time came.

If he could go through it.

Māhoe had been wrong: there were too many items here to remove in a quick and dirty grab. His estimation of a thousand items was low. Considering how dangerous each item was, even carrying one or two things out of here put everyone at risk without the proper equipment.

And right now, they did not have the proper equipment.

Iokua turned on his exterior comms. It was time to contact Olina, if he could from this depth.

He realized at that moment that Leimomi hadn't responded to his question, the one he had asked before going through that long corridor, and he wasn't sure if that was because of where she was, or because the comms didn't work in this part of the warehouse.

As he started to send the message, the mummies in the center of the room—or what he thought might be the center—lit up, a faint blue.

Their uniforms, that of the Ancient Denonites so familiar from Amnthran history, made him feel sick: he was looking at remains of real people, not some statue or random display.

He shook himself. He had been told the mummies would be in the room, but the reality of them stunned him. And the faint blue bothered him.

Near them, a giant piece of Spire, which looked like some kind of tree with branches going in all directions, also turned blue. He scanned the blue, trying to figure out what it was, then let out a breath.

Those were security fields. Strong ones. Not like the one near him at all.

If he had to guess, he would assume that the security fields were covering what the Enterrans believed to be the expensive items.

His stomach turned again, at the thought that the mummies were the first thing protected, not because they were being honored, but because they would be sold at a great price.

To hell with this. He was going to be trapped in here if he wasn't careful, and for what? A theft that couldn't happen.

This was an impossible job. Māhoe should have known that. He shouldn't have brought them here for this.

He should have destroyed the artifacts when he had the chance.

Iokua pivoted, and as he did so, the room shook. He had to grab the wall just to keep his balance.

He now felt isolated, without his hearing to tell him what was going on. So he asked the suit.

It had no idea. Only that something had made a large explosive noise outside, and the concussion had shuddered through the entire building.

A concussion. And he was in a room with weapons.

He needed to leave.

He turned around and started picking at the newly added security feature. He had to get through that door, through that corridor, and onto an upper level before the entire building came down around him.

He took a deep breath and calmed himself, making himself slow down.

And then he got to work.

TWENTY-SIX

Lebede was on her feet. She had no idea when she had stood up. Her hands were over her mouth as she stared at the holos in front of her. Fires burned across the entire acreage where the warehouses were.

Fires from the exploded flightwing.

She had just watched a lot of people die.

She backed away from her equipment, slamming into her chair and nearly losing her balance. All that calm that she prided herself on—it was gone. She wanted to flee, but she was afraid to go outside.

She didn't want to be alone, but she didn't know who to contact.

Then that thought registered, and she stopped.

Of course she knew who to contact. She was the one who had gotten the flightwing here in the first place.

She let out a small whimper. They would all be alive if she hadn't asked for more security.

Then she clenched her fist. She did not kill those people. She did not try to get into that warehouse.

She was just doing her job.

And she needed to continue doing it.

Those people, those *attackers*, they needed to be stopped.

She walked to her setup and stared at the holos, made herself look at them in depth, so she saw the destruction.

She did not cause it. The attackers did. If they hadn't been here, everyone would still be alive.

Once she had that thought clearly in her head, she leaned forward.

She cleared her throat, and spoke before she sent the message. A simple hello, which sounded like a croak. She practiced hello three times before it sounded like an actual word.

Then she contacted Fernsby.

She asked for a visual, even though she probably looked a fright. A small holo popped up over the burning ground.

Fernsby, hair sticking up as if he had put his hands through it, his eyes wild, snapped, "What?"

"The flightwing you sent," she said. "It blew up."

"We just got notification," he said. "This is the military's problem now."

"You should let them know…" She swallowed hard, feeling that croak return. Then she started again. "You should let them know that whatever destroyed that flightwing—it came from above."

"Above?" he said. "What the hell? Do these attackers have a craft above ground?"

"I looked." She was sure the flightwing's commander had as well, not that it mattered.

The only reason Lebede had looked was because she had been told that a military craft was coming. She hadn't wanted to be in the middle of some kind of fight.

"I haven't found any other air vehicle," she said to Fernsby. "Something could be cloaked though. Maybe the military has a way to see something, but I don't."

"So where is above?" he snapped, as if it was her fault that she didn't have all the answers.

"I'm worried," she said, "that they might have something really powerful in orbit."

He rocked backwards. Clearly he hadn't thought of that, but to be fair, the man ran ground security on *warehouses*. He didn't think about what was going on around the planet.

"I'll let them know," he said and signed off.

Nothing more. No condolences, no kind words. Just a curt dismissal, as if she was unimportant.

She sank into her chair. She *was* unimportant. She had set events into motion because she had found the ships, the people, the situation. But she couldn't do anything more here.

Then she let out a breath.

Except her job.

She could monitor. Maybe she would see more. She had no idea who to contact if she did, because her boss clearly didn't want to hear from her. But she would figure that out when she saw something.

If she saw something.

Then her hands paused over the controls. She had just misinformed her boss.

She hadn't checked for that strange ship. It had vanished, yes, but that didn't mean it was still parked like those skips.

Her fingers shook. She was going to have to figure out if it was still in place, but camouflaged like those people had been. The ones who had run as the flightwing descended.

All of them had appeared on her monitors when the flightwing's exhaust hit them. A few had disappeared again, but the others hadn't.

Maybe that ship had gone above the others. Maybe that mysterious ship had placed the killing shot.

If so, then everyone was still in danger.

Including her.

TWENTY-SEVEN

As Olina caught her breath, her planning mind returned, along with a coldness she hadn't felt in years. She stood upright and peered around the building.

That craft—that Imperial military craft—was in small burning pieces on the ground. There was damage in all directions, including a hole where the craft had been—where it had tried to attack *her* people, and maybe had done so.

Part of her team still huddled against the warehouse. Some were inside. She couldn't see at least six of her people.

She felt the ragged edge of fury—she had *told* Māhoe that they needed prep time. And he hadn't said anything about the military being so close. He should have said if they were going to attack when someone broke into the warehouse.

Or maybe he should have explained better what an active military facility meant. He'd lived here forever. He knew the culture.

He hadn't explained it well enough.

She tamped down the fury and contacted Halia.

"We lost two," Halia said before Olina could even speak.

That ragged edge of fury became something stronger. Olina

clenched her own fists to keep herself from telling Halia to shut the hell up. Olina didn't need to hear that right now.

"They hadn't moved when that craft descended. That was ugly, Olina—"

"Shut up," Olina said. Time for recriminations later—her own at Māhoe and Halia's at…whomever. Maybe even at Olina. "We need to be extracted *right now.*"

Halia didn't respond immediately. Time had slowed down, and that delayed response seemed to take hours, which was making Olina even angrier.

"We still have three in the warehouse and—"

"I don't care," Olina said. "We'll get them out."

She wasn't sure if that part was true or not. She didn't care about that either. All of the casualties were going to have to be on Māhoe.

"Can one of those skips be operated remotely?" Olina asked.

"Yes," Halia said in a tone that had an undercurrent of *I thought you knew that.* "But I can come—"

"You will come," Olina said. "You're getting us out of here. But first, send those skips away. They're beacons, proving that we're here."

"I think the owners of that warehouse already know you're there," Halia said.

Olina had to tamp back fury. Working with her own hand-picked team was better. They didn't talk back. They didn't have opinions or if they did, they kept those opinions to themselves.

"Get those skips out of here," Olina said tightly, "and then get yourself here immediately. I'm going to gather whomever I can and we'll meet you on the far side of the warehouse." In case that wasn't clear, she added, "On the opposite side of the craft that we destroyed."

"Yeah, got it. Be there shortly. How are you going to get everyone from inside the warehouse?"

First, it was none of Halia's business. And second, Olina probably wasn't. They might be on their own.

But she would try, without going in.

"Just get here," Olina said.

Then she signed off and leaned against the building for a half second. She was more fatigued than she should have been. So she had the suit run a diagnostic.

Nothing had punctured it. She was not visibly injured. But she was in some kind of mild shock, which irritated her.

Or maybe the irritation was that ragged edge of fury, some of it from the beginning of this job, at the way that Māhoe figured everyone could handle something that he should have known was impossible from the get-go.

She opened a channel to her surviving team members. All of them, including the ones inside the warehouse.

"We're meeting the ship on the far side of the building—" which she identified using the coordinates they had started with. "We have to leave within ten minutes. If you're not here by then, use the tactics we taught to blend into the area. We will find you later."

If they could. If they weren't captured.

Maybe she would take control of the *manu* and just destroy that warehouse. It would be for the best, after all. Then no one would have the weaponry.

But who knew how many people would be killed in that explosion. If there were as many weapons as Māhoe thought there were, an entire section of the city might be leveled.

Olina wasn't sure she was that angry. She wasn't sure she could have the deaths of thousands on her conscience.

She ran toward the far side of the building, following the three who had accompanied her. She didn't hear any real response on her comms, not that she had asked for any.

She realized as she ran that she hadn't asked who had died in the initial disaster. She hadn't been close enough to this team to really get to know them without anything but contempt.

And people who couldn't save themselves from an obvious threat? They truly did deserve her contempt.

She reached the edge of the building, heart rate too high, breath coming too fast. She was sucking oxygen out of the suit, which was telling her that the air in the area was filled with chemicals and smoke and a toxic stew of plastics or something, stuff that was either banned or not even made on Amnthra.

People would be damaged by this day no matter what she did.

She saw that for the rationalization it was.

She didn't care. She had reached the point where she needed to get through this part of the day.

Once she did, she would take matters into her own hands.

Whatever that meant.

TWENTY-EIGHT

Five flightwings took off from the base on the south side of Vaycehn. Combat Captain Henry Chester flew in the first flightwing, leading the V-shaped formation.

He sat in the back of the flightwing, studying what little they had on the situation. The back was wide and slightly oval-shaped, with a back end that opened and doors on the side as well. He could evacuate from any direction, not that he wanted to.

Instead, he was sitting just to the right of the cockpit, so he could see through the windshields as the flightwing hurried through the mostly empty night sky.

The flightwings had taken off even before anyone had a complete handle on the mission. A single flightwing had been preparing to respond to a call for backup from a flightwing commanded by Lieutenant-Coronet Felicity Dunstan, but that mission had changed suddenly when her flightwing was destroyed.

Now, the mission had expanded to five flightwings, and more might follow, considering they were going to a military warehouse in the warehouse district.

His own commander had no idea why anyone would attack a warehouse that the military had vacated fifteen years ago. The military still protected it, primarily because some of the tech built into its walls was still proprietary. No one in charge wanted any other entity to understand what kind of security technology the military actually had.

Other than that, the military had nothing to do with the entire area. And hadn't in years.

The flight across the city would only take a few minutes, not really enough time to watch the vids, get up to speed and figure out exactly what was going on.

Chester had been ordered to take out any interlopers in the area, but he was loathe to do that. He used to live in that warehouse district.

There were apartment buildings nearby, filled with civilians.

If he did this wrong, then it would haunt him for the rest of his career.

The problem was there wasn't a lot of time for caution—and there certainly wasn't a lot of room for error.

For anyone.

202

TWENTY-NINE

The ground had just rumbled beneath Hazleberg, as if a death hole had exploded somewhere in the vicinity.

Her loveseat had actually traveled across the floor, bumping and sliding with the rumble. The other furniture danced as well, and the lights above her had swayed precariously.

The only thing that hadn't moved had been the serving tray. It still waited patiently beside the space where the loveseat had been, hoping she would finish her drink. If, of course, a serving tray hoped. Or even waited patiently.

Hazleberg gave the corporate apartment scant attention. She had been assured when she moved in that it had been built recently enough to have all of the proper death hole precautions.

Instead, she was staring at the images before her, images of the storage area on the lower level of the warehouse. The security cameras were shaking and debris was falling in front of them. The artifacts—all of them—seemed to wiggle.

Maybe a death hole had opened underneath the warehouse. More debris was raining from the ceiling, at least on the working cameras. She now realized that at least two had quit.

She had warned Blasingale not to store so many precious artifacts below ground, but he had asked her *What does it matter? If a death hole blows, it'll take out everything nearby. One has to hope that the military knew what was beneath this warehouse when they built it.*

One did have to hope, but that didn't mean a whole heck of a lot. Death holes sometimes went straight up, sometimes they went sideways, sometimes they seemed to come out of nowhere.

And Blasingale should have known that. He probably did know it and didn't care. He had probably thought that a former military facility was the safest place he could find for a haul like this one.

Hazleberg couldn't change the locations now. She had two things to focus on—the breach in the storage area itself, and now, the rumble of the possible death hole.

When the death hole had blown, she had been watching a man in an environmental suit. He had broken into the storage area. She wished he wasn't wearing an environmental suit because she wanted to see his face. No matter how she tried to change the cameras, though, she hadn't been able to peer through his visor.

Somehow he had gotten through the normal security to that room, even though he wasn't supposed to. There were two other people in the warehouse, but none of them were as close as he was.

She had actually stopped watching them. She had been more concerned with the man.

Somehow he had gotten through the locked door and stepped inside just as she was activating her own protocol. She had stopped, startled to see him.

He was thin, his suit dark and of a make she had never seen before. She had no idea why anyone would be wearing an environmental suit in a warehouse, but she worried about it.

And now it niggled at her.

Maybe he had planned to tamper with the environmental systems. Was he there to destroy the artifacts? Because one man certainly couldn't steal all of them.

When he entered, he had stopped, clearly surprised at what he saw. And after she spent a good minute trying to figure out who he was —*what* he was—she went back to activating the security protocols.

What she wanted, more than anything, was for those protocols to trap him inside that room. Then someone could question him. And since the security protocols had gone off, that "someone" was going to be the Enterran military.

She would tell Blasingale that she needed to be part of that interrogation. She was the only one who knew what questions to ask, the primary one being how this man in his strange suit knew that there were artifacts on the lower level of that warehouse.

Now none of it seemed relevant.

The rumble—whatever it had been—had moved the cameras, and she had to move them back to see him.

He was carving his way through her security field near the door. Carving was the only word she could come up with, because he was using his hands to part the field as if it were water.

He didn't seem panicked. He moved with an almost military precision, which worried her.

He was getting through her security and she had no idea how to make it stronger.

At least he wasn't focusing on the artifacts—yet.

She hoped that beneath that military precision was just a spark of adrenaline, one that was demanding he escape the room quickly before the death hole opened up around him.

He grabbed the door handle, which shouldn't have been able to happen, and then flung the door open. He staggered out, without taking a single artifact, and staggered into the corridor—which, from the tiny vantage that Hazleberg got, seemed undamaged.

Then the door slammed closed, dislodging more ceiling debris around all of her cameras.

She didn't have access to the security cameras owned by the building. Now that he'd moved out of the storage area, she was effectively blind.

She needed to contact Blasingale. She didn't have the right codes to get her to track the man in the environmental suit, and he was probably getting away.

She cursed as she stabbed at her equipment with her right forefinger, ignoring a shaky feeling that came from her proximity to a death hole.

She hated working on Wyr. In the future, when she held events, she would hold them in space, so that there wouldn't be death holes or environmental problems, no outside access either.

She would be able to vet anyone who came on a ship, and she would deal with any problems that arose. Enough of this working with other people. She was going to have complete control or she was going to quit.

She grabbed the tablet. It shook as she activated it. Blasingale had better answer, because they were running out of time.

His face filled the screen, just like it had earlier, and if anything, he looked worse than he had before. His eyes had sunken into his face.

"This better be important, Ethel, because—"

"We have a runner," she said.

He blinked and frowned at her. He had clearly thought she was going to say something else.

"Someone in an environmental suit breached the artifact room," she said. "I thought I trapped him in our security, but he got out just a minute ago. You need to let the military know that he's coming out. We need to know who these people are—"

"There's no one," her boss said.

"What?" she asked.

"They—the intruders—they blew up the military flightwing that had come in to clear them out. They're some kind of attackers, Ethel. They're after the items in the warehouse."

He sounded terrified. His eyes glistened through the screen.

She had to look away. The panic that had threaded through her when the death hole blew—except that wasn't a death hole, was it? It was some kind of explosion, and she had felt it all the way here.

She straightened her shoulders, then stood, carrying the tablet as she walked to the windows. She didn't care what Blasingale was seeing right now. Probably sideways views of the uncomfortable furniture.

She saw the rows and rows and rows of buildings that stood

between her and the warehouse district. The buildings looked like toys from this height. They were all surrounded by mountains.

In the distance, near the warehouses, she could see smoke rising.

She'd seen similar things here before, rising smoke from someone else's tragedy. Only this time, it might be hers.

If that had actually been a death hole, there would have been smoke and dust and debris as far as the eye could see. The buildings would have disappeared into the maw of the hole, and the edges would have been visible even now.

Some kind of attack. She wasn't sure how to process that, but she was sure of one thing—reacting out of terror would help neither of them.

She moved the tablet so that she could see him. He was sweating, his eyes darting from side to side.

He was a panicker. That wasn't going to help at all.

She used her calmest voice on him. "You need to let the military know that there are people in environmental suits around the warehouse, that one of them breached that artifact room, and they need to catch him. They need to cover all the doors. They need to hurry."

"I think they're hurrying, Ethel," he said tiredly.

"He knows what's in that room," she said. "He might be making plans. We need—"

"Ethel, I'm not military," he said.

She made herself look at that smoke. It was floating with the wind, heading toward the mountains, a trail of black like a finger, pointing away from the district.

"Give me the information. I'll tell them," she said.

"All right," he said. "I'm sending it to you."

Then he signed off.

It was as if he had already given up. Maybe he couldn't deal with the loss of life, but she suspected it was more like he couldn't deal with the potential loss of money. If these people had blown up a military vessel, did that mean they were going to blow up the warehouse?

Was that why the man in the environmental suit had been so eager to escape?

She hadn't looked to see if he had planted anything or dropped anything or done anything. And if he had done so outside of the room, she had no access to that.

The tablet buzzed as the contact information appeared.

Her stupid boss. His passivity was going to cost them precious seconds as she explained her way into the chain of command.

But it was either that or try to make Blasingale do it. And that would waste even more time.

She pivoted, so that the cityscape appeared behind her, the smoke a beacon of the destruction and death around her artifacts.

Then she activated the contact that Blasingale had sent her.

She would get through, no matter what. She would make sure of it.

THIRTY

Khelan had moved his screens closer to Nani. He didn't want to sit on one of the pedestals from the monkey tree. They were too far away from her.

So he stood as close as it was possible to get to her pedestal. He still couldn't see her very well, but that was because they were both surrounded by four holographic screens. He had almost wanted to put one behind him, so that he couldn't feel Elikapeka's gaze on him.

She hadn't left the control center. She had gone to the back, sat on one of the pedestals of the loulu, arms crossed, almost as if she wanted to watch the two of them fail.

He wasn't used to working with someone like her. He vetted his own people and weeded out the difficult or egotistical (and stupid) ones. Elikapeka should never have been on any team.

But he needed to focus. One of his screens monitored all of the military bases in and around Vaycehn.

And the system had just flagged something he had been afraid of all along.

"Five flightwings just took off from the same base the original flightwing left from," he said to Nani. He wasn't sure she had seen it.

"Traveling at the same rate?" she asked.

"They've sped up in the past minute or two," he said. "They must have gotten word about the explosion."

He wanted to look over his shoulder, to give Elikapeka an evil glare, but he resisted the urge.

If the flightwings had sped up, then they would be here shortly. The timeline the team was facing was nearly impossible.

His stomach clenched. That meant he might have some hard decisions in the next hour or two.

He couldn't think about that, though.

He watched the skips take off. They headed in different directions, all under autopilot. He mentally thanked Halia for thinking that far ahead. Now, if she could get to the team...

"I'm still reading people inside the warehouse," Nani said. "What's your policy if they don't get out?"

"That warehouse stays intact," he said, deliberately not going any farther with his answer. He was going to do this moment by moment.

He had never presided over a disaster quite as big as this one. And if the team didn't get out of there, if Halia didn't get the *manu* out of there, the problems would be compounded.

The last thing he wanted to be was the guy responsible for the Enterrans learning about the Amnthrans—and their capabilities.

Not to mention what might happen if the Enterrans learned that they had acquired a cache of very powerful weapons.

He monitored those flightwings. They were the key.

And his options were terrible. He could shoot them down now, from orbit, which would make the Enterrans believe they were under attack—and they would be right; just not from another military power.

If they got to the warehouse before his people left, he couldn't shoot them at all. Too much chance of an accident with the facility.

And after that—

He didn't want to think about after that. He couldn't. He needed to focus on each second, and hope it would lead to something he could live with.

THIRTY-ONE

Lebede couldn't sit down. She couldn't stay still. She paced and worked and paced and worked, trying different consoles, kicking the chairs aside. There were only four, but each one had seen her wrath more than once now, because they always seemed to be in the way.

She knew what she was doing, or at least, what she was trying to do. She was trying to locate that weird ship, doing everything she could with the systems she had. Technically, the area where the ship had been wasn't in her jurisdiction at all. She was piggybacking on city systems, and hoping no one was going to care, considering what had just happened.

The office had a faint stink of smoke, which she hoped was her imagination. But her burning eyes were telling her that maybe it wasn't. Maybe she was smelling the smoke from the explosion—the smoke from the deaths.

She had turned on the cooling system, even though it was cold outside. She thought that moving the air might help, but the smoke smell seemed to grow stronger. Who knew from where the tiny tower drew its air.

It would be just her luck that it came from outside.

So she shut off the cooling with a simple voice command, and immediately everything felt stifling. But she pretended she didn't care.

The holos before her were filled with smoke and she had to scrub the imagery. She made herself focus on that strange ship.

The readings still suggested a gap where the ship should have been. And she hoped to hell she could trust those readings.

She contacted Fernsby as she continued to work.

His answer was curt. "What now?"

"I told you before that there were skips parked on the landing area not far from here," she said, not caring whether she sounded polite and deferential. "Next to them was a strange ship, and it's vanished."

"So it was the ship that attacked our flightwing," he said, his voice trembling with fury. "You said the shot came from above. You said—"

"And I was right." She wasn't looking at his image, superimposed on all of the holograms. She was looking at the data. The skips were powering up. "That's not why I contacted you. I contacted you because the ship is missing."

"You expect me to glean something from that," he said. "And I don't have time for riddles—"

"Sir." She stood up and this time she made eye contact. She had just watched a group of people die horribly and her office stank of the smoke, maybe from their deaths, and he was just being obtuse.

The last thing she needed right now was obtuse.

"Three skips and a strange ship arrived at the same time. Those people near the warehouse, their leader came from the strange one, then it vanished, like they did—some kind of stealth tech," she said. "I don't know, but I was tracking them, and then the flightwing came down and someone attacked it, and now I can see just a handful of those people on the far side of the warehouse, and I'm pretty sure they're waiting for pickup. From that strange ship. You have to let the military know. They might be walking into another ambush. Sir, it's on us if they do."

"It is now," he said, and signed off, leaving her breathless. What the hell was that?

And then she understood. Everything they communicated was

recorded. She had just put it all on the record, and he didn't want it to be.

She had thought she was being protective of her job, but he was really protective of his. Too protective.

The skips hovered, then rose, the way skips did when they were on autopilot.

She set up a tracker to keep an eye on them, even though that wasn't her job, but maybe they would tell her something. Maybe they would tell the company something. Maybe they would tell everyone something.

If they were moving, then that ship was probably moving too. She wondered how she could find it.

She was going to have to look for gaps in the light, just like she had done before. If the ship was picking up those people, then it wouldn't go far.

If it wasn't—if it was coming in to defend them, to attack again— then she had no idea where it was going to go.

She split the holograms into two extra, one to monitor the strangers gathering on the far side of that warehouse, the other to monitor the area where the ship had been. Then she used the center hologram to work the gap, to see if the data gave her any information at all.

The system was not designed for this, but she was bending it to her will.

Her back sent a spasm through her and she had to stand up, so she moved the hologram she was working on up to her line of sight.

And as she did, something registered.

There was a gap, a small one, in the light. It was ship-shaped and it was moving toward the warehouse.

"I'm tracking it," she said, for what good that did anyone. She tried to reach Fernsby, but he wasn't responding. She didn't even have a public contact for the authorities.

Except the one posted all over the apartment building for the residents. The emergency contact, complete with security video.

She opened the contact on her personal handheld, gave her address, and said, "I'm running security on the warehouse district, and I see a strange ship heading toward the central warehouse where there was an explosion of a flightwing earlier. I need someone there to reach the response team before it arrives, so they can patch into my systems."

The response she got was not automated. It was a person, sounding as adrenaline-filled as she felt.

"Who are you again? What do you have?"

"We don't have a lot of time," she said, as she repeated her message. "Please contact them right away."

"Already on it," the voice said. "I just need..."

Lebede let the voice fall into the list of needs, into the directions of someone who might be able to help. For the first time that night, she didn't feel alone.

She worked to patch the locals into her system, her boss be damned, and hoped to hell that all of this work would be finished in time to save lives.

THIRTY-TWO

Iokua ran through that ridiculously long corridor. The lights were fading in and out, and debris was falling from the ceiling. He had no idea what had just happened—he couldn't roust anyone on comms— but it was something bad.

All he could think about was the history that Māhoe had told them. Something about malfunctioning *anacapa* drives underground that were causing violent disruptions in the planet itself. The locals called those disruptions death holes for a reason.

That shaking could have been one of those disruptions. Whatever it was, it nearly knocked over parts of the Spire, and all he could think about was being trapped in that gigantic room with a thousand weapons and an unstable wall and the ceiling collapsing—

It was a tribute to his own quick thinking that he didn't start panicking until he started running. He got out of that security field with a minimum of fuss, doing the delicate work to extract himself, and then he bolted when he entered the corridor.

The run felt uncoordinated, headlong, with his limbs pinwheeling and his breath so ragged his suit was warning him that he was over-taxing himself.

Being underground in this place was the stupidest thing. He

wished he could tell his suit that, but it was inanimate, even if it acted concerned about him.

Then, as he emerged, as the stairs rose above him like a beacon, blissfully intact (oh, he had been worried about that, badly worried, in fact), a message filtered its way through his comms.

A message Olina had sent seven minutes earlier.

A message that sounded...not panicked, but breathless nonetheless, as if something horrid had happened, and just getting the words out was taking too much time.

She started with coordinates, and then added, *We have to leave within ten minutes. If you're not here by then, use the tactics we were taught to blend into the area. We will find you later.*

He cursed and started running again. The coordinates she had sent him were for the very door he had breached what seemed like a long time ago. It had taken him a while to make his way to this spot.

Even running, he wasn't sure he would get out of this hellish warehouse in three minutes.

Ten would have been hard, but three.

It seemed impossible.

Still, he had to try.

He sprinted up the stairs, two at a time, a little shallower than he would have liked, but the idea of tripping, of hurting himself, and taking *any* chance away made him even more cautious.

Olina knew what had happened. And she was willing to sacrifice everyone on the team to get away.

Maybe not one of those *anacapa* malfunctions, then. Maybe something else.

Something human-caused?

He didn't have time to speculate.

He just had to get out.

THIRTY-THREE

The flightwings were one minute out, and Henry Chester was receiving contradictory information. A possible attack from orbit, mixed with a concealed ship, as well as some kind of notification that a man in an environmental suit had breached the lower levels of that central warehouse, a man that the client—whoever that was (and why was there a client?)—wanted alive.

"Sir." Coronet Debra Bleeker spoke up from the middle of the flightwing. She had been assigned to monitor the security vids of the warehouse area.

Three other members of the team looked at her, as if they hadn't expected her to speak. Which was probably a fair expectation, since Bleeker rarely said a word.

"The two skips on that landing area?" she said, her softspoken voice carrying in the wing's belly. "They're taking off."

"Leaving?" he asked. He wasn't going to confirm on his own equipment.

"Leaving," she said, nodding her head as she spoke. She was looking down at her equipment, her blondish-brown hair wrapped in braids around her skull catching the light. He hadn't realized until that

217

moment that she wasn't wearing a regulation cap. "And they're empty."

"Flying on autopilot," said Ensign Rufus Rutherford, garnering him a series of annoyed looks. Rutherford was new to the crew, and he had annoying habit of correcting everyone sideways, trying to prove that he belonged.

Technically, he didn't outrank Bleeker—since they were the both lowest level of combat troop—but her title made it clear she came from a military family, which gave her certain privileges that he was not entitled to.

Chester hated it when the enlisted tried to prove themselves. So he wasted a precious half second to put Rutherford in his place.

"Is that true, Bleeker?" Chester asked.

"It seems so, sir." She gave Rutherford a sideways glance, as if expecting him to correct her. Chester would have to deal with this at some point, but not now.

He suspected the skips were some kind of diversion, but he wasn't certain.

"What about that mystery ship?" Chester asked. "Has it followed them?"

"We have no readings on it, Sir," Bleeker said. "But there's a security feed that I'm told we can tap into—"

"Do so," he snapped. They were now less than a minute out. Less than a minute to decide if he wanted to break formation and have flightwings follow the skips.

But skips, as far as he knew, had no stealth tech. They couldn't vanish from equipment. They could be tracked now or later.

His mission was to get to that warehouse and stop whatever this was. If those skips had taken off without personnel, then that meant the people he was after were still in the area.

"Let headquarters know about the skips," he said. "Do we still have visuals on those intruders?"

He asked this of the whole team, but only Rutherford responded. Of course.

"Yes, sir. They appear to be gathering on one side of the warehouse."

"Then that's where we're going."

Chester sent a revised attack formation to the other flightwings. They would go in, spread out, and get as close as they could, but not close enough that some random shot from orbit could take them all out quickly.

That wasn't going to happen again.

"Gear up," he said to his crew. "Our mission is to take these people alive."

Or at least, as many of them as possible. Headquarters needed to know who was behind this threat, and what it all meant.

And he was the one in charge of the answers.

THIRTY-FOUR

The roar of five craft drowned out every noise in the district, rumbling the ground with the power of their old-fashioned engines. The crafts were coming in quickly in a V-shaped formation, but just as Olina thought that, the formation split apart.

They were moving from a V to a rectangle, which meant they were going to try to surround either the warehouse or the district.

The timer running in the corner of Olina's visor gave the team thirty seconds to arrive, and those thirty seconds might be too many. The *manu* wasn't here though.

"Halia, where are you?" Olina said.

"Landing now," Halia said, and it suddenly became obvious. Dust and dirt rose from the downward pressure of the ship.

Leimomi ran around the corner of the building, her thin arms waving, screaming, "Wait for me! Wait for me!" so loudly that Olina could hear her over the roar of the craft.

With her arrival, two of the three who had breached the warehouse were here. The team was now missing only one person.

Leimomi shoved her way into the group, as if she was willing to shove them all aside to get out of this area.

"Where's Iokua?" Olina asked.

"Thought he was with you." Leimomi was breathless, but that didn't hide the fact that she also didn't seem to care.

The crafts were spreading out, except for one that was slightly larger than the others. It was coming directly for them.

"Get to the *manu*," Olina said.

They didn't have far to go, maybe two dozen meters, maybe less, but it seemed forever. And Halia was going to have to shut off the shield for just a moment to let everyone board.

"Halia," Olina said as she ran, "you'll need to use the *anacapa* drive to get us out of here."

"Already have it prepped," Halia said.

She was the only one who sounded calm.

The *manu* appeared, watery and unclear in the darkness. That meant Halia had partial shields up, away from the doors. If the team got into the ship quickly, the Imperial craft wouldn't have the opportunity to target and shoot—if Olina's understanding of their tech was correct, which she doubted.

Four members of the team had already reached the *manu* and were climbing the emergency ladder to a small emergency exit. Another entrance had opened, and Halia had released a ramp, which was taking its sweet time descending.

The rest of the team headed for that.

Shots—actual propellants again—starting firing around them. That slightly larger craft was above them.

Olina finished her sprint, then glanced over her shoulder.

No sign of Iokua.

She hoped he got the message. She hoped he had the right kind of training, so that he knew how to blend into this community.

She doubted he did. None of them really had Empire training. But he was a smart guy. Maybe he would figure it out.

"Pull up the ramp," she said as the last of her people went up it. The damn thing was taking so long to maneuver that she didn't want to wait for it any longer.

Then she headed for the ladder.

She was the last one to climb it, the last one to slide into the ship, the last one to get out of that stupid area.

She hoped that Halia had seen her, and hoped that the shield was back in place.

Because those propellant weapons were weirdly powerful. She didn't know if the propellants had other properties—some ships allowed shrapnel to embed, for example, but if these propellants had explosives that activated when they had embedded into a target—

She didn't want to think about it.

The airlock was open, and she rolled into it, then bounded up onto her feet. The other four were still there, their helmets down, but they all looked slightly green.

She thought that was from the run until she pulled her helmet up. The air, which had filtered in from the outside, stank of smoke and chemicals.

She brought her helmet back down.

"We have to get out of here, Halia," Olina said through her comms.

"Already on it," Halia said. "Brace yourselves."

And then the ship bounced and jostled and vibrated as if it was running across a road made of large stones.

Olina hated it when an *anacapa* got activated in atmosphere. The entry into foldspace was always unpleasant and hard and often took a bit of unnecessary ground with it.

But the jostling stopped. She had both hands on the nearby walls, a movement she didn't remember making.

Then she let out a puff of air, and made herself breathe.

They had escaped. Not with everyone, but that failure was on Māhoe.

She would deal with that later, when they rendezvoused with him. He had called this—the use of an *anacapa*—unnecessary. He had said it was a violation of his mission parameters. He had said that they would be revealing the wrong kind of tech to a backwards community.

She also had a sense that she had been right about the problem all along. It wasn't just her team that lacked the respect for the Enterran Empire.

It was Māhoe. He thought them backward, unable to handle a small incursion like this.

Yet he was the only one who knew how vast the array of artifacts had been. He thought that some private corporation wouldn't secure them very well, and he had been wrong.

A hundred people should have been involved in this recovery. There should have been a dozen ships, maybe more, trying to get the items.

Or maybe Māhoe should have had ships stationed all around Wyr, monitoring shipments and destroying them as they left the planet's orbit.

Anything but this.

This was the largest loss Olina had suffered in years. Three team members dead, another missing.

There was going to be a reckoning.

And she was going to make sure it all landed on Māhoe.

THIRTY-FIVE

In the last three seconds, Chester had moved to the pilot's board, sitting next to Lieutenant-Coronet Gert Talbot. She was the better pilot, fast and efficient, but he had to be in charge now, and ready to take controls if need be.

His flightwing was coming in low and tight over the warehouse. Through the windshield, the entire area had become clear. On his right, a group of people were huddled against the side of the building. On the other side, little fires still burned from remains of the first flightwing. He saw it, but didn't acknowledge it. He'd had friends on that vehicle, but he'd deal with the emotions later.

A person ran toward the group, waving their arms, clearly shouting. But the group didn't really look in that direction. Instead, they were looking to their right. Dust and debris started moving, and the air seemed to vibrate.

He made a quick double check. He was not looking at a hologram.

"Target that dust storm," he said, and then, when Talbot didn't respond, he did it himself.

As he started to fire, something appeared at the edge of the dirt, half of a ship, the rest fading into nothingness. A shield of a kind he didn't recognize, then.

The ship was bigger than the flightwing, maybe the size of a large cargo ship—if the front part was any indication. It was dark, not black, and had something painted on the side. A bird? He couldn't tell because half of it was gone.

Several people ran underneath the ship's giant nose, but several others ran to the side. A ramp was descending, and he targeted that.

His shots weren't bouncing off the front like he expected. They were hitting the ground full force.

"We land near that," he said. Then he opened comms to the other four flightwings. "When that ship takes off, shoot it out of the sky."

He didn't have to hear the acknowledgements. He knew that the other commanders were as furious about this as he was. They'd take that ship down.

The ramp slowly eased up. There were no more people on the ground. The ship would take off now, and he was ready.

It rose maybe a meter, and then a door opened in the air in front of the ship's nose.

A door. His brain tried to compute that. Double doors, more like, with a blackness inside them.

The ship lurched slightly and then eased through the door.

"Go after it!" he said to Talbot.

She took the flightwing into a dive, but as it reached the ground, that door—those doors—whatever the hell it was—vanished, as if it had never been.

He fired a shot in that direction, and the round slammed into a warehouse nearly a kilometer away.

There was nothing in front of him, not a ship, not a door, not anything.

"Anyone know what the hell that was?" he asked—and no one answered.

THIRTY-SIX

Lebede saw it. That partial ship, that weird doorway. She had been sitting in her chair, believing that the military finally had this, that the interlopers would be caught and this incident was about to end.

The skips were gone, and she had thought the strange ship was too, until it appeared. Partially appeared.

She had trained all of her equipment on that ship, trying to figure out what it was and how to read it.

Then that doorway opened—as big as the ship, like a window into another world.

The ship went through, and now it was gone.

The first flightwing landed. Then another, and another.

A handful of people got out in full uniform, helmets, weapons, body armor making them all look larger than they were.

And they walked toward that divot in the ground where the ship had clearly been.

It was gone.

That window to another world was gone.

Lebede leaned back in the chair. She had no idea what had just happened, but she had recorded it all.

And she was going to make a personal copy of everything,

because there was a good chance she'd be fired tonight. The bad guys got away, after all, an entire ship blown up, lives lost, maybe items inside destroyed.

The people in charge would need someone to blame, and she was the lowest-ranking person in this chain. Who was she kidding? She didn't have a real rank.

She was disposable, an easy target.

She had no idea how she would use all of the tech information, or if she would need to, but she knew she needed it.

Even if nothing happened to her, she would need proof of what she had seen. If only to convince herself.

She leaned forward again, peering at everything.

For the first time that evening, she didn't feel the urge to contact anyone. This was going to have to play out.

And she was going to get through it.

She always did.

THIRTY-SEVEN

Five minutes. It had taken Iokua five minutes to get up the stairs and across that damn warehouse. The white and silver lights were still strobing, and his suit told him the sirens were still wailing.

Iokua was trying to reach Olina—had been since he crested that top step, sending warnings and messages and yes, pleas to wait for him.

Nothing seemed to be getting through, and he had no idea why.

The top floor of this place seemed dimmer even with the rotating lights, and he didn't know, because he didn't take the time to do more than glance, whether that lurking shadow he saw in the direction he was not supposed to go was simply a shadow or some kind of destruction.

He reached the door and grabbed the handle, terrified it would stick, terrified it wouldn't work, terrified he would be trapped here.

He had placed the words *I'm coming!* on a loop, and as he pulled on that handle, he blared those words even louder through the comm system. Still no response.

He yanked the door open—and took a step backwards in horror.

A person stood in front of him, wearing some kind of thick body armor and cradling some kind of long weapon, a rifle of some kind.

Iokua nearly turned around and fled deeper into the warehouse, but what would that get him? Caught a few minutes later, and even more out of breath.

He opened his hands, showing that he held nothing, and ran scenarios through his mind.

They spoke Standard, these Enterrans, so there was that. He would have to tell them part of the truth. He had been hired to test the security systems here, but he wouldn't be able to say anything else.

The person stepped to one side, and another person appeared beside them. Then another, and another. Even if Iokua had thought of escaping—which he hadn't—it would have been impossible.

He moved slowly and nonthreateningly, trying to remember the little he knew about the culture. Was smiling a threat or was it considered reassuring?

He didn't even know that.

So he would ride this through.

He was on his own. Olina had made that clear.

Maybe, if he lied well enough, he would be able to get out of this entire mess.

Or maybe someone would rescue him.

He almost snorted a laugh. He'd been told he was expendable from the start.

Maybe he should have listened.

THIRTY-EIGHT

"We lost one." Khelan cursed long and hard, using words he'd forgotten he knew. "We lost one."

He needed a chair to sink into. His legs were wobbly, his entire body unsteady. He didn't want to sit on a pedestal. He didn't want to figure out where, exactly, he belonged.

He wanted to sit down. Easily.

He'd been in the Enterran Empire too long. All he wanted was a simple chair.

Nani looked at him through her screens, her tattooed face pale in the silver light. She looked terrified.

He *felt* terrified.

The worst had happened—well, not the worst. So far, that stupid warehouse was still intact and the neighborhood hadn't been destroyed—but something he'd been trying to avoid since he came to the Empire had just occurred.

They had gotten their hands on Amnthran tech, items that they *knew* were strange tech. And to make matters even worse, they had someone to explain it to them.

That man—whatever his name was. Khelan wasn't sure he had

ever known it—hadn't had training in how to deal with the Empire. None of this team had.

All Khelan could do now was hope that the man had had previous training and knew the Empire well enough to lie his way through the next few hours.

Khelan doubted the man could. He doubted anyone could. He knew he couldn't. The Empire had interrogation techniques that were effective if barbaric, techniques that had been banned in Amnthra.

No one could withstand those.

"It's not a crisis," Elikapeka said from the back of the command center.

Khelan had forgotten she was there. He didn't need her wry, knowing voice right now. He didn't need her.

He wasn't going to argue with her either, so he ignored her.

Apparently, that was Nani's plan as well.

"I've been tracking him," Elikapeka said.

"You're locked out of the system," Nani blurted.

"The *command* system," Elikapeka said. "I still have other access. And I've been tracking him."

"You say that like it's important," Nani said.

"Don't engage," Khelan said so softly that only Nani would be able to hear him.

"It is important," Elikapeka said. "They'll have to take him somewhere. They have facilities for dealing with prisoners, right?"

Nani looked at Khelan but he didn't answer. His hands were shaking. He knew where she was going with this, and he didn't like it.

He didn't like it at all.

"You know the rules." Elikapeka sounded almost gleeful. "He's a liability now. We can't let them know what he knows."

"We can't rescue him," Nani said. "We don't have the personnel."

Khelan folded his body over itself. He braced his elbows on his knees and covered his face with his hands.

Elikapeka was right: the rules really were clear. No Amnthran with special knowledge who was captured could be allowed to communicate with the enemy.

And all other cultures, from the Amnthran point of view, were the enemy.

If they were anywhere else, Khelan could argue that the man didn't have specialized knowledge. He was hired because he could access buildings and steal things without being caught.

But his environmental suit was far ahead of any suits that existed in the Empire. His knowledge on how to use it alone would qualify as specialized knowledge.

Khelan felt ill. He was a man who recovered things for Amnthra, not a man who dealt with these kinds of crises. Even though he had been trained in them...decades ago. Before he left.

Back then, he'd said he could do whatever it took.

Now he wasn't so sure.

"Would you like me to be in charge again?" Elikapeka asked. "Because I can do whatever we need to do."

She probably could too. And more.

Too much.

He sat up, and turned to Nani. "Track him," Khelan said.

"What are we going to do?" she asked.

"Nothing right now," he said. He was being truthful. They couldn't do anything right now. The man had been captured and he would be taken away from the warehouse, away from the neighborhood, and all of those weapons.

Khelan couldn't do anything until then.

He wished he didn't have time to think about his next steps. He wished he could just act.

But he had time. Which meant the move would be deliberate.

"I can do this," Elikapeka said. Clearly she understood that he was feeling overwhelmed.

Not that he was trying to hide it.

I'm sure you can, he almost said. But he was taking his own advice. He was not going to engage.

"Do what?" Nani asked.

Maybe she hadn't had the training. Most likely, she hadn't had the training. Or if she had, she hadn't understood it.

"Kill him, of course," Elikapeka said.

"What?" Nani said. "No! Iokua's a great guy."

Khelan could have done without the name or the summation of the guy's character.

"That's not true, is it?" Nani asked. "We're not going to do that, right?"

Khelan didn't answer her, at least not directly.

"Can you track him?" he asked quietly.

"Yes, I already am. He's with a group near one of their ships." Nani swiveled her head wildly, looking from him to Elikapeka. "We're not doing this, right? She's nuts, right?"

He still didn't answer her. He wasn't sure what to say. Normally, he would have told her to leave the command center, but he couldn't. He didn't know any of these systems well enough to get the *anuenue* out of here, let alone destroy something from orbit.

"Can't we rescue him? You know, send the team—"

"Tell me how." Khelan's voice was hoarse. "Your team just went into foldspace. They're unavailable for most of the day, if not longer. Who else do we have? Us? How would we do that?"

Nani started to put her hands to her mouth, then seemed to rethink it.

"There has to be another way," she said.

"There is." Khelan swallowed hard. "We let them interrogate him. They will break him. He will tell them about the suit, then he'll tell them what the artifacts really are, and eventually, they'll get him to explain foldspace."

She was looking at Khelan in horror.

"This culture," he said, then clarified. "The Enterrans, they're barbaric. They're militaristic, hierarchical, and they're unwilling to see anyone having worth other than themselves. Do you really want to give them the kind of power we have? Without them working toward it?"

"You just yelled at me for killing a bunch of them," Elikapeka said, as if she was part of this conversation.

He continued to ignore her.

233

"Do you?" he asked Nani.

"Those are our choices?" she asked.

He nodded, even as he said, sadly, "Yeah."

"It doesn't make us much better than them, does it?" Nani asked.

"Individually?" he said. "No, it doesn't. As a culture? We're doing what we can to protect our tech and keep it out of the wrong hands. Right now, you and I, we're making the kinds of decisions the Guard usually makes. We're normally separated from it."

And he preferred it that way. He didn't want this.

"We can destroy everything right now," Elikapeka said. "If this culture is so worthless, then hit the warehouse and be done with it. So what if other Enterrans die."

He finally looked at her. She was sitting on her pedestal, one leg crossed over the other. She had brought up a few palm leaves so that they looked like fans over her head, maybe thinking they made her seem regal.

Her eyes were glowing.

He hadn't expected to have someone this crazy on the mission. His own fault for not requesting help the moment he had seen the announcement for the auction featuring the Mummies of Wyr. If he had done that, he might've gotten a trained crew, one with Empire experience.

He looked back at Nani who, if anything, seemed even more horrified.

"I guess we have a third option," he said drily. "We can destroy everything."

"I can't do it," Nani said. "I can't do it. I just can't. I *know* him."

At least Khelan didn't have that problem. He'd met this Iokua, but he knew nothing more about the man.

"Talk me through it when the time comes," Khelan said.

"I'll do it," Elikapeka said, almost angrily.

"And keep her out of the system," Khelan said. "Okay?"

Nani squeezed her eyes closed so tightly the movement added wrinkles all over her face.

Then she opened them. They were lined with tears.

"Okay," she whispered.

He wasn't sure if she was only agreeing to keeping Elikapeka out of the system or if Nani was agreeing to everything.

He wasn't going to ask for a clarification.

Right now, he didn't want to find out.

THIRTY-NINE

Post Commander Aurelia Dickerson stood in the very center of the Wyr Battle Command, surrounded by nearly a dozen ranking officers of various levels, all of whom were pretending to be paying attention to their screens, rather than watching her reaction. But they *were* watching her. She could see the side-eyes, the quick looks away.

And even if that wasn't happening, the stunned silence in the too-small room told her everything.

Nothing was supposed to go wrong on the ground in Wyr. This was a pre-retirement posting, or according to some, a punishment posting. Every planet in the Enterran Empire had a ground-based Battle Command, but most of them hadn't see action in generations. Some of them hadn't seen action in centuries.

These were training posts as well, for troops that would get sent onto the ground in conquered worlds—although in the past few decades, the Enterran Empire had been held tightly within its borders.

Once upon a time, she had hoped to change that. But once upon a time for her had been a long, long time ago.

She had her hands on her hips. She was in a uniform, thank goodness, but only because she had to do some work with her assistants before the next round of fledglings (as she called them) came in.

The raw recruits would be put through their paces before they got their permanent assignments. Most of them had washed out of the Space Force because they weren't suitable there. What she got here were often the dregs, since everyone knew that any problems on the ground in Wyr would be grisly ones—recovering bodies from death holes or worse, recovering people who should have died and hadn't—yet.

A death hole had blown during Dickerson's very first week on this post. She had been in battle—she had more medals than half the commanders who outranked her—but she had never seen anything quite like the results of a death hole.

It didn't keep her up at night—nothing did, not anymore—but she had washed out half of that year's fledgling group, because they were not suited to any kind of recovery task. Most of them literally didn't have the stomach for it.

One of the survivors of that class had been on the destroyed flightwing. Felicity Dunstan. Dickerson had approved Dunstan's increase in rank two years before, and had harbored hopes that Dunstan would distinguish herself enough on some mission that she would go even higher.

She had been one of the few people training at this Battle Command who actually had the ability to lead invasion troops, should the Empire ever try to conquer anything again.

Dickerson had allowed herself a moment to feel both anger and grief at Dunstan's untimely death before coming to what she always told the trainees was the beating heart of Battle Command.

This room wasn't the beating heart of anything. It was barely big enough to house the personnel and equipment needed. She'd gone up the chain half a dozen times, trying to get a new building here, citing the death hole recovery as a reason to get a larger building with more room. She'd received a positive response to the last request, but it wasn't exactly a yes. They were going to monitor the next death hole recovery before making the final decision...and then there hadn't been a death hole for more than two years.

Not anywhere on Wyr. Not even that explosion in the SeBaze Mountains which had led to a very strange discovery. She hadn't been allowed to see any of it because it remained in private hands, but she had sources which told her about a bunker beneath the surface, filled with clothing and furniture as well as art. There were also rumors of a ship, but she had only heard that from one person, who claimed they had heard it from a woman on comms just before she died.

Dickerson wasn't sure what to believe about the ship. It didn't seem possible.

But she did know that most of the art from that bunker was being stored in the warehouse in Vaycehn, the warehouse that had just been breached.

She had made it up to this room in time to see the five flightwings under the command of Henry Chester arrive. At first, she had thought they were going to take on what she had been led to believe was a strange ship, but instead, they had shot at what looked like ghosts.

She already had sent the footage for analysis by several methods. She herself was haunted by a fleeting glimpse of an opening filled with darkness, an opening that appeared around that ghostly ship.

Then one of Chester's flightwings went right through it or over it and that doorway appeared to be gone.

She had already ordered his pilot to send their raw footage, the things the ship recorded that never got sent automatically to ground command.

"Ma'am, we have a prisoner." Her second for the evening, Captain-Lieutenant Anne Fleetwood, approached her from the left. Fleetwood was a tall bony woman who had asked for ground postings from the beginning of her career. She was too tall and broad to fit comfortably in most Empire ships.

Dickerson blinked, letting the news sink in. A prisoner. She had never been in charge of a prisoner before. Her postings as a commander had always been inside the Empire's borders and the Empire was rarely attacked inside its borders.

She would have said never a few years ago, but some strange incidents had changed her perception of that.

She would need to contact her own commander to find out how they wanted the prisoner handled.

But first she needed to get the prisoner here.

"The prisoner is completely secure?" she asked.

Fleetwood nodded. "Captain Chester is asking if we want the prisoner brought here immediately or if we want to wait to see if more are recovered from the warehouse."

"They believe they have secured the warehouse as well?" Dickerson had received no notice of that.

"No, ma'am. They can't guarantee it. But the three people who had shown up on scans as Captain Chester and his team arrived are no longer there, so they're reasonably certain that—"

"I'm reasonably certain that these attackers, whoever they are, have access to technology that we don't even understand." Dickerson was both intrigued and yet feeling a major sense of urgency.

These people had surprised everyone from the start. So Dickerson knew, the best thing she could do was expect more surprises.

"Which means," she said a little more slowly than she normally would have. But she didn't want to sound panicked, alarmed, or show any other kind of emotion. This wasn't a routine day, but it was the kind of day that showed who had absorbed their training and who hadn't, "That we need the prisoner here, now. Make sure they have a military escort, just in case these intruders want to try something stupid."

"Yes, ma'am," Fleetwood said.

Dickerson continued, "I want you to send more troops to the area. We're going to need them, a military cleanup unit in case the intruders are gone, and an investigative team. We need to know who these people are."

"Yes, ma'am." Fleetwood pressed her heels together and nodded. Then she frowned. "We don't have a brig or anywhere to keep the prisoner, ma'am."

Dickerson was aware of that, but she considered it the least of their worries. She doubted the prisoner would be here longer than a few hours.

"Be creative. Figure out how to keep the prisoner away from everyone else and secure." She didn't add her expected timeline, because it was better to be overprepared than underprepared.

"Yes, ma'am," Fleetwood said. She walked toward one of the

consoles, and Dickerson hoped she wouldn't stop there. Because Dickerson needed her to eyeball the rooms where they would stash the prisoner until someone—probably the corps commander—figured out what to do.

"One last thing, Lieutenant," Dickerson said, mostly because she didn't want to give any orders to anyone else.

Fleetwood stopped, then turned slowly. Her body had a bit of an attitude that didn't show up on her face. She could hide her annoyance only so well.

"Send someone who can brief me on this Corporate Treasures organization and what, exactly, they're stashing in our warehouse that enticed this particular group of thieves."

At the word "thieves," Fleetwood's eyebrows went up slightly. Apparently she hadn't thought that this might be nothing more than a high-tech theft of some kind.

"Yes, ma'am. I'll do that, ma'am."

Dickerson had half hoped that someone else in the room would have volunteered that information already, but no one did. When this was over, she would discuss the importance of initiative with all of them.

Everyone here was either on a training path or the path down. And most of them had risen somewhat in the ranks due to their behavior at death holes, which was good prep for working on Wyr and in a cleanup unit, but not really anywhere else.

Fleetwood waited half a beat, apparently to see if she was allowed to leave. Dickerson nodded at her, and almost made a shooing motion with her hand, but didn't.

Fleetwood was doing her best, and Dickerson had just overburdened her.

But she was going to have to overburden the others too. She had a feeling that whatever this was, it was just beginning.

Long ago, she had learned to trust those instincts.

She just hadn't had to use them in a very long time.

She turned to the rest of the team.

"Well," she said. "Time to stop watching me. You all need to get back to work."

People scrambled and turned toward their screens. If they didn't have any, they pulled out a handheld as if they'd been studying it the entire time.

"But," she said a bit louder, "work means this: You have to find that ship in orbit, the one who destroyed Dunstan's flightwing. You should have been looking all along."

"We have been, ma'am," someone said from the side.

Dickerson couldn't see who spoke, and didn't recognize the voice. It was in that medium register that meant the speaker's gender was impossible to determine as well.

"Good," she said. "Because you're going to have to figure out how to monitor the area around that warehouse."

"For what, exactly, ma'am?" someone else asked.

Dickerson stopped trying to figure out who was talking to her.

"I'm expecting another attack," she said. "We're going to need to find that ship and isolate it, before it can do any more harm on the ground."

"But if it's not shooting, how do we find it?" A third person asked.

She wanted to close her eyes, to hide the irritation. If this was a training exercise, she would have had them volunteer ideas.

But it wasn't.

"Figure it out," she said. "Work with Space Force. They need to know we've been attacked from orbit."

If they didn't know that already.

She had a feeling that this was bigger than it seemed. More than a theft. Something difficult and different.

Long ago, she had learned to trust those instincts.

She just hadn't had to use them in a very long time.

FORTY

Khelan was still standing, too restless to even attempt to sit down. He was surrounded by his screens. They felt almost like shields, so that Nani, and especially Elikapeka, could no longer see him.

He had finally figured out the controls, enough that he could actually track this Iokua by his suit. But Khelan couldn't do much more than that.

He hadn't figured out the subtleties of the weapons system. Whoever used those weapons had to be careful not to hit the warehouse.

The command center felt cold and damp, even though the humidity had been shut off. The ocean breezes were long gone. He longed for more sunlight, but didn't know how to turn that on either.

He didn't want to distract Nani by asking her to pull some of the plants out of the floor and create some kind of warmer environment. He wasn't sure he'd feel it even if he did, mostly because of the stress of what he was about to do.

How different it was, to tell the people who sent you on a mission that, yes, of course, he could do whatever was necessary. And then, when he was faced with whatever was necessary, he had to hold himself together to do it.

He felt lightheaded, and a bit nauseated. He was having trouble standing still. He swayed just a bit, but he kept himself upright.

He couldn't be the man who collapsed. Any more than he could be the man who gave the wrong kind of information to the Enterran Empire.

He'd seen how those people interacted with their little section of the universe. He had never approved. When he first got here, he had been appalled, over and over, maybe even for the first few years.

Sometimes he was still appalled. Those mummies...

He shook himself, and made himself focus. The weapons screen was near his right hand. Nani stood beside him, tears streaming down her face. They illuminated her tattoos, making them glow. It looked like someone had drawn on her skin in glittery gold paint.

She held her clasped hands against her chest, and her breath was coming in ragged gasps. He wasn't sure she would make it much longer, but he didn't know how to encourage her.

He needed her. He doubted he could move fast enough or be efficient enough to target one of those ships from orbit. He—or Nani—needed to be precise. If they hit the wrong vehicle or had the shot veer wildly into a neighborhood...

Now he was having trouble catching his breath. He couldn't think about those things.

"You know, I can do this," Elikapeka said for what had to be the thousandth time. She hadn't moved from the loulu pedestal in the back, and neither he nor Nani had the opportunity to throw her from the command center.

Khelan was doing his best to ignore Elikapeka, but it was getting more and more difficult as his nerves became more and more frayed.

"That ship," Nani said quietly, her voice a bit watery. She pointed at a ship on his hologram, which he had opened to her as well. The ship was in the middle of two others just like it. "That's the one he'll be on. It's powering up."

"The other two are powering up as well," he said.

"But not everyone has left the warehouse." Nani sounded confused.

"They're giving him an escort," Elikapeka said. "They think we'll attack on the ground. They're not expecting a shot from orbit."

Then they were fools and the Enterrans were not fools. They were running scenarios and guarding against every possibility.

"What kind of shields do those vehicles have?" he asked Nani. "Have you figured that out?"

"Not anything we have to worry about," she said. "They're really not designed to work on anything other than a small local level. They think they'll be shot at from the ground, and probably using those projectile weapons. They're not protected against something like this."

Yet, he would have thought they would have been. The Enterrans had had a space-based military for millenia. Surely, they had thought of attacking like this, which should have meant that they would have defended against something like this.

Maybe they believed the craft was too small.

He didn't have time to speculate. He watched both of his holo-screens, one showing what was happening on the ground as if he were watching through a window, and the other showing just heat signatures—except for Iokua, whose suit was showing up in a silver gray.

Part of Khelan was rooting for Iokua to break away, to flee the military, to see if he could survive somewhere.

But Iokua probably didn't know how to do that. Or maybe he was worried about the projectile weapons—rightly so.

Or maybe, he really didn't care. He knew the team had left him behind, and maybe he was one of those mercenaries who didn't think about anyone else. Maybe he didn't put Amnthra first or maybe he hadn't thought about the risks of telling the Enterrans all kinds of Amnthran secrets.

Khelan had never talked to him, so Khelan didn't know. He wasn't sure he could speculate either, because that speculation would favor his own actions. He would make up a compromised captive who didn't care about anything, in order to justify what was about to come next.

"You two need to listen to me," Elikapeka said. "I can—"

"Shut. Up." Nani spoke tightly. "I can't take your idiocy any more. Shutupshutupshutupshutup."

"Really, Nani," Elikapeka said. "You need to concentrate if you're going to do this. I mean—"

"Shut. Up. Shut up. Just shut up already." Nani was shaking.

Khelan put a hand on her arm. "I need you to focus," he said softly. "She wants us to fail. We can't."

Nani took a deep breath, and then nodded. She huddled inward before wiping the tears off her face.

Apparently the anger had calmed her. Or at least had made her focus on something else.

The vehicle rose, followed by the other two. Two still remained on the ground.

The three vehicles flew side by side at first, and then they began to move around, as if they were dodging an active threat, or maybe trying to confuse some kind of tracking. The vehicle's signatures kept changing too, which he found to be an interesting feature.

That word, "interesting," told him that he had separated from his emotions. He was ready to do this. He hoped Nani was.

"You're seeing this?" he asked.

"Yes," she said, and for the first time since she had learned what they were going to do, she sounded calm. "They're almost to our target."

Khelan braced himself, half expecting Elikapeka to say something, but she was strangely silent. He was relieved that she had been locked out of the system. He had no idea what she would have done otherwise.

The vehicles flew across the city toward the base where they had originated. He had hoped they would take the same flight path they had used when they arrived, and fortunately they were.

That meant they would veer slightly toward the SeBaze Mountains in a few minutes. It was the least populated part of the route, and the only one without homes and apartments nearby.

"Ready?" he asked.

"Yeah." Nani was still using the same calm voice. "Let me show you what to do—"

"No," he said. "You have to do it. I might do something wrong, and we can't afford to screw this up."

She gave him a sideways look filled with such hatred and pain that he wanted to tell her *Nevermind. I'll do it*. But he didn't.

She shoved him slightly aside and put her hands on the holographic controls. She twitched a pinky, activating the test beacon on the side of the control panel. It showed that she was connected.

Then she squared her shoulders, as if she was squaring herself.

Khelan didn't move. He would do what he could if she failed, but he hoped to hell she wouldn't fail.

The three vehicles flew over the rugged part of the foothills, at the place where Khelan suspected there was a secret military base. At that moment, Nani targeted the vehicle with their man on it.

Iokua. Their man Iokua. Khelan wanted to get his name out of his head, but he couldn't do so.

At the moment, the vehicle was flying slightly behind the other two. The target made it seem red, but that was only on their screen.

Nani leaned forward just a bit, her fingers moving slowly.

Khelan would have to shove her aside if she couldn't do this, and he'd only have a few seconds to figure that out.

Then she tapped the holographic controls and the laser, its power threaded through the bits of the Spire that were inside this ship, traveled into the atmosphere in a split second, hitting the target with amazing accuracy.

The vehicle seemed to expand on the screen before him, and then it split into parts, some of which went hurtling into the other vehicles. One moved up and around the debris. The other veered sideways.

He couldn't tell if they were damaged or not.

But the image, the little silver-and-white image that gave him Iokua's environmental suit, well, it had vanished completely.

He initiated a search for it, which he had planned all along, and then he made sure that the system found all of the suits on Wyr.

There weren't any at all. Not even bits of one.

Any evidence of those suits—anyone wearing those suits—had either gone into foldspace on the *manu* or been killed.

He put a hand on Nani's back. She stiffened, as if she hadn't expected the touch.

He pulled away, rather than offend her. He had wanted to give her comfort.

Or maybe give himself some.

"It's done," he said quietly.

She nodded. Then she looked at him. The tear tracks glistened on her cheeks, but her eyes were dry.

"I know," she said. "What's next?"

He wasn't sure if she was asking that to prepare herself for something else awful, or if she was truly curious. Not that it mattered.

"We get the hell out of here," he said. "They'll be searching for us."

"On it." She moved back to the controls. She was going to send them into foldspace, just like they had discussed.

And after that? He still couldn't collapse. He was going to need a lot of help. More than two poorly trained pilots on a ship too powerful for them.

The moment the *anuenue* emerged from foldspace, he was going to have to contact Amnthra. He was going to need a lot of help.

They all were.

Because the mission wasn't even close to complete.

FORTY-ONE

A collective gasp rose in Battle Command. Dickerson didn't even have to look away from her holoscreen to know what they were reacting to. If she hadn't had so many years of training, she would have gasped as well.

"That was a precision hit," she said, making sure her voice was calm and even. "Track it, find who sent it, and make sure our flightwings scramble." If they hadn't thought of it already. "And get me Alcott Quarles right now."

Alcott Quarles was Operations Commander for the Space Force here on Wyr. He too had little to do. It was a pre-retirement post for him as well. He even let his underlings do most of the training. From what she gathered, he spent most of his time at his home in Vaycehn, doing who knew what.

She had made certain that Fleetwood had contacted him and his posting as it became clear that someone had fired from orbit. But Dickerson had been too busy with the activity on the ground here to brief him.

She had figured she would give him enough time to put on his uniform and head into work.

Maybe she had given him too much time.

"Ma'am," said Lieutenant-Coronet Leslie Bright. Bright had been promoted in the same group as Felicity Dunstan. Of the two of them, though, Dunstan had been the one who shined. She had had bright eyes and an active mind.

Leslie Bright was round, despite her excessive exercise routines. She was strong and she was smart, just not as creative as her classmate had been.

Bright was standing near one of the consoles, her hand resting on it. "We found the ship that fired the shot, but it disappeared, just like the other one."

Somehow Dickerson was not surprised. These people, whoever they were, had amazing technology.

"Make sure their signal just hasn't vanished from our controls," she said. She was monitoring the other flightwings.

The escorts she had assigned had peeled off, just like they were supposed to do in an attack. But all of them were fine, as were the remaining flightwings on the ground.

No one else was attacking that warehouse.

"I have Operations Commander Quarles," said Fleetwood.

"I'll take it in the office," Dickerson said.

The room really had no name. It had been designed for a post commander to use as their base, rather than something on the floor of the Battle Command, but she had never liked being separated from her people in the middle of an action.

Which showed how out of practice she was. She hadn't been in battle—real battle—for a long time. So, she hadn't had the need for privacy, since the joint operations had no stakes.

She brought one holoscreen with her, trailing her like a balloon. The office was small and cold. The overhead lights were a thin white that actually hurt the eye.

And someone had put a table against one of the walls, apparently as storage or something. The room's only chair leaned slightly to the right.

She opened another screen, and there was Quarles's face, lined and covered with a three-days' growth of white beard. The collar of

249

his uniform looked tight, so the flesh of his neck draped over it like a loose cowl neck.

"What the hell is going on?" he asked.

"I don't know," she said. "Something destroyed two of our flightwings from orbit. I've been dealing with the ground matters."

She had to work to keep her tone level. She felt like accusing him of neglecting his duties. She could mentally make excuses for him, though.

No one expected an attack in this part of the Empire—although maybe they should have, after that strange attack in Vaycehn three years before.

"We saw the second attack," he said, and she could tell from his tone that he meant *he* had seen the second attack. His people had probably seen the first one as well.

But she knew commanders like him. They were people who used a plural, sometimes to hide their own culpability in something.

She mentally shook herself again. She needed to work with him, so she needed to treat him with respect.

"My people tell me..." he said, and with that phrase, she relaxed a little. She was clearly judging him on his appearance and their earlier interactions. "...that we've never seen a ship like this one, and now it's disappeared?"

That last part became the question. He wanted her to answer it, not his own staff.

Apparently, he did not believe them.

"I'm hoping it's an advanced cloak," she said. "It took us a while to figure out the first shot came from orbit. Once we did, we had to examine our older footage to find it. It had moved to a different orbit. More elliptical."

"Has it changed orbits again?" He should have known that. He was the one who was commanding the Space Force, not her.

"No," she said. "Or rather, not that we could find. But honestly, Alcott, my people aren't set up to track a ship in space. Yours are. I've been focusing on ground tactics all these years."

That slight rebuke—a hint that he should have been at work, even at this time of the evening, especially since her people had contacted his when they realized the shot came from orbit—slipped out despite her best efforts.

Maybe his people had reached him, and it had taken him this long to report to duty. Or maybe he just truly did not believe what the equipment was telling them.

"We've been tracking," he said, sounding almost defeated. "It looks like that ship flew through a door in space. Since that's not possible, I'm having our people recalibrate everything to find the cloak."

"It is possible, Commander," she said. "We saw the same thing on the ground with another ship."

"That is not proof," he said.

"Except that we were shooting at the ship at the time, and the shots went from bouncing off the ship to going through the area where it had been."

He was shaking his head, his watery blue eyes glancing sideways at someone she couldn't see. She had thought he had been alone in his office, as she was in hers.

His lips thinned. "We'll take it from here, Commander," he said to her, almost as if he was dismissing her as a crank.

She couldn't let him get away with that. "Apparently, you weren't briefed on the problems at the Room of Lost Souls a couple years ago," she said. "I was in one of the responding ships, so I have knowledge. When this is over, I'll send you what I can."

"The Trekov disaster?" he said. "That's connected to this?"

"I'm beginning to think so, Commander," she said.

He nodded, frowning. "So, not a cloak," he said.

"I don't think so, but again, I don't know." She straightened, adjusting the tunic of her uniform slightly. Then she glanced out of the room. She didn't want her staff to hear this next part.

The little window in the door was cloudy, so she couldn't see them clearly, which meant they couldn't see her clearly either. From what she could tell, they were all monitoring the crisis.

She turned her attention back to the screen in front of her. Maybe she had misjudged Quarles. Maybe he had been alone and had been doing the same kind of double check she had just done.

"Right now, we're lucky, Alcott," she said. "We—"

"Lucky?" His voice sounded strained. "We've lost...what?...two dozen soldiers so far?"

"Yes," she said quietly. "But whatever those ships were, they didn't knock out all of our flightwings. Just two. And they easily could have. These were surgical strikes. The flightwings they took out —the first was attacking their people—"

"Who were surrounding our facility," he said.

"Yes," she said, trying to calm him. It had clearly been a very long time since he'd handled anything like this. "But the second strike is the one that worries me."

"Really, Aurelia," he said, "they should both bother you."

She noted that he changed "scare" to "bother," which told her more about him than about her. He was unwilling to admit that he was scared as well, and he clearly was.

"That flightwing," she said, refusing to be derailed, "had a prisoner on it."

"Prisoner?" he asked. "The thief that you captured?"

At least he had been briefed that far.

"Yes," she said. "They took out that flightwing on purpose. They weren't attacking our people."

He blinked, his eyes still a bit watery, but sharper somehow. As if he had finally focused.

"They weren't attacking us," he said quietly, almost as if he was speaking to himself. "They were silencing theirs." It was a realization for him. "What the hell is this about? I mean, that warehouse is mostly decommissioned. We rented to it to some art gallery, for god's sake."

"It's an auction house," she said. "And they had some extremely rare items inside. My people think this is a simple theft, given the millions in artifacts housed in that warehouse."

Quarles's frown grew deeper, making his entire face into one giant frowny wrinkle. "But you don't."

"Not now," she said. "Not after this last strike."

He looked to the side again, then back at her.

"We're alone?" she asked.

"Yeah." He spoke softly, so he clearly was worried about being overheard. "What do you think is going on?"

"I think this is related to that attack on the Room of Lost Souls," she said. "I'll tell you what I can after I figure out what is not confidential, but I can tell you this: the intruders at the Room had taken something from that Room, which our analysts believe was some kind of weapon."

He rubbed his unshaven chin, then looked at his fingers as if the stubble surprised him. Then his gaze met hers.

"I thought that was Trekov's justification for her screwup," he said.

"And yet she still has a military commission," Dickerson said.

"Because her name is Trekov," he said.

"Or because she wasn't wrong." Dickerson had watched the disinformation campaign centered around Elissa Trekov for the past two years, and had wondered at it. No one had questioned the information being put out there, even though it denied logic.

Ships were destroyed. Six hundred people died. The Imperial military did not have weapons that could do that, nor had they found anything in previous years around the Room that could have caused that kind of damage.

But Dickerson wasn't sure she could say that much. She had never really paid attention to the rules of the classified material on that attack, because she never thought she would have a need to discuss it.

Quarles was looking slightly to the side. She could see his thumb and forefinger moving. He was looking up that attack while talking with her. He was using a screen beside the one he had been talking on to do research. That was why he kept turning his head.

"The attackers left in a Dignity Vessel," he said. "An ancient one."

"And that Dignity Vessel looked new. It was operational," she said.

"This is not a Dignity Vessel, this thing that attacked us today."

"But it left the same way, going through a door in space." She probably wasn't supposed to say that. She suspected that was classified. But she couldn't take the words back.

253

He looked at her directly through the screen as if her words shocked him. "You think what we saw was the modern equivalent?"

"I don't know," she said. "But humor me for a moment, Alcott. Assume that these people, whoever they are, came for something at the Room and that something was a weapon stashed there, which they took or tried to take."

His expression was impassive but his eyes weren't. They were focused on her.

"Then they came here to take something from that warehouse. *We're* not storing weapons there. What we have there is built into the facility and has been there for a very long time. What's new are the items in that auction."

"You think there's a weapon inside," he said.

"I don't know," she said, "but it's a good guess."

His lips flattened. He seemed to have straightened his spine, become stronger. Maybe he was recovering himself as he realized he had real work to do, work he actually valued.

Then he glanced to the other side, clearly checking something. "We can't seem to find this attacking vessel. No matter what we do, the cloak is either very good or they're gone."

"I'll bet that they're gone," she said.

He focused on her again. "What kind of items are in that auction?" The question was rhetorical, an acknowledgement that the auction's items were the vexing detail, maybe the only one they could all solve right away.

"I don't know," she said, "but we need to protect that warehouse and its contents now. We need to figure out what is there."

"You think there will be another attack," he said.

"Yes, I do," she said.

He tilted his head slightly, that frown still furrowing his entire face. He looked to his right, then to his left.

Dickerson waited. The two of them were going to have to work together on this, whatever that meant, so she needed him to understand what she understood.

"That weapon at the Room of Lost Souls," he said slowly, as if he were looking at a report, "it damaged a lot of ships and killed six hundred people. It shaved off part of the Room itself."

"Yes," she said.

"And if one of those weapons is stored in that warehouse..." He looked up at her. "It would destroy the entire neighborhood."

"Or more," she said.

"Do you think those strangers were trying to protect us?"

What an interesting question, and one she hadn't thought of. He had been trained, as she had, to assume that outsiders were the enemy. She wondered how he became a commander who thought outsiders might be benevolent.

"I doubt they're trying to protect us," she said. "I think they know something we don't. We have a death hole problem we can't solve, Alcott. We don't know what causes it. Two years ago, some people emerged from an underground cave and there was an attack here on Vaycehn."

"I remember," he said. "You handled it."

"I handled the investigation. The attack was over when I got to the site. And some of the things I learned were pretty unbelievable."

She would have to review to see if her memory was right. But she now had a feeling these events were tied together.

She continued, "What if the death holes are caused by some kind of weapon, randomly firing or deteriorating and going off?"

This time he didn't interrupt her. This time, he just let her speak.

"What if these people know what the weapons are and are stealing them for some purpose we don't understand?" she asked. "It would explain why they were unwilling to just fire at the warehouse when we arrived. They want the weapon."

"And that's why they killed their own?" he asked.

"These people have shown they're not averse to killing people to get their way. They did so at the Room," she said. "So the fact that they did not blow up the warehouse is not altruistic. It's because they don't want to destroy whatever is in there."

He shook his head. "There has to be more to it than that. The prisoner, he had to have more information than that for them to kill him."

"We don't know their customs," she said. "But assume for a moment that they're similar to us. Then he had a few other things."

Quarles waited. She was beginning to see the commander he had been before he got this pre-retirement posting.

"That prisoner had an environmental suit with its own shield," she said. "We had trouble seeing any of those people on any of our command screens, just like we had trouble seeing the two ships. That alone might tell us something important. Not to mention the way those ships left—those doors."

"It's all guesswork," he said, but not dismissively. Which was good, because if he had been dismissive, she would have reminded him that she had told him that up front.

"Here's an assumption based on the way that we as a culture behave," she said. "These just might be random thieves who've stolen some tech that's beyond them and don't want to be caught. This incident might be completely unrelated to the Room and that other event."

She seemed to recall both involved a Dignity Vessel and this didn't.

"It might be," he said reflectively. "But here's the upshot."

She started. She didn't expect analysis from him.

"They obviously didn't get what they came for. If it is a weapon, they'll be back. If they just wanted millions in art, they didn't get that either." He nodded. "They'll be back."

"Or they'll try something else," she said. "That auction house's contract with us only runs for a couple more weeks. By then, everything has to be vacated from the premises."

"We're going to have to inspect those items," Quarles said.

"And we're going to need to activate all of the security at that warehouse, maybe even evacuate the neighborhood," Dickerson said.

He looked very serious. "This will work its way up the chain," he said. "My superiors are going to want to know if I think this is the first volley in some kind of war."

"Why would it be?" she asked. "We're not a strategic location. And if these outsiders wanted to shock us, they should have destroyed more."

He gave her a thin smile. "You haven't worked Space Force, have you, Aurelia?"

"Not since my early years," she said.

"We operate under the assumption that battles can come from anywhere at any time for any reason."

"So you think your commanders might believe this *is* a targeted attack." She shook her head. "The outsiders only had two ships. That's not enough."

"From my understanding," he said, looking sideways again, clearly at something just past his line of sight, "there was only one ship at the Room of Lost Souls during that horrific attack. Maybe these ships, whatever they are, are more powerful than anything we've seen."

She felt a deep frustration.

"Clearly," she said, "we don't have enough information."

"No, we don't," Quarles said. "I think they killed that prisoner because he would have given us more information, which meant they're going to do something else."

"We can agree on that," Dickerson said.

"Let's figure out what's going on here," Quarles said, "as best we can. This is our turf, Aurelia, even though the powers that be parked us here, thinking we're too old to be useful."

She hadn't felt that way. It was interesting that he did. This entire event seemed to have awakened something in him though. She had seen it happen throughout the conversation.

"We have to tell our superiors," she said. "Or I do. I lost two flightwings today."

"Yes, we do," he said. "Let's see what we can find out, though, and tell them we have theories pending a bit of research. They might take this from us, but they might not. They might give us time."

Or they might treat the two commanders like they treated Elissa Trekov, as people with too much dangerous information.

"All right," Dickerson said. "We'll pool our resources. But we both have to be ready for more attacks, maybe even in the next few hours."

"I'm already on that," Quarles said. Because he'd had that kind of experience.

She hadn't. She needed to shore up that warehouse.

"Contact me with any new information you get," she said, "and I'll do the same."

He nodded and signed off.

She glanced at the holoscreen she had dragged in here. She had been using it to follow the flightwings' progress back to base. The two escort flightwings had just returned. She would talk with them shortly.

But first she adjusted the holoscreen. She looked at the warehouse. Many of her people were huddled outside, talking, and gesturing toward the flightwings on the ground. This entire situation was still so new that the pieces of the first flightwing—the one that exploded on the far side of the warehouse—were still burning. The smoke curled and traveled upward, looking white through the lights and the dark sky.

She moved away from that, looking for another trail of smoke. She had no idea if the second exploded flightwing caused destruction on the ground. She hoped not.

She followed the second smoke trail downward. She saw burning pieces on the foothills, near some trees. The lights of the emergency response were threading toward the area, but a cursory glance told her that no buildings were hit—and somehow that didn't surprise her.

These people, these attackers, whoever they were, they seemed focused on their task and nothing else. Maybe it was a coincidence that they had struck the flightwing over an area where the debris would fall without killing anyone on the ground.

Or maybe it wasn't.

That surgical strike bothered her.

She had to make sure her people—both the people under her command and the people above her—didn't underestimate these attackers.

They had an agenda and they were going to achieve it. No matter what.

THE RESPONSE

A FEW HOURS LATER

FORTY-TWO

The military didn't want Ethel Hazleberg on site, but she didn't care. Whatever had happened to that warehouse had happened because of the items Corporate Treasures had housed inside of it.

She had initially thought of the people who broke in as thieves, but she was beginning to wonder. Thieves didn't kill one of their own...did they?

She had no one to consult—not yet anyway. Blasingale, her boss, had spent fifteen minutes screaming at her, as if the entire disaster had been her fault. He seemed to believe she had done something horribly stupid, like giving the thieves the codes to the warehouse or something.

She realized he was covering his own ass, but she didn't have time for that garbage. She ended their conversation while he was still in mid-rant and sent a complaint to Blasingale's boss, the owner of the company, ending the complaint with an implied threat.

No one, she said, *should be treated the way I was, no matter what the emergency. I will continue to do my job, but I will not speak to Mr. Blasingale again.*

She had not received a response yet, which did not surprise her. It was the middle of the night, after all, not that she would be able to sleep.

And it was the very idea of getting sleep—which seemed profoundly ridiculous at the moment—that had her changing her clothes into her inspection attire, and hailing an aircar to take her to the warehouse site.

She also brought two of her tablets. She needed to record everything, including what (if anything) had been damaged or stolen.

Her inspection attire consisted of unflattering brown pants that were surprisingly easy to clean, a heavy gray shirt that fell into the same category, and a white medical garment that a doctor friend of hers had given her, the kind of full body covering that military doctors used when they were treating someone who had come in contact with some kind of unknown virus.

The suit was similar to an environmental suit, but didn't have the additional features like comms and computers that focused on the environment.

She didn't mind, though. She liked the fact that the suit told her about medical dangers—air quality, unknown items in the air. Or maybe she had just gotten used to the thing.

She had carried it over her arm on the aircar, along with a case that she used for her tablets. She hadn't left any tablets at the warehouse, as had been her wont during the auction, and she was grateful that she hadn't.

There was a lot of information on those tablets, which items came from where, proprietary information about the owner of the pieces, as well as information about the pieces that hadn't been put up for auction.

The aircar dropped her on the far side of a mid-range apartment complex at the edge of the warehouse district, which was as close as the aircar could get. The air smelled foul, some kind of mixture of smoke and chemicals. Each breath burned her lungs, and she wondered if she should put on the protective hood right now, but she didn't.

Several people stood outside, wearing coats against the rain and the chill. Most of those folks had their feet shoved into some kind of rain boot, but it was clear that underneath the coat, they wore night clothes.

"You an expert?" a middle-aged man asked her as she got off the aircar.

"Yeah," she said, even though she knew he was asking if she was going to investigate what caused the explosion. Apparently, everyone here had been too far away to see it.

She had seen it on the security feeds, as well as the arrival of a larger ship, and the escape of the thieves who tried to get something from the warehouse. She had been told, just before she got ready to come here, that there had been a prisoner, and he had been killed in another attack on flightwings.

So far, no one knew if he had given up any information.

She moved past the middle-aged man, and found even more people in the same kind of garb—clearly awakened from a sound sleep, clearly wondering what, exactly, was going on.

A woman wearing a slick yellow coat over red-and-green plaid pants looked pointedly at Hazleberg's white suit, and asked, "Do we need protective suits?"

"I don't know," Hazleberg said. "What did they tell you?"

"Nothing," the woman said.

"You weren't ordered to evacuate the building?" That surprised Hazleberg, given the number of people outside.

"No." The woman looked truly panicked now. "Should we have? My kids are in there."

"If they were going to order you to evacuate, they would have done so by now," Hazleberg said with a certainty she didn't have. She had no idea what the procedures were around here.

She hoped she was right. She suspected this was new territory for everyone in charge. She couldn't remember ever hearing about an attack on a military facility in the center of the Empire. But then, she had no idea if the military would admit to such an attack.

Keeping track of that kind of information was outside of her purview. She tried to keep her focus on collectibles, antiques and antiquities. That was usually more than enough to fill her brain.

She threaded her way around the knot of people and walked to the warehouse district proper. Blue and white lights illuminated the sky. Some gold lights flickered on top of floating aircars, but most of the vehicles ahead of her were military brown.

Large lights rising two stories into the sky were pointed down at the warehouses—probably at her warehouse—and made the entire area look washed out and brilliant at the same time.

People wearing yellowish-orange suits that made hers look like it was designed by a child walked with purpose around the area. None of those people had their hoods up, though, so they were breathing this noxious stuff as well.

She felt out of her depth. She had no idea if they were supposed to wear this stuff whenever they came to a scene like this, or if there was something onsite here that made them think such suits were necessary.

A perimeter was set up all around the warehouses. The perimeter was made up of yellow lights each about six inches apart. They looked like a fence made of glowing materials, which, she supposed, it was.

She had never seen anything like that either, but it appeared to have been built into the ground and raised because of this emergency. Or maybe those fence-lights had been built for a time when the warehouse district was used continuously by the military.

She didn't know. What she did know was that it had never been this hard to get to her warehouse before.

She walked up to the fence, and felt a slight heat from the lights. They glowed in the cool air, with a bit of steam rising around them as a mist started.

She had been so focused on where she was going she hadn't even noticed the mist. But it had been raining off and on all day, and with everything else going on, she no longer thought being wet was much of a concern.

No one seemed to notice that she was near the fence. She rose on her toes, looked over the fence and the dozens of people who were gathering information or clustered, talking. A few stood outside her warehouse. Others were near some of the nearby warehouses.

In the distance, she could see the two flightwings which had come with the initial group of five. They looked larger than they did on her holoscreen.

"Sorry, no civilians," someone said, and she started.

A woman with short-cropped black hair, a strong jaw, and suspicious eyes was standing just a few feet from her. This woman wore a greenish-gray uniform, which Hazleberg didn't recognize.

Of course, Hazleberg had never made learning anything about the Enterran military a priority. She had served her two years while she was in college, and had done so in a program attached to the university, which some said wasn't even really military at all. Fortunately, she wasn't graded, just analyzed. Told at the end she really wasn't career military material, which she could have told them without the two wasted years.

"I'm with Corporate Treasures," Hazleberg said. "We're the ones who rented that warehouse."

"So?" the woman said.

"So, I need to know what happened to our materials. And I can provide information to your people."

"We haven't cleared the scene," the woman said. "It's still considered active and dangerous. We can't have civilians here."

Hazleberg drew herself up to her full height—not that she was much taller than the woman. But still. It was the principle of the thing.

"I can tell you if they changed something, left something, or did some kind of important damage. I can also easily get you into a few of our protected areas where we have our own security."

The woman looked sharply at Hazleberg. "You're not supposed to add security," the woman said, which led Hazleberg to believe the woman was in charge of something, or she had checked records before coming here.

"We have items in there worth millions," Hazleberg said. "Of course we added some security."

The woman cursed under her breath, just loud enough for Hazleberg to hear, but probably not loud enough to get the woman in trouble.

"We can show you vids—"

"No," Hazleberg said. "I need to go in there. I doubt even your experts on antiquities have seen items like the ones we have in that warehouse."

She had to work hard to keep the sarcasm out of her voice when she said, "experts on antiquities."

"Excuse me a moment," the woman said and walked a few yards away, clearly to have a private conversation with one of her superiors.

Hazleberg waited, shifting from foot to foot. Now, the mist was bothering her. She felt it, chill drops on her face and the one hand that wasn't buried under the suit. The suit itself was irritating; it seemed heavier than it had before. She thought of shifting it to the other arm, but that also meant shifting her bag, which she didn't want to do.

The woman returned. "Do you have staff?"

It took Hazleberg a moment to understand the question. It was a military one. If she was the person in charge, how come she didn't have staff with her?

"I do," Hazleberg said, not wanting to undercut her own authority, "but I opted not to bring them. I figured you weren't going to let many people through."

"Good thinking," the woman said. She squeezed the thumb and forefinger of her right hand together, and a small section of the light-fence in front of Hazleberg shut off.

She still saw a faint glowing outline of the light-fence, but she wasn't sure if that actually existed or if her eyes were seeing the after-effects of such a bright light.

She stepped through, and the woman pressed her thumb and forefinger together again, reinstating the light-fence. It illuminated the ground around it, which was now covered with marks from all the vehicles.

Ahead, though, Hazleberg saw a few small fires. The remains of that flightwing were still burning, and for some reason, the military people here had not thought to put it out.

"You will follow me," the woman said. "You will not talk with anyone until directed, and you will do as I tell you."

Hazleberg nodded, but didn't verbally agree. That was an old trick she had learned long ago. Plausible deniability. She might not have agreed at all, but had simply been moving her head slightly as she took in the scene.

The woman seemed to think that Hazleberg had agreed, because she led Hazleberg through a maze of vehicles and equipment. The stench had grown here, and there was something organically foul, like waste matter, which Hazleberg really didn't want to think about.

Nor did she look at the lumps near her too closely, afraid she might see something connected to the people who died, something she would never be able to unsee.

The woman didn't ask a single question as they threaded their way toward Hazleberg's warehouse. If Hazleberg had been in the woman's place, she would have been throwing questions at Hazleberg—what's going on? What's so desirable about those items? Who *are* those intruders?

Maybe the woman didn't ask because she knew Hazleberg didn't have the answers. Right now, the only thing Hazleberg would let herself think about was the money. She had thought it all a simple theft (or rather, a not-so-simple theft) until the thieves had destroyed the flightwing.

She had passed two warehouses now, and was definitely soaked from that mist. She hadn't realized just how far it was from that apartment complex to here. She had always ridden in an aircar, and covered the distance in a very short period of time.

Fortunately, she had worn comfortable boots, because she knew she would have to be doing a great deal of walking. She just hadn't expected it out here.

Then they reached the area between her warehouse and this one. In the center, there was a large smoking crater. It was squarish with curved edges, and it wasn't as deep as it had looked on her holoscreen.

That was where the flightwing had exploded. Hazleberg couldn't look away. People had died here, so recently that the air was still charged with the aftereffects of whatever that weapon was.

Hazleberg had never been this close to a disaster before. She had seen the historic aftermath of several disasters, and she had held items that had come from war zones. But this was different.

She liked to think it was the smell, which had grown so strong that her eyes watered and was making her queasy, but she had a hunch it was not.

The woman led her around that crater without a word. There were still big pieces of broken flightwing here, some the size of boulders, others bits and pieces of metal. Most everything in this part of the debris field was just smoldering or had burned itself out.

The woman brought her to the edge of the warehouse—Hazleberg's warehouse—which was bathed in white light. The security lights for the warehouse were all on. Exterior lights were pointed at it, illuminating the clean white walls.

She remembered first seeing this place, thinking it was so pristine and perfect. The best place to keep items so expensive that they made her nervous.

She had convinced herself that keeping the items here was better than having them on some kind of spaceship because she felt that no matter the size of ship she would use, some pirates could come onboard and steal it.

Her breath hitched. She had thought of theft, but not here, at the edge of the Wyr's biggest city, in the center of the Empire, in a warehouse with active military security.

She wiped at her eyes, not that it did any good. The hand she used —the one holding her bag—was wet, so it didn't dry her eyes at all.

The woman glanced back at her. "You okay?"

The question didn't hold concern for her well-being. Instead, it was a business question, something filled with *are you able to move forward?* tones.

There was no way Hazleberg was going to answer that question honestly. "I would like to see the warehouse."

The woman nodded crisply and led Hazleberg to a cluster of vehicles. There, three people with handhelds were talking to a man who was wearing a military cap with a black braid and a large bill. Hazleberg recognized that cap. Her instructor at the university had worn something similar.

Hazleberg felt a faint jealousy over his cap. If she had been thinking, she would have worn a hat as well.

The woman who brought her here stopped in front of the man.

"Sir," the woman said, "this is the person who says she's from Corporate Treasures."

"You didn't check her identification?" he asked, as if the woman had done something wrong.

"She's in the system, sir. The moment she went through the gate, it identified her as Ethel Hazleberg." The woman mispronounced Hazleberg's last name. "She's apparently the person in charge of this installation."

The man nodded, and then dismissed the woman with barely two words. The woman walked off.

The man pivoted so that he was facing Hazleberg. He had a dark face, made light by his silver eyebrows and mustache. His eyes were such a pale blue that they accented that silver.

"I'm Unit Commander Harald Corbyn," he said, his voice filled with gravel. "I'm in charge of figuring out what caused this mess."

Hazleberg clicked her heels together and nodded, using the most polite greeting she knew. Then she said, "I might be able to help you figure out what happened here."

"That's the only reason we let you through." He glanced at her suit. "You should have worn that from the start. Your clothes will never lose this smell."

She nodded. "I realize that now, sir."

He walked her to one of the doors at the warehouse. "We've gone inside, mostly to clear it and make sure that none of the intruders remained. From what we can tell, they haven't touched anything."

She wasn't going to agree, because she couldn't be sure without checking herself. But she was going to give him one thing.

"I looked on my holoscreen, sir, through our security, and except for one person—the one you captured—none of the others made it into the area where our auction items were being kept. Did he say anything before…?"

She had no idea how to delicately mention the thief's death, considering the entire flightwing had been destroyed.

"Before he died?" Corbyn asked. Apparently, he had no qualms talking about that part of the disaster. "No. We hadn't even tried to get information out of him. We figured we could do that at headquarters." Then he let out a small snort of derision. "Obviously, we were wrong about that."

She had never met anyone so calm in the face of a disaster, which was probably why he was in charge.

"What is this auction, anyway?" he asked. "What's so important about it, besides the money?"

"For these thieves?" she asked. Because the question had several answers. The owner believed the items contained important information about the history of the Empire. The collectors were interested in the art. And Corporate Treasures, if she was honest, cared mostly about the money.

"Yes," Corbyn said, his gaze solidly on hers. Given all that was going on around them—the lights, the smoke, the people using equipment to search the debris—he was remarkably focused.

"I don't know, then," she said. "It could be many things."

Considering how they had planned, though, whatever they wanted was extremely important to them.

"If you had to guess," he said.

She shrugged. "We had some exceptionally rare items."

"Which came from a cave, I'm told."

He had been briefed more completely than she expected. But the briefing must have been quick, which was why the details were slightly off.

"No, sir," she said. "It was a bunker. One discovered in a box valley. The man who found it, he initially believed that a death hole had created the site until he found stairs."

Corbyn looked at her. "Stairs? Were they ours?"

"Stairs that the military had built?"

He nodded.

"No, sir. We researched the area as best we could after he contacted us, and we found no signs of military presence there." Then she gave him a bitter smile, glancing at the warehouses. "Which, as you know, means nothing."

He nodded, then scanned the area around her, clearly keeping track. Considering everything that was going on, he was giving her quite a bit of time.

"What caught all of our attention, sir, was that there were mummies in that bunker. They were wearing uniforms that we can't identify."

He grunted, and seemed to think for a moment. Then he said, "Just like ships we can't identify. Technology that appears to be more advanced than ours. Weaponry that seems a bit extreme for a simple theft—wouldn't you agree with that, Hazleberg?"

At least he pronounced her name correctly.

"I would, sir. This is unlike anything I've experienced, and I've had to deal with thefts before. Nothing successful, mind you. Corporate Treasures has always been able to ensure the safety of our items."

Until now, she almost added, but she had no idea if one of those other two thieves had taken anything. She had no idea how they could have.

"What else can you tell me about that bunker?" he asked.

"Not much, sir," she said. "I did not see it. A different team of ours extracted the artifacts."

Corbyn's strange pale eyes narrowed. "There's more, though, isn't there?"

It took her a moment to step past her training. She was so used to keeping things secret. "As I said, I haven't seen it. But there was talk of more items deeper in that bunker, things that the owner would only allude to."

"Things you would like to sell or things you think are a lie?" Corbyn asked.

"Things I believed fantastical until tonight," she said, surprised at hearing the truth emerge from her mouth before she had time to think about it.

"Such as?" he asked.

"The owner, he mentioned that there was a large ship under one of the mountains at the edge of that box valley."

"Under?" Corbyn asked.

"Under," she said. "And if you saw the map, you would understand that no ship could get down there, unless it was built there.

Which meant little to me, because why build a ship underground with no way to get it out."

"Why indeed," Corbyn said, sounding bemused. He looked at the crater where the flightwing had been, his expression reflective. "You think now that he was telling the truth?"

"I don't think he's ever lied to me," Hazleberg said.

"Then why don't you trust him?" Corbyn asked.

"He was injured, sir. Severely." She swallowed, tasting that chemical smoke. The metallic edges made her teeth hurt. "In an explosion, sir. In that bunker."

"An explosion," Corbyn said.

"Yes, sir. Right after he found the bunker. His partner died, and there was a cave in."

"Hm," Corbyn said, still studying that crater. She had the sense that he could see her through the corner of his eye, and he was studying her reaction maybe more than he was studying that crater. "What caused the explosion?"

"Honestly, sir, we don't know. The owner believes that there might have been some security that he hadn't understood near the door they had gone through. His partner was trying to remove one of the artifacts. He hadn't been carrying anything and he had gotten through."

Corbyn nodded, then turned toward her. "Do you believe that?"

"I don't know what to believe, sir," she said. "When we sent our team in, we prepped for the possibility of heightened security. They never found anything that would trigger if they removed items."

He grunted again, frowning.

"But," she added, "our team entered after the explosion. Maybe the security was a one-time thing."

"You took precautions," he said.

"We did."

"Perhaps they were enough...?"

She shrugged. "I don't know, sir. I just know we were able to remove everything, from the mummies to the clothing in the back to the collectibles and artifacts stacked in one of the rooms."

He grunted again. "And the ship?"

"We did not see a ship. But that area, where the owner had seen the ship, it was the only part blocked off. He wouldn't let anyone go there."

Corbyn nodded. "You didn't find that suspicious?"

"I wasn't involved then," she said, knowing she wasn't answering his question. She did find it odd, but then she found everything the owner did odd.

"This is bigger than some collectibles," Corbyn said, still looking at that crater.

She wasn't willing to say that. "I don't know, sir. There is a lot of money involved. People do strange things for money."

He pivoted slightly, maybe so that he could see her better or maybe so that he could watch her and look past her to see what was going on with his people.

"I'm not sure you understand the cost of what you saw today," he said.

"The lives," she said, trying to follow what he meant.

His lips turned downward slightly, but that was his only reaction.

"Yes, the lives," he said almost dismissively. "But more than that."

More than that? She was always so careful with her words, that his surprised her. Surely he didn't mean that something else was more important than the loss of life.

"The ships," he said, "the personnel. The weaponry. The attack itself. It all cost money. I have no idea how much money you believe those collectibles are worth—"

"Millions, sir."

"—but I can guarantee that it makes no sense for a group to spend millions to steal something worth millions."

"Oh." She shook her head. "I'm sorry to disagree, sir, but this is my area now. Sometimes, collectors want an item and will spend more than it's worth to get it. That's common behavior, especially if the item is rare."

"Would they steal it?" he asked.

"If they couldn't buy it." Her cheeks flushed. She had been so distressed by everything that was going on that she hadn't thought about her buyers. "Sir, I had a number of buyers who tried to pick up the entire collection. We refused to sell everything in one bundle, per instructions from the owner. I couldn't change that."

"Did these buyers offer more than the collection was worth?" he asked.

"Yes," she said. "And they were angry that they couldn't get it."

"Do they have the capability of conducting an operation like this?" he asked.

"I—I don't know, sir," she said. "They certainly have the money. But the contacts? The ability to use this kind of technology? That's not something we vet for."

"You only vet for money?"

She didn't like his tone.

"No, sir," she said. "We make sure they are who they say they are. We make sure they have no criminal records or criminal contacts. We do a very deep dive into their backgrounds and their personal histories."

He shifted, his first sign of impatience. "Then you would know if they have the capability to conduct a raid like this."

Raid. She hadn't thought of it that way.

"No, sir, we wouldn't," she said. "We learn how they made their money, but if it checks out as some corporation or some such, then we don't go any deeper. We don't look at what they manufacture, if anything, and we certainly don't examine the corporation's security capabilities."

He frowned at her. "Security—oh, that's what you think this is?"

She was getting cold, and she was very wet. The smell of that smoke was giving her a wicked headache, which she didn't need. Or maybe the headache had come from the stress.

"No, sir." She glanced at the door. She wanted to go inside and see what had become of her warehouse. "I'm out of my depth here."

He nodded, almost as if he had been trying to get her to make that realization. "I will need a list of the buyers," he said. "The ones who were upset that they couldn't get everything."

"Tell me how to send it to you and I'll do so once I'm inside," she said, with a small pointed twist on the word "inside."

"You will also tell us what, if anything, is missing," he said.

"I will," she said.

Then he nodded, and reached for the door. He stopped, though, just before grasping the handle. "We have security inside. They will escort you through the building. You will not have privacy."

She was surprised to realize she was relieved about that. Normally, she wouldn't want anyone to see some of these items, particularly the ones that she had held back from the auction.

But she really didn't want to go in there alone, not after what had happened.

"Thank you, sir," she said.

He opened the door. The interior was light, but some blue lights flashed. Security lights. She had only seen them a few times before. They were there, she had been told, to let her know that the security was on its highest setting.

Small comfort, given all that had happened.

She nodded at him, and went inside. She had never felt so unsettled before in her life, or so far out of her realm of experience.

She supposed she could give this over to some other employee at Corporate Treasures. She'd certainly thought of that more than once on her journey over here.

But she had to see what happened for herself.

She needed to know what the company's liability was—and whether she was somehow responsible for the entire mess she had just seen.

The lost lives. The first steps in something that Corbyn seemed to think was bigger than a simple theft.

And, truth be told, she thought that too.

She just didn't know what it all meant.

FORTY-THREE

Operations Commander Alcott Quarles couldn't keep the extent of this attack to himself any longer. He was going to have to notify his superiors with a plan.

He stood in the half-empty bridge of the *Dryland*, silently cursing himself. He had let half of his recruits go home two weeks ago, for one of Vaycehn's weird regional holidays. It was some religious something or other that the entire local culture liked to celebrate.

He had given the recruits this time in previous years, and that had made them a lot happier, a lot more cooperative, and made them feel understood.

He had never, in all of his time here, needed everyone he had on his staff...until now.

He stuck a finger between his collar and his neck. He hadn't realized how much weight he had put on during his time on Vaycehn. He hadn't worn his uniform, formally anyway, with the shirt buttoned and the collar properly fastened, in years. He was going to have to unbutton the damn thing, even though it wasn't proper.

But he couldn't breathe. His staff wouldn't notice.

The skeleton crew running the *Dryland* included a handful of others also on their way toward retirement. They wanted to keep busy and to feel useful, but they didn't want to patrol or fight along the border or deal with miscreants throughout the Empire.

They didn't mind training, but they didn't even do that very well, not that they wanted to.

He looked at the six people on the bridge. They hadn't changed into their proper uniforms. The team was working, as they were supposed to be, and he was just a bit surprised.

There were three levels of ambition in the Wyr Space Force operation: the stark ambition of the young recruits, particularly the provisionals, who had gotten here either to escape a terrible life at home or to better themselves; the lackadaisical ambition of the officers, who believed they had already done enough to get some kind of plum assignment (and resented that they hadn't); and the almost complete lack of ambition on the part of the people he privately called the adults—the ones in charge.

They wanted everything to be as smooth as possible, and so far, it had been.

Until this very long night.

Apparently, his lackadaisical attitude about the staff and that stupid holiday had gotten rid of the crew members who didn't like working. If he wasn't so preoccupied with everything that was going on, he'd make a mark in their files, just like he was supposed to do, but never really had.

He truly had let a lot of his work go, just like he had done with himself.

Then he silently cursed, and unbuttoned his collar, taking in sweet air. His neck ached, but he could focus on the console in front of him now.

He was working it because everyone on the bridge needed to concentrate on what was before them. This was the first real emergency Wyr had had since he had arrived—maybe since the Empire had expanded its borders enough so that Wyr was in the middle of the Empire instead of along its edges.

He was reviewing what his bridge crew was doing, not because he didn't trust them, but because everyone was out of practice, including him. And if he went to his superiors, then he needed everything to be perfect—not just for his career, which was waning, but for the crew.

He glanced at them again, feeling oddly nervous. Then he realized what he was experiencing. It wasn't really nervousness, the way a young recruit would experience it, worry over something new.

It was anticipatory nerves. He wasn't certain if this team was going to have to fight an unknown enemy, and he wasn't sure they were up for it even if some had been in battle before.

He had to trust them, though. Or maybe trust Ruth.

Commander Ruth Chivington was literally three months from full retirement. She probably had more experience than everyone else on the bridge, including him. She had served in the Space Force for more than fifty years, the last five here.

She was bent over her console, her silver-black curls falling around her face. When he had contacted her before he left his home on Vaycehn, she had been asleep, and hadn't taken the time to change from her silky red sleepwear. She wore boots beneath the shiny pants, and it didn't look like she had put on any socks. Her arms were bare, and she had to be cold because he kept the bridge at the lowest temperature possible.

But she didn't complain. She had been digging into all of the information as if they were in the middle of a battle, which they might be. No one knew.

Most of the rest of the crew had taken the time to dress a little better. They might've been wearing a non-regulation shirt underneath their unbuttoned uniform top, but mostly, they looked like a bridge crew.

Chivington was the only one who destroyed that illusion, but then, she had hurried to the bridge the moment she heard about the trouble. Even Quarles had taken his time getting here, needing a skip, since he had been in his house on the outskirts of Vaycehn when the news came in.

By the time he arrived, Chivington had already isolated the coordinates of the ship that had destroyed the two flightwings. She had been trying to isolate it after the first shot, but had been unable to, because of what she called "an amazing cloak."

It was only when the ship changed orbits, leaving a tiny trail of unfamiliar energy, that she had been able to locate it.

Too late, though. That ship, too, had opened one of those strange doorways in space, and had flown through it. He wouldn't have believed it if Chivington hadn't shown it to him. In fact, he hadn't believed it when Dickerson had told him about it.

After looking at the imagery from the Room of Lost Souls two years before, he agreed with Dickerson. The Empire was being targeted by an unknown group, for unknown reasons.

And now, Dickerson had just contacted him to let him know that the Unit Commander on the ground heard from the woman in charge of Corporate Treasures that there had been a massive explosion in the bunker where the auction items had been originally found.

More evidence for my theory, Dickerson had said.

Her theory had caught Quarles from the moment she uttered it. There was a lot of ancient tech abandoned throughout the Empire, things he'd had to deal with from the beginning of his career. Wrecks of old ships, like Dignity Vessels, that were claimed by salvage companies. Ruins on several planets.

Enough evidence that some group had been here before the Empire, but that didn't correlate with the incident at the Room and now here. This was an active unknown force.

"I can't figure out what these ships are," Chivington said, still looking at her console. "I'm searching every single database we have, including the abandoned ships base. I'm not finding anything."

"Me, either," said Commander Raymond Upton, who stood to Chivington's left. Upton was a small man with an attitude that had gotten him demoted twice.

Technically, he should have been a sub-commander by now, but a person with that level of experience should have requisite rank, at least on Quarles's ship. Quarles hadn't submitted the promotion paperwork up the chain, yet, because Quarles thought of Upshaw as being on temporary probation.

"This is truly disturbing, sir," said Katie Bradshaw, who was a sub-commander, usually helping with the recruits. She was on her way up, one of the few people here with ambition and a higher rank.

She was moving back and forth between consoles, as if she was getting different information from each one. Quarles wanted to remind her that she could just open separate screens, but he didn't want to interrupt her workflow.

Bradshaw tugged on a small braid that had somehow slipped out of the pile of braids that ran down her back. That single braid qualified as sloppy for Bradshaw, whose uniform was always perfectly pressed and appropriately buttoned.

Quarles's finger went to another button on his shirt. He needed to find a shirt that was one size up.

"This ship," Bradshaw said. "It's—"

"Which ship?" Upton asked, his tone combative.

She gave him a sideways look. "The one that was in orbit," she said, her tone not as ruffled as her expression. "It was here for days."

"How many days?" Quarles asked.

"I'm not sure yet," Bradshaw said. "At least three. I think they were trying to scope out the warehouse before they sent a team."

"That's an assumption," Upton said.

"It's as good as we have right now," Quarles said. He usually kept the two of them on opposite sides of the bridge, but this small crew made that impossible.

Upton seemed to resent Bradshaw, either it was for her still-remaining ambition, her perfect record, or something about her personally. Quarles had been too tired to care about their interpersonal problems before.

Now, they were getting in the way.

And, if he was honest, *they* didn't have interpersonal problems. Upton was pushing too hard against Bradshaw, something he seemed to do with a different person at every posting.

"Expand your search," Quarles said. "Figure out when they got here."

"That's the problem, sir," Bradshaw said. "They seemed to have just appeared."

"Excuse me?" Upton sounded offended by the imprecision.

Bradshaw twirled that loose braid, then moved away from Upton, closer to Quarles.

"Sir," she said. "I meant what I said. They didn't travel here through the Empire. We have no record of them anywhere, and then they just showed up here."

He felt the hair rise on the back of his beleaguered neck. That sounded very similar to the records from the Room of Lost Souls.

"You're certain of this?" he asked her.

"Yes, sir," she said. "I worry that they're heading somewhere else now."

"Or that they're lurking," Chivington said. "This might be a very sophisticated cloak, one that lets us believe they're gone when in fact they aren't."

Quarles didn't like that idea either. But he knew what all of this was. It was pure speculation.

"Set up some kind of monitor," he said to Bradshaw. "We need to know if they return."

"Or reappear," Chivington said.

He looked at her, not sure if he should reprimand her for interrupting. He decided against it. He had been lax for years. It wasn't the moment to return to the hard-ass he had once been. He needed to find a place in between.

"Sir," Upton said. "We have to—"

Quarles held up a hand. "I'm aware of what we need to do, *Commander*." He leaned into the word as a reminder that Upton's rank was on Quarles's sufferance.

"I want us to have weapons at the ready," Quarles said. "If that ship reappears, I want you to damage it. I want the environmental and weapons systems compromised enough that they have to abandon ship or ask for our help. We need to know what the hell they are and the best way to do that is to capture some of them."

He felt a shiver of concern, though, one he did not share with his team.

If that ship was carrying unusual weapons, weapons they were all unfamiliar with, then nearby ships could be damaged. Something terrible could happen.

But at least it would be in orbit, and the something terrible might just happen to the *Dryland*, not to any other ship.

"Set up some protection for our ground forces too," he said. "Keep an eye on that warehouse. The last thing we need is another of those mystery ships to swoop in and destroy the warehouse."

And maybe the neighborhood.

Then he pivoted, and headed into his ready room, which was decidedly unready. Half the equipment didn't work in there, as he had discovered in his discussions with Dickerson.

Not that it mattered at the moment. He needed to contact his superiors. This last bit—the fact that the ship's travel to Wyr hadn't been obvious and the thing had been in orbit for more than a day—was enough to worry Quarles.

He had no idea how many of these foreign ships were nearby or what their intent was.

He mentally apologized to Dickerson. He had initially agreed with her plan for the two of them to handle this crisis.

But this crisis was clearly beyond them and their deliberately mediocre staff.

This unknown group attacking Wyr, they were sophisticated, and they might actually have abilities beyond anything the Empire had developed.

That meant egos had no place here. What was important was saving the Empire.

Normally, he would have laughed at his own dramatic thought. But he didn't believe he was being overly dramatic.

He had a hunch he wasn't being dramatic enough.

FORTY-FOUR

Hazleberg wanted to say that the interior of the warehouse was just the way she had left it at close of business that afternoon, but that would be a lie. The flaring white and silver lights, the unusual darkness, the presence of the military security team that Corbyn had assigned her made the interior of the warehouse feel different.

Or maybe the feeling was the consciousness she had of the break-in. It had upset her more than she wanted to acknowledge.

The large empty room looked strange in the alarm lights. Flashing silver, then flashing white seemed to reveal different aspects of the warehouse, things she had never seen before.

"I'd like to do two things," she said to her chief escort, a man who had not introduced himself. "I would like to turn on the normal lights. May I do that?"

"And the second thing?" he asked. He had a stentorian voice, but that was the biggest thing about him. He was slight, and probably had been raised in space—unusual in the Empire, but not unheard of. Former space children were often stronger than they looked.

"I have an office here with a change of clothes. I'd like to change before I get to the artifacts. I'm worried that I'm so wet I'll damage something."

He studied her for a moment, then glanced at the two female members of the team. They were larger than he was, and hadn't yet said a word. Both of them had grunted in acknowledgement outside when Corbyn waved them over.

One of the women, older, with a slightly angry mien that made her small mouth narrow, said, "I suppose. If you think those artifacts, as you call them, are that fragile."

"They are," Hazleberg said, although she didn't know that exactly. Still, she had never forgotten what the owner had said about his companion carrying one of the artifacts just before the explosion. The owner—heck, everyone who had heard the story—had believed that the bunker itself had security measures that had triggered the explosion.

But Hazleberg had a nagging worry that the destruction might have happened because of the artifact itself. Once they were all in her custody, she had made certain her people had handled them with extreme care, as if each artifact would crumble beneath their fingers.

"In fact," she said to the security team, "it would be better if no one touched the artifacts without someone from Corporate Treasures present."

And right now, that meant her.

"You'll have to discuss that with Commander Corbyn," the man said.

"Well, I need a guarantee from you all right now that you won't touch anything without my permission," Hazleberg said as if she was talking to new employees at Corporate Treasures.

Part of her had detached, finding the fact that she sounded like her usual self astonishing. Another part of her was absolutely terrified.

Something Corbyn had said was rattling around in her brain, worrying her: *Just like ships we can't identify. Technology that appears to be more advanced than ours. Weaponry that seems a bit extreme for a simple theft...*

What if those strangers hadn't been thieves at all? What if they had been trying to activate something? What if everything inside this warehouse was different now?

Corbyn had assured her that his people had gone through this place and secured it, meaning—she had been given to understand—that there were no weapons stashed, no bombs were put into place. There was nothing his people could find.

But something unidentifiable...?

She let out a breath. She was scaring herself.

"I'm talking to you," she said to the security team in her most forceful voice. "I don't want you to touch those artifacts. Are we clear?"

The older woman shook her head ever so slightly, as if she couldn't believe that Hazleberg was talking to them like that.

The man gave Hazleberg a thin smile.

"I can make no promises," he said. "If we believe anyone in this group is in danger, we will do whatever is necessary. That includes touching one of your artifacts if need be."

Something in his expression told Hazleberg that he wasn't going to change his mind.

"Fair enough," she said. "Just no random or casual touches. I want to make sure that everything remains as pristine as possible. And for that, I'd like to change."

"We're wet as well," said the other woman. She was younger and stood toward the back, her posture a bit hunched for someone who was working military. She kept her distance from the older woman, as if the older woman frightened her.

Hazleberg looked at them all. "Not as wet as me," she said. "You're wearing suits that are already drying."

The team hadn't left wet footprints on the floor. She had.

"I will change before we see the artifacts," she said. "I need to check the office anyway."

Giving commands was going to be the only way she got anything done. She could see that now. They were not happy to be with her, and she wasn't happy about them, but Corbyn had insisted on a security team, and so she had one.

She had just imagined that they would be a lot more malleable, or quiet, or people that stayed out of her way, not a group that would shadow her like trainees on their first day.

They hadn't answered any of her questions, and she wanted to get out of here, not discuss each move.

"I'd like the lights on," she said. Then she walked across the large empty room toward the office she had claimed for herself.

She no longer cared if the team walked with her. No one could hide in this room. If she stepped on something, well, then it would be because she couldn't see what she was walking on with the silver then white then silver lights.

Her shoes squished and squeaked as she walked. She had other shoes in the office, but she didn't want to subject them to that rain.

Then she smiled at herself. Petty. She hadn't expected that of herself.

She had nearly reached the small office when the overhead lights came on. Either someone had checked with Corbyn or they had taken some initiative. She didn't care which.

Now, if they would only shut off the alarm lights. The overhead lights illuminated the space, but the light kept flickering between a silver base and a white base. The changing light still made the warehouse feel horribly unfamiliar.

She was cold too, which never happened inside this place. If anything it was usually too warm.

The office was on one of the back walls, near the room housing the elevators. She used her handprint to activate the lock and then uttered the code she had been given, which was tied to her voice print. If the strangers had gotten in here, they were even better than she thought.

Still, she paused before opening the door. And as she did so, the older woman shoved her aside.

"We go first," she said to Hazleberg. A chill that had nothing to do with her wet clothes went through Hazleberg.

The military hadn't checked the office. She wondered if they had even known it was there.

That made her wonder how many other rooms in this gigantic warehouse they had missed.

The man and the other woman pushed open the door while the

older woman stood beside Hazleberg, effectively preventing her from even looking inside.

The two disappeared into the room, then the light came on.

The office wasn't very big, so they didn't have a lot to search. It only took a few minutes before they pulled the door open all the way.

"All right," the man said.

Hazleberg went inside. The office, at least, felt like it was hers. Extra clothing hung on a rack near the door. Some tablets graced the built-in desk, and three extra pairs of shoes were scattered along the floor, just like she had left them. The only thing different inside was the smell. It smelled like wet clothing, and smoke.

She probably would have to destroy all of her clothing, including the outfits she had stored in here.

"Give me a moment," she said to the team.

"No," the older woman said. "Our orders are to keep you in sight at all times."

Hazleberg had been afraid of that. So, she looked directly at the older woman. "One of you can stay," Hazleberg said. "The other two can wait outside."

They glanced at each other, clearly not used to receiving orders from civilians. But the two left, pulling the door closed behind them.

Hazleberg had extra of everything. Her undergarments were in a drawer to one side, and she pulled them out now. Then she changed as quickly as she could, putting on the warmest outfit—a casual white sweater and some scratchy wool pants she'd been meaning to get rid of.

She stared at her shoes for a moment, then decided she couldn't face putting them back on. She grabbed another pair, deciding they were worth sacrificing.

"Do I need to put on the medical suit?" she asked the older woman.

"It's your decision," the woman said. "But it is wet, so…"

For the first time, Hazleberg saw some humanity in her.

"I'll leave it hanging, and grab it on the way out," Hazleberg said. Then she peered at the tablets. They looked undisturbed, which was good. They were non-networked, and had a lot of important information, some of which she had duplicated and sent to the head office.

But some she had not, most of which was information that Corbyn would ask for once he thought about it. He was going to want the background information on the collectors.

Hazleberg slipped those tablets into a bag she kept in her desk. Then she grabbed the tablet she had been most worried about.

It contained the full list of the items recovered from the bunker, including the items that remained in Corporate Treasures' vault far from Wyr. Corporate Treasures had held back 10 percent of the items, just like it always did, for future sales.

The point of that was to generate interest years from now, when the collection became legendary—if the collection was going to become legendary. If that didn't happen the decision to hold back was still a good one, because that 10 percent prevented the market from getting flooded.

Corporate Treasures reserved the right to sit on the extra items for ten years, with an option for renewal. That was usually all it took for interest to peak and grow again.

"What are those?" the older woman asked.

"Proprietary information," Hazleberg said, her tone as cold as she could make it. "Since this building is not as secure as promised, I need to get it all out of here. We'll be moving the artifacts as soon as we can as well."

The woman looked startled, as if it hadn't occurred to her that this place was no longer secure.

Hazleberg realized, as she spoke, that once again her mouth was ahead of her brain. She would be able to recover a lot of money from the Enterran military because this facility wasn't as secure as promised. She made a mental note of that.

"I'm not sure you'll be able to move anything from here," the woman said after a moment to digest her surprise.

"And I'm not sure you can make that call," Hazleberg said. "Let's just make sure that the artifacts are even here, shall we?"

The woman frowned at her, but put a hand on the door. "You're ready?"

As I'll ever be, Hazleberg almost said. But she didn't. At least she was dry and warm and thinking a lot more clearly than she had been since this disaster started.

She had tasks ahead of her, and she was going to do them as quickly as she could.

She needed to protect the artifacts, of course, and the company as well. But she also needed to make sure that this disaster was contained, and she wasn't exactly sure how she was going to do that.

She knew now, though, that she would figure it out.

FORTY-FIVE

Group Commander Rusty Wilton bent over a table covered in tablets. Information literally swirled around him in open holographic screens, each showing a different segment of his command at different times in the past month.

He was in his office which was adjacent to the main headquarters for the Central Imperial District. The headquarters were on Trekov Station, located at the midway point in the entire district, theoretically equidistant from every important planet under his command.

But, of course, the definition of important had changed over the centuries since the space station was first built, and Wyr, the planet now in question, was farther away than Wilton liked. He hadn't even been to Wyr in a decade, maybe more, and he was beginning to think he had made a mistake by not visiting every single capital city under his command.

He couldn't remember the last time he had been to Vaycehn— long enough ago that parts of the city had been relocated because of the death holes that plagued the place.

And now this.

He had three dozen researchers reviewing files and information that had poured into District headquarters in the past month. He had his programmers create a specific program, looking for images of the ships Quarles had sent him, as well as information about any ship that magically appeared somewhere, only to disappear just as easily.

Normally, Wilton would have ignored such information—and part of him worried that maybe he had—but right now, it all seemed urgent. Targeted shots from orbit, killing two dozen ground troops in the space of an hour.

The ground commander, Dickerson, seemed to believe that the second target hadn't been a flightwing, but the prisoner on board, but at the moment, Wilton wasn't going to believe anything.

Something was happening in his district, and he needed to know what it was.

His office had clear walls, a design he insisted on. He could see his people moving through headquarters, many of them rousted from a sound sleep to investigate this strange emergency. His staff was the best in the Empire—he had seen to that—but one reason they were was because of him.

This office reflected his attitude toward his command. He was straightforward. He didn't hide anything unless he was ordered to by his superiors. The clear walls signified his openness, but they also had two other added benefits.

The clear walls allowed him to see his staff at work, so they knew he was monitoring. His staff had fewer breaches of protocol, ethics, and security than their counterparts in the other districts.

But there was a symbolic benefit. The clear walls made them see him as part of the team, but separate from it. The separation was almost hinted at, rather than something obvious, but it was there enough to make them all aware of it.

Right now, his staff was swirling through the large room, some with holoscreens surrounding them. The screens looked like smudges from a distance—hard to read by anyone other than the authorized users. So the room had a lot of people, a lot of control panels, and some dark screens up front, but scattered throughout were tiny gray clouds that reminded Wilton—who was raised planetside before running away to the Space Force at the age of fourteen—of nothing more than a gathering storm.

The storm didn't look that threatening at the moment, but if those clouds combined with each other, the storm could form into something deadly.

He stood, put his hands on his back, and stretched. He was reviewing the work from his teams, and finding nothing. He had expected to find other hints that these ships were active in the Empire. It wasn't enough that his people were looking for them. He also had them think about the rumors they had heard. And he cast back in his memory, trying to recall any strange ships that had breached the Empire's borders.

He couldn't ask his team about "strange" ships, because that would include the ancient Dignity Vessel that had been rebuilt and somehow attacked the Room of Lost Souls. Dignity Vessels weren't strange. They had been littered all over the Empire, damaged and old, many kept in place because they had become salvage. Some were considered historical wrecks and diving companies had permission to take tourists to them.

It wasn't a practice he approved of, but then, that was outside of his purview. His purview was maintaining the military in this part of the Empire and monitoring for problems. He didn't really have a border to protect, surrounded as he was by other districts with a different mandate.

So it surprised him to find himself in the middle of something like this.

The entire Space Force in this region was on high alert. His superiors had also notified the ships patrolling the Empire's borders. His superiors hadn't yet sent more ships to the borders, though, because no one was certain how or where these intruders had entered the Empire.

Once someone figured that out—if anyone could—then a defensive perimeter would appear.

And there was the problem of these ships appearing and disappearing, seemingly at will.

That bothered Wilton more than anything. These ships clearly had technology greater than any seen in the Empire before, and he wasn't sure they had a defense against it.

Someone rapped on the window beside his open door. He looked to his left, saw Commander Hollis Radellia standing in the doorway, a tablet clutched to her chest. Her right fist was still up, as if she expected to knock more than once.

She was a big-boned woman with auburn hair pulled back in a bun. Her gray eyes had more intelligence than those of half the staff working in headquarters. He had promoted her quickly enough to cause rumors among those prone to jealousy, but he had only done so because she was the most competent person he had ever worked with, and he needed her loyalty.

"Sir," she said, revealing the only part of her that grated on him. She had a nasal voice with a regional Hector Cluster accent that made her sound distinctly uneducated. "I found something."

He beckoned her into the room, and moved some of his holo-screens aside, sending them to corners as if they had been naughty children.

She came inside, standing in the gap where the screens had been. She was taller than he was, which meant he had to look up slightly.

She took the tablet she'd been hugging and shifted it from her left hand to her right and back again, as if she wanted to show him what she found.

But she knew better than to do that. He preferred to hear news, particularly from her, so that he could ask questions. Besides, sometimes her brain worked so quickly that he couldn't always make the same connections she did, not without a lot of help.

"Fifteen years ago," she said, "a cargo vessel on its way to Mehkeydo University got waylaid near our border with the Nine Planets."

He waited.

"The vessel was attacked by pirates, sir," she said.

He didn't find that unusual. The Nine Planets tolerated all sorts of misbehavior. Pirates had been a problem along that border. He was happy he wasn't in charge of that region, because he didn't want to have the endless discussions about whether a cargo vessel needed an escort.

Some believed that escorts were signs to pirates that the vessel was worth protecting. Others believed that the escorts prevented a more serious attack.

He didn't stop Radellia, though. He had learned it was better to have her speak uninterrupted.

"The cargo vessel was carrying parts of an Ivory Tree," she said.

He had to think for a moment. Ivory Tree. He almost had to look back through all the data he'd been absorbing in the past hour.

"The warehouse is full of bits of Ivory Trees," she said as if she had seen him try to remember. "And, from what I understand, at least one intact one."

He nodded. He recalled that now. But it still confused him, because he was uncertain what an Ivory Tree was. Art was not his forte.

"Ivory Trees are unusual," she said. "That's why they're so valuable. It's not just because they're pretty, but because they're rare."

She must have seen his confusion, even though he had tried to keep his expression impassive.

"So that was how I conducted my search," she said, "to see if anyone had stolen an Ivory Tree."

That kind of thinking was why he had promoted her. He could have guaranteed without checking at all that no one else on his staff had thought to search for Ivory Trees. And certainly, no one else in the Imperial military would have made that connection either.

"The cargo vessel was not destroyed, sir," she said. "It was boarded."

He frowned. That was different from what had happened here. Or was it?

"The pirates took off with everything in the cargo bays. It didn't take them long to transfer about a hundred items to their ship."

She made that sound significant too, and he couldn't contain himself.

"I take it that's unusual?" he asked.

"Yes," she said. "They had a large team and some kind of transfer vehicle that was large enough to handle most of the items."

"All right," he said. "But it's my understanding that in the art and collectibles business theft can be a problem."

Meaning, he was saying without shutting her down, that thefts were not unusual.

"Yes, sir," she said. "I found a number of thefts, even a few that including parts of an Ivory Tree. Usually they were from poorly guarded museums or a private collection."

She was still shifting that tablet from hand to hand.

"But this one was different, sir. It happened in space, just across our border, and there was a type of ship involved that the pilots of the cargo vessel had never seen before."

Now, she had his full attention. "Do we have images of it?"

"No, sir," she said. "The pirates did something to the cargo vessel that shut down almost all of its systems. The vessel was able to send for help, and that was it. The repair couldn't restore any of the logs from the theft."

She was still shifting the tablet from hand to hand. He wasn't sure why she was so nervous. He usually didn't make her nervous at all.

"The authorities," she said, "especially the folks at Mehkeydo, thought the cargo ship's crew was making this up, and that the crew themselves stole the items. But an investigation couldn't locate any of the items at all."

He wanted to make a circular gesture with his hand, encouraging her to hurry up. But he didn't, even though he still wasn't seeing the reason for her interest, besides the Ivory Tree stuff.

"You see," she said, "the sticking point for everyone, the reason no authority wanted to believe them, was that the cargo ship's crew was adamant about one thing. They kept saying the strange pirate ship disappeared after it stole the items."

"Disappeared," he said.

"As if they had gone through a door in space."

He let out a breath. Ivory Trees and doors in space. Now he got it. He shouldn't have worried that what she had been telling him was Irrelevant. He should have trusted her.

"Do we know what these tree things are?" he asked.

"They're sculptures," she said.

"Are we sure?" he asked. "This is a lot of interest for something that is just a decoration."

She smiled at him. The smile was condescending enough that he noticed it, and she must have felt the condescension, because the smile slid off her face.

"The last intact Ivory Tree sold for nearly a million, sir," she said.

He swore and turned away. People and their money. They wasted it on all kinds of things he did not understand.

He bent over his table again, looking at the tablets. At least one had a history of the Ivory Tree inside the Empire. Bits of Ivory Trees had been discovered near an unclothed Mummy of Wyr a few decades ago, but that was the only detail he remembered about the stupid trees.

He shoved the tablets away, then shook his head. He might not understand art, but he understood risk.

He stood back up.

Radellia was hugging her tablet again, both arms wrapped around it as if she was protecting it. She was watching him, a slight frown on her face.

"I'm going to stand by my question," he said. "Are we sure these are just art?"

"Just art," she repeated mostly under her breath. She seemed to tighten her grip on that tablet. "What are you asking, sir?"

"These people, whoever they are, have technology more advanced than ours. The ships do things ours can't. Could these tree things be some kind of technology that we don't understand?"

She tilted her head. Clearly she hadn't thought of that.

"I have no idea," she said.

"Neither do I," he said, "but I'm going to flag it. We don't have time to figure that out right now, but this seems important to me. These tree things have to be important enough to risk incursion into our territory. It was one thing when we all believed that these trees things were art, but this is something else."

"Sir?" she asked, for once not understanding him. Hell, for once not being ahead of him.

"Look," Wilton said, "pirates, we all understand. Even I do, a man who doesn't understand art."

Her cheeks flushed, the red clashing with her auburn hair. She held up her free hand. "I didn't mean any insult, sir, I—"

"It makes sense for pirates to cross the border to get something worth a million or more," he continued, as if she hadn't spoken. He didn't need an apology, and she didn't need to give it to him. It was a distraction.

She nodded, still frowning

"But, to come here? In the very center of the Empire?" Not that Wyr was the *very* center, but Radellia had to know what he meant. "That's a risk, particularly since we seem to have no idea who these people are. And if they were trying a simple theft, then why kill their own man?"

Quarles had mentioned that when he brought this to Wilton, and that detail had caught Wilton's attention from the beginning. It took a lot of balls—or an intense coldness—to kill a team member who had been captured.

The Empire frowned on it. Regulations stated that any captive deserved rescue or, if held by a hostile foreign power, be the subject of a trade.

Wilton didn't know of any battle in which an Imperial soldier was killed instead of being allowed into enemy hands—not even deep within the Empire's past.

"Speculation among the staff, sir," Radellia said, clearly failing to understand that he was asking a rhetorical question. He let her finish. He wanted to hear this. "Is that they believe that the prisoner had secrets worth dying over. Perhaps the technology he was wearing...?"

"Perhaps," Wilton said. "Which then begs the question. Why don't they want us to get our hands on their technology?"

"Because it's advanced compared to ours, sir?" she said.

"Maybe," he said. "That assumes they're trying to protect us from their technology or control our behavior in some way."

"We have a long-standing policy that any culture not as sufficiently technologically advanced as we are cannot buy our technology," she said, as if he was a raw recruit.

"Yes," he said, not bothering to point out what she had just done. "But you're assuming that they act the way that we do."

She stiffened.

"We know nothing about them. And what if this isn't about *all* of their technology, hmmm?" He couldn't resist that little *hmmm*. He didn't get a chance to school Radellia very often, so he enjoyed it when he could.

"I'm not sure what you mean," she said, sounding as confused as he sometimes felt when he was talking with her.

"What if," he said, "we already *have* their technology, and they don't want us to learn how to use it."

"Sir?" she asked, then blinked as the realization came to her. "You mean the Ivory Trees?"

"Yes," he said. "We need to figure out what those things are."

"Sir?" she asked.

"Let these auction people know that we're confiscating everything in the warehouse," he said. "We'll send it all to our research divisions."

Radellia opened her mouth and then closed it, as if she had thought of something to say, but then thought the better of it.

"Can we do that, sir? I mean, this business—it has invested millions."

He looked at her, knowing his expression was incredulous. Hadn't she paid attention to the things the Empire had done in the past?

Then he shook off the idea. The history the cadets received in training wasn't complete. They learned Imperial history the hard way or in some of the civilian universities around the Empire. Not from the military itself.

"Yes, Commander," he said, regretting her rapid promotion for the first time. There were significant gaps in her knowledge that might get in the way of her conduct. "We can do that."

"Oh, my," she said. "Are you sure it's the Ivory Tree, I mean, there might be something else in that warehouse they want."

"Like those foul mummies?" he asked.

She nodded. "Or some of the other artifacts, or something."

He hadn't thought of that. "Were other items stolen when that ship you found was boarded?"

"No, sir. Just the Ivory Trees," she said.

"Then it's a good assumption that these people, whoever they are, are after those tree things." He paused as something hit him. "However, we have no idea what else was on that old ship. Maybe the tree things were the only items in common with the warehouse. So, you're right. We should just confiscate the contents of the warehouse and be done with it. We don't even have to move everything."

He regretted the words the moment he said them, but before he could clarify—or, really, acknowledge that he was changing his mind, Radellia was already responding.

"Oh, sir," she said. "There's a residential area very close to that warehouse. We're lucky that no civilians were killed, but should these attackers return, we might not be that lucky again."

He nodded. "I had second thoughts even as I said that." Then he gave her a slight smile. "I want us to study these things, to figure out if indeed they are just art, or if they're something more."

"Just art." This time she didn't say it under her breath. She half-smiled in return, as if she knew that she would never convince him that art was something he could value.

"Let's keep them in this district," he said. "Send them to research and development and have them figure out what these items can do."

"After we secure the warehouse," she said.

"Yes," he said.

She hadn't moved yet. She clearly had something else to say.

"What?" he asked, knowing on this he would have to prompt her.

"Any research we do," she said. "If these are actually art—*just* art, that is..."

"Yes?" he asked.

"Um, then, sir, studying them might damage them. It would hurt the value."

He didn't care about the fake value of something that had no real use. He almost said so and caught himself in time.

"We'll compensate the company," he said. "And I'm sure they're insured."

"Sir," Radellia said, using a tone he'd never heard from her before. "If we damage them, there's no more. They're ruined."

He almost snapped at her, but caught himself. They would never resolve this disagreement between them. It was fundamental.

"And if they're some kind of tech and we never figure that out? Isn't that a problem as well, Commander?" he asked.

She sighed, almost imperceptibly. "There's no good way of handling this, is there, sir," she said.

It wasn't a question, but he answered her anyway.

"I don't know what you mean by 'good,'" he said. "There's a right way. We have to protect the Empire. That means figuring out who these people are and what they're about. They're after these tree things, so we need to understand the tree things. That part is pretty simple."

She straightened, still clutching that tablet.

"The rest isn't as simple," he said. "We have to figure out how to defend ourselves from these people. That means figuring out who they are, what kind of ships they have, and what they're doing in our territory. *Deep* in our territory."

As he spoke, he realized that she had never fought. Most people in this command hadn't fought. The Empire had a tight control on its territory, and there were very few challenges to it.

He was going to have to take up the lack of critical military thinking with his own superiors. Training on this crucial area had fallen by the wayside.

"We've beefed up security at our borders," he said, "but I want Wyr protected. We need more ships and we need more surveillance. The one thing we do know is that this mysterious ship had been in orbit for days. We should have questioned that. We did not."

"We didn't think anyone would be interested in Wyr," she said.

"That's true," he said. "That's a serious mistake. It cost over twenty lives so far."

She winced at the words *so far*.

"Let's get on this, Commander," he said. "I want the mystery of who these people are and what they want solved by Central Imperial District Command."

"Yes, sir," she said.

"And at the same time, I want us to be prepared for more incursions. *Serious* incursions, not just two ships and...what...eighteen people?"

"That's what it looked like, sir," she said.

"Imagine," he said, beginning her new combat training now, "if they had come with ten ships and hundreds of people."

Her breath caught and her eyes widened. She clearly hadn't thought of that.

"Now, do you understand why I'm interested in those trees?" he asked, "and why I don't give a cold shit about their artistic value?"

She bit her lower lip.

"They might be worth millions," he said. "But measured against human lives? Those trees are just junk. It would do you good to remember that."

"Yes, sir," she said. "I will, sir."

"Good," he said. "Now, get on this."

"Yes, sir," she said, but she didn't move.

He leaned toward her and made a shooing gesture with his hand. She flushed again, and pivoted, heading out the door.

He watched her through the clear walls. She made her way past the rest of the staff, walking with purpose.

He wasn't sure if he got her to agree with him, not on a deep level. But he knew she would think about what he had said.

And more importantly than that, she would execute his orders.

He would have those trees and he would have his defense.

He hoped both of them would be enough.

FORTY-SIX

By the time Hazleberg had left her office, the security team—or someone—had shut off the alarms. The lights were the familiar golden overhead lights she had been using since Corporate Treasures rented this facility.

Still, the interior felt strange to her. She was slowly beginning to realize the source of the strangeness was the stench of smoke, which was still filtering inside.

She slung the bag with the tablets over her shoulder, then led the team to the secret room, the one that the rental agent had been the most proud of. That room was three times the size of Hazleberg's office, and located not that far away.

But the room didn't appear on any of the standard architectural maps, nor did it show up to the naked eye. The door was hidden in the wall, and revealed itself only when an authorized person touched the lock, just like she had.

The wall looked solid here, although if someone compared it to the elevator room, they would have realized that there was enough space for two more elevators that hadn't been built.

Hazleberg was banking on the fact that the strangers hadn't compared the elevator room to the rooms that could be accessed from the main warehouse floor. The three strangers hadn't been inside long enough to do that.

Although, they did have what appeared to be advanced technology. That meant that they might have equipment that could penetrate walls.

She didn't want to think about that.

She was going to go with the idea that they simply had not had enough time to explore this place thoroughly.

She placed her hand on the space she had memorized, where the hidden lock was. The wall was cool against her palm. For a moment, nothing happened, and she wondered if all the alarms had deactivated her access.

Then the lock appeared, scanning her face and asking for her personal code. She recited a different code from the one for her office.

The door's outline formed, and behind her, one of the women cursed.

"I can guarantee no one checked out this space," she said.

"I would hope not," Hazleberg said. "I was told that it was a need-to-know space and that any intruders couldn't find it."

That might be wishful thinking, though. She pressed two spaces simultaneously with her thumb and forefinger, and heard the click as the door unlocked and swung open.

"We need to go first," the older woman said.

"No," Hazleberg said, surprising herself. "I'm going in."

"That's counter to our orders," the man said.

"I understand," Hazleberg said, "but you could damage items inside by blundering forward. I'm going to take the risk."

Then she slid through the door before any of them could. She wasn't being stupid; she was being cautious. She had set up personal security protocols in here that were as sophisticated as the ones she had used in the rooms below, protocols she wasn't supposed to activate in this warehouse.

Lights came on, a soft yellow that illuminated a full Ivory Tree, as well as extra clothing found in the back rooms of that bunker. There were also square metallic things that some had speculated were some kind of technology that no one understood.

She didn't look at those nor did she look at the small jeweled rocks that were found near the entrance to the large room past the living quarters. She didn't want to think about those.

Instead, she grabbed a pulley she had placed beside the door. A tablet hung from it as a decoy. When she touched the pulley, a small holoscreen opened up, and she was able to shut off the security measures she had put into place.

According to the information the security system gave her, no one had entered this room since she had left it three days before.

"What the hell's that?" the older woman asked from behind her.

Hazleberg pretended to misunderstand. "What you see in the center of the room is the largest Ivory Tree ever found in the Empire. Be careful around it and the items in the back, because Ivory Trees and their broken parts are extremely fragile."

She pulled out one of her tablets and scanned it over the items. Nothing had been moved, and her alarms had not been triggered in here, despite the warehouse alarms.

"I meant the holoscreen," the older woman said, clearly not deterred.

She shouldn't have been able to see what was on the screen. Hazleberg had to trust that.

"It is a double check on the items here," Hazleberg said. "As far as our records go, it seems that nothing in here was tampered with."

"What are these, the most valuable items?" the other woman asked. There was an eagerness in her voice that Hazleberg didn't like.

"No," Hazleberg said truthfully. "These are items that the owner wants donated to smaller, less wealthy institutions. He wanted the artifacts scattered all over the Empire, rather than allowing them to stay together as a collection."

She wasn't going to be able to look at each item in detail, not on this strange night. So she made a small shooing gesture with her hand.

"This room seems secure," she said. "Let's check the others."

In particular, she wanted to see the room that was actually breached. She didn't believe that everything in that room was fine.

She waited until the security team left, then she turned her own security measures back on. Her stomach twisted as she did so. She wasn't sure where the strangers had gotten their information about this warehouse, but the fact that they had made her very sensitive to loose information.

And now, she had shown the three security escorts this secret room. Technically, as military, they shouldn't speak of it, but she didn't trust them.

She glanced at the items one more time, then pulled the door closed, and reset the warehouse security.

Her military escorts waited outside. The man was standing slightly ahead of the other two, looking around as if he expected someone to jump out of the shadows and attack them.

The older woman had her arms crossed as she stood sideways, so that she could see both the man and Hazleberg.

But the younger woman was still looking at the door, as if she had seen something tantalizing.

"These are protected items," Hazleberg said. "No one outside of Corporate Treasures was supposed to know they were stored here. If I learn that any of you mention their presence to someone unauthorized—"

"We understand how to keep a secret," the older woman said.

"Forgive me if I don't trust that, after the night we've just had," Hazleberg said.

"*We* didn't breach anything," the older woman said. "The military had no knowledge of your little auction—"

"Which is completely untrue," Hazleberg snapped, "since we're renting this warehouse from the military. So I'm going to repeat. If I hear *anyone* discussing this room, or if this room gets breached, I will blame the three of you."

The man turned, his expression calm, as if her words did not distress him at all. "Commander Corbyn will need to know," he said.

"And I will tell him," Hazleberg said. "I will let him know where everything is and the condition it is all in. So far, we've been lucky. No one breached my office or this room. But I do know that at least one of our other rooms has been breached. I will want to see that before I leave here."

The man nodded as if she was now his superior officer. The older woman looked annoyed.

The younger woman gave the door one last longing glance. "You're giving them to institutions?" she asked. "Like museums?"

"I'm not," Hazleberg said. "The owner is. He insisted."

"So I'll be able to see them, and maybe study them?" the younger woman asked.

"That's his intent," Hazleberg said. "He believes art should be open to everyone."

She didn't. If she had, she wouldn't work the job she was working.

But this young woman seemed eager, and Hazleberg didn't want to step on the enthusiasm, at least at the moment.

She did find it odd to have the younger woman so intent, though. Maybe it was the woman's way to focus on something other than the destruction outside the building.

"We still have a lot to do," Hazleberg said. "So we should probably get to it."

Then she pivoted, and headed away from the supposedly secret storage room. The elevators weren't far, although she wasn't sure if she wanted to take them to the lower level.

She would have to ask when she got there. Sometimes alarms interfered with other technology, like elevators—and door locks.

She wasn't going to focus on that, though. She was going to get this job done, and then head back to her apartment.

She had a lot of work to do, and she still wasn't certain exactly what that work would be.

FORTY-SEVEN

The *anuenue* dropped Khelan at his space yacht almost twenty-four hours after the failed mission began. The *anuenue* remained cloaked, even as one of the skips took Khelan to the yacht.

Khelan worried that the Empire would be searching for the *anuenue* and he didn't want to be tied to it in anyway. Even the skip that was being used to get him from *anuenue* to his yacht was an Empire-built vessel, one that wouldn't attract attention.

He had insisted, though, that the skip was not one that had been used on Wyr, just in case someone was smart enough to be monitoring for that.

He entered through one of the cargo bays, primarily because it was easier to land the skip in the empty bay than it was to dock alongside. If anyone asked (and he hoped to hell no one would), he would tell as much of the truth as he could.

He would say he had come from a trip scouting artifacts. The ship that brought him back to his yacht was cloaked, for reasons he did not question. They pulled the skip into the cargo bay so that It could be unloaded—and the implication would be that there had been something besides him to unload.

Then the skip left...which it just had.

He stood in the center of the empty cargo bay. It looked small compared to everything on *anuenue*. The ceilings were low, the walls a light gray that was never used in Amnthran vessels, and the standard cargo containers, the ones that could be used in a pinch, were clunky and large.

The cargo bay was ugly, and oddly enough, it felt like home.

He had no one to admit that to. Idil was still on his personal Amnthran vessel, which he had ordered moved as far from Wyr as possible. She kept it cloaked as she had done so, moving to a part of Empire space away from the shipping lanes, a part that didn't get a lot of traffic, military or otherwise.

She had sounded shaken when he spoke to her, after *anuenue* had emerged from foldspace in yet a different part of the Empire. He had a hunch he had sounded shaken as well.

He hadn't expected the mission to go this horribly wrong.

He left the cargo bay, and took the yacht's internal elevator to the cockpit. The yacht's cockpit was small—able to fit five people maximum—but it had lovely views from the long portals, should he decide to open the shields over the windows themselves.

But there were no plants, no soft ocean breezes, no programmed sunlight. If anything, the cockpit smelled faintly of sweat and spilled coffee from a mistake he had made early on.

He sank into the captain's chair—large, plush, soft enough to sleep in, and reached for the control panel. He meant to take the yacht out of here, and pilot it himself.

He kept the yacht in a private docking facility that housed at least twenty other space yachts at one time. The reason he had booked this place was because it did not track anything. He paid premium rates to keep the yacht protected while he was not there, but to keep his own comings and goings private.

The contract he had with the company stated that all information about his yacht, his own arrivals and departures, and the arrivals and departures of the yacht would be destroyed. If they reported anything to anyone, he had grounds to sue the company out of existence.

He was going to have to check the contract though. He couldn't remember if there were exceptions for the Enterran military.

He would wager that there were.

He pulled his hand back from the control panel. Right now, he was too exhausted to take command of the yacht. He was going to leave it here, and get some sleep.

If he could sleep after the disaster he had just lived through.

Or if he believed no one tracked him.

Although he wasn't sure how they could have—at least, how the Enterrans could have.

He leaned back in the chair. It felt familiar, almost as comfortable as the bed he had in the captain's suite. He had lived on this yacht for years, and had, apparently, grown accustomed to Enterran technology.

Maybe that was why he was so shaken.

Or maybe—most likely—it was because he had just ordered the death of someone he had met.

He ran a hand over his face. He had done everything he could. He had contacted Amnthra the moment *anuenue* emerged from foldspace, sending them all of the pertinent files and giving the required post-event interview.

Once he was done, the interviewer had reminded him of his mission. His mission had been to recover Amnthran weapons and return them to Amnthra. If for some reason that did not work, Khelan was supposed to destroy the weapons.

The interviewer, whom he never saw, had sounded sympathetic. That sympathy had gotten him through the interview, and through the next with his superiors. They did not seem upset, even when he had told them he would need ships here in the Empire.

From what he could tell, he would need fighters and a warship or two. But, as he had told his superiors, he wasn't military. He had no idea how to conduct anything at scale.

They would have to send someone in who knew exactly what they were doing. He would advise. And, he had said, he hoped that person understood the Empire.

Khelan was told that he was heard. They said they'd get back to him. No one blamed him for anything that had gone wrong. No one acted like they were surprised.

He leaned his head back in the pilot's chair, wondering if he should just sleep here. It might be better than walking through the corridors of the yacht, seeing all the collectibles he had placed inside this ship to convince any Enterran that he was really someone he was not.

Or maybe that was someone he had become.

And the one thing he hadn't confessed to that faceless interviewer, to his superiors, not even to Idil, was the unsettling feeling that he was carrying inside of him.

Not just because of Iokua's death, but because of something else as well.

Khelan felt like he was pitting two parts of his life against each other. He had grown up on Amnthra, but he hadn't been there in more than two decades. He professed—to Idil, to anyone who had come from there—that he preferred Amnthra, and on some levels he did.

He preferred the technology, the commitment to beauty, the relaxed nature of his people—at least in the various cities—and the common sense attitudes they seemed to have toward living.

But he had dwelt in the Empire for more than twenty years now, and he had become accustomed to it. He knew more about this place than anyone from Amnthra did—at least, anyone he had ever met. He rather liked some of the art he had chosen for this yacht, and there were some resort towns here that he actually enjoyed.

He hated the government. He really hated the military. But he had met some Enterrans who seemed like good people. He wanted to cure them of their ignorance, let them know that they were dealing with dangerous items when they found Amnthran artifacts. He wanted to tell the Enterrans about the real cause of the death holes.

But he had done none of those things and now, he was stuck. He couldn't tell the people he lived near that they were playing with weapons they didn't understand, and he couldn't tell the people he worked for that there was no malicious intent in what the Enterrans were doing.

Intent didn't matter. The Amnthrans had a strict policy, one that had given him a good life. No Amnthran technology could leak into other cultures.

None.

Not even a little bit.

He closed his eyes, hoping to rest a little.

But his mind wouldn't shut off. He had too much to do.

He had to work with his people when they arrived, making sure they got to the Spire pieces, as well as the other weapons. He had to figure out how to get his hands on the manifest that he knew Corporate Treasures would generate.

They still had contracts with collectors, universities, and museums. The one thing he did know about Corporate Treasures was that it honored its contracts.

Which meant, as he had told his superiors, all the Amnthran technology would be on the move, possibly in the next two weeks.

It's an opportunity to take it back, he had said, and it was. But that theft had to be done very carefully.

The Enterrans had already seen Amnthran technology in action, and they would be curious about it. That was a problem, but a solvable one, since one of the strange things about the Enterran Empire was that it had a lot of superstitions.

If the Amnthrans conducted themselves correctly, the glimpses the Enterrans got of Amnthran tech might just go down as lore, rather than as something to be sought out.

If the Amnthrans listened to him, and did it right.

But that wasn't all he had to do.

He had to find the owner of all of the artifacts and figure out where they came from. Khelan had to find the source.

He couldn't just speculate, either. He needed to know now if his hunches were correct—if those mummies were actually Amnthran, or if this was something else.

Finding the owner was much more suited to Khelan's skills than helping warships and fighters get their hands on the existing artifacts. He had no idea how to recover anything using force.

He took a deep breath and realized he was still shaking.

He had no one to discuss any of this with. He hadn't realized until tonight just how completely alone he was.

Ordering a man's death.

Maybe starting a war—even a small one—with the Empire.

All over weapons that could destroy an entire neighborhood in Vaycehn. Or maybe do something worse.

He had to get a hold of himself. He needed to calm down.

He just wasn't sure how to do it.

FORTY-EIGHT

Hazleberg saved the breached room for last. It frightened her. Even though she had seen the intruder leave that room in real time, she was worried. She had also seen dust fall from the ceiling and the artifacts sway—probably as the flightwing exploded.

She and her military escorts opted for the stairs. The lighting was dim here. It looked like parts of the warehouse had suffered damage in that big flightwing explosion. That crater kept coming to her mind.

The force of the explosion had gone downward, not upward, so if there was damage to this warehouse, the damage was underground.

She was getting tired. The headache she had thought she lost in the middle of her work here had returned with a vengeance. She wondered if that was because the air felt gritty. There were probably things floating in the air that she couldn't smell.

Or maybe her nose had become numb to the stench. It had seemed powerful earlier, even inside this warehouse, and seemed to be gone now.

She made herself take the stairs slowly, even though she wanted to finish now. She was feeling overwhelmed. There were two other rooms filled with artifacts, none as valuable as that first room she had checked.

The other rooms were for the schools and museums whose directors had attended a different auction a few days before the auction she had held for the collectors and the schools with enough money to bid on items.

No one had breached those rooms, even though they were not hidden like the first room. Still, there had been dust on the artifacts from a crumbling ceiling. The Ivory Tree parts inside those rooms had looked like they were made of dirt, not ivory, and the writing on their sides had vanished.

The floor had been slick with dirt, which meant—at minimum—she was going to have to rehire a group of experts to make certain the artifacts were properly cleaned a second time.

She needed them in top condition before she sent them to their final homes.

And that was a whole new problem. She wasn't sure how she would be able to do that. She wasn't sure the military would let her remove items from the warehouse. She was going to have to figure out who to talk to about that, because she was contractually bound to make deliveries in the next few weeks.

With that thought, her headache got even worse—which meant that some of this was pure stress. And probably fear, not to mention her own attempt at controlling her emotions.

Her escorts seemed able to do that, all except for the younger one, who was too interested in the artifacts. At some point, if she had the opportunity, Hazleberg would have to treat the younger woman the way she treated people she sometimes hired to carry materials from one place to another.

If they were young, she asked about their dreams, pointed them to a program that would enable them to work with collectibles and rare artifacts, and promised to help them. The implication always was that she'd help if they remained quiet about what they saw. And she wouldn't if they didn't.

Sometimes she had to do more than imply. Sometimes she threatened, but she didn't think she could do that here.

And she wasn't sure it was appropriate. Or would even be effective, given what had happened. At least twenty of their colleagues dead, not to mention the constant threat of attack.

She shuddered as she hurried down the stairs. They seemed wider than she remembered, but that might be the dim lights. The lights seemed to have dust on their surface or inside the fixtures.

She wasn't sure it was safe down here at all.

Yet another problem to add to her growing list. Did she need to hire someone to move the artifacts out of the lower levels of this building? Could she do that? Or was she going to have to beg for military help?

She kept one hand on the railing as she hurried down, her breath coming in short gasps. The adrenaline wasn't fueling her as much as it had before. Now, she was getting tired, but she had to keep going.

This was the part she was the most worried about.

There was a long corridor that took her to the room. The corridor felt smaller and closed in. She wasn't sure if that was the lighting or if it was just how she was feeling.

She could hear the escorts behind her, their feet slapping against the floor.

The older woman moved ahead of her. "We're going first," the woman said, as if Hazleberg had argued with her.

Hazleberg hadn't. She just wanted to be done. She was beginning to feel completely out of her depth.

She emerged from the corridor. The door to the room looked like it always had, except for a blue light above it. She had never seen the blue light before. The light made the door look metallic gray.

"Your people checked this room, didn't they?" she asked the older woman.

"We checked everything we were notified about," she said, as if the lack of notifications was Hazleberg's fault.

The man moved in front of Hazleberg.

"We did," he said. He was looking at a handheld. He had been using it to check the areas that were already inspected. "The alarm light means there are possible hazards inside."

Hazards. The hair rose on the back of Hazleberg's neck.

"Did it say what kind of hazards?" she asked, although she had a hunch she knew. She had watched debris fall from the ceiling as she also watched the intruder try to escape.

She hoped it was nothing more than that.

The man eased her aside with his own body. The younger woman stood behind them all, and the older woman stood as she had twice before, facing the group, arms crossed, as if the entire job offended her.

Maybe it did. Maybe she blamed Hazleberg and Corporate Treasures for the loss of life, the reasoning being that if the auction hadn't been held here, no one would have died.

That was somewhat true. But not entirely true. Because if these intruders wanted something that Hazleberg had, then they would have attacked any other place she had held the auction.

A different group might have died.

She might have died.

The man propped the door open and the smell of burned dust filtered out. Dust swirled out, coating him and his uniform.

Hazleberg closed the bag with her tablets inside, nervously running her fingers along the top. She didn't want to go in there. She didn't want to know what she would find.

Besides, that burnt dust smell overrode all of the other smells. She could actually taste the dust in the dryness.

The man looked back at her, as if he expected her to push him aside. She had essentially done that in all of the other rooms. She probably should do so here.

But she couldn't move. She had stopped looking at the interior of the room on her tablet back in her apartment when the intruder got out. She had then contacted everyone, trying to alert them to the break-in. She hadn't watched the room.

She had no idea what level of disaster she might find.

She squared her shoulders. The disaster wouldn't change whether she went inside or not. The only way she could handle it was to know the extent of it.

She resisted the urge to take a deep breath, which might only lead to coughing or an increased headache.

Instead, she took a few steps forward, tugging at her sweater.

Corbyn had told her she would need to get rid of the clothes she had worn outside. It was clear she would also need to get rid of the clothes she was wearing in here.

The dust had already changed the color of the sweater.

She passed the man, then peered inside. The blue alarm light had filtered in, mingling with the overhead lights. They looked brown. The light seemed like the sky on a cloudy morning just before a terrible storm.

This time, she didn't ask for the alarm to be shut off. It looked like the regular lights were on, and they were the ones that had become that muddy brown. If anything, the blue light from the alarm made the room clearer, crisper.

She wished she had some kind of mask. She wished she had brought her medical suit. But she had left it to drip-dry in her office, which was utterly useless.

The room seemed smaller than it had before. The dust coated the walls, more dust along the floor than near the ceiling. That was because much of the ceiling had fallen in, revealing metal rods, some tiny lights that were probably part of a computer system, and a lot of darkness that she couldn't see through.

Somehow the debris had missed the intact Ivory Trees, and the branches stored to the side. The debris had fallen on some of the smaller items as well as two of the mummies, making them look more human than they had the last time she had seen them.

She wanted to close her eyes against this mess, but she couldn't. Nor could she catalog it all right now. The debris field seemed to go down a center line that went all the way to the back of the room.

The amount of cleanup would take weeks, weeks she didn't have. She needed to send these items, by contract, to their new owners. Those owners could reject the items if they were damaged. And if the damage was severe, the owners could ask for a full refund plus 25 percent.

Blasingale had insisted on the 25 percent when he came on board, citing Corporate Treasures' perfect record of deliveries and pristine product. Hazleberg had argued against it, trying to remind him that sometimes events were out of their control.

He had pooh-poohed her, something he did often.

If she couldn't get these items cleaned in time to put them on some kind of shipment, then they would be liable. She needed to record all of this now, and let Blasingale's superiors know that this wasn't her fault.

It wasn't any of their faults, really. Not that it would matter to the client.

"This is a mess," the younger woman said.

Hazleberg could feel the woman's warmth against her shoulder, the first clue that the temperature down here was degrees cooler than it had been on the upper level.

That part of the environmental system was still working, then. She always like to keep artifacts cooler than regulation, simply because they didn't deteriorate as badly in cool temperatures as they did in hot ones.

Hazleberg didn't respond to the young woman. After all, what was there to say? Yes? That was obvious. The fact that this would cause a lot of work—maybe dangerous work, given the ceiling? Also obvious.

"I need to make a record of this," Hazleberg said. The security feeds probably had it, but she needed to make sure.

"I don't think we should go in there," the older woman said. "Not at least until we know that the ceiling is stable."

"I agree," the man said. "This thing could come down at any minute."

It probably could. And what did that say about the stability of this entire lower level?

Hazleberg didn't respond directly, though. She said, "I won't go in."

She removed one of her tablets and set it up to record. She had to look through a viewfinder, something very old-fashioned, but she needed to make sure she got the room from as many angles as possible.

The viewfinder had its own low-light monitor. As she started, an incredibly bright white light beamed out of the tablet, illuminating each thing she pointed the camera at.

First the near wall, showing items that seemed spattered with dust, then the Ivory Trees which were remarkably untouched, given the debris on the floor near them, and finally the mummies. All of them were dust-covered, but the two closest to the middle were the worst.

She didn't even want to think about cleaning those. Thank goodness she wouldn't have to. It wasn't her job, although it was her responsibility.

She would probably be the one to deal with everything, now that she had made her feelings about Blasingale clear to the owners of the company. She would have to talk with them, and she needed to know what she would do before she spoke to them again.

Should she contact the owner and let him know that his precious items were nearly destroyed? Or the customers and let them know that their items would be late due to...what? An attempted theft? A military-style attack? Some kind of problem in the warehouse?

Then she felt her breath catch. She had no idea if this would become media fodder or if it would be covered up. Usually internal military actions in the Empire never hit anything resembling news. But that didn't stop the rumors and innuendo.

In addition to cleaning (and maybe fixing) all of the artifacts, she was going to have to address what had happened here without admitting any liability by Corporate Treasures.

The blue light behind her seemed to grow darker, almost a navy blue.

"I think we need to cut this short," the man said, as if she had given him an actual timeline.

She said, "I'm almost done." And she was. She only had the floor to cover, and the ceiling itself.

When she turned the camera on the ceiling, she could see past the metal rods to the equipment. The camera tried to zoom in, and at that moment, the older woman knocked the tablet downward.

"You don't have permission to film that," the older woman said.

Hazleberg's cheeks warmed. Of course she didn't. That was some of the proprietary technology that the military had threaded through this warehouse. It had been one of the reasons Corporate Treasures had rented this place.

But Hazleberg wasn't going to admit a mistake. No apologies. She wasn't going to lose the control she had gained on this visit.

She slowly shut off the camera and shoved the tablet in her bag. Then she deliberately turned to the man, not the older woman, and said, "I think we have everything."

For the moment anyway.

Hazleberg was overwhelmed by the work that faced her as well as the politics ahead. The destruction of the ceiling and the smell of smoke made her realize just how dangerous even being here was.

The deaths hadn't hit her yet, but they would.

Occasionally people died recovering artifacts, but that never happened on her watch. Instead, she would report that as a fact to the collectors or the administrators who were purchasing the items.

Tonight, she was in the middle of all of it, and she felt odd. Not just because of the smells or the headache, but because she had never really thought of the deaths that had come before as anything more than the history of whatever artifact she was selling.

"Let's go," the man said. He had somehow managed to make his stentorian voice gentle. He seemed to have noticed how shaken up she was.

He put a hand on her shoulder and slowly turned her around. As he did, she realized she was shaking.

"It's shock," he said quietly. "You'll be all right."

She nodded. She wasn't sure if she was in shock or if she was just overwhelmed. Her entire worldview had changed in the course of one evening.

She loved collectibles, antiquities, and artifacts. Loved them. They were about history to her at best, and at worst, they were beautiful items that needed to be treasured.

Yet they all had pasts, and some of those pasts were dark. She would recite them as if they meant nothing, as if the pain that had occurred around the artifacts was a thing of the past.

This was not in the past. This, whatever it was, was ongoing. And she was in the middle of it.

The man's hand became a bit more insistent, forcing her out of the room and into the corridor. The blue light had grown darker and there were other warning lights on throughout the corridor.

"Are we going to be all right?" she asked him.

"If we hurry," he said.

She nodded and let him lead her through that long corridor. She had the information she needed. She knew what kind of disaster she was facing.

She just wasn't certain what she would be allowed to do next.

REGROUPING

ONE WEEK LATER

FORTY-NINE

At first, Hazleberg couldn't tell where the yelling was coming from. She had fallen into a deep sleep for the first time in a week, and it took her a few moments to climb out of it.

The bedroom in her apartment was dark. She had brought all of the shades down so that she couldn't see her hand in front of her face. She hadn't been able to sleep much at all since the attack on the warehouse, and she was trying everything she could just to get her mind to shut off.

So when the yelling started, at first, she thought it had come from one of the other apartments. It took her a moment to remember that in this building, she had most of the top floor. So then, she figured someone was having such a huge fight that she could hear them yelling through the floorboards.

But she wasn't sure how that was possible, since the floor was airgapped.

Still, her sleep-fogged mind couldn't quite grasp what was happening. She sat up, shoved a silk-covered pillow behind her back, and blinked hard, unable to see anything except a flashing blue light that was coming from the living room. Or maybe the kitchen. Or maybe the door.

Terror spiked through her. Maybe whoever had attacked the warehouse had found her and wanted to do some kind of damage. What kind, she didn't know.

She wasn't sure what, exactly, to do. Raise the lights and call attention to where she was? Keep them down and be unable to see?

Then she realized that the yelling included her name.

I swear, Ethel, if you don't answer me, I'll fire you right now. You're about to lose us millions and our insurance...

She blinked again, made herself take a deep breath, and then told the lights to come up.

The voice belonged to Blasingale, and judging from his tone, things had just gotten worse.

Technically, the owners had assured her, this would be the last job she would work on with Blasingale. She was supposed to keep an eye on him, and report any bad behavior privately to them.

She had protested, saying that all of Blasingale's behavior had been bad lately, but the owners had been adamant. She hated having to deal with Blasingale while she was working on the most difficult job of her career.

He was yelling about things getting worse.

She wasn't sure how they could have gotten worse while she slept. And she had spoken to him as she left the warehouse, informing him that the estimates she had gotten for cleaning the artifacts were in the hundreds of thousands. And, the experts told her, to clean the artifacts without causing more damage might take months. Maybe even years.

She hadn't yet contacted the buyers because she wanted to have news for them, and she didn't have any, not yet. At least, not any that wouldn't cause them to panic.

Hazleberg! Blasingale's voice seemed to get louder. The lights were flashing all over the front area now, which irritated her beyond reason. That meant that somehow he had accessed the controls in the apartment, probably because *she* hadn't bought this place. Corporate Treasures had.

That meant he couldn't see into places designated as private, but he could see the so-called public areas. That infuriated her. Someone should have informed her.

At least he couldn't spy on her in the bedroom.

She debated whether she would just stay in here, not give him the pleasure of talking to her, but eventually, she would have to deal with him.

She very quietly ordered the bedroom door to close. Then she brought up the lights. This place was so exclusive that the lights came up slowly, so as not to hurt her eyes.

She grabbed her white silk robe off the nearby chaise lounge, slipping her feet into a pair of mules as she did so. Then she realized that her outfit was personal and private, and she wasn't going to give Blasingale the satisfaction of knowing he had awakened her.

If she did that, then she worried that he would try it again.

He was just that kind of person.

So, she went to her closet and grabbed a casual sweatshirt along with a loose pair of pants. She decided to keep the mules, just because she didn't want to bother with socks.

Then she went into the stupidly large luxurious bathroom, and brushed her hair.

She wasn't completely dressed up, but she didn't look like someone who had been so soundly asleep that it had taken her a few minutes just to figure out that her boss was screaming her name.

Then she walked into the living room. The lights were as bright as they got, and Blasingale was still yelling.

His voice was coming out of all of her tablets as well as a wall screen. All of that irritated her too. She was going to talk to the owners again, because she was done with this.

She had been working her ass off, while he'd been sitting in corporate headquarters pretending to care about what had been going on.

Now he contacted her in the middle of her night because something had gotten to him?

"I'm here, Bertram," she said. She was done calling him "Mr. Blasingale." She had been done for weeks now. She wasn't even sure he had noticed.

The lights stopped blinking. The wall screen remained on, but some of the tablets went dim.

She pivoted so she could face the wall screen. She had no idea what camera it was recording her from, but she had a guess, based on the angle of the tiny image of her in the upper righthand corner.

The camera was to the left of her and slightly above her. It didn't catch her best side.

Blasingale was at his desk, which she could only tell because the wall behind him had images of his kids at a variety of ages. He loved that moving mural and would point it out to anyone who came into his office.

The mural looked odd in two dimensions, but in no way was Hazleberg going to put Blasingale on a holoscreen. He looked weird enough here, with his hair sticking up at all angles, and his normally florid face bright red with fury.

The anger made his blue eyes brighter, but smaller somehow. Or maybe she was just so tired and so overwhelmed that she wanted him to seem smaller.

"Where the hell have you been?" he snapped.

"Working," she said. "Where the hell have you been? I could use some other executives here. We have a mess on our hands."

"I'll say we do." He didn't even seem to notice that she had insulted him. "Why didn't you tell me that the military is confiscating everything?"

She froze in place. She'd been working with the military. They'd been guarding their warehouse as if they were afraid she had been breaking in to steal their secrets.

Every single person she had had to bring inside, and she had had to bring in dozens just to assess the damage, had to go through a rigmarole of approvals and security clearances and identification badges that made it seem like she had somehow moved to some top secret lab.

She was never renting anything from the military again.

"What do you mean, everything?" she asked.

"You know what I mean," he said. "I've just been informed that they're taking everything we had in this auction, except the mummies. They have no interest in the mummies. That's the official word."

She had to focus. Waking up as she had plus the exhaustion made her feel fuzzy. The last thing she could be right now was fuzzy.

"Official word from where?" she asked, keeping her voice calm. Maybe if her voice was calm, she could be calm.

"You already know," he said. "You've been keeping this from me."

She was going to snap, and if she snapped, it would be at him. So she let just a smidge of the anger she had been feeling out at him.

"I have been keeping nothing from you, Bertram," she said. "If you'll recall all of our previous contacts over the past week, I've been urging you to come here and handle some of this yourself. The task is too large for one executive to control right now. I could use backup."

"Well, you're not going to need it now," he said. "The military wants everything. They're taking it to some secret facility to protect it, they tell me."

"I thought we were protected in this warehouse," she said.

"Obviously not." He spat the words. "If we were protected, none of this would have ever happened."

She wanted to argue with him, except she had made that argument herself with the woman who had been in charge of renting the entire warehouse.

You had promised us great security, Hazleberg had said to her, not yelling like Blasingale was right now, but with tight control, *and instead, your people didn't respond immediately to the incursion. It took fifteen minutes from the moment the intruders entered the warehouse to some kind of activity on your part, and no one arrived for at least ten more. That allowed them access to our artifacts. Who knows what they took? I haven't been able to complete a full inventory.*

But Hazleberg didn't know how to respond to Blasingale right now. Because he was right, but he was angry. And she was confused as to what exactly was happening now.

"I meant," she said as smoothly as she could, "that the military has assured me we are protected right now."

He opened his mouth as if to respond, but she kept talking over him.

"You have no idea what I have to go through just to get onsite. Everything is monitored, everything I do must be given to them for approval, and even the experts we bring in are vetted three and four times." She shook her head, unable to completely control her frustration. "If we had had that kind of security from the start, none of this would have happened."

"If you hadn't argued to bring the artifacts to Vaycehn, then this wouldn't have happened," he said.

That was it. He had just destroyed her final nerve.

"I did not argue for that," she said. "I said we needed a neutral site. You wanted to keep the artifacts in that bunker that blew up. Have you forgotten that you tried to talk Mr. Hogarth into letting us down there with the collectors? Because I haven't. He was *appalled*. I believe his exact words were, 'You want your really rich clients to access a place where someone died and we don't know how?'"

She took a breath, expecting Blasingale to jump in, but he didn't.

If anything, his face had gotten redder, his eyes smaller, and his mouth even more twisted. She had just put his stupidity on the record, and he knew it, and someone could check it if they wanted to.

"Be that as it may," he said carefully, as if he were trying to control his tone now. "You did not inform me that the military wants to confiscate everything."

"Because they didn't inform me," she said, her voice shaking. This was infuriating to her too, but she wasn't quite sure where to put it all. "They do believe in something called the chain of command, Bertram, or don't you remember that from your mandatory service?"

He started to answer again, and again, she talked over him.

"I'm sure they went to your bosses because they wanted to deal with the person in charge. I guess they didn't think that you all seem so worried about your reputations and so averse to actually doing work that you leave all the messy details to me."

She couldn't quite believe she had said that last thing. But she had. If that wouldn't get her fired, then nothing would.

He opened his mouth, closed it, looked at something below his chin—probably a control panel. Knowing him, he was probably trying to figure out how the hell he could delete this entire conversation, pretend it never really happened.

Well, too bad for him. He had accessed everything in her stupid apartment so probably more than one device was recording this conversation and in a variety of different ways. This one could haunt him—if she wanted it to.

"Look," he said, sounding somewhat contrite. "We have a real problem here, Ethel. They want everything, and we have nothing in our contracts to protect us from military seizure. We're liable in two different ways."

She understood that. Their contract with Hogarth, the owner, said nothing about the seizure, so he would suffer a loss that they would be responsible for. They had promised to protect his artifacts and to get him a fair price for them.

And then there were the buyers. Their contracts also lacked some kind of seizure provision—probably because something like this had never happened, not in Hazleberg's memory, anyway. If it had, it hadn't happened to Corporate Treasures.

If it had happened to one of their rivals, that rival wouldn't have mentioned it. She knew she wasn't going to broadcast this to anyone, because if she did, not only would Corporate Treasures' reputation be ruined, so would hers.

She needed to check her contract with the warehouse. Because she wouldn't have signed anything that allowed them the right to seize anything Corporate Treasures represented.

She ran a hand over her face. The last thing she needed was a prolonged legal battle. That would hurt Corporate Treasures as well.

At least she was waking up. She was able to focus.

"What, exactly, are they telling you?" she asked.

"*They* aren't telling me much," he said. "But I saw the conversations they've been having with my superiors, and the upshot is that there's some kind of technology that these attackers have, and the military thinks that the technology might be hidden with the artifacts. So they want everything."

"Except the mummies," she said.

"Yeah, they're not interested. They think the mummies are something that happens on Wyr, so they don't care about the mummies."

She nodded. This was a mess, but she could figure this out—at least, well enough to keep Corporate Treasures alive—to keep her career alive.

"Tell them to deal with me," she said.

"They've already been dealing with the owners of the business," Blasingale said. "They won't deal with you."

"The owners are going to destroy what they built. Tell them I can resolve this."

"Don't make promises like that, Ethel," he said. "It'll make me look bad."

There it was. What he was most concerned with. How he looked.

It took all of her self-control to keep from rolling her eyes.

"I can resolve this," she repeated. "And I can save your career—unless you're not interested..."

Not that she planned on saving his career at all. But she could save hers.

"I don't want you to be overconfident," he said. "If you can't pull this off—"

"We're no worse off than we would be if I didn't try," she said. "We'll never work in the industry again."

He stared at her as if he hadn't thought of that. Hadn't he thought of it? Had he been deluding himself that much?

"What are you going to do?" he asked, his voice barely above a whisper.

She wasn't about to tell him. He would ruin it by trying to do it himself.

"Get that permission," she said, "and I'll have this resolved in a day."

His mouth thinned. He understood, just from her evasiveness, that she wasn't going to share. He had to understand why. He would have done the same thing.

"All right," he said. "This better work."

"Or what?" she asked, because she couldn't stop herself.

He let out a small sigh and winked off the large screen. She stood alone in the middle of the gigantic apartment the corporation had rented for her.

If she was smart, she would just walk away from this. Get a new job, figure out a new life.

But she wasn't ready to do that.

Besides, she found herself looking forward to a challenging negotiation.

She hadn't had one of those in a very, very long time.

FIFTY

Edward Quintana, whom everyone knew as Quint, stood in the viewing room just off his office, hands clasped behind his back. The room was small, and unknown to almost everyone on the research station, even his own security people.

The room was essentially a box. Most of the high-level offices on the research station had starlight views, as someone called it— windows that showed the space around the station. The station was far away from the shipping lanes, and so there wasn't a lot of space traffic. Mostly what anyone could see was the blue-blackness of space, littered with thousands of stars.

His security office had a view like that. He used that office as much as he could. It was his cover. He was in charge of security for the station, yes, indeed, but he also worked for Imperial Intelligence.

Only a handful of others who also worked for Imperial Intelligence knew that he held both jobs. The two jobs dovetailed with each other. He could monitor everything at the research station in his job as chief of security, but his main focus was on intelligence, usually making certain that the research being done here remained secret.

He also had to stay on top of it, so that it was reported to the proper channels. That was where his science degrees came in handy.

This small box of an office, unprepossessing and not even on any architectural renderings of the station itself, was the important office. It was his Imperial Intelligence office.

Only he could get into it, with all kinds of redundant security features. He could change a few of the features so that his two cohorts in Imperial Intelligence could use the room, but he hadn't yet.

And he doubted he ever would. If something happened to him, this room might end up being secret forever.

Which did not bother him. Everything in this room was classified. He liked to joke (to himself, of course) that even the desk that he had shoved into a corner and the highly uncomfortable chair he had been issued long ago were classified.

For all he knew, they probably were. Like the room, they probably weren't on any inventory sheet.

He was keenly aware of everything he brought into and out of this place. He never brought a drink in here or any kind of food. Nor did he use trays or anything that could be tracked, if he forgot about it.

As a result, the office had a sterile feel that, if he were honest with himself, he rather preferred. It made him focus on whatever was in front of him.

And what was in front of him right now was highly classified. It was also disturbing and intriguing at the same time.

He had been sent all of the information on the assault on Wyr because, he had been told, there were artifacts from Wyr that would have to be housed and studied on this station.

He hadn't really looked at the artifacts yet. Instead, he studied the attack. Not many would get to see it, so the more eyes on it, the better, at least in his opinion.

He stood in the middle of the room, letting the images play around him in three dimensions. It still didn't feel like he was actually there, because what he was seeing was small and compressed. But he watched the imagery several times, and ran a program for anomalies.

He hadn't looked at the program's results yet, but what he had seen had thrown up many things which bothered him. He had seen little discussion about the planning and coordination that had gone into the attack.

The detail that caught his eye was the use of actual skips. Everyone else had been focusing on the two strange ships, the one that had landed near the warehouse storing whatever those items were, and the other that had been in orbit around Wyr longer than it should have been without someone flagging it.

He had already sent an inquiry through channels, wondering why Wyr Battle Command hadn't noticed that ship before it attacked. It had arrived out of nowhere, and it was difficult to trace.

Not impossible. Even now, Quint did not believe in the impossible. He had seen too much.

But he did understand difficult.

He had set those ships mentally aside at the moment, focusing on the skips. The skips told him that whoever had planned this attack understood the Empire. He would have wagered that the initial attack had been planned with skips only.

If he were a guessing man—and sometimes he was, because his hunches usually played out—then he would have guessed that whoever brought in the smaller foreign ship was either disobeying orders or overriding them.

He knew this attack was all about technology, and he didn't know that because he had been told about it.

He could see it, in the skips, in the murder of one of the attackers by the other attackers, in the environmental suits that the attackers wore, suits that seemed to have their own cloaking ability.

Quint had been told that something in the warehouse had attracted them, but it was more than that. They weren't attracted to a single item, or they might actually have performed a successful theft. After all, when thieves hit various sites, they didn't try for large groups of items.

They usually stole one or two, particularly when the items were as rare and expensive as these seemed to be.

Whoever these people were, they were after the technology, and not the technology of the retired military warehouse.

The question was, what kind of tech were they trying to steal? Was it theirs? Was it someone else's?

Those questions intrigued him.

Other parts of this attack worried him. Others had commented on those doorways in space, which apparently had shown up in an attack on the Room of Lost Souls two years ago. The doorways bothered him, but in an entirely different way than they bothered everyone else.

He kept the images of the two large ships heading through those "doorways in space." He wasn't really looking at the "doorway." He was looking at the light around it.

He had seen that light before, as a younger man, just before a disaster at Mehkeydo University. Students had triggered something in an unauthorized stealth tech experiment, and they had died.

These ships he was looking at now weren't using stealth tech as *stealth* tech, at least as he understood it. They hadn't been cloaked.

But that light had a quality that reminded him of the light he'd seen around more than one stealth tech disaster. He had left the research area of science long ago, although he kept a hand in. But he was never the best at understanding how any of this worked.

That had been his wife, Rosealma. Before she left him. Before she decided that their philosophies of life were so different they couldn't be together.

Now, though, he wanted her to see this, but he knew he didn't dare contact her. She wasn't even in the Empire anymore. She was in the Nine Planets. She wouldn't listen to him anyway. If only he could figure out a way to get her back to the research she had abandoned decades ago.

She, more than anyone, had understood stealth tech, and he had a hunch she would understand this.

He shook her out of his head, reminding himself that she always rose to the forefront of his mind when he was dealing with stealth tech. For him, the two were badly intertwined.

Besides, stealth tech was not the issue here. Although this was one of those hunches again. Something about that light and those doorways made him think of stealth tech. Something about the cloaks on those environmental suits reminded him of stealth tech.

This was one of those times where he wished he had more cachet here in the station. He would talk to some of the researchers, and point out the link.

But here, they thought of him as the security chief and little else.

Ironically, he wasn't watching these images in his capacity as Imperial Intelligence. He was watching them because the contact had come to the chief of security for this particular research station.

He had been ordered to find a place on this station to house what the military believed to be more than a thousand artifacts. He had already looked through the history of those artifacts.

He had been sent a list—the same one that had gone to collectors —and he had been told that the items coming his way would not include the six mummies, which struck him as odd.

How did those in charge know that the mummies weren't what the attackers were after? Right now, the military knew nothing about these attackers, which meant—at least to Quint—that everything should remain on the table, including the mummies.

He would probably mention it, and he would probably be ignored. He had a hunch he knew what the arguments would be. Someone would tell him that the mummies were a feature of Wyr, and the artifacts that had been found were rare, and found outside of Vaycehn.

But no one knew where the mummies had come from. They were almost always found underground, which made no sense scientifically.

He left the images up, let them float around the small room, and then headed back to his regular security office. He needed to find enough room for all of those artifacts.

Once he had that, someone would farm the artifacts off to select researchers, none of whom were on the station yet. Everyone who was working on the station at the moment had their pet research projects, and wouldn't want to give it up to do some kind of guess-work for the military.

That urge to contact Rosealma hit him again. Maybe he could lure her here. Maybe he could figure out a way to catch her attention, and then he could lead her to these items. Or maybe to the light surrounding the doorways.

He smiled at himself. He was such a practical man on almost all matters, except anything dealing with his ex-wife.

He knew that, and he supposed he should change it.

But he didn't want to.

He sighed and started the procedure to get out of the room. He had to make sure no one else was nearby. He had to be cautious.

Which was probably something he needed to consider as well with these artifacts.

He would have to keep their presence here secret, and he wasn't yet sure how to do that.

But he had—what? a few days? Maybe a week? Maybe more?— to figure that out.

And he would.

Because he always did.

FIFTY-ONE

The money arrived in Corporate Treasures' accounts two days after
the negotiations were finished. Two very long days during which
Hazleberg believed the military would change its mind.

She had gone up the chain of command, using documents that gave
her permission to negotiate for her company, and treated the Imperial
military like a hostile client. She was kind, of course, but she didn't trust
them, so she always asked for three times more than she actually needed.

By the end of the negotiation, she had everything she needed and
a few things she didn't. She got the Imperial military to agree to pay
her twice what the artifacts had sold for (negotiated down from her
original price).

She had gotten them to purchase only the items in the warehouse,
not telling them that there were other items off-site.

And she got to keep the mummies—all of them. Not just the
mummies but their clothing and anything found on them.

She didn't have to give up Hogarth's name as the owner of all of
this, nor did she mention the bunker.

She had a hunch the bunker and Hogarth himself would be in play
one day, but not right now.

It was not her problem.

She had made enough money for Corporate Treasures that they could repay their clients and take on an extra 10 percent bonus for the trouble that this entire incident caused.

The clients wouldn't be happy, but they would have no grounds to sue Corporate Treasures. And she would give each client hope that they could appeal to the military to recover the artifacts, should need be.

Of course, she wasn't going to be the one to inform Hogarth of this. He wanted everything in the open and in public, and that had just been thwarted.

She would leave that little discussion to Blasingale or whomever he could pawn it off on.

The money in the accounts made her feel better, but Blasingale had managed to make her life miserable one last time. (She knew it was going to be the last time because she had started dealing with his bosses directly; they had promised her a raise and a large promotion if she pulled this off—which she had.)

Blasingale made her stay at the warehouse and handle the transfer. If she was being honest, she didn't mind. She wanted to see this through—especially now that she didn't have to supervise the cleaning and restoration of the artifacts.

The problems with that would go with the artifacts. She had no idea if the military would try to clean and repair the artifacts or if they would simply take them apart.

She didn't care. Or rather, she had to convince herself that she didn't care. Because the artifacts were art, and they were going to be destroyed, and she couldn't stop it.

The day she received confirmation of the funds' arrival, she was standing in her office in the warehouse, looking at all of the non-networked tablets. So much information. She was now going to have to decide what she would give to the military—what they actually needed—and what she wasn't.

Someone knocked on the door. She suppressed a sigh. She hated all of her interactions here. Her emotions had been rubbed raw for more than a week. She hated being watched and monitored and having someone question her every move.

She hated being the only authority on site, as if there was something to be an authority over.

But she squared her shoulders, and adjusted the cheap shirt she wore over even cheaper leggings. All of the clothes she had stored here had a not-so-faint odor of chemical smoke, with an underlying tinge of burning flesh.

Maybe she had imagined the burning flesh. It was just that she had made the mistake of looking at the security feeds, to see how the intruders had broken in here, back when she thought she was going to be responsible for the damage to the artifacts.

She had watched the destruction of the flightwing with sheer horror. She had been able to see the faces of at least two of the soldiers on board as the flightwing turned red and expanded, just before it exploded.

She hadn't slept for two nights after that—or rather, hadn't slept well.

She shook the thoughts out of her head.

"Yeah?" she said, not really willing to tell anyone they could come into her office.

And yet the door opened. Corbyn filled the doorway. He wasn't in uniform, although his posture told anyone who saw him that he was in charge of this place. He wore a bright blue shirt that accented his eyes, but made his silver eyebrows and mustache look almost white.

"Did you hear from your bosses this morning?" he asked.

She supposed she could play dumb, but she wasn't going to. She was too tired for games.

"I did," she said. "But I'm not sure you and I are talking about the same thing."

He stepped inside, making the small room seem even smaller. She wanted to back up to the desk, brace herself on it, and keep away from him. It wasn't him, though. This reaction was new for her. She didn't want to get close to anyone anymore.

She probably should investigate that reaction when this job was done.

"Apparently, you no longer own the artifacts," he said. "We do."

"Yes," she said. "I'm aware of that."

"My orders are to get them out of this warehouse and deliver them to their new home as soon as possible," he said.

She nodded. "I know that you're now responsible for everything."

He closed the door. Her heart rate increased, even though, on every level that mattered, she trusted him. She had watched him interact with his people, with some of the nearby residents, and with at least one family of one of the victims, and he had been both professional and kind to all of them.

"It's just..." Then he frowned at her. "I'm making you uncomfortable."

She gave him a thin smile. Honesty would help them both. "Everything makes me uncomfortable now."

They had already established days ago that this was her first in-person disaster. He had actually argued for her to get some help from the military counsellors. She had brushed him off, knowing that if she focused on everything that had happened to her, she wouldn't get her work done.

She supposed that didn't matter now.

He glanced over his shoulder. "You want the door open? I should have asked..."

She wasn't used to this side of him. She preferred the man who gave orders.

"It's fine," she lied. "What do you need?"

He nodded, almost reached for the door, then seemed to think the better of it.

"I...um..." He opened his hands. "I've been listening to you. You said these artifacts are fragile, and now I'm supposed to get them to..."

He almost told her where they were going, which she guessed was not something she was cleared to know.

"...um," he said, "to their destination. I'm not even sure how to handle them, pack them, what to do about them. I've had no real instructions."

"Don't you have experts who can handle them?" she asked.

343

"I'm sending them to the experts," he said.

She nodded. She suspected the word *expert* meant something different to him than it did to her.

"Do you have people who can pack them? Or get them loaded on ships? I'm not sure how to transport them or what kind of ship to use or anything."

She let out a small breath. "I work for Corporate Treasures," she said, "and we're no longer responsible for the items."

"I know," he said. "Can we hire you? Or them? We need someone to help us with this. It's not what I'm trained to do."

"I'm sure you have historical experts you can tap," she said, knowing she was being a bit unreasonable.

"At some of the universities, yes," he said. "But..."

But the military had just undercut almost every university in the Empire by taking the artifacts.

"You don't think you can trust them," she said.

He nodded. Apparently, he didn't want to say that on the record, even though they really weren't on any record.

That she knew of, anyway.

"Give me an estimate of what it would cost to have you and your people pack up these artifacts," he said.

"As is or repaired?" she asked.

"What?" He frowned at her.

"The artifacts have been damaged by the explosion and the collapsing ceiling." She felt odd explaining that to him since his people had been helping her shore up that ceiling. She had been afraid to work in the room otherwise, and she couldn't remove the artifacts on her own. "That's why I've been bringing in the experts. I wasn't sure how to proceed."

He frowned at her. "Do we still need those experts?"

She felt a surge of frustration. Wasn't he understanding her?

"I don't know," she said. "It depends on what the military wants."

He opened his hands in a gesture of futility. "They want the artifacts moved to one of our research sites. That's what I know. I was asked if your people could pack everything. Does that clarify?"

"No," she said. "Our normal way to pack would be to catalog all of the damage and give you a full list of the problems. Judging from what I've seen so far, it will take months to generate that list, and to properly pack everything."

He peered at her, then looked around her office as if the stacks of tablets, piles of ruined clothing, and minimal desk furniture held more answers than she did.

"You don't have the personnel," he said.

"Not here at the moment," she said. "But I could bring in a team."

"Oh, for..." He didn't finish the sentence. "What if we just pack it up, then?"

"You will have to sign a damage waiver for each item," she said.

"*I* will?" he asked.

"Someone will," she said. "We would be giving you the items as is, and then you would be responsible for all the other damage that will happen in transit."

"*Will* happen?" he asked.

"Ivory Trees are delicate," she said. "They can shatter if you touch one part of them wrong."

He swore, then sighed. "I did not expect this to be such an issue," he said. "I wanted that stuff packed up and on some ships to our research facility within the week."

"I can tell you now that it won't be moved within the week," she said.

"Well, I don't want it here," he said with more force than she expected. Almost as if packing everything up correctly was her fault. "I suspect those intruders will come back, and this time they'll bring even more firepower. I've been talking to my superiors about evacuating the area, but they don't want to do that. They want these items out of here as quickly as possible."

And she had just delayed *as quickly as possible* by negotiating.

"What's the fastest you can get the things itemized, packed, and out of here?" he asked.

She shifted slightly from foot to foot. All of this went against her training—against her inclinations, really. She valued the artifacts. She understood Hogarth's desire to give some of them to institutions, so that the items could be studied.

She believed all of the artifacts were important, not just for their collectible value, but because they existed, because they were beautiful. They were history and art.

Corbyn raised his eyebrows and gestured with his left hand, a quick way of hurrying her along.

She wasn't going to like any of this. Maybe she wasn't supposed to.

She rubbed her hands on the cheap fabric of her pants. Her palms were actually sweating.

"How long will it take?" she repeated. "The fastest we can do it is about two weeks, but we'd have to sign a lot of documents, clearing us of any responsibility for damage."

He shook his head. For a moment, she thought he wasn't agreeing to the terms, and then she realized that he was just disgusted with what she was saying.

"You people are all about condition, aren't you?" he said.

"Actually, yes," she said. "Condition is everything."

He was about to say something, when she held up a hand.

"Look," she said. "You're going to want to check with your people, the ones who want to research these items. If they don't care what condition they're in, then fine, but if they want the items intact, it'll take us longer."

"You really think these things will get damaged in transit, even if you pack them?" he asked.

"Yes," she said.

He rolled his eyes. "This is not my forte. All I want is to get these things out of Vaycehn and somewhere that we can protect them. *That's* my priority."

"I understand it," she said quietly. "Do you really think I want to be here much longer?"

His gaze met hers. There was a lot of intelligence in those ice-blue eyes. "Your contract with us ends in less than a week. What would you do to get the items out of here?"

"I've already negotiated an extension," she said. She wasn't going to cost Corporate Treasures any more money if she didn't have to.

"In an ideal world," he said, "where there was no interference and damage. You had, what, two weeks after your auction?"

"A little over, yes," she said. "We would have been working nonstop to prepare the items and ship them to the correct addresses."

"They were going to different places." He sounded bemused.

"Yes," she said.

"Have you notified those folks they're not getting their items?" he asked.

"Not yet," she said.

"Hold off on that," he said.

It was her turn to frown at him. She had already decided not to tell the collectors and Hogarth about the changes, not until the military had full possession of the items. Then she would pay each collector and organization who had invested in the artifacts.

The one thing she had been unable to figure out was what she was going to do with the organizations that were getting donations.

But she didn't say that. She wasn't sure she liked having Corbyn tell her what she needed to do.

"Why would I do that?" she asked.

"Because we don't know if one of those people was behind this theft," he said. "You've never given me the list of collectors."

"Oh." She felt unsettled. No, she hadn't given him the list. She had forgotten. She wondered what else she had forgotten. She was aware on many levels that this incident had distracted her and left her feeling unsettled.

She just hadn't realized that it was also having an impact on her efficiency.

"I'll do that right now." She had made a second tablet for him in the day or so after the incident. (And when did she start calling it an incident? The explosion—the...and then she shook her head. A clear sign that this last week has been messing with her mind.)

She paused, then focused. She had already done the work, but she double-checked herself to make sure she hadn't left anything out.

Then she handed him the tablet.

"I forgot to give it to you," she said. "It's all here. We vetted everyone, just like I had told you."

He took the tablet from her. "And what guarantee do we have that no one on this list was a spy for the Nine Planets?"

"It would have shown up in our background check," she said.

"Really?" he asked.

Her breath caught. She had no idea, not really. She was out of her depth here.

She waved a hand at the tablet. "You can figure it all out. I just want to finish this and go home."

Not that she had one. She had a condo near corporate headquarters, but she hadn't been there for longer than a week in years.

She just wanted to get away from Wyr, and these artifacts, and this place.

He gripped the tablet tightly in one hand. She was afraid he might actually break it.

"Back to the original question," he said. "These items are already damaged now, right?"

"Some of them," she said. "At least, I think so."

He nodded. "Does it matter where the damage happened?"

"To collectors—"

"We're not taking these as collectors," he said. "We're taking them for research."

She paused. It mattered. If something changed on the tree, then wouldn't a researcher want to know that the change had occurred in the explosion or in transit?

"From what you're telling me," he said into her silence, "letting us know the details of the damage means that all of us would be here for months, which isn't good for any of us. Or maybe even for those artifacts, if the ceiling does fall in."

She closed her eyes. She didn't even want to think about that.

"Not to mention that we're vulnerable for another attack." Without seeing the intensity on his face, his voice actually sounded soothing.

She was so tired that keeping her eyes closed actually felt like an option.

And it wasn't just physical tiredness. She was emotionally exhausted.

She opened her eyes. Was he looking at her with compassion? Or maybe she was just hoping he was.

"We're going to get these artifacts out of here as quickly as we can," he said. "We're not going to worry about condition. You have an itemized list, right?"

"Yes," she said.

"We'll use that as our list. Can my people pack these things?"

"No," she said almost reflexively. "We have specific packing equipment and ways of protecting the items. If you don't do that, then the damage will increase exponentially."

"I could order you off the premises and just do it," he said.

"You could." She wasn't sure how that made her feel. Better? Worse? Both at the same time? "We'd need waivers, so that we're not responsible for the damage."

"You're convinced there will be more damage," he said.

"Yes." She spoke softly.

"How quickly can you get your people here to pack?" he asked.

"They're already scheduled," she said. "They've been waiting in another part of the city until we knew what we were doing."

He let out a breath. "Why didn't you tell me that?"

Because you didn't ask, she almost said, then realized how defensive it sounded.

"We just finished negotiations this morning," she said.

Then she thought about the logistics. The items actually had to leave this warehouse, and go somewhere. She hadn't ordered up any cargo ships yet. She hadn't known exactly how many she would need. She had been waiting until she had finished designing the routes.

That felt like plans she had made years ago, instead of just two weeks ago.

"We'll get them out of here," Corbyn said. "That's non-negotiable."

She leaned back, startled. "You…?"

"I don't want anyone outside of our organization to know where these artifacts will end up. I'm sure you understand." His voice was flat and so was his expression.

Shock ran through her. "You think one of my people was trying to steal these artifacts?"

"We have to look at all possibilities."

"They would have had ample time and opportunity to do that before the auction," she said.

His expression hadn't changed. "You're the one who keeps mentioning money. And didn't you tell me that some of these collectors wanted everything?"

"Yes, but—"

"Couldn't one of your people be bought off so that the collector *could* buy everything?" he asked.

She almost blurted that no, it hadn't happened that way. Because one of her people would have known that she held items back away from this warehouse. Those items would have been easier to go after, and she had checked on them already.

They were fine.

But she didn't want to tell him about the other artifacts. The ones he was taking were already going to get ruined.

She couldn't stomach losing the entire collection. She had to preserve some of it.

"I suppose someone could have been bought off," she said, sounding as unconvinced as she felt. "But that's not your real reason, is it?"

His lips moved a miniscule amount. Had that been an aborted smile? She couldn't quite tell.

"You don't want us to know where this research base is, do you?" she asked.

He did smile now. Just a small one, as if he was proud of her for figuring this out.

"There's a lot in my business that's need-to-know," he said. "And you don't need to know this."

"I don't want to know it," she said.

She took a deep breath. There was an end to this nightmare, at least for her. She hadn't realized just how much she welcomed it.

"Get your cargo vessels here," she said. "I'll work with you on packing them properly. Make sure these vessels can handle delicate items. No vibrations or rumbles or leaky atmospheric problems. Make sure the cargo bays are roomy, so that we can put everything in there, without cramming it all together, which could cause other problems."

His smile grew. "You're going to do this."

"My people are," she said. "And we'll get it done as fast as we can. Then you and I can both leave this place...hopefully before the bad guys return."

"The bad guys." He chuckled. "I like that description, even if it isn't apt."

"You don't think they're evil?" she asked. "They killed one of their own."

"I don't make judgments like good and evil," he said. "Such things have no value in my work."

The implication was that he didn't seem to understand their value in hers either.

But she hadn't been thinking about work. She'd been thinking about the loss of life, and the willingness to kill.

Maybe he was used to it, but she wasn't.

He must have seen something on her face, because he said, "We'll make sure this place is protected while you're working here."

She nodded. He had made that promise before, and she trusted it. She'd seen the patrols, had to deal with the security, and knew that there were warships now in orbit around Wyr.

"Thank you," she said, because what else could she say?

"We'll get you out of here as fast as we can," he said. "You'll be safe."

Surprising tears pricked her eyes. She hadn't expected it. She hadn't realized how terrified she was feeling.

"Thank you," she said again. "I just want this to be over."

He nodded. "So do I," he said. "Believe me. So do I."

FIFTY-TWO

Khelan was having second, third, and fourth thoughts before he even approached Longbow Station. It was at the edges of the Empire—at least according to some maps—and others actually placed it inside the Nine Planets Alliance.

He'd heard of Longbow over the years, because it was one of those trading hubs that no one was willing to shut down.

But he had never visited it. If he had researched it better, he wouldn't have brought his yacht. As he got closer, he realized he had made a mistake, but he wasn't about to dock the yacht far away.

There were rumors of actual pirates in this part of space, and those pirates would have no trouble taking over his Empire-designed yacht. He hadn't upgraded most of the tech on the yacht to Amnthran tech, because he always planned to have visitors here, even though the visitors hadn't really panned out.

His mistake. He should have pressed Zimmer to meet on the yacht. Or maybe, Khelan should have done what his instincts had told him and ignored Zimmer's protests. All this secret talk from a man who had too much money and time and little else annoyed Khelan.

Zimmer claimed he had information on Corporate Treasures. He was afraid someone would listen in if they discussed it the usual ways. Things were just strange enough that Khelan felt compelled to hear Zimmer out.

Khelan couldn't send anyone else to do it, either. Idil hadn't been with him long enough to know the players. And no one else understood the Empire.

Zimmer and Khelan were colleagues, at least as far as Zimmer was concerned. The fact that they had never really had a meaningful conversation didn't seem to bother Zimmer. They had both bought something from this last auction, and Zimmer needed to discuss that.

For all Khelan knew, Zimmer had just heard about the attack and wanted to talk about it. Khelan had seen no media coverage of the incident, even though everyone in Vaycehn had known about it. (How could they not?)

But the military seemed to have put a clamp on the information flow to and from the site, so even Khelan was having trouble learning what was going on.

He hadn't admitted it to anyone, but he was beginning to get worried. He knew the artifacts had to leave the warehouse. The original timeline had been a little over two weeks after the auction, but he didn't believe anyone could keep to that schedule now.

Although Corporate Treasures had surprised him in the past. Maybe they had enough staff to pull off some kind of miracle. After all, they had gotten the artifacts into that building.

Getting them out and in the proper groups for each set of buyers was going to be hard.

What worried him was that he and Idil had been trying for days now to get the shipping manifest, and they had been unable to. Idil had gotten into Corporate Treasures' systems deep enough to realize that the military was going to handle the transfer of the items.

As a customer, he had received no notice of that. He found it disturbing. He had no idea how an Enterran would react, though. Would they think it normal to have military involvement after an attack?

After all, these were people who all performed military service as part of their educational process. Maybe the indoctrination was deep enough that they wouldn't question anything.

Idil had been frustrated, though, and he was too. She had been unable to get into the military systems. She did everything Khelan suggested, but she wasn't as creative (yet) in Enterran systems.

Khelan should have tried to dive into the system, but he couldn't. He was afraid someone would backtrace his incursion and find not Khelan Māhoe, but Khelan Madani, the collector.

And that would destroy everything he had built.

What he and Idil had to do was wait until the team arrived from Amnthra. That team could figure out how to hack Wyr Battle Command, and do so secretly.

He hoped they would have enough time to delve in. With each passing day, he got more and more nervous, especially as information seemed to have dried up.

Which all went a long way into justifying his presence here, at Longbow Station. He liked to think he wouldn't have responded to Zimmer if Khelan knew what was going on at Corporate Treasures.

Longbow had existed forever in Empire terms. Khelan had researched it enough to learn that the station had been one of the earliest built and maintained by the Empire, created for trading back in the day when the Empire actually traded with places in the Nine Planets Alliance — before there was even a hint that those nine planets would ally with each other.

His research had warned him that there were places in the center of the station that no outsider should go. In particular, there was a bar in the center core that catered to long-timers, people who were known to each other and the trading game.

He suspected all of that was a euphemism for pirate activity, but he didn't know.

Instead, he was going to stick the edges of the station.

Zimmer had suggested another bar there, one with a view of the docking rings, and Khelan had agreed.

As he approached the station and saw the docking rings, his uncertainty returned. Those rings weren't rings. They were more like tentacles from some kind of mythological space creature, something fanciful that was organic but looked like it had corded arms and legs.

Amnthra had a lot of art like that, beautiful renderings of creatures that did not exist outside of legends and stories. There was nothing like that in the Empire. Everything here was utilitarian and bleak.

He had docked as safely as he could, used all of the security built into the yacht to protect it, and then, at the last minute, added a small little protective measure over all of his files, and his true identity. That extra measure was Amnthran, because the Empire didn't build anything like that.

The little added bit of security would let him know if anyone breached the ship and tried to enter its databases.

According to the station's official map, the bar he was supposed to go to wasn't far from the docking rings.

Judging by how far he had walked, and the circuitous route he had to take, the official map was woefully inadequate.

Still, he had found the bar. It was small and dark and didn't have a view of the rings at all. It was next to a viewing area that looked like it hadn't been open for decades. The doors to the station, made of some kind of clear material, had yellowed and cracked.

A hazard sign in Imperial Standard warned that the environmental system no longer protected anyone in that viewing area and that the very floor itself was unstable.

That made him wonder if the entire floor all along this level was unstable, but there was no one to ask.

The people who walked through this part of the station looked like they would rather be anywhere else. Most wore clothing that looked worn and frayed. Much of it was black, and some of it he recognized as tight pieces that were designed to be worn underneath the standard Empire environmental suits.

No one wore any kind of official identification or wore Empire military uniforms. Only a handful of people were well dressed, many of them in fabrics that had to be grown or nurtured like silks and cottons. Those clothes were also brighter—pinks and blues and bright greens.

Those people had to be tourists, not just because of their clothing, but also because they looked panicked. Which was, if he was honest with himself, exactly how Khelan was feeling.

The sense that he had made a mistake was growing with each passing moment.

The bar was called, unoriginally, The Docking View, which was probably why Khelan had assumed there was a view. He started through the wide open doors, only to be stopped by some kind of invisible barrier.

A sign went up in front of him in Imperial Standard. A mechanized voice asked him what language he preferred.

He felt momentarily flustered. He'd never encountered anything like this before.

Then he said, "Standard is fine," in Standard, which had to be some kind of weird recursive exercise.

The voice then read him the sign. It was a notification, really, a warning. To sit in the bar, he had to order something. The bar only took payment in Imperial currency and would verify the payment before anyone was allowed inside.

He had to order a drink, in other words, and pay for it right there, before he entered.

Which he did. He ordered a honey-butter ale that was supposed to be a specialty of the station. The drink sounded disgusting to him. He didn't plan on sipping any of it, because he had no idea what he would be subjecting himself to.

The stupid drink was five times more expensive than a comparable ale on any other Empire station he'd ever had the misfortune of going to.

But he didn't mind. He wanted this meeting over as soon as possible.

The barrier went down, and the mechanized voice told him he could enter. A floating tray waited for him, a large stein of ale sitting in the center.

The surface of the tray was covered in multicolored foam—some white, some yellow, some gray, and one little area was bright blue. He made himself take the stein. The handle was grimy, as if the glass hadn't been washed at all.

It didn't help that the interior smelled fetid—unwashed bodies, old urine, and sour wine. He resisted the urge to put a hand over his nose. He regretted not wearing some kind of mask or an environmental suit.

He hadn't expected a toxic hazard in the Empire, though. For all its utilitarian design, every place he had gone in the Empire had been fanatically clean.

Except here.

The light was dim. There was no real bar, which surprised him, given the name. (Most places in the Empire that called themselves a bar had an actual bar, sometimes with railings, often with stools for patrons.)

There were a dozen tables, scattered around the dark dingy space, and no other patrons—except Zimmer who sat in the exact middle of the room.

Zimmer had brought his own light source, which he had set in the middle of the table. He was wearing a loose-weave brown tunic over matching pants. An untouched bottle of something green sat in front of him, with a tall glass beside it that had a coating of yellow gunk along the surface of the green liquid inside.

Or, to be more accurate, the somewhat greenish liquid. It had separated into something that matched the blue foam on the tray and a puke yellow along the bottom. Only the middle of the liquid was anything approaching green at all.

Khelan's stomach turned. The sooner he got out of this place, the better.

He carried his stein to the table, pulled back a chair that looked like wood but was some kind of metal, and debated whether or not to sit down. The chair's seat was brownish black, and he couldn't tell if that was wear or if it was the source of one of the smells that was still wrestling with his nose.

"This is charming," he said, lowering himself slowly. He set his horrid stein on the table next to the bottle of yuck that Zimmer had already ordered.

"Yeah, well, it's one of the few places that I knew we wouldn't be monitored," Zimmer said. "I've been here before. I'm surprised you haven't."

Khelan frowned. "It's new to me."

"Hmm. I guess every collector has a first time." Zimmer said that without humor.

Khelan wasn't sure Zimmer had a sense of humor. Right now, he looked even angrier than he had at the auction. His small eyes glinted and a red flush had worked its way up from the folds in his neck to his round cheeks.

At least this time, Zimmer was wearing a shirt that fit over his stomach. The shirt was frayed, like the ones Khelan had seen on his way to this bar.

Khelan gestured at Zimmer's clothing. "You could've warned me."

"I figured you were the kind of man who did his research," Zimmer said. "Guess I was wrong."

Khelan bristled, just like he was supposed to. "The public information about this place is sparse."

"And there's a reason for that," Zimmer said. "I figured you would have known that when information is sparse, you should dig."

"I figured you'd recommend somewhere safe." Khelan kept his fingers on that filthy stein, because if he didn't, he would wipe them on his own pants, and who knew what kind of gunk he would take back with him to the yacht.

Zimmer raised his eyebrows, comically stretching his face, and making his forehead look like someone had shoved a series of small horizontal tubes under his skin.

"You figured..." Zimmer laughed. "You figured. I said we had to go somewhere that no one would listen in. That's not the wealthier parts of the Empire. You never struck me as naïve before, Madani."

"This is far from wealthy," Khelan said.

"And yet it's not." Zimmer's smile faded. "You really didn't research this, did you?"

There had been hints of a different type of wealth. Pirates. A secret core. Khelan really hadn't been paying the right kind of attention when he agreed to come here.

"I'm not used to mysterious summons," he said. "You want to tell me what's going on?"

"You heard about the thieves who broke into the warehouse,

right?" Zimmer pushed the glass of yuck farther away from him. The so-called liquid inside didn't even slosh.

Khelan had thought about how to answer that question for the entire trip here.

"Only the rumors," he said. "And judging by the fact that the military is the one putting a heavy lid on the information, I figure the theft had to be a lot worse than they're letting on."

"Twenty-some people dead, killed when they were responding to the alarms," Zimmer said.

Khelan didn't even have to fake his surprise. He *was* surprised, surprised that Zimmer had that much information. As far as Khelan had been able to learn, no one outside of Vaycehn, Corporate Treasures, and the military itself had known about the deaths.

"How?" Khelan asked.

"That's something I can't find out," Zimmer said. "The intruders —thieves—whoever not only fought when the military arrived, but escaped too."

"With our artifacts?" Khelan asked, raising his voice.

Zimmer waved his right hand downward in a *shush* movement. The man really was worried about someone overhearing them.

Khelan couldn't see anyone in here, not even through that supposedly open door. The serving trays were lined up against a wall, which had a window that they probably went through to get the drinks, but he saw nothing else that could be used for overhearing their discussion.

At least, with Imperial tech. The fact that the table's surface was wet with some kind of liquid meant that any tech built into it would glitch.

Zimmer leaned forward. He almost braced his arms on the tabletop, but stopped himself at the last minute.

"No," he said. "Our artifacts are fine, although I'm hearing that they might be damaged."

"Damaged?" Khelan really was surprised now, and about the thing Zimmer was talking about. The very idea that the artifacts could be damaged made Khelan even more nervous than he had been.

He hadn't had a chance to really look at the Spire parts. He didn't know what would happen to them if they were badly damaged.

"This sounds...fantastical," he said. "I've heard nothing about this."

"No one has," Zimmer said. "That's one reason why I wanted to talk with you. I wanted to find out what you've heard."

"It's been frustratingly silent," Khelan said truthfully. "I heard the rumors about some attack, and then nothing. I don't even have my shipping manifest yet."

"That's what I wanted to talk to you about," Zimmer said. "I haven't gotten mine either."

Khelan frowned at him. "I've never worked with Corporate Treasures before. Is this normal behavior for them?"

"No," Zimmer said. "I've done business with them three times before. If anything, they've been too responsive, giving me too much information."

"But now, when we need it, they're silent," Khelan said.

Zimmer nodded. He seemed to be waiting for something.

Khelan had to separate himself from the man from Amnthra who was trying to recover weapons, and the collector. The collector would be upset about the money and the collectibles.

"What are you thinking?" Khelan said. "You're worried they're covering up the damage?"

"We stand to lose a lot of money if they are," Zimmer said.

"We're covered," Khelan said. "They have to report all the damage to us and give us a choice as to whether or not we want the items. It's in the contract."

"With hundreds of pieces, that'll take weeks," Zimmer said.

"So that could be why they're stalling?" Khelan asked.

Zimmer shook his head ever so slightly. "You worry me, Madani."

Khelan's heart rate increased. What could make Zimmer make that comment? And right now?

"I figured you were a guy I could trust, but the fact that you haven't done any research on Longbow makes me wonder. I thought you were as anal as I am and as savvy. I think I'm wrong." Zimmer stood, wiping his hands on his pants, and making Khelan wince. "Sorry to waste your time."

This was a negotiation ploy that Khelan was familiar with. It was annoying to discover Zimmer using it in a normal (or semi-normal) conversation.

"Sit down." Khelan used one of his most forceful voices. "If you want me to pay you for information, you've come to the wrong man. If you want a conversation, I'm willing. But you're giving me rumors and not basing them on anything. You want to tell me how you supposedly know all of this?"

Zimmer glanced around, then looked at the serving trays. For a moment, Khelan thought Zimmer was going to suggest leaving the bar. Khelan didn't want to. He had no guarantee that wherever they went next wouldn't be worse.

Then Zimmer slowly sat down. "I'm only telling you this because I can't sit alone with it anymore," he said.

Khelan tilted his head in surprise. He hadn't expected Zimmer to say something like that.

"I'm not sure what to do, Madani, but I'm not sure you're the guy to ask."

"Try me," Khelan said.

Zimmer took a deep breath, then choked a little and coughed. Khelan almost told him that breathing too much in this fetid place was a bad idea. The stench had settled into something less powerful, but ever present, particularly that smell of old urine.

Khelan was beginning to wonder if that smell was coming from one of the drinks.

Zimmer finally stopped coughing. He reached for the glass, saw it, and brought his hand back, his lips curled upward in disgust.

"What I wouldn't give for a clean glass of water," he said quietly, then glanced at the serving trays. None of them moved.

Maybe Zimmer was being honest, or maybe he was testing them. Khelan couldn't tell.

"I wouldn't trust clean or water here," Khelan said.

That got Zimmer to raise one eyebrow and half smile. Then he nodded.

He glanced at the trays again, but they didn't move. Then he shrugged, as if finalizing a debate with himself.

"I, um, have someone inside," he said so quietly that Khelan had to strain to hear him.

"Inside...?" Khelan didn't understand. "The warehouse?"

Khelan had thought that the only people inside were military and security. But he didn't know.

The frustration he'd been feeling grew. That was the real problem. He didn't know.

"Corporate Treasures," Zimmer said. "They can't get near the warehouse, even though that woman—Hazleberg?—she's still there. She was trying to hire experts to assess the damage, but she's stopped."

"Inside," Khelan breathed.

"Headquarters," Zimmer said. "But they have information, and they can share it with me."

"Your inside man," Khelan said, to clarify.

"My inside *person*," Zimmer snapped. "Are you usually this dense? Because you never seemed that way before."

Khelan ignored the insult. "Your person," he said. "They know about the damage?"

"That's what they told me about first, but what made me contact you was this." Zimmer took a deep breath again, rolled his eyes as he choked again, but didn't cough quite as long.

Khelan waited, making certain to breath shallowly.

"They sold everything."

"Okay," Khelan said. He was there for that. They both had been.

"To the military," Zimmer said. "We're going to get reimbursed."

"What?" The word came out before Khelan could stop it. "You're kidding."

He'd never heard of that, but it made sense. That would be why the military was in charge of delivering the artifacts.

"No," Zimmer said. "That's what my person said, but I wanted confirmation. I was hoping you had it."

"I've been dealing with silence. That's it. Just silence," Khelan said. "Why would the military want it?"

He was worried about the answer, but he didn't want to tip his hand. And he needed to know what Zimmer's inside person had to say.

"I guess they think this isn't a simple theft. Something about strange weapons?"

Khelan's breath caught. "What does that mean?"

"Whatever killed those soldiers," Zimmer said. "They can't identify it."

Khelan let out the breath. That made sense. But the rest didn't.

"And they think the artifacts have something to do with it?"

Zimmer shrugged again. "It makes no sense to me. But my source says they're going to some kind of research station as a unit. I don't know if the military thinks the artifacts will draw the thieves again or if there's something else going on. I was hoping—"

"I'd know, yeah." Khelan shook his head. "I don't know anything."

And he really didn't. But he was worried. If the military guessed that the artifacts were weapons, and were taking them to a research facility, that meant they'd reverse engineer them.

The best thing anyone from Amnthra could hope for was that someone would mishandle a bit of the Spires, and the entire research station would explode.

But that wasn't something to hope for. Khelan couldn't even casually think that anymore, not after what had just happened.

"Maybe you have an idea how to stop it?" Zimmer said.

His words so closely echoed Khelan's thoughts that Khelan had to peer at him. Zimmer was operating from an Empire collector standpoint, not an Amnthran viewpoint.

"I suppose we talk to the institutions," Khelan said. "We pool our resources with them, figure out how to get Corporate Treasures to stop this handover."

"The handover is a done deal," Zimmer said.

"Not if they don't pay us," Khelan said, but he wasn't sure. "I think we band together, get a lawyer to contact them, put a stop on the whole thing."

Zimmer nodded. "I thought of that. I don't think it'll work."

"It won't hurt to try," Khelan said, but he was just speaking reflexively. He didn't know a lot about imperial law. It was complicated and there were a lot of exceptions for the government and the military.

He'd met a few lawyers due to his Madani identity, but he didn't know if theirs was an effective profession in this culture or not.

As a result, he had no idea what the collectors could do or what they should do. And he really didn't care.

But he wanted more information, so he was going to continue this conversation.

"Is everything going to that research station?" he asked.

"I guess," Zimmer said.

"Talk to your person," Khelan said. "Make sure. Because if the institutions were still getting theirs, then we don't want to involve them. We need to go after Corporate Treasures ourselves. We need to figure out who the other collectors are too."

"I already know," Zimmer said. "They're pretty self-involved. I just figured you'd be the one open to this."

In other words, he'd already contacted a few of them, and they weren't interested.

"Find out about the institutions," Khelan said. "And do it fast. By then, I'll have some options for us."

"I can't contact anyone from here," Zimmer said, "and I really don't want to talk—"

"All you have to do is tell me yes or no," Khelan said, tired of the subterfuge. He wasn't sure it was necessary.

Or rather, he knew it wasn't necessary, not for him. It might be for Zimmer, but deep down, Khelan didn't care about Zimmer. Khelan wondered if it showed.

"Once I know," Khelan said, "I'll have a plan. Maybe they will have paid us by then."

"I don't want the money," Zimmer said. "It's the Ivory Trees. I wanted them for my beach house."

Khelan almost asked about that, then decided against it. He hadn't realized that Zimmer had Ivory Trees. Or Ivory Tree parts.

Were there more in the Empire than Khelan realized? He hoped not.

But he couldn't react to Zimmer's comment—at least, not in an Amnthran way.

So Khelan smiled and nodded sympathetically.

"Yeah," he said. "I was hoping to buy all of the Ivory Trees for that very reason. I only have a few bits."

"Even those bits are pretty," Zimmer said. "My visitors always comment."

Khelan nodded. "I have yet to show mine off," he said. "But you're right. I want the items, not the money. However," he added, "if we can't have the items, repayment is essential."

Zimmer's mouth thinned. He didn't seem to like that argument.

"I'll give you a yes or no in a day or so," he said. "I want a plan to get us our artifacts. I hope you can come up with something."

"I have some folks I can consult," Khelan said. "But you seem to be the operator. You have someone inside. I would never have thought of that."

"You might consider it in the future," Zimmer said. "You'd be surprised what I've learned over the years. These auction places, they try to screw collectors more often than not. I'd worked with Corporate Treasures before and never had a problem. But I figured, pay off someone in the middle of it all, and make sure. I'm glad I did."

"I am too," Khelan said. "Thank you for consulting me."

And he hoped that Zimmer would get back to him shortly. Because now, Khelan was going to have to figure out how to get deep into the military databases, something he had avoided in his entire time here.

He hoped that the new team would arrive before he got too involved in the research, and of course, he'd go through Corporate Treasures' systems first.

He couldn't base everything they were going to do on Zimmer's word.

But Zimmer had no reason to lie to him.

There was nothing easy about this job. Too many artifacts, too many people involved, too much to do.

Too much death.

Khelan slapped his palm on the filthy table and immediately regretted it.

"I appreciate all of the news," he said to Zimmer. "We'll figure out a way to get our items. I promise."

Zimmer looked at him, maybe not with hope because Khelan wasn't sure that man could hope. But with something akin to agreement.

"I don't like any of this," Zimmer said.

"Me either," Khelan said. "But the sooner we control our artifacts, the better."

"If we ever get that chance," Zimmer said.

THE SOLUTION

SIXTEEN DAYS LATER

FIFTY-THREE

Lieutenant Percival Tattersol settled into the pilot's seat of the vessel that was unoriginally called *Cargo One*. The cargo ship actually had a name, based on the military battalion that it was usually attached to. The name was complicated, with lots of initials, numbers, and subdesignations, all so that that cargo ship wouldn't get confused with its identical counterparts attached to different ships in the same battalion.

He didn't pretend to understand all the designations and markings. He didn't usually command a cargo ship, and would have said it was beneath him if someone had asked him a month ago.

He tugged on the right sleeve of his environmental suit. The sleeve kept digging into his wrist, a problem he always had when he wasn't wearing the gloves that adhered to the suit. The gloves were on his console, and his helmet was on the floor beside him, which was probably not the brightest plan.

But he didn't want to put on those last bits of the suit unless he needed them. No one else on his five-person crew was wearing their helmets either, although most of them were wearing the gloves.

He would have preferred to wear no environmental suit or a full suit. He had asked his superiors if he could just shut off the environmental controls and wear the suits, and he had received a loud and almost angry denial.

After that, he hadn't asked for an explanation, although the deeper he got into this mission, the more unsettled he got.

Right now, he was toggling between annoyance at the bulky ship he was commanding and pride that he was chosen to lead this cargo convoy to a secret research base in a part of Imperial space that he (and others) thought had no real value at all.

He had been read into program after program after program, received a small promotion so he could even see the location of the research station, and had to sign waiver after waiver promising to protect classified data should it inadvertently cross his screen.

For the rest of his life, he would not be able to discuss this mission. As his own commander put it: *This mission isn't happening. None of you are working on it. You will have a cover story prepared for you once you have delivered the artifacts safely. You will stick to your cover story. If you ever deviate from it, you will be subject to sanctions, possible court-martial, and loss of your commission.*

Then Tattersol had to sign his life away, go through some psych evaluations that he hadn't expected, and agree one final time to handle this job.

He had no idea what was so important about the cargo on this vessel. Only once had he been told he was carrying "artifacts," but when he boarded *Cargo One*, the cargo was already in place.

The mission was structured. He was not allowed any input in the job whatsoever. He was not allowed to speak with the other pilots on the other two cargo vessels—unimaginatively called *Cargo Two* and *Cargo Three*—and he certainly was not allowed to give orders to the twelve escort vehicles that surrounded them, three vessels on each of the convoy's four sides.

Apparently there had been some debate about whether they needed more than twelve vessels, and Tattersol's commanding officer told him that he shouldn't be surprised if more escort vehicles showed up, should more protection be needed.

Tattersol wasn't even allowed to discuss the cargo with the five other officers in the cockpit of *Cargo One*. Only one had a real rank, and that was Hester Ralston, his second-in-command. She was an actual sublieutenant.

She was a small woman who sat to his right. She wore her bright red hair in a coronet of braids that looked like a hat. He had made the mistake of commenting on it, and she had given him a look that would have made a lesser man quake.

Her face was narrow, and her lips pursed most of the time. He tried not talk with her at all, which she seemed to be fine with.

The talker was F. O. Ludlow, who had told them all upon introduction that he did not like his given names and they were to call him Luddy. He had been given one of those fake promotions that changed his status from Provisional to Officer, which Tattersol had known before he checked the files. Clearly, Luddy, with his out-of-control mane of brown hair, round cheeks, and large nose (which looked like it had been broken more than once) had not been raised in a military family. He had gotten into the military through some other means, and he was not yet refined.

Tattersol had learned in the two days the so-called team had been together not to ask Luddy a question unless they wanted a monologue on the history of or the mystery of or some irrelevant sidetrack on whatever it was that they needed.

Still, Luddy seemed to know everything there was to know about this make of cargo vessel. He knew how to operate systems that Tattersol had not been trained on, which actually relieved Tattersol.

They had been told that there was a possibility of pirate attack on these vessels, which was why they had the escorts and the secretive route.

They had also been told that they had these cargo vessels instead of something larger and faster because this version had an extensive weapons system as well as an effective cloak.

Tattersol and his team had received training on the weapons and the cloak, but not on all the details of the cargo ship's navigation system.

It's a complex system, said the officer who was training them, *and usually you'd have months to practice with this ship. But you don't. And we don't have the personnel with the proper experience...*

Which Tattersol had heard as rank and clearance.

...to handle these vessels on short notice. So we're teaching you the main systems, and you'll just have to guess at the rest.

Tattersol had not liked that any more than the rest of his cockpit crew had. He had surreptitiously moved Luddy from his position on communications to assistant navigator, a move that the real navigator, Wilber Offley, hadn't minded at all.

Tattersol had the sense that Offley didn't mind much, so long as he didn't have to work at whatever was thrown his way. The man had what Tattersol privately called "loose muscles" which meant that he wasn't in the best condition.

That happened to a lot of older officers, who felt they no longer needed to keep up with the condition requirements for their branch of the military, but it rarely happened with someone as young as Offley. Offley was clearly not an ambitious sort, like Luddy, and would most likely leave the military entirely once he had put in enough time to get a minimal pension.

Twice already, as the ships headed out, Offley had leaned back and let Luddy program in the slight corrections in course that their superiors wanted them to do by hand.

The cockpit was large enough that the six officers did not have to sit close, although Luddy was at Offley's side almost from the beginning. The only other officer to take advance of the space was Maud Pixton. She was to monitor the cargo bay—for what, Tattersol did not know—and the egresses throughout the ship.

The crews of all the ships—from the three cargo vessels to the escort vehicles—had all been told that these pirates had sophisticated equipment and might be able to somehow get around the escorts and breach the cargo vessels.

No matter how often Tattersol asked how this would be possible, no one would tell him. The first time he asked, Operations Commander Alcott Quarles gave Group Commander Rusty Wilton a sideways look as if Quarles expected Wilton to answer the question.

Wilton's face had remained impassive, and he had said nothing in response to the question. In fact, all of the commanders who had been giving the presentation paused only slightly then moved on as if Tattersol hadn't asked a question at all.

Tattersol had later talked with Lucinda Vance, the only officer in this cargo crew that he had known before they were all thrown together what she had thought of that non-answer.

She had widened her dark eyes, as if she had been afraid of the question itself, then shrugged one bony shoulder. It was the only time in this entire short run that she had turned away from him, moving to a different part of the room.

She had clearly heard something and she had clearly believed she was not at liberty to say anything about it.

That irritated Tattersol enough that he had assigned her the only seat in the cockpit that was behind him. He had asked her twice what she knew, and both times she had frowned, and looked away.

The final time he had said, "Luce, I can't command this mission well if I don't know what we're up against."

She had given him a pitying look, which really didn't fit well on her harsh features, and had said, "If they believed you needed the information, they would have given it to you."

And that was all he could get out of her.

Her position here was weapons' specialist. She also handled the cloak. She had more training on both than the rest of the crew; *just in case,* Quarles had said.

Tattersol had thought that Quarles was in charge of this mission until Group Commander Wilton had shown up. And from Wilton's behavior, he was dealing with someone on a regular basis who outranked him.

This mission was important, and everyone in charge was nervous, which made Tattersol nervous. He had never seen his commanders worried about any other group—not that there were many.

There was the Nine Planets Alliance, but they weren't trying to overtake—or even to bother—the Empire. The Alliance just tried to keep the Empire from adding more territory.

Every now and then, there were rumors of some kind of incursion from some other culture or organization that made the mistake of confronting the Empire. He'd often wished he could be part of one of the rapid-response teams.

He'd also heard rumors of the Empire investigating expansion, taking ships into other territories with the idea of bringing them into the Empire.

He had never heard how that went.

But this, he didn't entirely understand and no one would explain it. When he left the training sessions, he would go to his assigned room and investigate the known pirates around the Empire. Most of those pirates operated out of the Nine Planets Alliance, which was nowhere close to Wyr, and about as far away from the research station it could be.

He had no idea how pirates could even get into this part of the Empire, let alone be some kind of threat.

So the only thing he could think of was that these so-called pirates weren't outsiders at all. Maybe they had come from the Empire. Maybe they used Imperial technology. Maybe they were an internal threat that no one wanted to discuss.

He glanced at the crew, all of whom (well, all but Offley) were working hard at their various stations.

This trip was supposed to take eight hours at the designated speed. He had been told not to exceed that speed unless the situation warranted it. He had been told that their cargo was delicate, and even though it was packed well, it needed to be protected from jolts and other problems.

He was also supposed to keep an eye on the artificial gravity. If he had to make a choice between keeping the normal temperature and oxygen levels and keeping the gravity, he was to keep the gravity. Followed by strict temperature controls.

The oxygen—the breathable air—was the last on his list.

He hadn't asked for an explanation of that, because he had received it with the order. Those delicate things in the cargo bay needed to remain packed as they were, and at the best possible temperature. Zero-g might cause unexpected damage, just like extreme cold could.

And that was pretty much all he knew about the items he was

carrying to the research station. The items were delicate, especially in zero-g and extreme cold. They were also the targets of some pirate group, although he was not allowed to know which one.

Protecting the cargo was more important than his crew. He'd also gotten that message, although he had not told the team that.

Quarles had pulled him aside after the little *sacrifice might be necessary* speech that Wilton had given everyone at the end of the instructions.

"I know you have a desire for action," Quarles had said to Tattersol, "but don't get overeager. If something happens in transit, let your escorts handle it. Your weapons are a last resort. You use them only if there is no one else to defend you. Remember, there are two other cargo vessels with similar cargo, and any errant shot could be disastrous."

Tattersol had nodded. He had used that moment to ask one final question.

"If it's so important to make sure no other cargo vessel gets harmed, how come we're not traveling separately?"

"Good question, son," Quarles had said. "I'm not allowed to answer it. So just follow orders, all right? Maybe someday you'll get enough clearance that you can look up this mission, and actually get the answers to your questions."

Then he had laughed, as if that amused him.

It hadn't amused Tattersol. He knew that being part of the Space Force meant doing things without pushback, but this just seemed strange enough that the lack of knowledge about what exactly was happening worried him.

He had a hunch they were all being lied to, but he didn't know about what. The other cargo ships' commanders knew no more than he did, and he was not allowed to meet the commanders of the escort vehicles. They could communicate with him. He could not communicate with them, except on an emergency basis.

The route to the research station was programmed into the autopilot. As Quarles had told him, if they were all lucky, he wouldn't have to touch the controls at all.

Luddy had investigated the route, though, and saved it somewhere, just in case the autopilot went down. He had suggested that Offley find some kind of alternative route, but Offley had said that if their superior officers had wanted them to know about an alternate route, someone would have told them.

The only thing that Ralston had said, and she had done so quietly, after they had embarked, was that she wondered why they weren't taking the shipping lanes as far as they could before heading into the region of space near the research station.

"Shipping lanes," she had said, "have built-in protections against pirates."

"Sounds like these aren't your average pirates," Tattersol had said, and had to leave it at that.

Speculating was getting them nowhere. They were merely the drivers, the group that was getting the ships from one place to another.

Their presence, he had come to understand, was an added factor, a failsafe in case something else in this plan—whatever it was—fell apart.

Or maybe in case the entire plan fell apart.

Eight hours. He'd looked at the route that Luddy had saved. Most ships could make it in four.

He worried that whatever was in their cargo bay was volatile. Not just delicate, but so delicate that going fast would endanger all of them.

But he wasn't allowed to know if that was true.

He knew he should act like Offley and just relax into the journey.

But Tattersol had too many questions to relax. He wanted to get up and pace, but he knew that would probably upset his crew. And if he paced, he'd have to put on the gloves and helmet on his environmental suit.

He was just going to have to be patient, which usually wasn't a problem for him.

But he had a bad feeling about this entire journey, and it wasn't just because of the weird warnings and rules.

Something was off.

He just wished he knew what that something was.

FIFTY-FOUR

Chief Mele Wong of the Amnthran Territorial Guard's warship *'iliahi* sat on the center pedestal, legs crossed at the ankles as she studied the convoy surrounding the three cargo ships heading to a research facility deep inside Enterran Empire space.

Twelve ships, plus the three, all looking formidable—and perhaps they would have been if they knew that the *'iliahi* was near them. But they had no idea. Their primitive systems could not pick up the *'iliahi's* cloak, nor had anyone in the various military organizations near the Enterran planet of Wyr discovered that the *'iliahi* waited just outside of orbit, observing everything.

The command deck smelled of jasmine this morning. Someone had programmed the jasmine to bloom, even though she had not ordered it. Plants—some real and others not—decorated each station on the command deck.

She couldn't see the rest of her crew through the greenery, even though that was not a real problem. If she wanted to see the crew working the command deck, she could either call up holos, or make the plants recede into the flooring.

Right now, the command deck did not have to be at its most spare and utilitarian. It could be the jungle they were all comfortable in.

The air was humid, because it was good for the plants. Everyone left the deck every eight hours or so when the plants were up so that the misters could tend to the greenery.

Before the air filled with mist, the equipment—what little couldn't handle the water—would cover itself. Then the environmental systems would dry the floor, wall, ceiling and pedestals, while leaving the nearby leaves just a little damp.

The misting had occurred early this morning. Another was due in a few hours. Right now, though, the command deck was in its sunshine cycle. The lighting was bright as midday on an Amnthran beach, which the beautification scientists had determined provided the best light for plants all over the ship.

Knowing she would be here in the day's summer cycle, Wong wore her lightest uniform, a thin pale-pink shirt over slightly darker pants. The materials were made of a loose weave that would let in cool breezes—should the environmental system determine that the command deck needed them.

Sometimes a breeze would come up in the middle of a stressful situation which this was going to be.

She was trying not to obsess about anything here, although it was hard. The *'iliahi* had never been this far away from Amnthra before.

This mission was unlike any that had ever been done before. Should someone raise an objection, she wasn't sure if they were protected under Amnthran law. So far, no one had. She had a hunch the *'iliahi* was chosen because its crew was the least likely to make a fuss, should the mission go sideways.

The mission was defensive. Amnthran space law gave the Traveling Division the right to leave the boundaries of Amnthran space to retaliate against attackers, to retrieve or destroy stolen technology, and to investigate possible threats.

What they could not do was initiate a battle or participate in any situation that might begin a war with another culture.

That was a gray area, as many had acknowledged in the past, and it was never more gray than this mission. The Traveling Division of the Space Division of the Territorial Guard had a mandate to deal with technology that had fallen into enemy hands.

To knowingly allow Amnthran technology to exist outside of Amnthra was a crime, not just in the military codes, but in the civilian ones as well.

So when Khelan Māhoe had notified the Amnthran authorities that the Enterran Empire had a large cache of pieces from the various Spires, as well as other weapons, the Amnthrans had no choice but to recover their lost technology.

They had tried, using standard methods. But they hadn't thought through the difficulties of dealing with a military culture like the Enterrans.

The theft had gone sideways, leaving the Guard no choice but to attack. Inside the Space Division, this was being called a retrieval mission.

But Wong had been in the service long enough to know that if some outside culture attacked a convoy of fifteen Amnthran vessels inside Amnthran territory, that attack would be looked at as an act of war.

The mission made her uncomfortable. Her second-in-command, Sub-Chief Liko Eusebio, had said to her after they had received their orders that the entire mission made him nervous.

Eusebio never admitted to nerves. But his emotions were strong enough that the ship's gardeners were noticing some side effects on the plants around his pedestal. There had been an increase in yellow leaves, and one particularly delicate fern that had been with him throughout his entire career was getting brown spots on its oldest leaves, something that the gardeners had never seen before.

They believed that plants reacted to stress of their main caretaker, which was why the gardeners had their own deck, filled with relaxation tools. But Eusebio did not tend to his plants. His gardener stated that either his stress was strong or the plants had formed a bond with him anyway.

The rest of Wong's deck crew had no such issues. They were unaware, however, of the full orders that the 'iliahi had to carry out.

Only the six leaders on this crew, and Weapons Chief Kalena Akana, brought in from the Defense Division, knew exactly what the 'iliahi's mission was. All of the others had looked worried as they were briefed on the orders, but only Eusebio had expressed any misgivings at all.

When asked if he wanted to be replaced for this mission, he had immediately shaken his head.

We have a duty, he had said, but he had sounded sad as he spoke. They did have a duty, a sworn duty, to make sure no other culture was getting Amnthran technology.

And this was one of the most flagrant violations of that rule that Wong had ever seen. This mission was necessary, if disturbing.

She had a lot of discretion in the way she went after the convoy. She had more tools than she had ever had before. The *'iliahi* was at full capacity, filled with thirty two-person fighters, four orbiters, and several small vessels that could travel a short distance in a relatively quick time.

That didn't count the armory, the vast weapons systems, and the various storage systems that would allow the *'iliahi* to handle a mission that lasted years without landing anywhere, not that it had ever had to.

On top of that, Akana had brought her own weapons' specialists. They needed to be here to deal with problems from the Spires themselves.

According to Māhoe's reports, the Spire bits and pieces were ancient.

There was plenty of history on how the ancient Spires had once worked, and their various mechanisms. But there was no real technical understanding of how the old and decaying Spires would respond to any kind of threat.

In fact, no one actually knew if Spires, removed from their natural environment, decayed at all. The Spires were replaced on a regular basis on Amnthra, often the entire Spiral system, not just section by section.

The Spiral system was powerful, and no one wanted something to accidentally go awry with it.

Not only were the Amnthrans protective of their technology leaving its culture, they were also protective of its operation. Technology was constantly tested and improved, with anything that was out of date, or wasn't functioning to capacity, replaced immediately.

That included ships as well as weaponry. Any time Wong left the *'iliahi* for an ordered vacation or a land-based trip to Division headquarters, repairs or replacements were made on the warship. She often had to return and learn new systems.

She had tested all of those systems before leaving Amnthra. The *anacapa* drive had worked to perfection. She had never arrived exactly on target before, and this time, the *'iliahi* had appeared at the exact coordinates.

It hadn't taken long to break into the Enterran military systems and learn not only the plan for the materials found on Wyr, but the route for the convoy, the specifications of each vessel traveling to this so-called secret research station, and any contingency plans should something go awry.

She could also see into the defensive systems around Wyr, such as they were. She had been shocked, as had her colleagues, at how breathtakingly behind the Enterran government was, particularly since the sector had once housed a Fleet sector base.

So far, the convoy was following the route it had planned. It was avoiding shipping lanes and populated areas. It wasn't even going near space stations or planets.

It was traveling as far from anything as it could.

On some level, that made her sad. She didn't want this mission to be too easy. It might create some guilt, not just for her, but for her crew.

On another level, though, the distance made her job easier. She would have no trouble remaining hidden.

And, if she did her job right, the Enterran Empire would have no real idea what happened. They could investigate all they wanted with their backwards technology, and they would never really be able to figure out what, exactly, went wrong.

She had an hour before the convoy reached the target location on the route. Farthest from anything, away from all of the various buoys and monitors that the Empire had set up along some of the military routes.

An hour.

She was ready.

And she knew that they would never be, no matter how much they had planned.

She wished she could be happier about that, but she wasn't.

She would just complete the mission, and then she'd be able to go home.

Not victorious. They would never be victorious on a mission like this.

But at least they would get the job done.

FIFTY-FIVE

Khelan was hiding in the captain's quarters on his space yacht. He had shut down most of the networking and had isolated communications to Enterran channels only. He had told Idil, who was piloting the yacht, that he did not want to be disturbed.

But he was already disturbed. He was trying hard not to think about all the things he had put into motion, and he found himself unable to do that.

He had prepared one of his favorite meals. Lemongrass soup, jasmine rice, and a light curry with Amnthran chicken—not real chicken, like they ate here in the Empire, but chicken-flavored food, made from local plants. The meal, along with some pita bread, steamed on the table he had set up near one of his favorite holostations.

He was staring at the soup bowl, watching the spices blend with the golden broth. He clutched a spoon, but so far, he hadn't used it.

He had poured himself some wine, but he had left it on the counter. He had a hunch alcohol would not be good for him right now, nor would drinking alone.

The captain's quarters were as utilitarian as most suites on Enterran ships. The walls were a light beige, so that images from

383

various holoscreens could be easily seen against them. The original furniture had been very uncomfortable, so he had bought high-end furniture made for land-based buildings, and actually had the bottoms modified so that they would function on the yacht.

Two couches, one long enough for him to stretch out on, and several plush chairs, usually gave him some sort of comfort while he relaxed in here.

But he was finding no comfort, and he was not relaxed. He wasn't even sure he was going to enjoy the food, even though he was forcing himself to eat it.

His work was going to be done after today—should the mission go well, anyhow. He had made up his mind: he was returning to Amnthra. He had seen the beauty of Amnthran ships, and they had reminded him just how much he missed all the details of home.

He knew he wouldn't fit in anywhere on Amnthra anymore, but he no longer cared.

He wasn't set up for the conversations that he knew were coming here in the Empire among the collectors, auctioneers and specialists.

Did you hear what happened to that big collection from Corporate Treasures? Do you think it's worth buying from an organization like that when they can't even protect a collection that big…?

Oh, and then Zimmer would get involved, and talk about what he had known, and there would be speculation about the value of any remaining Ivory Trees. Not to mention the discussion of the mummies, and once again someone would mention the ethics of them.

Khelan got up from the table and went back to the small galley kitchen. The glass of wine, paler than the soup broth, looked unappealing.

Nothing looked appealing any longer.

He resisted the urge to leave his quarters and join Idil. She would have questions. She had been eager to monitor the activities of the convoy and what little they were being fed about the *'iliahi.*

And she was diligently researching the next part of their job—her job, really. Finding that bunker, where all of this began.

It wouldn't be hard, especially now that Khelan knew that Zimmer had a person inside of Corporate Treasures. Zimmer had proved very useful, in surprising ways.

His inside person had learned that the institutions weren't getting any Ivory Trees. And the smaller colleges and organizations weren't getting their free gifts.

Zimmer's person, whom he steadfastly refused to identify, hadn't revealed the name of the owner so far Khelan had a hunch the inside person didn't know it yet, but they would, the moment that the owner discovered that none of his wishes were carried out.

Everyone at Corporate Treasures would know—if the owner was like most rich people in the Empire. If not, then Khelan would research who Zimmer's person was and talk to that person himself.

Khelan already had ideas, just from the details that Zimmer had dropped. He wasn't as surreptitious as he thought he was. If the inside person could be bought off by Zimmer, that person could really be bought off by Khelan.

Or Idil. Or whoever would replace Khelan in the next few months.

He leaned on the counter, and stared at that glass of wine. It smelled slightly sweet with a tang of bitterness. He really didn't want it, but he did want the oblivion that a lot of wine promised.

He pushed away from it.

He hadn't imagined his work here would end like this, with a mission so difficult that several warship crews had to be vetted by the High Chiefs of every division.

Part of Khelan felt like this was all his fault, when he knew it wasn't.

Rules were rules. He had done all the work he was supposed to do. He had even gone over and above these past two weeks and made notes of loose bits of Spires scattered around the Empire—such as at Zimmer's beach house.

Those bits would be the focus of his successor.

Idil seemed interested and enthusiastic about all of it.

Khelan hoped that enthusiasm would hold after today.

He doubted it would.

But he had learned long ago never to put his own emotional reactions on someone else.

He grabbed the wine. The glass was warm against his fingers. He sniffed, and nearly downed it.

Then he set it aside one more time.

He would make himself eat, and then he would find some entertainment to amuse himself. Something to distract him. Something to make him think about a universe other than the one he lived in.

He had no idea what that something would be right now, but he would come up with it.

Or, at least, he hoped he would.

FIFTY-SIX

Officer Garrick Leighton, copilot and navigator on *Wyr Fighter Five*, studied the holoscreens before him. The pilot of the fighter, Officer Fern Davies, sat slightly in front of him, looking calmer than Leighton was.

The cockpit was small. It fit only the two of them. The old-fashioned design put the weapons officers in their own separate compartment, which Leighton thought a terrible flaw in the design.

Even though they could use comms to communicate, what would happen if the comms went down? How would they communicate then?

When he'd been assigned to the fighter a year ago, he'd asked his commander that very question, and the man had laughed.

Who would attack us, son? We're not going to the border.

Now, Leighton could answer that question. The door-ships, as some of the other soldiers who had been at the briefing had started to call the strange vessels that had killed twenty-four of their number on Wyr, would attack.

Ships no one understood with weapons that seemed outrageously powerful, and a way of traveling that was mysterious.

Plus, as he had pointed out in the briefing (okay, asked questions about), these ships appeared to have a cloak that the Empire couldn't penetrate either.

His superiors had pushed back at that. They contended that they hadn't tried to penetrate the cloak because they hadn't known the strange vessels were targeting Wyr.

It was a logic that Leighton didn't like, and because he didn't like it, he was taking initiative.

He had programmed one of his holoscreens to find what he called the watery-wave that seemed to appear just before the large vessel had uncloaked. That watery-wave appeared about thirty seconds before the vessel had emerged from its cloak. He had checked and rechecked that wave, and saw it no matter what kind of equipment he was using.

Some of his colleagues thought he was imagining things, but he wasn't. He knew what he was seeing.

And then there was the light. There was a bright light that wasn't gold and wasn't yellow but had tinges of both that appeared whenever those doors opened, just before the ships vanished forever. That light had a unique glow, something that seemed almost alive.

He programmed another holoscreen to find that as well. He figured if the ships used that light when they left, the light might be present when the ships arrived.

He had given his programs to his counterparts in the other escort vehicles. One of his colleagues threatened to report him for not following orders, until Leighton had reminded him that they had no orders preventing him from creating a program to keep them all safe.

Leighton had reminded that idiot that the idiot didn't have to use the program if it was beyond him, and maybe that would guarantee compliance, but probably not.

At least one part of the convoy, then, was unprotected if any more strange vessels uncloaked around them. But not Leighton. And not *Wyr Fighter Five*.

At the moment, they were taking point, along with two other vessels. Davies had pushed the fighter slightly ahead of them as if she had been trying to make the fighter the tip of some spear.

Leighton had flown with Davies for a year now, and he had found her to be both determined and competitive. She liked leading this convoy. She had appreciated the work he had done on this program, because she felt they could see and destroy whatever those ships were, by surprising them—and maybe some of the other vessels in the convoy as well.

The cockpit was a little cold, because that was how Davies liked it. The area also smelled faintly of spearmint, because she chewed some kind of gummy spearmint thing when she was nervous.

He had tried it once, and it had made his teeth hurt.

But otherwise, she would grind hers together. She had had to ask for special permission to use the gum stuff, but her superiors hadn't minded, so long as it wasn't some kind of drug. When they were certain it wasn't—just a regional habit from her home in the Hector Cluster—they approved it, for her only.

Usually, the weapons specialists kept the small screen between their two compartments closed, just because of the smell, but they didn't do that today.

Both of them seemed nervous. They had used every single weapon in the Empire's arsenal, but never in combat. And if this mission went awry, they would all be in combat for the first time in their lives.

Watery waves appeared just ahead, too many to count. But his program told him that there were six in front of him, six beneath, six behind, and a dozen more at the back of the convoy.

"Crap," he said. "We got incoming."

His heart rate jumped, and Davies, bless her, didn't question him.

"Let the others know," she said.

He did. He sent the images to the other escort vessels, just like he said he would do, while Davies asked the weapons specialists, "You all ready?"

"Ready, hell," Leighton said. "They should be firing now."

"You heard the man," Davies said. "Fire."

Technically, they were all supposed to wait until they saw an actual ship, but they had privately agreed that order was stupid. They had all made a pact to fight the moment they saw any kind of strange ship. If they hit something of the Empire's so be it. They were doing so in defense of the cargo vessels, and if something had arrived that close, it was their fault they got fired upon.

The weapons specialists fired at the watery waves in front, below, and above them. The most powerful lasers the fighter had streamed toward those waves, arriving seconds after ships actually appeared.

The ships were small, not large enough to carry more than a person or two. They were streamlined, black and narrow, with something that looked like a stinger on one end. Little stingers hung off the sides of the ships.

Leighton had just a moment to register them, before the lasers hit an invisible shield, illuminating it, and brightening the entire area around those ships.

"Again!" Davies shouted, even though she didn't have to. The weapons specialists were unloading on those ships, and from the brightness of the space around them, the other escort vehicles were firing as well.

The attack was bigger than Leighton expected, and there were more ships involved. Small ships that couldn't take any cargo from the cargo vessels.

The hair rose on the back of his neck.

These weren't pirates. Pirates would have ships big enough to carry cargo or to at least tow the cargo vessels. Maybe the pirates might board and take over the cargo vessels, but that would still take more than two people.

These little ships—they were killing machines.

"We've got to take them out," he said to the weapons' specialists. They were probably trying to do that, but he wanted them to try harder.

"We'll get them," someone said from behind him, but there was doubt in that voice, as the laser weapons again hit shields.

"We have to," Leighton said. "We absolutely have to."

FIFTY-SEVEN

Noa maneuvered the fighter sideways, changing speed and position at the same time.

"What the...?" his copilot Kimo said. "They're firing on us!"

And they were. About half of the Imperial escort vehicles were firing on the fighters that were uncloaking around them. Noa shook his head.

They had been told that the Enterrans didn't have the ability to locate cloaked vehicles, and yet they had. At least half of the fighters had been made before they even finished uncloaking.

At least the shields were holding up.

Enterran weapons were doing no damage at all.

Noa moved the fighter just slightly, getting into the proper position with the six other fighters in his group.

The fighters were small, ostensibly big enough to handle two people, but when one of them was Kimo, two was a stretch. Kimo was twice Noa's size—hell, Kimo was twice most people's size. Kimo's family was land-based, and Kimo was one of the few land-based people to sign up for Territorial Defense.

He had more tattoos on his arms and face than Noa had on his entire body. The tattoos made Kimo seem fierce, even though he was not—except at moments like this.

His entire expression was tight, focused, and that momentary shock of them being fired upon seemed to vanish.

"You ready?" he asked Noa.

"As I'll ever be," Noa responded.

They were to fire and peel away. No one knew if there were Spire pieces in these escort vehicles. And if there were, then hitting one of the vehicles might cause a larger than usual explosion.

Half of each squadron was assigned one of the escort vehicles. Noa's squadron had the first vehicle, the one that was the apparent leader of this convoy.

That vehicle had fired on them first too, seconds before the others.

He focused, poised to move.

"Go," he said.

And Kimo fired.

The shot cut through the old-fashioned laser weapons that the escort ships were using. The shot made them dissipate. Starbursts of light appeared where Kimo's shot hit the lasers, but after that, no laser weapon existed at all.

And Kimo's shot continued to move forward, as if the touch of the lasers had had no effect on it whatsoever.

It moved faster than it had when it started, gaining so much speed that the first escort vehicle couldn't move away from it.

The shot hit the escort vehicle, illuminating it for a moment. Noa thought he could see faces through some of the portals, but he knew that was impossible.

Then the vehicle expanded, turning red as the heat from the shot made its way through the old-fashioned metallic hull.

He peeled his own fighter away, turning it upside down and speeding to the place he had uncloaked, while he continued to watch the slow-moving explosion on one of his screens.

Two of the other escort vehicles were red now, and others were starting to expand.

His heart pounded. If they all exploded at once, and they all contained bits of the Spires, then the explosions would be huge.

If they didn't—

The first escort vehicle came apart, tiny pieces spinning off in all directions.

The other fighters in Noa's squadron sped to his side, and they all turned around. With shots like that and the escort vehicles coming apart slowly, there was no need to continue to move away.

The disintegration of the nearby escort vehicles didn't even have an impact on the nearest cargo vessel. It kept moving, but it had shields up now, for what good that would do it.

He gave the signal.

The fighters in his squadron flipped around, moving swiftly back to the convoy—or rather, what was left of it.

Bits of the escort vehicles floated like dust in an ancient house. The cargo ships were the only things that remained.

And that wouldn't be for very long.

Noa paused, just like he was supposed to do.

The cargo ships belonged to the *'iliahi*.

The show was about to begin.

FIFTY-EIGHT

With shaking hands, Tattersol pulled on his helmet. He had already put on the gloves when the shooting started. The gloves dug into his wrists, too tight as usual, but he no longer cared.

The escort vehicles were gone. And he was now in charge. Or rather, all three of the commanders of the cargo vessels were in charge.

He hadn't expected thirty small ships—fighters of a type he didn't recognize—to decloak all around them.

Nothing in his equipment, no scan, no announcement, no nothing, had told him or anyone else on his crew that those fighters were approaching.

Nothing.

He was trying not to panic. He'd been trained not to panic, but training and actual warfare were two different things.

He fully expected to be boarded, but how, he had no idea.

"Let's destroy those assholes," Ralston said. She wasn't supposed to be giving the orders, but he was stupidly silent, so she had stepped in.

Tattersol's voice had locked up. He wasn't even sure how to give an order right now. His heart was pounding.

"Fire, for goddsake," Ralston said. "Give those assholes every-thing that we've got."

Tattersol's team moved swiftly. Luddy was surprisingly silent too, but he was slapping his hand on a console. Offley had put his body between Luddy and another console, and was poking at the surface, as if the console was delicate.

"I'm not seeing anyone trying to board," Pixton said from the side. She sounded surprised. "Nothing has changed in the cargo bays."

The crew had been briefed about potential boarding. *Someone* should be trying to board right now.

The escorts were gone, so boarding was next, right? Right?

Tattersol realized he had thought this, but he hadn't said any of it.

Cargo One shook ever so slightly as the laser canons fired. Not that it would do any good. Didn't anyway see those fighters' weapons? They had actually cut through the weapons from the escort vehicles.

Then some missiles zoomed past *Cargo One*, probably from one of the other cargo ships. The weapons missed.

All of the weapons missed. They didn't even hit the fighters' shields like the first shots from the escort vehicles.

Behind Tattersol—his weapons' specialist, the one who was supposed to send out a barrage of inexplicable weapons—swore.

"Are you seeing this?" she asked, but he couldn't tell who she was asking.

"Seeing what?" Ralston's voice was tight. She shot a sideways look at Tattersol, but all he was seeing were little bits of escort vehi-cles and probably bodies, floating around him.

"This."

A screen moved in front of all of them. There was a ship above them—way above them, above where the top escort vehicles had been, above the remaining cargo vessels.

The ship was the biggest thing that Tattersol had ever seen. He had seen smaller space stations. The part that was above *Cargo One* (the bottom of the ship?) covered kilometers. *Cargo One* looked like a fingernail clipping in comparison.

"I guess that's what's going to board us," Luddy said. He was standing up now, arms crossed, as terrified as Tattersol.

"I'm not getting any message about that," Pixton said.

"Well, they don't have to ask," Vance snapped.

"Maybe they can just absorb us," Oxley said. "Who knows what they can do."

"How're we supposed to fight that?" Luddy asked, voice shaking.

"We're not," Ralston said. "Regulations. Lives are more important than cargo."

Except when they weren't, Tattersol thought, but he couldn't move at all.

"Sir," Luddy said to Tattersol. "Are you going to let them know that we give up?"

Somehow that phrase caught Tattersol, and sent a shudder through him. Give up? He wasn't supposed to give up, not yet.

He cleared his throat.

"No," he said. "We keep going."

"And lead them to the research station?" Oxley asked. "It's supposed to be secret."

"If they knew where we'd be, they know where we're going," Tattersol said.

"There's no guarantee of that," Ralston said. "I'm going to let them know—"

"No," Tattersol put a hand over hers. He looked at her. "Just, no."

She shook her head, as if she didn't understand.

"They want something from us," he said. "They have to take it."

"You're thinking of our *careers* right now?" she asked.

"No," he said. Career hadn't even crossed his mind. For a moment, nothing had. But he'd been a bullied kid, and he had learned one thing.

You make the bully do the work. You don't do it for him.

"We can't fight them," he said. "We can't run from them. They have us surrounded. So we keep our dignity. They have to take the action. Not us."

Ralston tilted her head. Luddy visibly relaxed. Vance let out a small bitter laugh from behind Tattersol.

Pixton opened her hands just a little, in an *oh-well* gesture. "If nothing else," she said, "we'll have a hell of a story for our grandchildren."

"Oh, it'll probably be too classified to tell them," Oxley said, and everyone laughed. Not because it was funny or even true, which it was.

But because they needed to release some of the tension.

"Let's keep going," Tattersol said, and so they did.

FIFTY-NINE

The three cargo vessels didn't stop. They didn't surrender. They had stopped firing, apparently understanding that to fire on the *'iliahi* and her fighters was futile.

So they kept moving forward.

Wong mentally saluted them. She admired determination, enough to make her curse her orders just for a half second.

Then she recessed the plants around the flight deck, and shut off the perfumed air. She ordered up cleaners. She didn't want this memory brought up every time there was jasmine in the air.

Suddenly the flight deck was clear. Only the pedestals and the floating screens were visible.

In moments like this, the pedestals looked like tree trunks carved into seats, just like they had been in some of the primitive parts of Amnthra, millenia ago.

"We could tow them," Eusebio said without a lot of conviction. "I mean, their defenders are gone, and—"

"And if the weapons blow?" Akana asked. Leave it to the weapons' specialist to put everything in context.

"We don't know that they will," Eusebio said.

"We don't know that they won't," Akana said. "If I had to bet—"

"We have our orders," Wong said. She didn't like them either, but the orders made sense. No witnesses. No chance for any information to escape. They had already blocked all communications between the cargo vessels and the Enterran Empire, although she doubted any of the Enterrans knew that.

Even once the attack started, they hadn't tried to send for help.

But they also couldn't send a record of their last moments either.

The Enterrans would never know how powerful the weapons were. They would never know exactly what they had.

Wong watched the cargo vessels crawl along, making their way through the debris of their escorts, heading to the fighters in front of them.

"Pull the fighters back," she said.

Technically, she should probably have them return, but she didn't want to do that. They had to move to a safe distance. If something somehow got out of the perimeter, the fighters could destroy it.

The fighters moved back, double the distance that they had established during the original attack.

"All right," Wong said, with no charge in her voice at all. She kept her tone flat. "Fire."

She didn't have to repeat the order. Akana opened three shots, more powerful than anything the 'iliahi had ever fired.

The High Chiefs had opted for obliteration here, hoping that would stop any internal explosions. That's why the shots were so very powerful.

There was no warning—at least for the cargo vessels.

These shots were dark and invisible on most Amnthran equipment; they would be undetectable on Enterran equipment.

The shots didn't surround and destroy the way that the fighter shots had. These shots cut through, obliterating as they went.

The cargo vessels evaporated—or at least, the exteriors did. But the Spires floated free for a moment, and Wong wondered, with a half second of concern, if she was going to have to figure out how to destroy those too.

Then they exploded, each individually, one at a time as they scattered across space—or at least, one at a time at first.

Then they combined into a massive explosion, the largest Wong had ever seen.

"Nifty," Akana said. "I'd heard that they could do that—"

"Chief," Eusebio said. "The fighters…"

At least a dozen fighters hadn't pulled back far enough. They were trying to escape now, but they weren't going to make it.

Wong held her breath. Maybe their shields would hold. Maybe they could survive. Maybe—

But no. They disappeared in the massive outpouring of energy that had come from the bits of the Spires and who knew what else was in those cargo bays.

She was glad she wasn't standing. Her knees would have buckled.

She hadn't expected to lose fighters, even following regulation. She hadn't expected an explosion this big to come from the cargo.

But the High Chiefs had clearly known that some kind of disaster was a possibility.

No wonder they didn't want this stuff towed. The wrong move and half of the *'iliahi* would have been obliterated.

"All right," she said to her team. She wasn't going to mention the fighters. Not yet. "Let's make sure there's nothing left of that cargo."

No one responded. They didn't have to. They were all shaken, but they knew their duty.

And they were doing it.

Just like they had been trained to do.

AFTERWARD

ONE DAY LATER

SIXTY

The body count was more than he could bear. Khelan Māhoe had been briefed decades ago on the risks of this work.

You could die, he'd been told.

You might have to kill someone, he'd been told.

You will have to take extreme risks, he'd been told.

But no one had told him that he would be responsible for hundreds of deaths.

Maybe he wouldn't have cared back then. Back then, the Enterran Empire was just a name.

But now he knew people here. He had lived here for a long time. He understood them.

And he knew they were going crazy, trying to figure out what had happened.

He was trying to figure out how to avoid anyone he knew. So far, no one had contacted him, not Corporate Treasures, not Zimmer. But that would change at some point.

He was going to have to destroy the yacht or take it back to Amnthra, maybe in the cargo bay of his own ship. He hadn't figured that out yet.

He had remained in the yacht's captain's quarters, obsessively monitoring the destruction and the communications from the *'iliahi*. They'd lost more than twenty fighter pilots, a completely unexpected result.

It wasn't because of the Empire, either, but because of the Spires. There had been some chain reaction explosion that the theorists expected and only the High Chiefs believed would happen.

And there were bits of the Spires all over the Empire.

Khelan was obsessively making notes about the ones he knew. He would leave a copy of the notes with Idil, and he'd give the rest to the Amnthran government for his successor, whoever that might be.

He suspected it wouldn't be Idil. He had seen her only briefly in the past few hours, but she looked as shaken as he felt.

They had thought they were dealing with recovering stolen property. It should have been easy, but it wasn't.

Maybe it never was.

This cache, though, it was so big that it brought everything into sharp focus.

There was a lot of work left to be done, but he wasn't going to do it.

Someone needed to find that bunker. Someone needed to research where all these artifacts came from. Someone needed to figure out if each and every piece of the Spires from this particular cache had been recovered.

That someone wasn't him.

He wasn't going home in defeat. He suspected he'd be hailed as a hero. He had gotten a lot of Amnthran weapons out of enemy hands.

But he wasn't going to feel like a hero. He wasn't sure he was going to feel anything again.

Or if he dared feel anything. He had a hunch the emotions would crush him.

If this was what success felt like, he wanted no part of it.

He wanted no part of it at all.

SIXTY-ONE

The convoy never showed up, and given what he knew about all of the events on Wyr, Quint was not surprised. There had been something in that list of items that he had received from Corporate Treasures that someone wanted destroyed.

Because he was the one with contacts, and because he was the one who was supposed to receive the shipment at the research station, he was the one who noticed the lateness first. He was the one who ordered nearby ships to investigate what happened to the convoy.

Part of him—a hopeful part that he hadn't realized still existed—hoped they were in some kind of pitched battle to protect the cargo ships.

But there had been no battle. There was barely debris. He had sent ships all along the route and off the route and throughout the Empire, trying to find the vessels.

He didn't. No one else did either.

Instead, tiny little unidentifiable pieces, most no bigger than a speck of dust, really didn't even form a cloud where the convoy had last been. There were some strange energy readings there, though, so he had his people from the research station collect all of it—each speck, each piece of debris.

He wondered if the cargo was stolen away before the ships were destroyed—because, as far as he and the others were concerned, they were gone—or if the cargo was destroyed too.

Given what had happened on Wyr to the one poor sap who had broken into the warehouse, Quint believed that the cargo had been destroyed.

But a few others still held out hope that it hadn't.

He found the debriefings annoying and he had finally put his second-in-command, Yves Beltraire, on them. Quint didn't have time for recriminations.

There was something on this list that was so dangerous, so important, another culture was willing to destroy it all rather than have it in the hands of the Empire.

Quint could understand that impulse. It was something he would do.

He had already set up a base far from here to take in the cargo from Wyr. He wasn't going to dismantle that base.

Instead, he was going to confiscate every remaining mummy and Ivory Tree in the Empire. He was going to get each part of any strange artifact and he was going to do it fast, before this new all-powerful enemy found out.

He was going to make sure that no one besides his team knew where this base was.

Then he was going to set the best scientists he knew on all of the items, and they were going to figure out what they had.

Because whatever it was, it wasn't art. It was something else.

Something powerful.

Something that could benefit them all.

Unlock more secrets about the ancient Amnthran technology in *The Spires of Denon*. Available now!

Meklos Verr took over once the command ship entered Amnthra's atmosphere. He was a better on-planet pilot than anyone else on board. Besides, he preferred to do most things himself.

Even though he had the coordinates, Meklos flew hands-on. He opened the portals so that the cockpit, which jutted out in front of the small ship, seemed like it was encased in sky. He didn't have quite a three-hundred-and-sixty-degree view, although it was close.

Only the area directly behind him, where a door led to the area the crew usually called the bunkhouse, blocked the view.

It had taken two days to get to Amnthra from base, and that was about twelve hours longer than any group should have been in this vessel. But no other space-to-ground vessel had been available on short notice, so he had to take this one.

This part of Amnthra was isolated and sparsely populated. According to rumor, the ancients still lived in these mountains. However, no matter how hard he looked, he couldn't find any independent confirmation of those rumors.

The Naramzin Mountain Range had some of the tallest peaks in this sector. It ran from east to west along Amnthra's largest continent. In fact, except for the beaches along the edge of the continent, the range and its small hidden valleys *were* Amnthra's largest continent.

Most of Amnthra's people now lived on islands and the four smaller continents, which were mostly flat. The weather was good in those places, the soil rich, and life spectacular.

Or so the travelogues told him.

They also told him to avoid the Naramzins. Hostile terrain of surprising beauty, the travelogues said. Easy to get lost in.

Easy to die in.

Meklos had no intention of dying.

He also had no intention of getting lost.

He was heading to the largest valley on the continent—the Valley of Conquerors—where he and his team would camp before they hiked to the Spires of Denon—and the city beneath them.

The Spires of Denon were the reason he had to leave the ship so far away. They were delicate, so delicate that scientists believed that the wrong harmonic vibration would shatter them, and one of the great treasures of the Lost Age would disappear forever.

He could see the Spires in the distance, rising like Earthmade skyscrapers into the clear blue sky.

Right now, he didn't care about the Spires. Right now, he worried about landing, hiking, and working under such restrictive conditions.

He had agreed to those conditions—had, in truth, hired on for them. But he didn't like them.

And he liked them less as the peaks of the Naramzin Range came into view. The Naramzin was unconquerable—that was what the ancient texts said, which was why the Denonites had, for a time, conquered every known civilization on Amnthra.

It wasn't until Amnthra got rediscovered by the other peoples in the sector that the Denonites actually got defeated.

And then they disappeared.

One of the great mysteries of the Lost Age.

And one he wasn't about to solve.

He was just here to provide security—not that he could find any real reason for it. He had done some research, in the limited time he had before taking this job, and it looked like no one and nothing threatened the group of archeologists who worked the ancient city of Denon.

His people needed a rest. They'd gone on a rescue mission two months before and found themselves in the middle of a civil war. Two weeks and four deaths later, they managed to rescue some university professors who had wandered into the wrong encampment.

He'd given the bulk of his team a vacation. Fifteen remained—the fifteen who, like him, didn't believe in time off.

So he'd force them to take it with this easy job in one of the great sites of the Lost Age.

He had a hunch he might even enjoy this job himself.

Follow Kris on BookBub!

I value honest feedback, and would love to hear your opinion in a review, if you're so inclined, on your favorite book retailer's site.

Be the first to know!

Just sign up for the Kristine Kathryn Rusch newsletter, and keep up with the latest news, releases and so much more—even the occasional giveaway.

So, what are you waiting for? To sign up go to kriswrites.com.

But wait! There's more. Sign up for the WMG Publishing newsletter, too, and get the latest news and releases from all of the WMG authors and lines, including Kristine Grayson, Kris Nelscott, Dean Wesley Smith, *Pulphouse Fiction Magazine,* and so much more.

To sign up go to wmgpublishing.com.

ABOUT THE AUTHOR

International bestselling author Kristine Kathryn Rusch writes in many genres, from science fiction to mystery, from western to romance. She has written under a pile of pen names, but most of her work appears as Kristine Kathryn Rusch. Her Kris Nelscott pen name has won or been nominated for most of the awards in the mystery genre, and her Kristine Grayson pen name became a bestseller in romance. Her science fiction novels set in the bestselling Diving Universe have won dozens of awards and are in development for a major TV show. She also writes the Retrieval Artist sf series and several major series that mostly appear as short fiction.

She has won more than thirty awards for her fiction, including the Hugo, *Le Prix Imaginales*, the *Asimov's* Readers' Award, and the *Ellery Queen Mystery Magazine* Readers Award. Publications from *The Chicago Tribune* to *Booklist* have included her Kris Nelscott mystery novels in their top-ten-best mystery novels of the year. The Nelscott books have received nominations for almost every award in the mystery field, including the best novel Edgar Award, and the Shamus Award.

Rusch broke a number of barriers in the sf/f field, including being the first female editor of *The Magazine of Fantasy & Science Fiction* and being the only person in history to have won a Hugo Award for writing and editing. She has owned two different publishing companies, and she also writes a highly regarded weekly publishing industry blog.

To keep up with everything she does, go to kriswrites.com and sign up for her newsletter. To track her many pen names and series, visit those websites at divingintothewreck.com, retrievalartist.com, krisnelscott.com, kristinegrayson.com, wmgholidayspectacular.com, and pulphousemagazine.com.

f facebook.com/kristinekathrynruschwriter
BB bookbub.com/authors/kristine-kathryn-rusch
|● patreon.com/kristinekathrynrusch

Milton Keynes UK
Ingram Content Group UK Ltd.
UKHW040036111123
432318UK00001B/23